A GOD IN EVERY STONE

A GOD IN EVERY STONE

KAMILA SHAMSIE

BLOOMSBURY

LONDON · NEW DELHI · NEW YORK · SYDNEY

First published in Great Britain 2014

Copyright © 2014 by Kamila Shamsie

The moral right of the author has been asserted

Bloomsbury Publishing plc
50 Bedford Square
London
WC1B 3DP

www.bloomsbury.com

Bloomsbury Publishing, London, New Delhi, New York and Sydney
A CIP catalogue record for this book is available from the British Library

Hardback ISBN 978 1 4088 4720 6
Trade paperback ISBN 978 1 4088 4721 3

10 9 8 7 6 5 4 3 2 1

Typeset by Hewer Text UK Ltd, Edinburgh
Printed and bound in Great Britain by CPI Group (UK) Ltd, Croydon CR0 4YY

For the sisters – Saman, Magoo, Maha

Author's Note

Ancient Caria, including the site of Labraunda, is in present day Turkey. In 515 BC it lay at the western border of the Persian Empire; at the other end of the Empire, on the eastern border, was the settlement of Caspatyrus. The exact location of Caspatyrus has never been determined but some historians have placed it in or near Peshawar.

BOOK I

The greater part of Asia was discovered by Darius, who had wished to know where it was that the sea was joined by the River Indus (this being one of only two in the world which provides a habitat for crocodiles), and so sent ships with men on board whom he could trust to report back truthfully, including Scylax, a man from Caryanda. These duly set off from the city of Caspatyrus, in the land of Pactyike.

The Histories, Herodotus

FOR KING AND COUNTRY

515 BC

Fig leaves and fruit twirl in Scylax's hands. As
he turns the silver circlet round and round, animat-
ing the engravings, he imagines flexing his wrist
and watching the headpiece skim down
   the

               sloping

                           desert of the mountain,
across the jewelled valley of streams and fields
and fruit,
  to land
        splash!
in the muddied tributary along which it races
towards the crocodile-filled Indus.

Beside the distant riverbank, his ship is a brown
smear. His crew think him mad to have spent all
night on the mountain; but why explain to them, if
they don't already understand, the wonder of waking
with the sun and, in the clear morning air, looking
upon the rushing course of the Indus which is laid
out before him like an offering. He places the
circlet on his head, runs his rough sailor's hands
over the delicate figs embossed on it — in honour of
his homeland of Caria, where men are barbarians but
the fruit is sweet. So the Persians say — and yet
here he is, one of the barbarian men, entrusted to

7

lead the most daring of missions in the Empire. No
man has ever navigated the mighty Indus. No man has
ever attempted it. Not even Odysseus.

A flock of white birds swarms around his ship. No,
it's the sails. His crew has worked all night to
surprise him with this gift. The ship is ready; the
sails catch the wind and billow towards him. He
whistles sharply and his horse, tethered further
down the mountain, responds with a whinny. Scylax
runs towards the noise; the distance between him
and the ship suddenly enormous. Today it begins.
Today they set sail from the city of Caspatyrus,
edge of Darius' empire, edge of the known world.
Caspatyrus — the doorway to glory.

July–August 1914

Vivian Rose Spencer was almost running now, up the mountainside, along the ancient paving stones of the Sacred Way, accompanied by an orchestra of birds, spring water, cicadas and the encounter of breeze and olive trees. The guide and donkeys were far behind, so there was no one to see her stop sharply beside a white block which had tumbled partway down the mountain centuries ago and rest her hands against its surface before bending close to touch her lips to it. Marble, grit, and a taste which made her jerk away in shock – the bones of Zeus' sanctuary had the sweetness of fig. Either that, or a bird flying overhead might have dropped a fruit here, and the juice of it smeared against the stone. She looked down at her feet, saw a split-open fig.

– Labraunda! she called out, her voice echoing.

– Labraunda! she heard, bouncing back down the mountain at her. That wasn't her voice at all. It was a man, his accent both familiar and foreign. But no, she was the foreign one here. She picked up the fig, held it to her nose and closed her eyes. She never wanted to return to London again.

The reports of the nineteenth-century travellers hadn't prepared her for this: on the terraced upper slopes of the mountain enough of the vast temple complex remained intact to allow the imagination to pick up fallen colonnades, piece together the scattered marble and stone blocks, and imagine the grandeur that once was. Here, the Carian forces

9

fled after losing a battle against the might of Darius' Persians; here, the architects of the Mausoleum, that wonder of the world, honed their craft; here, Alexander came to see the mighty two-headed axe of the Amazon queen held aloft by the statue of Zeus.

Viv walked slowly, trying to take it all in: the ruins, half lost in foliage; the sounds of earth being turned, tree limbs hacked, voices speaking indistinct words; the view which held, all at once, the vast sky, the plain beneath, and the Aegean Sea in the distance. She had yet to become accustomed to the light of this part of the world – brilliant without being harsh, it made her feel she'd spent her whole life with gauze over her eyes. Something small and muscled charged at her, almost knocking her down.

– Alice! she cried out, and tried to pick up the pug, but the animal bounded ahead, and Viv followed, through a maze of broken columns taller than the tallest of men, until she saw the familiar lean form of her father's old friend Tahsin Bey crouching on the ground next to a man with sandy-blond hair, pointing at something carved onto a large stone block – a serpentine shape, with a loop behind its open jaw.

– A snake, the man with sandy-blond hair said, in a German accent.

– An eel? suggested Tahsin Bey in that way he had of putting forward a certainty as though it were a theory he was asking you to consider.

– An eel? Why an eel?

It was Viv who answered, though she knew it was impolite to enter the conversation of men unaware of her presence.

– Because Pliny tells us that in the springs of Labraunda there are eels which wear earrings.

The two men turned to look at her, and she couldn't stop herself from adding:

– And Aelian says there are fish wearing golden necklaces who are tamed, and answer the calls of men.

Tahsin Bey held out his hand, his smile of welcome overriding the formality of the gesture.

– Welcome to Labraunda, Vivian Rose.

His palm was calloused, and a few moments later when she raised her hand to brush some irritation out of her eye she smelt tobacco and earth overlaying fig. The richness of the scent made her linger over it until she saw the German looking at her with a knowing expression she didn't like. Briskly, she lowered her hand and rubbed it on her skirt, all the while wondering how she would ever rest her eyes in this place with so much to see.

She woke up early the next morning, still wearing clothes from the day before. She had done little the previous afternoon beyond measure and sketch the columns of one of the buildings – a temple? an andron? a treasury? – but her muscles ached from the walk up the mountain and the half-delirious scrambling up and down the terraces before Tahsin Bey had instructed her to take her sketchbook and make herself useful. By dinnertime it had been all she could do to place her food in her mouth and chew while conversation buzzed around her, good-natured about her inability to participate.

She arose from her camp bed and changed her clothes quietly without disturbing the two German women in the tent, before stepping out into the hour between darkness and light. There was almost a chill in the air, but not quite, as she walked among the ruins, both hands held out to touch every block, every column she passed. A sharp yip cut through the silence. Looking around for Alice she found Tahsin Bey instead, sitting on the large rock with a fissure running through it – the split rock of Zeus – holding up a mug to her in greeting. Alice was dispatched to guide her up through trees and broken steps, and a few minutes later she was drinking hot tea from the cap of a thermos, watching the sun rise over the ancient land of Caria.

– So that's what a rosy-fingered dawn looks like.
– You must write and tell your father that. He'll be pleased.
– Oh, I'm going to write and tell him everything!
Her father, a man without sons, had turned his regret at that

lack into a determination to make his daughter rise above all others of her sex; a compact early agreed on between them that she would be son and daughter both – female in manners but male in intellect. Taking upon himself the training of her mind he had read Homer with her in her childhood, took vast pleasure in her endless questioning of Tahsin Bey about the life of an archaeologist every time the Turk came to visit, and championed her right to study history and Egyptology at UCL despite his wife's objections – even so, Viv had barely allowed herself to believe he was being serious when he'd asked her one morning, as if enquiring if she'd like a drive through the park, if she'd be interested in joining Tahsin Bey at a dig in Labraunda. Outrageous! Mrs Spencer had said, slapping a napkin onto the polished wood of the breakfast table. Did he want his daughter running up the pyramids in her bloomers like Mrs Flinders Petrie? Did he have no thought for her marital prospects?

Father and daughter had shared the smile of conspirators across the breakfast table before Viv rose from her chair to throw her arms around Dr Spencer's neck. She had been more disappointed than she'd ever revealed during her just-concluded university years when he'd said no, she would not be among the students who Flinders Petrie took to Egypt over the summer – and assumed that meant all future digs were out of the question, too, as long as she was unmarried and under his roof. But there he was, pushing aside his plate, showing her the letter from Tahsin Bey and saying of course she mustn't miss such an opportunity, and his old friend could be trusted to ensure all proprieties were observed which was more than could be said for Flinders Petrie with that madcap wife of his, and how he wished he could set aside the responsibilities of his life and join them.

– He's very proud of you, the Turk said, turning his body slightly towards her on the rock.

– I know, but I haven't given him any reason to be proud. Not yet.

– No? You don't think he should be proud of your courage?

– Courage? That's something I certainly don't have. You

remember my friend, Mary? She's become one of those militant suffragettes, I regret to say. But even though she's completely wrong, I see her facing prison and force-feeding, and I recognise courage. But it isn't there when I look in the mirror.

– It takes considerable courage to come to an unknown part of the world, away from everything you've ever known.

– This isn't courage. You're here.

She felt herself blush as she said the words, which had more heat in them spoken aloud than she had anticipated. All she meant was that she wasn't away from everything she'd ever known when in his familiar company – he and her father had tumbled into an unexpected friendship as young men who met on a train in France, and there had scarcely been a year she could remember when Tahsin Bey hadn't come to London and walked with her through the British Museum, talking about his hopes for one day convincing the Ottoman authorities to grant him a firman to excavate at Labraunda. And I'll come along! she had always said. Oh of course, he'd replied when she was a child and, if your father approves, once she'd started to approach adulthood.

But his company wasn't familiar in the old way, she saw as he blushed too. She was twenty-two now, and though she'd always thought of him as old the muscles of his bare forearm and the thickness of his dark hair which she'd never noticed in the muffled light of London made her sharply aware that a twenty-five-year gap grows narrower over time. She had friends from school who'd married men in their forties, and had children.

She swivelled away from Tahsin Bey, and opened her sketchbook so she could pretend the change in angle was necessary only to allow her to draw the ruins of the building which she'd been sketching up close the previous day. Of course, she'd often thought that marrying an archaeologist was the only way she might ensure her place in the thrilling excavations of the age – as opposed to the irrelevant digs at the edges of knowledge to which the recent fad for women-led excavations was relegated. But to think of Tahsin Bey in that manner was absurd. He was her father's friend; she couldn't begin to imagine . . . not that she'd ever really known what she was supposed to imagine about men in that way; she'd seen enough fertility totems to understand the mechanics of it, but that wasn't really the point. The point was, she would die of embarrassment if he even knew what she was thinking.

– You have a fine hand.

She looked up, startled, but his attention was entirely on the page which she had filled with a quick, precise sketch of the stumps of columns – Ionic on two sides – which formed the rectangular outline of the building. He held out his hand, she gave him the sketchbook, and watched as he turned the pages.

– Not a fine hand, an exceptional one. When you show these to your father, he will be proud.

She returned his smile – a child again, in the presence of an adult whose assurances made the world better.

That night there were ten at dinner around a long wooden table under the night sky. Three Germans, six Turks, and Viv. They started the meal in near-silence, all attention on the stew which Nergiz the cook had prepared, but when it was over they pushed their plates away, and everyone other than Viv – even the two German women – lit up cigarettes and fell into rapid chatter about their day in a mix of languages in which French dominated. Viv was seated next to the blond German man, Wilhelm, who was particularly interested in the necropolis surrounding the Temple complex and talked to her in painstaking detail about the coins and inscriptions he'd already found in one of the rock tombs. She nodded and listened, which was clearly all he expected of her, while her ears caught wisps of the conversations she'd rather be in – an increasingly heated discussion about whether the largest building within the complex was the Temple of Zeus particularly intrigued her. At some point she caught Tahsin Bey's eye, and he winked – she could never imagine him doing such a thing in her parents' home, but it didn't feel as though he were taking a liberty.

– Bored? he mouthed, and she nodded.

The next thing she knew he was standing on his wooden chair, Alice tucked under one arm, the stars clustered around his head like a band of silver.

– Ladies and Gentlemen, if we lower our voices we might be able to hear them.

He placed one finger on his lips, and pointed down the mountainside. They all turned to look but there was nothing to see except white columns cut out of the darkness.

– The remnants of the Carian army. Listen – you can hear their weary footsteps as they drag themselves and their wounded brothers up the Sacred Way to the Temple of Labraunda. It isn't the physical wounds that make their steps falter – it is failure. This morning they were men of hope and courage, a brave people at the edge of a vast empire, ready to cut through the chains that bind them to their Persian over-lords. Now they are a tattered, spent force – not one of them hasn't lost someone he loves to a Persian sword. There they go now, limping past us, towards the Temple of Zeus . . . no, Mehmet, not that one . . . their hearts filled with either sorrow or rage towards the god who has deserted them.

Since her childhood, this had been his role. The Storyteller of the Ancients. In her first clear memory of talking to him he had told her he was from Anatolia – ancient Caria – like Herodotus the Father of History and Scylax the Great Explorer.

– In the temple they argue: should they give themselves up to the Persians or try to flee their homeland? Only one man says nothing: Scylax, who knows the Persians best of all – has travelled with them, drunk with them, and worn Darius' mark of favour on his brow.

– Stop him!

The words whispered in her ear by Tahsin Bey's nephew, Mehmet, the archaeologist nearest to her in age but until now distant around her, almost distrustful.

– Please. He'll listen to you. Please.

The edge of panic in his voice made her act without think-ing. Picking up a slice of pear she flicked it towards the pug who leapt from Tahsin Bey's arms, tiny legs paddling the air as though it were water; the Turk lunged forward, caught her, and somehow managed to regain his balance on the chair to the sounds of applause. It had worked; the mood shifted to the jubilance which accompanies averted disaster, Mehmet called out, A song! A song! and the Germans around the table broke into 'Greensleeves', Wilhelm catching hold of Viv's hands and pulling her into a surprisingly light-footed dance around the table as he sang.

A little later, she apologised to Tahsin Bey. For some reason, I was convinced I could toss the pear directly into Alice's mouth, she said. He waved away the need for any explanation. Mehmet, sitting near by, watched impassively.

– Why did I really do it? she asked the young man when they were out of everyone's hearing.

– Oh, I've heard that story so many times I'm sick of it, he said, and though she knew he was lying she couldn't begin to fathom why.

During the second week, her discovery: a fallen slab of stone, which had once been part of the ceiling, was moved away from the rectangular building with Ionic columns and an inscription stone was revealed. It was Viv who'd insisted the foreman ask his men to move the obstructive slab – no one but her took much interest in the small building while there were grander structures to excavate – so she was the only one of the archaeologists present to read the Greek words, step back, read them again, and race down the terrace in search of Tahsin Bey.

– I've found it! I've found the Temple of Zeus!

Although it was early in the afternoon all the archaeologists broke away from what they were doing to cluster around the inscription stone and toast Viv with the wine which her tent-mate, Gretel, had been saving for A Great Occasion.

– Vivian Rose Spencer, archaeologist! Tahsin Bey said, and the others raised their glasses and echoed the words in their different accents. She wished her father were there to witness it.

* * *

Every night Viv placed a bowl of figs beside her camp bed, and fell asleep with her hand resting among the plump fruit. She had always been a fitful sleeper but in Labraunda the hours of physical toil followed by wine meant that she woke in the same position as she had fallen asleep, pulled out of dreams by the snuffling of a pug who knew how to lift up the end of a mosquito net with her teeth and squeeze under. One paw on the rim of the wooden fruit bowl, Alice rocked it this way and that without quite tipping it over. Too well-behaved to cause disorder or too imperious to serve herself, Viv could never decide.

Either way, within minutes of waking Viv, while the other women in the tent slept on, Alice would be tucked under the Englishwoman's arm, having thin shavings of fig delivered to her mouth just as she liked them. Tahsin Bey would pretend surprise every morning when woman and dog caught up with him as he was walking, very slowly, up the slope.

– Did she wake you? She runs off as soon as I open the tent flap; I'm so sorry. But as you're awake, would you care to . . . ?

Viv was increasingly grateful for the pretence as the summer drew on; it allowed her to avoid the question of what she was doing, contriving – with a pug – to have a few minutes of the day alone with Tahsin Bey, sitting on the rock with a fissure created by Zeus' lightning bolt, drinking a morning cup of tea as the rising sun lifted the ruins of the Sanctuary of Labraunda and the surrounding forested mountains out of shadows. There was a beauty in this piece of the Ottoman Empire which sank down into her as nothing in England ever had – the terraced slopes, the plane trees, the brilliant cloudless blue of the skies, the bones of a temple which she would always and for ever be the first person to have identified. She pressed her palms together, the hard skin and calluses giving her more pleasure than anything else about her body ever had.

One morning near the end of the dig they were sitting together as usual; Tahsin Bey on the rock with one leg folded under his body, the other leg dangling over the edge, elbows tucked in as he held the hot mug of tea near his face. It was a posture she had sketched from memory by the light of the full moon in her calfskin notebook – more private, more precious than all the sketchbooks.

– Are you disappointed that you haven't found it? she asked, watching him as he looked down towards the Temple.

– Found what?

– What you've always hoped to find at Labraunda.

– How do you know . . . ?

– You told me. The first time we talked properly.

– You were five years old the first time we talked properly. We discussed the spiritual life of dolls.

– Well, all right. The first time I remember us talking properly.

Their voices lowered, teasing, their hands resting side by side on Alice's fur.

The girl followed the lights, the music and the gabble of voices as they spilled from the door into the garden. As she progressed closer to the edge of the property she realised everything that had preceded her out was being swallowed up by the darkness, so that soon only she would remain. Unless the darkness swallowed her up, too.

– Where are you going?

The darkness didn't sound as she'd expected; its voice foreign.

– Away from that.

She flicked her hand behind her at the house filled with New Year revellers waiting to cross into 1904. What she really meant was that she wanted to escape from her mother who was attempting to send her to bed as though, at eleven, she was still a child.

The darkness lit a cigarette and a man's face appeared, attached to the end of the glowing white stick. The girl had known this man all her life but he had only become interesting to her earlier that evening when her father whispered into her ear, 'He's an archaeologist who grew up where Herodotus did'. She repeated this fact back to the man, who pulled on his cigarette, his cheeks sucking in until the girl was sure they must have met inside his mouth.

– Yes, the ancient land of Caria, on the cusp of Persia and Greece. Home of Herodotus, the Father of History, it's true. But before Herodotus there was Scylax – the greatest of the ancient

18

travellers. Now reduced to a speck in the corner of history's eye.

– He travelled to India! Herodotus writes about him.

The man looked at her as if she had just become a person worthy of interest.

– Yes. It was the least he could do, Herodotus, after he stole all Scylax' tales of India for his Histories. *What do you know of him?*

– Only what Herodotus tells us. The Persian emperor Darius sent a group of men he trusted to India including Scylax –

– Especially Scylax! Kai de kai, that's the emphasising phrase he uses. Especially Scylax. The most trusted. Go on.

– Scylax travelled along the River Indus, and later Darius used the information he brought back to go down the river and conquer India, just as the British have done.

– Learned that last part from Herodotus, did you?

He laughed, and she saw the gentle mockery as a sign that he recognised her as an adult worthy of the light-hearted teasing which he exhibited often with her father and never with her mother.

– Let me tell you the part Herodotus never mentioned, Vivian Rose: Darius so trusted Scylax he gave him a silver circlet fashioned with figs – a mark of the highest honour. But twenty years later when Scylax' people, the Carians, rebelled against Darius' Persians, Scylax was on the side of his countrymen, not his emperor.

– But Darius trusted him!

– Oh, English girl, how quickly you side with Empire.

She knew she was being chastised, but couldn't understand why. The Turk must have seen her expression change to bewilderment, hurt even, because he stood up and his voice lost its sharp edge.

– I'll tell you a secret, if you promise to tell no one: one day I'll find it. The Circlet of Scylax.

He swept his arm from side to side, rippling the air with fire.

– Somewhere, beneath a patch of earth, it's waiting for the man with the will to unearth it.

– Where will you look?

– A place called Labraunda.

* * *

19

– I told you that? I thought I'd never told anyone.

Tahsin Bey sat back on his elbows and looked at her, amazed.

– Well, you did. So – disappointed?

– Disappointed? The impatience of the English! One day, I'll hold the Circlet in my hands. Why must it be today? And anyway – how can anyone feel disappointment here?

Tahsin Bey unfurled his long limbs and stood up, his arms spread wide to encompass the Temple complex, the plains of Mylasa below, the mountains around, and the Halicarnassus peninsula in the distance.

– Caria! Vivian Rose, if you're going to give your summers over to excavating one of its most sacred spots you must know the rest of it as well.

There had been no talk until now of Viv's participation in future digs, no talk of next month, let alone next year. But she stood up beside him, ignoring the annoyed bark of Alice who disliked it when the tininess of her own legs was brought to her attention.

– I want to see all of it before I go. Mylasa, Halicarnassus, Alinda, Caryanda . . .

– That English impatience again. Here's an idea – if you're willing to cut short your time in Constantinople, why don't you travel up the coast with us? We'll see some of Caria, and places beyond. Ephesus. Troy!

– Us? You and Alice?

– No, no. Wilhelm and Gretel and me. You've heard us talk about it.

–Yes, of course. I am sorry. Of course you wouldn't have suggested . . .

– Of course I wouldn't! Your father – !

– He'd never speak to either of us again.

– Either that, or he'd force us to get married to preserve your honour.

She would have thought it a joke if not for his own startled response to the words out of his mouth. He picked up Alice, mumbled something she didn't catch, and hurried down the slope towards the sound of spades and chisels, leaving Viv in the silence of the plane-tree grove, breathing in the sacred air of Labraunda, trying to understand the rapid staccato of her heart.

The dig ended. The archaeologists disbanded with promises to meet the following summer; the foreman and his team picked up their spades and walked single file down the mountain towards the construction work that awaited them; Alice was sent ahead to Tahsin Bey's home in Bodrum, along with Nergiz the cook and her family, and the donkey train carrying the season's finds. Several of the archaeologists including Anna and Mehmet departed for Constantinople. Viv, Tahsin Bey, Wilhelm and Gretal set off on horseback towards the coast of Anatolia.

They rode in single file or two-by-two. The configurations changed at first, but soon a pattern was established: the two Germans together a little way ahead, Tahsin Bey and Viv following. When they stopped to walk around a town or a site, it was the same – the Germans striding away, the other two moving at a slower pace. At first the atmosphere between Tahsin Bey and Viv was strange, due to the absence of the pug. Alice had always been the diverting presence to whom they could turn when the silence between them lengthened and threatened to change shape. But soon they learned to be as comfortable in silence as in conversation, and Viv's suspicion that no one in the world was more interesting than Tahsin Bey became conviction. In Labraunda they had spoken mainly of the site and its discoveries, but as they rode she saw there was nothing he didn't hold in his mind – the story of every ancient stone, the call of individual birds, the plays and sonnets of Shakespeare, the overlap and contrasts of the Bible and Qur'an, the history of the tango.

One afternoon, they stood on a low cliff overlooking the Aegean Sea, the salt of it in their mouths and on their skin while the Germans waded in the water below. It was their last day in what-had-once-been-Caria.

With the toe of his shoe Tahsin Bey – almost daintily – drew a shape in the sand on the clifftop. Viv plucked leaves and fruit off the fig tree beside which they were standing and placed them, alternately, within the Circlet's outline.

– Oh! There it is. You've found it for me, Vivian Rose.

There are passages of time a person enters into knowing unshakeably that they will always retain a rare lustre, one that will gleam more brightly as disappointments attach themselves to life. That was once me, Viv thought, anticipating the reminiscences of her future self; that was once me, plucking figs off branches and cramming them into my mouth while watching the sun glitter from the Carian coast to the horizon, across water as blue as ink and clear enough to see all the way to the rocks at the base of the cliffs. Almost driven mad by the purple on my tongue, the blue in my sight – a moment to understand Sirens weren't creatures of the sea, they were the sea itself. Tahsin Bey laughed as though he'd heard her thoughts and said look, your eyes have changed colour; the Aegean Sea is in them now. Lightly touching her wrist, at the jut of her bone, he added, and the sun is in your skin. The metamorphosis of Vivian Rose Spencer.

– I prefer this version.

– I've been thinking. It's been so long since I saw Christmas in London. I thought I might visit at the end of this year.

– I'd like that very much.

There was nothing further either of them needed to say. For now they would continue on as colleagues, without any word or gesture to indicate what was understood between them so that he could approach her father from a position of honour. Papa would be taken aback at first, but there were few people in the world he regarded with more admiration than this generous, learned man – 'more English than most Englishmen' he'd once said – and surprise would soon give way to delight. Next summer Viv and Tahsin Bey would return to Labraunda as husband and wife, and all the summers after that. She had never felt so much at peace in her life.

* * *

They reached the south coast of the Sea of Marmara, from where they would take a ferry to Constantinople, and it was there that news of the war in Europe finally reached them. It had started just after they set off from Labraunda, and the Ottoman Empire was still neutral, though that situation wasn't expected to last long. The Orient Express? said the man at the ferry terminus. Oh no, that had been suspended. The Germans and the Englishwoman would have to find another way home, but not together, of course, now that their nations were at war. But – was the Englishwoman's name Miss Spencer? Her countrymen had been leaving messages for her all along the coast. Here – he held out a letter.

From the moment he said 'war in Europe' – everyone there had enough Turkish to understand the phrase – Gretel and Viv had taken each other's hands, and now Wilhelm took the letter from the Turkish man and gave it to Viv, his fingers touching hers lightly.

The message, from the Embassy in Constantinople, was brief. Her father was worried about her. She must contact the Embassy immediately and arrangements would be made to get her home safely.

After that everything moved too quickly. A telephone was found, the Ambassador himself spoke to her and said it was a stroke of luck, a ferry was on its way to where she was with an English couple on board who were returning home via the sea route. They knew about her – every English person in Constantinople had been worrying about her – and would be only too happy to accompany her home, so she must wait at the terminus and make herself known to them.

– But surely there isn't such a great hurry?

– Miss Spencer, you should have left a long time ago. I'll telegram your father immediately – he has been more worried than I think you can understand.

There was no time for proper goodbyes, no time to accept what was happening. The Germans said they shouldn't be with her when the English couple arrived, it would only create discomfort. Gretel embraced her, Wilhelm shook her hand vigorously, and then they were gone, and she was standing on a dock with Tahsin Bey, watching a ferry approach. When she stepped close to him, he moved away, holding up his hand in a rejection of whatever it was she intended.

– They may already be able to see us, he said, gesturing to the ferry which was moving too quickly towards the dock.

– You'll still come for Christmas, won't you?

– Of course. This will all be over by then.

– But if Turkey does join the war, which side will she join?

– That crazy Enver will want to side with the Germans, but I'm not sure about the others.

– It won't matter. I mean, to me. It won't change anything.

– Perhaps nothing will change, perhaps everything will. This sick man of Europe – a war may be the thing that kills him finally.

– I don't understand.

– All empires end. The Ottomans have been on their death-bed long enough.

– Oh! How terrible.

– Terrible? Why?

– For you, I mean. To contemplate that.

He raised himself up on his toes as he did when turning an important thought in his head, hands clasped behind his back. She wondered if he were trying to keep himself from touching her; she wanted to place her hand on his arm, grip the muscled forearm beneath the sleeve, and feel herself anchored.

– Did you know Nergiz and I are related?

– Nergiz the cook?

– Yes. Distantly. From my mother's side. Do you understand what that means?

He was trying to explain something to her about class, or social status. A scandal, a taint on the family name which he thought she might care about. She didn't know whether she was touched or offended.

– It doesn't matter, she said.

24

– It matters very deeply. My grandmother's people are Armenian. To my brothers, this is an irrelevance. But from the time I was a child, I've loved that part of my family most. The Bodrum relatives, the family home in Caria. And when I was a young man at university in France the Ottoman Empire's first socialist party was founded – an Armenian party, with independence from the Ottomans as its goal. For the first time I could stop feeling ashamed around the French students who compared their tradition of revolution to my despotic empire. Though even then I understood the world well enough to hold these loyalties in my heart, not on my tongue.

– That's why Mehmet made me stop you talking about Scylax.

– Yes. I knew that was what had happened. Scylax the seafarer who was sent on the greatest of adventures by the Persians, just as I was given permission to excavate the most astonishing site by the Ottoman authorities. We take from the Empire what it has to give – but in the end, our loyalties are with the people we loved first, love most deeply. As Scylax ended his days writing a heroic account of the Carian rebel prince Heraclides, so one day I'll write of my Armenian cousins, the ones braver than me who lived their life in rebellion regardless of the cost.

– You mustn't speak like this.

– I've never said any of it before. Only to you.

He unclasped his hands, touched her for the second time at the jut of her wrist bone, and her pulse leapt as though the touch had travelled all the way through bone and into her blood. Then he clasped his hands again, stepped even further away, and said nothing else.

The ferry docked; an elderly English couple was among the first to disembark; they greeted Viv as though she were their long-lost daughter.

Thank you, we'll take care of her from here, the Englishman said to Tahsin Bey when Viv introduced them. The suspicion in his voice was unmistakable, and it was for this reason that Viv

25

went up on her toes to kiss Tahsin Bey's cheek. He didn't embrace her in return, but instead whispered in her ear – a promise, a proposition, a caution:

– When the war ends, Vivian Rose.

January–June 1915

And then Tahsin Bey said, in this place every gift horse is a Trojan horse.

The young soldier threw his head back and laughed, slapping his hand down on the blanket in the place where his right thigh should have been. Viv's old schoolfriend and fellow VAD nurse, Mary, caught Viv by the elbow and said, Nurse! There's work to be done.

The soldier, six months earlier a student of Classics at Oxford, touched Viv's hand.

– That was the first laugh since they took my leg. Come back and tell me more about Troy if you have a minute?

Viv smiled back – kind but distant, in the manner she'd rehearsed until it had met with Mary's approval – and followed her friend to the door leading out of the ward, where she turned and gave the soldier another smile, a promise in it that she would return, before continuing on to the kitchen.

– You're worse than Matron, Mary. Narse! There's work to be done. Narse!

Mary, as sleek and imperious as ever, even ten hours into a twelve-hour shift, didn't say a word until the kitchen door was closed behind them. You wash, I'll dry, she said, with a gesture towards the piles of dirty mugs in the sink. Viv took off one shoe, raised it above her head and turned the tap as far as it would go with a quick twist of her wrist. The gush of water threw the beetles in the sink into panic. Darting here and there, they upturned mugs and milk jugs, fleeing the deluge. Viv and

27

Mary, practised now, smashed the shining dark bodies while balancing on one foot.

– Prison life probably seems a luxury after this, Viv said, bending to put her shoe back on when the scurrying had ceased.

– Well, the headwear here is nicer, Mary replied, indicating the white hat on her own head. In prison, they make you wear bonnets. Actual bonnets. With a bow tied beneath your chin.

Viv tried to picture it, laughed disbelievingly, and scooped a floating, upturned beetle out of the rapidly filling sink before rolling up her sleeves and turning her attention to the mugs. It still didn't entirely make sense to her that Mary had transformed so rapidly and completely from the suffragette who smashed windows, to this zealous supporter of the war who had taken Viv off to the Red Cross to start her VAD training the day she returned from Turkey, but it was a relief to find that they were no longer staring at each other in bafflement from either side of the Votes for Women question.

She looked out of the window over the sink; the lowered skies, the greyness of London. Not yet 5 p.m. and already the sun had given up any pretence that it would play a part in the day. She sighed, thinking of the Labraunda evenings, and the sound was met with clicking-tongued disapproval from Mary.

Viv pulled another mug out of the brown soapy water in an excessive gesture which flicked soap-suds onto Mary's uniform. At least the gruelling twelve-hour days meant there was little time to think of Tahsin Bey, or the refusal of the war to end, or the slow trickle of post between London and Turkey. She hadn't yet received any correspondence from him, though she continued to write weekly letters which she slipped into the postbox near her house when no one was watching. Her parents couldn't know about the nature of her feelings for Tahsin Bey, of course, not yet – and the one person who she might have talked to about it was Mary who was now entirely unreasonable on the subject of Germans and Turks. Viv had tried at first to make her see sense: What did the world of Agamemnon and Priam have

28

to do with the commoners of Greece and Troy? Despise a sultan or a kaiser, but why hate those who were born in his realm? Pity them, yes; pity all those who didn't have the good fortune of Englishness as their birthright – though some could approach Englishness via their education, yes, they certainly could – but why hate them? But she soon gave up.

Anyway, soon there would be even less time in the day to think of Tahsin Bey – her father, acting briskly on Mary's suggestion, had pulled strings to arrange for transfers for them both at the end of their probationer's period from this convalescent hospital to a Class A auxiliary hospital where the mugs and mops and dusters would be supplemented by septic wounds and death-rattles and gangrenous limbs. Mary said it would all soon become as unexceptional as the black beetles which had Viv shrieking just a few weeks earlier, which might be true, but who would want such a thing to become unexceptional? And yet every time there had been an opportunity to say she was content to stay right here with the mops and black beetles she remembered her father's response when Mary first asked him if there was anything at all he could do to place them where they were most needed. A daughter nursing in a Class A hospital was almost as fine as a son going into battle, Dr Spencer had declared. That 'almost' had struck at Viv's heart and prompted her to say if only she were twenty-three already she would volunteer straight away to join the nurses at the Front. Her father's proud smile a reward that would carry her through the worst of the Class A hospital's horrors.

The car pulled up to Cambridge Terrace and Viv stepped out into a world of wind and rain. Mary's chauffeur walked her partway to the front door with a large umbrella held above her head, and the one-armed ex-soldier who Dr Spencer had brought into the house as a footman to replace George – now Private Roberts – rushed out with an even larger umbrella to accompany her the remainder of the way. A month of living-in at the hospital, emptying bedpans, scrubbing bandages, washing cutlery and then, at the end of it, this return to a

29

world where a drop of rain mustn't be allowed to touch your skin – just before you were sent out again into the world of a Class A hospital.

– Miss Spencer. There's a gentleman to see you from the War Office.

– To see me? That can't be right.

– Your father said you must go in immediately on arrival.

Without changing out of her nurse's uniform? The one-armed footman said yes, Dr Spencer had been clear in his instructions. Viv took off her cap, smoothed down her hair, pinched colour into her cheeks and walked into the parlour where an unknown man was filling an armchair though his frame was slight. Her father stood up to greet her with the broadest of smiles, while her mother covered her mouth with her hand in horror, managing to make Viv feel it was her fault that she'd had to come in without brushing her hair or changing into more presentable clothing.

– There you are! We were just talking about your summer in Turkey, her father said. Those wonderful maps you've made of your walk up the coast.

Her sketchbooks from Turkey were piled onto a table next to the unknown man – whip-thin with a pince-nez balanced on the end of his nose – and one of them was in his hands.

– These are remarkable, the man said, standing up and directing a slightly awkward smile at her, as though his mouth wasn't accustomed to forming that shape. Such detail! When the Ambassador suggested you might have something interesting to impart about your time in Turkey none of us could have imagined this.

– I'm sorry – imagined what?

– The gentleman from the War Office believes your drawings could be useful to the Maps Division, her father answered. He intends to send them to Cairo.

– No, she said, her voice almost a shriek. You can't have them.

The man was still holding on to one of the sketchbooks, splayed open. She could see her drawing of the cove where

30

Tahsin Bey had found a length of emerald seaweed and draped it over her wrist.

– Vivian.

Her father kept his voice low, the slight edge to it all that was necessary to silence her, and the whip-thin man gestured to her to take a seat, as if this were his house.

– Miss Spencer, I assure you, they'll be returned to you very soon, in perfection condition. I just need to make copies and send them to Lawrence and Woolley.

– T. E. Lawrence? Leonard Woolley?

– Our men in Cairo.

– But they're archaeologists.

– They are the great travellers and explorers and linguists of the age. In times of war, such men are indispensable.

– What about such women?

Both men laughed at this, and her father said, I told you she wasn't like other men's daughters.

Viv lowered her head and looked away from the laughing men. For just a moment she had imagined herself in Cairo, standing in the shadow of the Pyramids with Lawrence and Woolley, drawing a map of the Turkish coastline in the sand to their cries of admiration. Her mother caught her eye, pursed her lips together and shook her head with that sharply honed ability to know when Viv was thinking a thought that might harm her marital prospects.

– You're already halfway to indispensable with these draw-ings, the whip-thin man said. And as to the other half – Dr Spencer, would you mind if I spoke alone to your daughter?

The speed with which Dr Spencer left the room, ushering the resistant form of his wife ahead of him, was remarkable.

For a few minutes thereafter, Viv understood how it felt to be of singular value to Empire. There was no one – no one! – in her position. No one else had spent an entire summer in the company of Germans and Turks and then walked along one of the most militarily significant stretches of land in the world, and observed it so closely. She tucked her hair nervously behind her ear – a habit of childhood she thought she'd long since left

31

behind – and said she wanted nothing more than to be of use, but she didn't see how. The man – she still hadn't been told his name – rested a pad of paper on his knee and said to start with she could tell him everything she knew about the Germans who were in Laboonda.

– Labraunda, she corrected him and his smile told her the name was irrelevant.

It soon became clear that everything she knew was irrelevant. He wanted to know about Wilhelm's political opinions, whether Gretel's last name meant she was related to a particular general, where Anna had learned her Arabic. She knew none of these things, though she could have told him of Gretel's theories about the religious practices of the Carian Satraps, or Anna's almost uncanny ability to match up the jigsawed edges of shards of pottery, or the gracefulness which entered Wilhelm's frame when he danced. Soon, the whip-thin man stopped writing down her answers, and a dullness entered his voice as though he were asking questions because it was his nature to be thorough but not because he expected anything useful to come of it. She was acutely conscious that she had proven to be a waste of time, and her father would soon come to know of it.

She cut off the man's question and said, It might be more helpful if I were to tell you what I do know rather than what I don't.

– Right you are, he said gamely, though with little expectation.

She stood up, walked over to the tea-trolley to pour herself a cup of tea, offered the man a slice of cake, which he accepted, with thanks – for a few moments everything was familiar, and known. This was her house, those were her sketchbooks, she could reveal a certain amount without revealing everything.

– The Ottoman Empire is very different to our own, she said.

– How do you mean?

– Take, for instance, the Indian soldiers at the Western Front. Thousands of miles from home, fighting with exceptional valour.

– They do us proud.

– That's just it. There was that one, an Indian, who won the Victoria Cross. I read about him, and I thought, there is a . . . a compact between us, the Indians and the English. We'll honour their bravery as we would that of an English soldier and, in turn, they fight our wars with as much fervour as any Englishman would do.

She hadn't really known she felt this way until she started to speak but now she touched the apron of her nursing uniform, and was momentarily silenced by the strength of her own feelings. The whip-thin man was nodding as he took off his pince-nez and polished it on his handkerchief, his expression that of an Englishman having an emotion he didn't want to deny but couldn't fully find a way to express.

– Fairness, morality – these aren't just lofty abstractions. In times of war they work to everyone's advantage, binding ruler to ruled, Natives to Englishmen. The Ottoman Empire, by contrast, is crippled by its own savagery.

She almost laughed at the sound of her voice – here she was, with a man from the War Office, explaining to him the contrasts of empires as though she were a university lecturer.

– Crippled, how? he asked.

– There is no love there, no admiration, for the Ottoman Sultan. No loyalty. That's what I think the War Office should know – they do not have their people's loyalty. How are they to win a war without that?

– If I understood more specifically what you meant . . . ?

– Well, just as an example – the Armenians.

– Oh, I see. Of course, no, the Ottomans aren't relying on the loyalty of Armenians to get them through the war.

He had been leaning forward towards her but now he sat back, that look of slight boredom returning.

– The point is, it isn't just the Armenians. There are those who the Ottomans would imagine to be loyal Turkish subjects who simply aren't that. Their sense of justice won't allow it.

– Such as?

– I'm speaking generally.

– Miss Spencer, I don't believe you are.

There was a long, stretched-out moment in which she wondered what to answer, and that became confirmation.

– Who? the man said, softly, as if he understood this were a matter that should only be whispered. She shook her head, her mouth very dry, unable to lie to the man from the War Office.

– You'd be breaking a confidence if you told me? Is that it?

– I'm relaying my observations.

– I wish we could leave it at this, I genuinely do. But you see, what you've said, it's of enormous interest.

– It is?

– Without question. It could certainly guide significant decisions in the propaganda department. But I need to know the source to evaluate the statement. It means one kind of thing if it comes from a workman on your dig; another kind of thing if it comes from a general in the Army.

He put aside his notepad, tucked his pen into his breast-pocket, and held his hands wide.

– I won't write the name down or even whisper it to anyone else. You must know that giving a piece of vital information to His Majesty's representative in a time of war is a quite different matter to betraying someone to the Ottoman authorities. If you like I could ask your father to come in and explain that distinction to you. I'm sure he'd grasp it right away.

It had been a declaration of love. She couldn't explain that to this man, and certainly not to her father. I've never said any of it before. Only to you, he'd said, and they had both known he wasn't talking about Armenians or empires, not really. But the world had changed beyond all recognition now – that's what the whip-thin man was telling her, his voice as understanding as it was insistent. Every day, the numbers killed or maimed – I don't need to tell you, he said; you've nursed those boys, and they're the lucky ones. Of course, many women are nurses, but you alone, Vivian, may I call you Vivian, you alone can tell me what I need to know.

How proud Papa would be to know she had said something

useful to the man from the War Office. But even at the cost of betraying one of his closest friends. All those who felt about this war as Viv knew she should were putting their personal lives to one side for the greater good. Mary had convinced her own brother to sign up, though it would break her heart if the slightest hurt came to him. Papa would most certainly have sent his own sons to war. Yes, Papa would do what was right for the war; and that was a sign of his strength.

– You can't betray a man to his friends, only to his enemies, the man from the War Office said. What you say will do no harm, and it may do our boys at the Front a great deal of good. I can't put it more simply or honestly than that.

For a few moments there was no sound, not even breath. He waited, his expression grave, and, yes, trusting. Was this how it felt, every day, to be a man – relied upon, responsible, in a position to guide decisions about how to conduct a war? The weight of it was terrible and wonderful all at once.

– Tahsin Bey. Part of his family is Armenian.

She had expected her heart to stutter, her breath to snag, but once she'd said it, it felt inevitable.

– I see. Are his sympathies well known?

– No one knows. His nephew, perhaps, to some extent.

– Would you tell me, please, exactly what he said?

– It was the day we parted company . . .

She kept her eyes on his hands as she spoke – the certain strokes of his pen, the half-moons in the nails of fingers balancing the notepad on his knee. He didn't interrupt, and when she was done he thanked her and said no one, not even her parents, would come to know the details of what she'd said. Then it was over; he departed; minutes later her father re-entered the room, and there was no 'almost' in his tone or in his words when he said he wouldn't press her for details but it was clear from what little the man from the War Office had revealed that she had done as much as any man's son on the battlefield.

– Oh Papa, she said, placing her arms around his neck, certain then that she had made the right decision.

*　*　*

35

Once, there were calluses from spadework, cypresses against the blue skies, the scent of figs, the fellowship of curiosity, ancient words imprinted on her palm, the slow headlong journey towards love. Now there was metal probing wounds, the stench of rotting flesh, the weeping of men too deep in suffering to remember shame, the leeching of colour from her skin, her eyes, but never her dreams in which men died as she stood helplessly by, again and again and yet again. This was the world of the Class A hospital, and she would never become accustomed to it.

One day of the week was a half-day, though it was considered bad form to take it when there was any shortage of hands – which was almost always. So it was a rare Friday on which Viv finished at 1 p.m. and had a beautiful April afternoon all to herself. From Camberwell she rode the buses home, her heart expanding as she saw the tops of the trees in Regent's Park – in the three months since she'd started at 1st London General Hospital she hadn't set foot in Cambridge Terrace, though she was entitled to seven days' leave during the period of her six-month term. (Even the men in the trenches don't work as hard, one of the VAD nurses had said, and Viv suspected that Mary was the reason the poor woman was placed on a double shift the next day.)

– Good God, Vivian, her mother said when she walked through the door. You look terrible.

But her father swung her up in his arms and said, My returning soldier! He had thought of shutting down his own practice and offering his services to the military hospitals but a delegation of expectant mothers had arrived at his door to say wasn't it enough that their husbands in the trenches would miss the births of their children – did the best gynaecologist in London have to miss them too?

– This soldier refuses to speak of the war today. Except for this.

From her pocket she pulled out a column of newsprint, carefully folded, and watched as he read the account of Armenian

36

intellectuals in Turkey rounded up and deported. The article had no information about what happened to them but said the worst was feared.

– I read it this morning. Dreadful business.

– Papa! she said, laughing to be the one to explain the world to him. It's propaganda. I think I may have played a role in placing it there.

She'd never seen him so amazed, so delighted.

It was near the end of the evening, and she could no longer delay returning to the hostel, back into her life of drudgery broken up by horror. She stood up to leave and it was only then that her father said oh yes, there'd been a Christmas card from Tahsin Bey addressed to all of them – it had been posted months earlier, but perhaps it was a wonder it had arrived at all. There was a message in it particularly for Viv so they'd kept it – where was it? Long awful minutes passed before the one-armed footman remembered it had been placed in Miss Spencer's room. Should he bring it down?

– No need, said Viv, surprised by the calmness of her voice. I need something from up there – if you'll excuse me, Papa, Mama.

My dear family Spencer

I have no way of knowing if this will reach you – I've had no post from London since the war began, and I like to hope this is a failure of the postal service. Regardless, in times such as these the rituals of friendship seem more important than ever so please accept my Christmas Greetings! I hope another Christmas doesn't pass before we're able to meet again.

I am well. I spend my days cataloguing the Labraunda finds at a long table under the cypress tree in my garden, Alice asleep on my feet. And although there is a great deal of unhappiness in the world I am daily reminded of life's capacity to find new ways to delight and enrapture – most recently while reading D. B. Spooner's account of the excavations at Shahji-ki-Dheri, on the outskirts of Peshawar. Vivian Rose, you'll find it in the

'Archaeological Survey of India, Frontier Circle 1908-9'. I'm sure you'll be as taken by it as I am. Since reading it I've had a great longing to go to Peshawar (which was once the city of Caspatyrus from where Scylax set off on his great voyage down the Indus. Caspatyrus! Where journeys begin and end). I would rush to Peshawar tomorrow to see the Sacred Casket of Kanishka discovered there by Spooner if I could. Perhaps you'll have the chance to do so before I'm able?
With warmth and best wishes
Tahsin

The card was written in a miniature version of his usual script; he hadn't wanted to waste the opportunity for a single added word. Viv leaned her back against the wall, the legs which endured twelve-hour shifts in a hospital suddenly too weak to support her.

The librarian at UCL remembered Miss Spencer and, seeing her VAD uniform, was happy to let her search through the shelves for a particular reference. When she left a few minutes later he waved goodbye, not thinking to check if her handbag might have the ripped-out pages of a journal folded up inside.

What had he been trying to tell her? Viv, sitting on the window-sill of the hostel's top floor as dawn light squeezed through the tall elm trees, unfolded the pages of D. B. Spooner's report to try and make more sense of them than she had when she'd read them the previous night – first, standing on the paving stones of UCL; then in the taxicab on the way back to the hostel; and again by candlelight in bed. So, a casket containing the relics of the Buddha had been found in Shahji-ki-Dheri, near Peshawar in the ruins of the Great Stupa of Kanishka. What of it? Why, of all the discoveries of the world, should this one 'delight and enrapture' Tahsin Bey?

It is with special pleasure that I turn now to the subject of the excavations at Shahji-ki-Dheri.

38

This time, the first sentence of D. B. Spooner's report sent a tremor of discovery along her spine, so overwhelming she had to grip the windowsill to steady herself. She rubbed her thumb along the fingertips of her right hand – with these she had brushed away the clinging mud of the inscription stone and watched Greek letters emerge. Now the fingers were chilblained, the tiny cut on her thumb plastered to guard against a soldier's septic wound discharging into her bloodstream. She rubbed her hands together, palm sliding against palm – she was in a different skin now.

She leaned back against the grey stone which together with the tall encircling trees kept the hostel in a state of perpetual gloom. Perhaps Tahsin Bey just wished to remind her of this – she was an archaeologist, as was he. In the shiver of their spines they were of the same tribe, regardless of wars and kings and sultans. Could that be all there was to it? *Caspatyrus! Where journeys begin and end.* Another puzzle. Scylax began his famed journey down the Indus from Caspatyrus – the ancient name for Peshawar – but he didn't end it there. *Perhaps you'll have the chance to do so before I'm able?*

– Oh, she said.

Somewhere across the oceans a Turkish man sat at a table of discovery under a cypress tree, and understood what no one else seemed to: that she, also, needed a place in the world where she could sit in sunshine, examining ancient coins, fragments of gods, while the war she didn't understand washed over her and disappeared into the horizon.

– Nurse Spencer! You've missed your breakfast and it's time to leave for the hospital.

City of Men,
City of Flowers,
Land Beyond the Mountains:
Caspatyrus, Paruparaesanna, Paropamisadae, Gandhara, Parasapur, Purashapura, Poshapura, Po-lu-sha-pu-lo, Fo-lu-sha, Farshabur, Peshawar.

They all had a name for it, century after century – the Persians, the Greeks, the Mauryans, the Indo-Greeks, the Sassanids, the Kushans; kings and generals and Buddhist monks and travellers, everyone felt the tug of Peshawar. Everyone, including an Englishwoman in a Class A hospital who wanted nothing more than a refuge amidst antiquity.

Now there were nights she dreamed different dreams and woke up with a longing even more unbearable than dread.

Private Andrews, twenty-one, who died of wounds; Private Smith, eighteen, who died of septic shock; Corporal Grimes, thirty-three, who died of pneumonia. The one with the bow-lips, recovering well, who never woke up and no one knew why. The one who called her 'Queen of Sheba', and didn't live long enough to explain it. The one – sandy-haired, blue-eyed, the inexplicable scent of apple on his breath – who clutched her hand and asked her to sit with him, which she said she couldn't do because it was against hospital rules, even though she knew he was very near the end and everyone understood when exceptions were permitted.

He was the one from whom she couldn't recover.

She stood in the shadow of the red-brick hospital building, shaking and shaking. It wouldn't stop. Matron told her to pull herself together; the doctor slapped her sharply across the face; Mary put her arms around her and sang a lullaby.

– Send her home, she heard Matron say. She has a few leave days due. After that, she'll be right as rain.

Her bed felt unfamiliar, the colourful motifs of the wallpaper hurt her eyes. Her parents' voices were raised outside her door, words coming through which made no sense. The shaking had stopped, outwardly, but her mind couldn't hold a thought for any length of time without splintering apart. She took a deep breath, thought of a cliff above the sea, the taste of figs on her tongue, a man's index finger touching the jut of her wrist, the sea so blue she thought it might drive her mad though she understood nothing of madness then. She closed her eyes, and slept without dreaming.

– So, your father thinks you're ready to go back?

Mrs Spencer bent to examine a half-opened bud in Regent's Park Rose Garden, flicking an insect away from the petals.

– Papa knows best, said Viv, wondering why her mother had insisted that they take a walk together when the swift summer shower ended and a rainbow looped across the sky. There was a sound remarkably close to a snort, before Mrs Spencer straightened and looked at her daughter.

– Are you to spend the rest of your life making up for my womb's insistence on killing his sons?

Viv scuffed her shoe in the rain-damp grass, and didn't know what to say to that, the unmentioned topic of their lives.

– There's a war on. We all have a duty.

– Oh yes, we certainly do. How quickly everything that was inconceivable for a woman has become her duty. Isn't it miraculous that competence has sprung up in us in the exact shape of men's needs?

Viv looked around anxiously, hoping none of the other women or the wounded serviceman out for an evening stroll could hear. It had been the most welcome of surprises to find Mama all consideration when Mary half-carried Viv into the house two days earlier, but she had gone right back to being the difficult Mrs Spencer now that Viv was up on her feet and feeling foolish about her behaviour, which her father assured her was down to nothing but exhaustion. Two days of solid sleep and you're fine, Dr Spencer had cheerfully declared this morning when Viv came down to breakfast and ate three eggs and five rashers of bacon.

– Have you even thought about the fact that you're almost at the end of your six-month term at the hospital?

– It doesn't mean anything. Everyone signs on for another term as soon as one ends.

– Everyone isn't my daughter. Do you have any idea how

41

terrifying it was when Mary brought you home? What you looked like? Empty. Your face – just a shell.

– It was exhaustion.

– That was only part of it. You father, he doesn't want to see or can't see, I don't know which, but I don't share his blindness. Not about you, not about how far this war is from ending. Will you give your entire youth to it? Give your health, and your heart and your sanity?

– Mama, you're being dramatic.

– Every time I see you there's less of you there. I don't think you have any idea what you want for your life other than pleasing your papa. Making up for the fact that he doesn't have sons to send into the trenches to have their heads blown off. Next month when you turn twenty-three and he reminds you you're old enough to join the mobile nursing units at the Front – what will you say then? You know he'll do it, don't you?

They walked in silence after that for a while, around the circle of the garden; raindrops dried on the petals of yellow and pink and red roses, and the sun moved further beyond the reach of clouds.

– Peshawar, Viv said finally, tentatively. That's what I want for my life. I want to go to Peshawar.

She waited for her mother to look outraged or disbelieving, but Mrs Spencer only said, Why?

– Because there's more past than present there.

– There's no need to be so coy about it. You mean you want to be away from the war?

– Yes.

– Thank God there's some sense in you. Why Peshawar?

– Two and a half thousand years of history beneath its soil. How long a list of reasons do you need?

– Tahsin Bey mentioned it in that Christmas card.

– Yes. He knew it's a place I very much want to see.

The explanation sounded false to her own ears, but Mrs Spencer merely nodded. It began to occur to Viv that this conversation was in earnest.

– Papa would never agree. And I can't just go off half way around the world, in the middle of the war.

Mrs Spencer picked up a rose which had tumbled off its stem into the grass, and brushed its softness against her cheek, her eyelids drooping with the pleasure of it. Viv had the strange sensation of witnessing her mother as she had been as a very young woman, when the world had more possibilities than disappointments in it.

– You went off to Turkey, to live in a tent, on a hillside, with no one within hundreds of miles known to any of us except an unmarried foreign man. That was your father's doing. He's in no position to object when I find you a situation far more conventional than that in the heart of our own empire.

She nipped at a petal, pursed her mouth in distaste and threw the rose back into the grass.

– I don't understand. What will you say to him? What conventional situation?

– Leave that to me.

Viv began to see she hadn't the faintest idea what kind of woman her mother really was. Until now, it had never seemed particularly interesting to find out.

April 1915

Qayyum raised the buttered bread to his nose, the scent of it a confirmation that Allah himself loved the French more than the Pashtuns. Beside him, Kalam Khan, impatient for the taste of fruit, bit right through the skin of an orange to get to the flesh beneath, eyes closed in pleasure as his jaws worked their way around the peel.

– How is it?

– Tasteless.

Kalam wiped a smear of butter off Qayyum's nose and spat a mix of peel and rind onto the train tracks, grinning – a boy who grew up in fruit orchards delighted to discover that his father's produce in the Peshawar Valley was superior to anything France could grow in her soil. No matter that everything else here was better than the world they'd left behind – the cows sleeker, the buildings grander, the men more dignified, the women . . . what to think about the women? One of the men coming out of the station made a gesture as if holding two plump melons against his chest, and there was a rush of men towards the doorway just as Lt Bonham-Carter stepped out, followed by a Frenchman and a woman whose dress was cut to display her breasts as if they were wares for sale.

– Whore, Kalam said cheerfully, but Qayyum looked away when he saw how the woman first crossed her hands in front of her chest and then, raising her head to stare down the men, lowered them to her hips.

Lt Bonham-Carter asked for the regimental band to gather

44

together. The Frenchman refused to take any money for the cigarettes, coffee, oranges and bread the men had purchased, and had asked instead for the band to play the 'Marseillaise', as it had when the 40th Pathans disembarked at the port of that city and processed through town. Lt Bonham-Carter smiled as he relayed the information – he'd been the one to teach the dhol and shehnai band how to play the French tune on the journey from Alexandria. The brilliance of the English was to understand all the races of the world; how the French had cheered the 40th Pathans as they made their way from the docks to the racecourse in Marseilles. *Les Indiens! Les Indiens!* A cry of welcome that made the men heroes before they had even stepped onto the battlefield. How much finer this was than Qayyum's first deployment to Calcutta where the Bengali babus were trying to cause trouble for the Raj and required a few Pathans in their midst to instruct them how to behave.

The band followed up the 'Marseillaise' with their regimental song, 'Zakhmi Dil', all the men joining in, including most of the English officers. Kalam turned to Qayyum, arms spread in resignation as he sang the opening words on a platform in rural France where the Pashto language might never have been heard before: There's a boy across the river / With a bottom like a peach / But alas! I cannot swim. When the song ended the Frenchman, for whom none of the officers had provided a translation, declared, *Magnifique!* And the woman rested both elbows on the back of a bench and leaned forward, looking straight at Qayyum. *Magnifique,* she echoed.

Embarrassed at himself for wondering if she wasn't talking about the song, Qayyum looked away and around the platform; how proud they were – Punjabis, Dogras, Pashtuns, all! – to be received with such warmth by these strangers. The generosity of the Frenchman was all it had taken to allow them to set aside the disgruntlement they had been carrying around since Marseilles, where they were told they had to give up their turbans and drab-and-green regimental wear in favour of balaclavas and badly fitting, prickly uniforms of grey that were better suited to the climate. And their guns, too, had been taken

45

away because they weren't right for the French ammunition; the new rifles were unfamiliar, the weight, the shape of them not yet a natural extension of the soldiers' bodies.

But a few minutes later, in the storage room where the smell of coffee beans soon fused with an even earthier scent, the French girl showed Qayyum how quickly an unknown body could become joined to yours. He was tentative until that became impossible. His only previous experience had been in Kowloon, the night before the 40th shipped off to France, with a woman who didn't pretend he was giving her anything she wanted other than the money he'd been told to place on the table before they started. That had been less troubling in some way than the responses of this girl who seemed to derive pleasure from things that made him worry he was hurting her. Would a Pashtun woman react this way? he wondered, almost as soon as it was over, the thought making him feel ashamed both for himself and the French girl who kissed him on the mouth and said something he couldn't understand. It was only then he realised they hadn't said a word to each other, and when he spoke to her in his broken English she shook her head and laughed. He had assumed all white people could understand each other's language in the way all the Indians in the Army had at least one tongue in common.

Kalam was watching for him when he stepped out of the storage room, his expression mocking, slightly hurt.

– Watch out, brother. You are too much in love with these people already.

– Salute your officers, Sepoy.

– Yes, sir, Lance-Naik, sir!

His salute was so sharp it meant to draw blood. Qayyum – his promotion from sepoy just days old – dismissed him with a lazy wave of his hand, refusing to take the challenge. Yes, he was in love with these people, this world. The shame had passed as quickly as it had arrived, and he drew himself up to his full height as the train whistled its arrival, understanding at that moment what it was to be a man – the wonder, the beauty of it.

* * *

They arrived in Ouderdom in the rain, Kalam hobbling on the ankle he had twisted when he slipped on a slick cobblestone. The fall had been a bad one, and Qayyum fell out to help him up, putting Kalam's arm around his own shoulders, prepared to support him for as long as they needed to keep marching. But a Belgian woman came out of her house and put salve on Kalam's ankle, bound his foot in a bandage and disappeared back inside without a word. Kalam had felt shamed by that and hadn't said a word since, except to tell Qayyum that he could walk on his own feet.

But now Kalam looked up across the farmland and smiled – there, walking across the field, were men whose faces were known to the 40th, not personally but in the set of their features, their expression. The soldiers of the Lahore Division, the first of the Indian Army to arrive in France. Above the howl of the wind a voice called out in Pashto, What took you so long? Too many peach bottoms distracting you along the way?

– We thought we'd give you some chance at glory before taking it all for ourselves!

Kalam, restored to good humour. Qayyum looked around at the men of the 40th grinning, name-calling. Not just the Pashtuns, but also the Dogras, the Punjabis. Brothers recognising brothers with a jolt of love, a shot of competition. What Qayyum felt on seeing battalion after battalion of Indian soldiers bivouacked on the farmland was something quite different – a deep, inexplicable relief.

The havildar-naik of 57th Wilde's Rifle fell into step with Qayyum as he walked across the moonlit stretch of grass. No sound except that of snoring soldiers and the call of a solitary night-bird.

– Worrying about tomorrow, Lance-Naik?

– Sir, no, sir.

– I don't want to be 'sir' just now. Mohammad Khan Afridi, from Landi Kotal.

– Qayyum Gul. Peshawar.

– Do you think one day they'll tell stories about us in the Street of Storytellers?

The Afridi lit a cigarette, handed it to Qayyum, and lit another one for himself. Qayyum's shoes squeaked on the wet grass as he rocked back on his heels, blowing smoke up into the air, watching the ghostly trail of it ascend and dissipate.

– Did you hear about the 5th Light Infantry? the Afridi asked.

– No, sir. What? Are they here also?

– No, Singapore. On trial for mutiny. Not all of them, but many.

– Pashtuns?

– Pashtuns and Rajput Muslims. They heard a rumour they would be sent to Turkey to fight fellow Muslims, so they mutinied. Killed their officers.

Qayyum swore loudly, and the older man nodded his head, held the tip of his cigarette against an oak leaf and burned a circle into it. The smell carried a hint of winter fires.

– They join an army which fights fellow Pashtuns in the tribal areas, but they'll mutiny at the thought of taking up arms against Turks. That's our people for you, Lance-Naik.

Qayyum shook his head, looked over the encampment. At 5.30 tomorrow morning they'd be on the march again. He cleared his throat, moistened his lips.

– What's it really like? Fighting the Germans?

– Go and sleep now, Lance-Naik. Dream of Peshawar. That's an order. You'll have the answer to your question tomorrow, at Vipers.

Again and again the pain plunged him into oblivion and a fresh burst of gunfire pulled him out. Then there was silence, and he waited for the darkness to claim him but there was only fire racing along his face, licking deep into his eye-socket. An ant climbed a blade of grass and his laboured breath blew it off in the direction of the stream, a few feet away, unreachable; the sun that made the fire burn more fiercely on his face turned playful as it dipped into the balm of the water. I will die here, Qayyum thought, and waited for Allah or his family or the mountains of Peshawar to take hold of his heart. But there was only the fire, and the blood drowning his eye and the stench of dead men. Was he the only man alive, or were there others like him who knew the gunners would find them if they twitched a limb?

Perhaps he was dead already, and this was hell. The eternal fires, yes. It must have happened just as they ascended the slopes – the Germans were right on the other side of it, just over the crest of the hill. But the first round of bullets must have killed him and flung him into this devil-made world in which men had to run across a field without cover, stumbling over the corpses of their brothers, and when the tattered remnants of one division reached the enemy lines on the slope across the field, a yellow mist entered their bodies and made them fall, foam at their mouths. Cover your nose and mouth, the order came, swift and useless; if they'd had their turbans they would have wound them around their faces but there were only the balaclavas. Qayyum remembered the handkerchief in his pocket, the one Captain Dalmohy had instructed him to dip into the buckets of liquid they passed, and he held it up against his face even as he watched the breeze move the yellow mist eastward. So this wasn't hell. The mist would have leapt into his lungs if it were.

The emerald green of the grass turned to pine green; the sun sank entirely into the water. His hand had gone to sleep but he was afraid to shake it awake even though the numbness was moving up his arm. There had been a sepoy sitting upright in the field as men advanced around him, one arm ending at the wrist. Qayyum picked up the severed hand he'd almost trodden on, and passed it to the man who thanked him, very politely, and tried to join the hand in place. I think there's a piece missing. Can you look? he said, and died. Qayyum had forgotten this, though it had happened only hours earlier.

Qayyum tried to pray, but the Merciful, the Beneficent, had abandoned this field and the men within it. Something was moving along the ground, a heavy weight; a starving animal, wolf or jackal, with its belly pressed against the ground, smelling meat; a German with a knife between his teeth. Grass flattened, the thing entered the space between Qayyum and the stream. Any movement was pain, any movement was target practice to the gunners. And then a whisper, his name.

– Kalam, stay there. They'll shoot you.
– Lance-Naik, sir. Shut up.

One afternoon in the Street of Money Changers, Qayyum and his brother Najeeb had stumbled on an object in the road – a dead rabbit with its lips sewn together, foam at its mouth. A man walked past a hundred cruelties in Peshawar every day, and nothing about the rabbit made him slow his stride, but Najeeb knelt on the street and carefully cut away the thread, the animal's fur-and-mud-caked head in his palm. When Qayyum put a hand on the boy's shoulder, Najeeb looked up and asked, Do you think its family was near by and it tried to call out to them? As if that were the real reason for distress, not the needle lancing the animal's lips, the hand which would have stopped the breath at its nose. Oh Allah, the cruelty of the world. How had Najeeb known this terror, this loneliness of dying alone? Kalam's hand clasped his ankle and he felt tears dislodge the blood in his eye, which he couldn't touch without feeling as if he was wiping off his whole face.

– Don't leave me.
– Brainless Pashtun, do you think I came all this way just to smell your socks?

Time had never moved more slowly than in those minutes – or was it hours? – in which Kalam inched himself along the ground until his face was level with Qayyum's, and he could see what the fire had done.

– Tell me. How bad is it?
– Don't worry, Yousuf, all Zuleikhas will still want to seduce you and so will the Potiphars.
– Kalam, don't joke.
– It's this or tears. Just be patient, we'll retreat when it's dark.
– The sun has gone.
– My friend, you've forgotten the moon, large and white as

50

your Frenchwoman's breast and climbing through the sky. Still a few more hours. But I'm here, don't worry. Your Kalam is here.

The end of his sentence disappeared in gunfire. Qayyum's body jerked in anticipation of the bullets that would rip through him, but Kalam had a hand on his chest, telling him to hold still, the gunners were aiming at something else. You stay still too, Qayyum said, but Kalam braced on his elbows and used them as a pivot for his arms, the rest of his body motionless as – again and again – he lowered his palms into the stream and slowly, hardly spilling a drop, brought them to Qayyum's parched mouth, washed the blood from his face and tried to clean the mess that was his eye. With the stink of blood all around, the only light in the world came from those cupped palms, the shifting water within them.

May–June 1915

−I'm sorry, no, it won't recover like a knife-cut on your arm. We must remove it.

The Indian doctor stepped back and switched off a torch which Qayyum didn't realise he'd been holding. When the doctor patted his shoulder and moved to the next bed, the white-skinned woman, grey-haired, and with lines all around her mouth, stayed to replace his bandages, her touch impersonal in a way he'd never imagined a woman's touch could be. Where was it they had brought him? Brighton, they said, but all he knew of it was the pebbled beach, the damp smell of the ambulance, and then this place, this page out of a book of djinn stories into which they'd carried him. Everything ever seen or imagined painted upon its walls, its ceilings – dragons and trees and birds and men from Tashkent or Farghana like those in the Street of Storytellers. Such colour, such richness. More than a single eye could hold. He was floating above it all, beside the gilded dragons on the leather canopy of the ceiling. England had made the pain stop. But the woman was speaking to him, he must return to the bed to hear what she was saying.

− We'll fit you up with a glass eye, and you'll be breaking hearts again in no time.

− I don't want to break hearts.

− Oh, love.

He didn't know why she looked at him in that way, or what a woman was doing among all these men but when she said 'love' in that sad tone of voice he understood, even through the

52

glow of painlessness, that he was maimed now, a partial man, and from here on he would never be admired, only pitied.

He used to be a man who climbed trees just to see the view from the top, one who entered a new city and sought out its densest alleys, a man who strode towards clamour. Now he couldn't think of a branch without imagining the tip of it entering his remaining eye. Everything everywhere was a threat. Every branch, every ball arcing through the air, every gust of wind, every sharp sound, every darkened room, every night, every day. The elbows of a woman; her sudden movements towards him in desire; her hands searching his face for those expressions that only revealed themselves in the dark. He traced the skin around his bandaged eye. Who was he now, this man who saw proximity as danger?

A warning, brother, if you see me walking through the streets, stay far from me. What I want I will have – women or men, wine or gold. A blade through the heart of anyone who tries to stop me. This is how it is when a man walks into hell and survives it. When you return to Peshawar, tell my father he was right. I should have stayed in the orchards.

Qayyum looked up from the letter. Through the mist, the arched gateway and green dome of the Pavilion entrance seemed insubstantial, a fantasy thrown up against the English sky by the force of the soldiers' homesickness. He wound his blanket tighter around his shoulders, his eye aching from the strain of reading only a few sentences. Was there a taunt in the letter beneath the rage directed at the world, or did this unease all come from within himself? One day at Vipers, and his war ended. Now here he was in the grounds of a palace in Brighton while Sepoy Kalam Khan wrote to him from the trenches at Aubers Ridge.

He raised his hand to his eyelid, permanently closed, and pressed down gently, feeling no resistance. There were men here who envied him this, his ticket home. 'When you return to

53

Peshawar'. But he wanted neither Peshawar nor Aubers Ridge – wanted only this domed pavilion by the sea, this place which did all that human hands could do to repair broken men and asked nothing about a soldier's caste or religion to make him feel inferior but understood enough about these things to have nine different kitchens where food could be prepared separately for each group, and where the meat for Muslims was plentiful and halal. The King-Emperor himself had sent strict instructions that no one should treat a black – and this word included Pashtuns – soldier as a lesser man. The thought of the King-Emperor made Qayyum rest a hand against his chest and bow his head. He had given his own palace to wounded Indian soldiers. What nawab or maharaja would do as much?

This thought first came to him when he looked at the great chandelier in Ward 1, its immensity hanging from the claw of a silver dragon; the long-tongued beast, in turn, descended from copper banana leaves which seemed to grow straight out of the painted foliage on the ceiling. Was it beautiful or ugly, he couldn't decide. But he knew that this one chandelier had more grandeur than all of Peshawar. In time, he came to see the chandelier as Empire – the King was the silver dragon, one single claw bearing the weight of smaller dragons, glass lotus flowers, a star of mirrors. He repeated this to one of the English doctors, and thereafter he was called upon whenever there were important visitors to explain that when he looked at the chandelier he gazed upon the glory of the King. What he said was a source of marvel equalled, if not exceeded, by the fact that he said it in English. When the supervising nurse was there to hear the compliment she'd wink at Qayyum and place a finger on her lips – she was the one who had taught him the English words he hadn't known, polished the grammar of his sentences, explained that the glass objects were lotus flowers and not replicas of the dusters which the staff used to clean the chandelier.

It was astonishing how easy the nurses here made it to be in the presence of a woman who wasn't mother or sister or wife. In the wards the soldiers talked endlessly about white women

– not just the nurses but also the French farm girls some of them had bivouacked with and the female aviator who one of them swore he'd met (no one believed him, but everyone asked him to tell the story over and over). Nothing about France or England was more different from India than the women – and from here it was a step some of the soldiers made to declare that if India's women changed then India too would become prosperous like the white nations, and everything from the livestock to the people would have a gleam to it. Qayyum listened to them and tried to imagine telling his mother she should be more like the women of Europe – she'd hit him about the ears with a shoe as if he were still a child.

Without warning, the air became driving rain and Kalam's words smeared across the page. Qayyum ducked his head and, as quickly as his fumbling hands could manage, threw the blanket over his head, covering it completely. The day his youngest sister put on a burqa for the first time she wore it backwards, no face-mesh for sight or breath, and she had burst into tears until Qayyum lifted it off and put it on the right way round; she was still young enough to throw her arms around him and say, Lala, forget the Army, stay here and defend us from our mistakes. Even the lost eye didn't make him wish he'd listened. Here he was, in the King's own palace.

But there was another side to this world and Kalam Khan was in it, regretting his soldier's uniform, the brotherhood of the 40th, the honour of service. Qayyum wondered who had written Kalam's words for him now that he wasn't there to do it, and if the letter-writer had left anything out. Qayyum recognised a process of selection as part of his own duty as letter-writer to the wounded, unlettered men at the Pavilion. So many of them asked him to write home for God's sake don't don't don't allow my brother my cousin anyone from our village to sign up. Such words would never get past the censors, and they would reflect poorly on the Indian troops who had been trusted to come halfway round the world to fight for their king though there were many in England who thought their loyalty would fail the challenge.

– Any doubts about you are held only by those who've never had the honour of serving beside you.

That was the only thing the English officers said, or needed to say, when the 40th set sail for France.

The rain was knocking on the blanket and pain was responding, yes, yes, I'm here, I haven't really gone away. He peeled the wet wool away from his face and held it above his head like a canopy; the relief of emerging from the clinging fabric was immense. Across the garden he saw a limping figure. It was the sepoy whose ankle had been shattered by a bullet and whose lungs were weakened by chlorine gas; soon he would be sent back to France. His letter had been addressed to the King-Emperor himself, complaining that wounded Indians were sent back into the field with injuries that would allow an English soldier to return home. Qayyum wrote down every word the man said, knowing it would never reach the palace. The letter ended: *If a man is to die defending a field, let the field be his field, the land his land, the people his people.*

Two nurses approached, umbrellas held above their heads. Flanking Qayyum like bodyguards, they each placed a hand on his upper arms and guided him back to the ward, his one remaining eye closed to protect it from the piercing rain.

He saw the supervising nurse approach when he was in the Pavilion garden reading aloud a letter which one of the sepoys had received from his wife. The sepoy wept in his wheelchair, knowing that his wife's dreams of the children they would have together when he returned would never be realised. Qayyum thought the nurse was there to let him know that the car was ready to take him to the glass maker's to be measured for an eye, but despite his eagerness to walk through the world with the semblance of a whole man he finished reading the letter and sat with his hand on the sepoy's shoulder for a period of time until the man's sobbing quietened before walking over to where she stood beneath a tree.

– You are very kind with the men, Lance-Naik. I think you must spend half your day reading or writing letters for others.

– It helps the day become night.

– Yes. Well, I wanted to say goodbye, and good luck.

– I am going?

– Not you.

She glanced over her shoulder, and spoke to the Englishman in civilian clothes who had approached unobserved.

– Put this in your report. Tell them a fifty-six-year-old widow was seen giving signs of favour to a Pathan boy. Let the Empire tremble at that.

Turning back to Qayyum, she pressed her handkerchief into his hands.

– When you have your new eye you may want something to wrap it in at night.

He didn't immediately understand. Not that day or the one after, not even when he realised all the female nurses had left. But later in the week, on an excursion to the pebbled seafront, he met two fellow NCOs of the Lahore Division – a Sikh and a Rajput – who said all the women had been removed from York Place Hospital as well.

– Have the English decided women shouldn't see wounded men? Qayyum asked.

The Sikh merely grunted, picking up a pebble with the hand that remained – his left – and concentrating all his attention on readying to throw, the sleeve on his right side flapping. It was early in the morning, the sun had barely risen; the hour when disfigured men went out into the emptied world.

But the Rajput with half a face in bandages and the rasping voice of one who has swallowed gas made a sound of derision.

– They haven't removed them from all hospitals. Just the ones with Indian patients.

– Why?

– Why do you think? Why do you think the Englishwomen who come to visit you in the wards and tell you how much the Empire owes you are never young and never out of sight of an Englishman?

The Sikh flung the pebble, his entire body pivoting. Qayyum stepped away from him, shielding his good eye. If the Rajput hadn't been there to steady the Sikh he would have fallen to the ground. The pebble landed on another pebble – a sharp clinking sound – and the sea rushed in to cover it. The Sikh pushed the Rajput away, tottered, regained his balance, and when he spoke his face was a snarl.

– They're right to worry. I'm going to find every Englishwoman whose husband is at war and quench her thirst for a man.

– Watch what you say. You Sikhs have to be twice as loyal as the rest of us now.

The Rajput spoke with sympathy, but his words were met with a string of curses. In Lahore, a conspiracy trial was under way for almost three hundred men – most of them Sikhs – accused of trying to start a rebellion in the British Indian Army, backed by the Germans. The supervising nurse had said to Qayyum, If a whisper of doubt should attach itself to any of the soldiers here because of this wicked plot I'll go to Lahore, and hang the conspirators myself. He had found himself imagining an embrace with the old lady. The conspiracy itself, which never had any real chance of success, wasn't as unsettling for Qayyum as was the fact that some of the sepoys in the Pavilion had already started to use the name 'Kirpal Singh' to mean an informer, a double-dealer, one who couldn't be trusted. Kirpal Singh, the man who had informed the English of the plot and sent his fellow Sikhs to prison and soon – it was inevitable – the firing squad.

One of the Indian doctors from the Pavilion, the one on the night shift, was walking towards them along the seafront. Qayyum called him over, and asked about the nurses. The doctor spread his hands to indicate the strange workings of the English and said their withdrawal had followed the outrage created in official circles by a newspaper photograph of a nurse standing beside the bed of Khudedad Khan, the first Indian to receive a Victoria Cross.

Neither the Rajput nor Qayyum knew what to say about that. All three men stood silently watching the Sikh who had the end of his empty sleeve between his teeth, pulling it taut, and was dragging the sharp point of a pebble back and forth against the fabric just below the stump of his arm. The word 'dishonour' entered Qayyum's mind and would not be dislodged.

Qayyum, I am here, in Brighton. At Kitchener Hospital. Don't worry, it is bullet wounds in places where the flesh will heal and soon they will send me back to France. But I am here now, in Brighton. I pray to Allah you haven't left for Peshawar yet. Kalam Khan, Sepoy.

He walked through Brighton's streets, the sunshine sharp. Previously he had only walked the short distance from the Pavilion to the seafront in the early morning. Now he gathered a group of curious children who followed after him whistling 'It's A Long Way To Tipperary' until he turned round and, expression blank, mimed playing a flute. One of the nurses had told him this was a useful way to make a crowd of children disperse and, astonishingly, it worked, though why they screamed and ran he didn't know. On Queen's Park Road a car stopped and the driver offered to take him to the hospital, but he was enjoying the grand houses and the quiet street and the feeling of anticipation with which he was walking towards Kalam so he thanked the man and continued on. Further along the road an Englishman with large whiskers tipped his hat to Qayyum, and his wife murmured, Thank you. His strides lengthened, the sun flung its warmth at him, extravagantly. He was still Qayyum Gul, despite everything.

Kitchener Hospital was a vast building, four storeys high with a clock tower against which Qayyum checked his wrist-watch, stopping to wind it up and move the minute hand forward by a tiny degree. One of the doctors on the hospital ship to Brighton had strapped it onto his wrist, and no explanation was asked for or received. He would give it to Kalam, he decided as he slowly approached the gate, squinting at every open window to see if a familiar form might be leaning out of it, waiting. With his attention on the upper storeys he didn't see the man in the sentry box and would have walked right

59

through the open gate if the man – a military policeman – hadn't commanded him to stop, and asked what he wanted.

– Lance-Naik Qayyum Gul. Here to see Sepoy Kalam Khan.
– No visitors allowed.
– What time I should come back?
– No visitors allowed.
– Because today is Sunday?
– No, because no visitors are allowed. Any day. Any time.
– My friend is in there. We were at Vipers. 40th Pathans.
– No. Visitors. Allowed.
– I am a lance-naik. 40th Pathans.
– That won't stop me from arresting you if you don't move along.

A car, with three Indians and an Englishman in it, drove out of the open gate and stopped next to the sentry box. What's going on? the English officer said in Urdu, and Qayyum, immeasurably relieved, saluted and said there was some miscommunication, his English wasn't very good, could the officer please tell the MP he was here to visit one of the sepoys under his command.

– Sorry, Lance-Naik, hospital rules. No visitors.
– Can you find out if he's well enough to come out? I don't know how bad the injuries are but maybe he can walk, or use a wheelchair.
– No Indian personnel, except NCOs, are allowed out of the hospital grounds. Except on supervised marches.
– Sir?
– Look, Lance-Naik, I didn't make the rules.
– But how do I see him?
– I'm afraid you don't.
– But we were at Vipers together. Sir? We fought at Vipers. He was at Aubers Ridge. He was under my command. 40th Pathans.
– I understand what you're trying to say. I'm extremely sorry, there's nothing I can do, not even for men who were at Ypres.

Qayyum looked frantically at the three Indian NCOs in the

car, two of whom had their heads turned away from him. The third – with the insignia of a naik – reached out of the car and touched his arm. Tell me his name, the naik said. I'll make sure he knows you were here.

Qayyum tilted his head back, cupped his hands around his mouth and called out through the hospital gates as loudly as his lungs would allow:

– Kalam Khan!

His voice was cut off by the hand at his throat. The military policeman brought his face close to Qayyum, who could see the man's eyeball, the yellowish tint of it, the blood vessels. What was he doing, this Englishman, young and able-bodied, standing outside a hospital keeping one soldier away from another?

– You are no one, Qayyum heard himself tell the Englishman.

– What did you just say?

The MP's hand closed around Qayyum's throat and Qayyum knew he could do it – he could strike an Englishman. But before that 'could' became 'would', the naik who had reached out towards him jumped out of the car, interposing himself between Qayyum and the MP, one hand on Qayyum's chest.

– He's only obeying rules, Lance-Naik. You need to leave.

The waves crashed over pebbles again – no, it was the gate closing, scraping the gravel beneath. The MP slid the bolt in place, and stood in front of it, arms crossed.

– Rules? Are there rules against saying a friend's name?

Again he raised his voice, drawing it out from deep in his belly:

– Kalam! It's me, it's Qayyum. Kalam!

The naik rested a finger just beneath Qayyum's good eye, the pad of his finger caressing the skin. Qayyum's voice stilled.

– Good man. Don't cause any trouble now.

Leaning in closer, he whispered, Even I can't go out unsupervised. We are prisoners here. You will make it worse for your friend.

That last sentence made it impossible to do anything but leave. When Qayyum returned to the Pavilion he saw, as if for the first time, the barbed wire around the walls, the sentries at the gate, the boarded-up gaps in the hedge. For the briefest of moments he believed he was in a German prisoner-of-war camp, with English-speaking men and women all around – an elaborate plan to turn the Indian soldiers against their King-Emperor.

But no, this was England and Kalam Khan was locked up in a hospital waiting for Qayyum to come to him as he had gone to Qayyum across a field of moonlight and dead men and German gunners. Tomorrow, Qayyum would find a way to see him, even if it meant petitioning the King-Emperor himself.

The next morning came a note from the naik at Kitchener to say Kalam would soon recover, and in the meantime he had been transferred to Barton-on-Sea. And that afternoon Qayyum's eye arrived from the glass maker's and the doctor said he could return to India.

On the last day in Brighton, Qayyum stood for a very long time near the doorway of Ward 3. Along the length of the walls were paintings of slim-trunked trees. A caged bird and an uncaged bird looked at each other, their gazes undeflected by the black and white butterflies flitting between them. The caged bird was the same muted orange as the door to its prison; the uncaged bird was the brown of the branch on which it stood, the tips of its wings the green and red of surrounding leaves and flowers. Qayyum took a step back – the birds, the flowers, the butter-flies, and the tree itself were enclosed in a gold frame, its shape that of a cage.

It wasn't until he was on the hospital ship, on his way back to India, that Qayyum realised the reason he hadn't received any response to the letters sent to Barton-on-Sea was that the message from the naik was a lie. He rushed out onto the deck, prepared to leap into the cold waters of the Atlantic, but it was too late, Britain was just a pinprick – such a small, small island.

CITY OF MEN, CITY OF FLOWERS

July 1915

At last, the two-rivered river.

Brightness scythed through the air into Viv's eyes as the train trundled out of the fortified entrance to the bridge; a dark imprint of river, hills, fort behind squeezed eyelids. What the negative couldn't reveal was this: two rivers running parallel to each other in one body of water – the blue of melted snow running down from the Himalayas, the brown of silt and turbulence racing across from Kabul. Progressing side by side until they passed beneath the Campbellpur Fort and merged.

Here, two and a half thousand years ago, Scylax sailed in on the muddied arm of the Cophen River and dived – how could anyone imagine he would do otherwise? – right into the jewelled blue.

Viv reached for her calfskin notebook even as the train crossed into the Peshawar Valley, splaying it open against the window, quickly sketching before memory could commence too far with its tampering. Had the light reflected differently off the two rivers in one? Did she really see a dolphin leap repeatedly in and out of the water along the border of the rivers, as though it were a needle stitching them together? She must keep as accurate a record as possible for Tahsin Bey.

She wrote *Indus* along the north-south length of the blue river, *Kabul/Cophen* beside the east-west muddy river, before turning the pages to find the lines she had copied out from Arrian's *Anabis Alexandri*: *The Indus emerges, already immense, from its sources, and after receiving the water of fifteen rivers, all of them larger than the rivers of Asia, and imposing its name upon them, empties into the sea.* Arrian, citizen of the Roman Empire, writing about Alexander's empire, his phrase still echoing in Britannia's empire: imposing its name upon them. Wasn't that what the British were doing when they glued the names of empire-builders onto Indian suffixes, resulting in Campbellpurs and Abbottabads and Forbesganjes. What she wanted was not to impose names onto the ancient places but to peel them away, back and further back, to locate the Cophen beneath Kabul, the Peukelaotis beneath Charsadda, the Caspatyrus – most of all the Caspatyrus – beneath Peshawar.

– Caspatyrus!

The syllables detonated in the silence of the second-class compartment, and Qayyum Gul's hand jerked up to cover his left eye. He must have done something to indicate pain because the Englishwoman who had expelled the strange sound – was it a name, a sneeze, a foreign language? – glanced in his direction, if not quite at him, before resuming her vigil at the window.

He had no idea why she was here; an hour or so earlier she had entered the compartment while Qayyum was stretched out, half-asleep, and had deposited herself and her large bag onto the row of seats opposite him with the words, This berth is free, isn't it? He had sat up quickly and watched the door for a few moments, expecting a husband to walk in or perhaps a father, but it quickly became obvious that he was alone in a train carriage with a young Englishwoman whose physical appearance was a cluster of contradictions: the blue eyes beneath long lashes were entirely feminine, but the hair was cut short like a boy; the sun-darkened skin suggested she worked in the fields, but everything about her manner indicated affluence. The skirt, halfway up her calves, might have meant she had the cast-off wardrobe of a shorter woman, but there was something in her brazen confidence which convinced him she was choosing to make men look at her ankles. Of course he had left, seeking out the conductor who said the only

66

available place was in the compartment with two English ladies which was where the other English lady should be seated. With Qayyum standing outside in the corridor the conductor entered to speak to her, and emerged a few seconds later, shaking his head at Qayyum. The Englishwoman followed him out and smiled brightly at Qayyum. You'll make me feel terrible if you skulk outside; you must come in, she said. As if it were that simple. But he had gone in, remembered anger from Brighton guiding his steps; let them object, any of the able-bodied Englishmen in the other compartments – he would stand up tall and say, Lance-Naik Qayyum Gul, 40th Pathans. But the compartment was at the end of the train, and no one had walked past.

He looked over to the Englishwoman who had paid him no attention since he re-entered the compartment – whether through propriety or indifference, he couldn't tell. What did she see, or hope to see, outside the window which allowed her to meet the sun's ferocity head-on, impervious to the red patches at her uncovered throat? Qayyum angled his body deeper into the shaded part of the leather-covered seat, which now burnt where the sunlight reached it, knowing the Englishwoman must be entirely aware of his discomfort.

A man in a starched white uniform entered the compartment, carrying a dripping wet khus blind in each hand, a stool under his arm. The Englishwoman moved away from the window, saying Jaldi, jaldi – one of the first things any Englishman or woman learned in India was how to tell the Natives to hurry up – and the uniformed man apologised even as he stood on the stool, untied the dried khus blinds and replaced them with the wet ones. As soon as the first one was up, the fan positioned behind it blew cool, fragrant air through the compartment and Qayyum heard himself exhale loudly. The world turned beneficent.

The Englishwoman made an impatient rotating motion with her finger and the uniformed man rolled one of the blinds up and secured it with string so that a large square of glass was again visible, heat ballooning towards it from the plains. Immediately the Englishwoman smiled, thanking the uniformed man as though he'd done a favour rather than carried out a command, and handed him a coin – the man touched his hand to his forehead, his body language shifting into obsequiousness. In the Army, hierarchy allowed for pride, insisted on it; the salute of a sepoy to a general was always straight-backed.

The Englishwoman reached into her bag, pulled out a bread roll and broke it in two. The faint scent of it an echo carried across the sea. Fresh loaves of bread at the station stop in Marseilles on the way to the Front.

– You're a Pathan?

The Englishwoman was standing in the space between the two rows of seats, holding out half the bread roll. Her hand freckled like the shoulder of the French girl. Qayyum shook his head, far more vigorously than was needed to indicate a lack of appetite. She gave him a look before she sat down, one which said, Are you in any position to refuse a kindness? He put a hand up to his face.

The fluttering of the blinds, the dripping of water which streaked the window and created the illusion of rain – these sounds grew louder, magnified by the silence between the man and the woman which was entirely different to the silence which had preceded it. Qayyum cleared his throat, leaned forward.

– Yes, I am Pathan.

He never thought of himself that way before the Army. His great-grandfather had left the Yusufzai lands decades before Qayyum was born, and so Qayyum was a Peshawari, a city-dweller, with Hindko not Pashto as his first language. Those Pashtuns! his grandfather liked to say, with the superior air of a man who believes he has escaped into a better destiny. But in the Army Qayyum was told he was a Yusufzai of the 40th Pathans and, in the company of the other Yusufzai of the regiment who called him their kinsman and said the air of Peshawar couldn't thin Yusufzai blood, he learned to think of himself as just that. Why, in the Army, would you be anything but a Pathan – the word itself exploded from the lips of the English officers like a cannonball, straight and true.

– You're going to Peshawar?

– Yes. My home.

– Have you ever heard of Scylax?

– I don't know any Englishmen in Peshawar.

She laughed at that, and he wondered if this Scylax was a Scot, like Captain Dalmohay. He, Allah rest his soul, had understood that to the Indians all the British were English, and wouldn't have made a man feel foolish for not knowing an English name from a Scottish one even though he could tell Dogra from Pashtun, Hindu from Muslim.

– I'm sorry, I'm laughing at myself. Did you learn English at school?

– The Army.

Until now the Englishwoman's gaze had been remote, as if she were trying too hard to pretend there was nothing of particular interest in Qayyum's face, but now she looked directly at the permanently closed eyelid.

– Mesopotamia or France?

– France. Belgium.

– Ypres?

His nod was brief, asking for the conversation to go no further. The Englishwoman stood up, rolled down the blinds, and for a time there was quiet and fragrance and shade. When she spoke again, her voice was different.

– There were ferocious arguments in London when it became known an Indian division was being deployed to France. But the old military men who had served in India insisted the loyalty of the Indian troops to the Crown was beyond question.

Beyond question. It wasn't a phrase Qayyum knew. Beyond question. If question was the Allied line, the loyalty of Indian troops was somewhere beyond, all the way across the field without cover and up the slope where the German gunners waited.

He stepped out of the compartment, into the corridor.

The light coming through the gaping compartment door turned harsh. Viv looked out through the open doorway, through the windows on the far side of the carriage. A barren plain scattered with slate, and rock the same reddish colour as the distant hills. As if young giants had gouged them out from the hillsides and hurled them into the plains in competitions of strength. The games continuing on through the centuries. How had the landscape altered so dramatically? But when she lifted a corner of the blind the view to the north was as before – the Cophen River and fertile ground; sugar-cane fields and orchards; beyond, the terraced tops of hills dotted with the domes of ancient stupas.

At last, she had the solitude she'd yearned for since leaving London as companion to an aged spinster on her way to Karachi. Finding someone in need of a travel companion had been her mother's idea – a way of ensuring a facade of propriety to Viv's journey, at least until Karachi where she and old Miss Adamson had said goodbye without very much regret on the part of either, and Viv had boarded the train. Now, it was an enormous luxury to look upon the Peshawar Valley without distraction, imagining Tahsin Bey beside her, exclaiming along with her at every new sight. It wasn't just Miss Adamson she'd had to rid herself of to achieve this but also the woman from Norfolk and her daughter in the compartment at the other end of the carriage. When she had entered the compartment the woman had taken one look at her – the V-shaped neckline which was an inch beneath the base of her throat, the short skirt, the flesh-coloured stockings, and most of all the short 'Castle Bob' hairstyle which Viv had daringly acquired during the sea-voyage – and conclusions had hurled themselves viciously across the carriage. In two directions, if Viv was honest. At least she was prepared to despise the laced and hooped creature silently – but the other woman had decided to embark on a lecture to her daughter, a bored child of no more than ten, about the importance of a woman's dress in maintaining standards in the Empire. Viv fled, finding refuge in a compartment which had appeared empty when she had looked in. It was only when she entered that she saw the man, lying down with his hands behind his head, and thought, oh God, that's beautiful.

70

A statue of Herakles brought to life – broad-shouldered and crinkle-haired, every bone chiselled. More like a Greek hero of antiquity than any Greek she'd ever seen. But then the man woke up and turned his head towards her and – God forgive her – her heart had been struck with a cold joy: this was the Monophthalmus, the single-eyed man of India of whom Scylax had written.

Even though it was solitude she had come in search of, from the first instant she'd seen the Pathan raise a hand to his eyeless eye, fingertips barely skimming the gashes around it as if he couldn't bear the touch of his own skin, she found herself wanting to say something to him. She had treated enough men who'd lost an eye to understand why the other eye was so chapped and reddened – this great, strong man, reduced to panicking over every speck of grit that might threaten what sight remained.

What did you think you were doing it for? was what she really wanted to ask the man who had lost his eye at Ypres. Was it loyalty to the Empire or something more mundane – travel in a second-class compartment, a pension, the promise of progressing through the ranks. She leaned forward towards the open door, watching the man, trying to imagine what she might say to him. The only sentence which came to mind was, Have you tried a glass eye? But if she said that the man would realise that his closed eyelid forced her to imagine the emptied cave within. She shuddered, remembering too much what she was trying to forget, and turned her attention back to the view.

The landscape coalesced as they approached Peshawar, the outside world a rush of fruit trees. Unexpectedly, Qayyum felt a generosity – or no, it was close to the obligations of a host – towards the Englishwoman who had been sketching every crumbling old structure the train had passed.

– Peshawar. You want to see?

The Englishwoman stepped into the corridor.

– Bala Hisar.

Qayyum pointed towards the elevated fort which cast its

71

shadow over the Walled City. The monuments all seemed closer to each other when viewed through one eye, so he saw Peshawar as accordioned, all breathing space pressed out of it.

– The City Walls. Gor Khatri. Mahabat Khan Mosque.

His fingertip touched the window as he pointed out each landmark, and faint dots appeared. A constellation in a sky of dust.

– And the excavation site: Shahji-ki-Dheri. Where the archaeologists dig. Do you know where it is?

– No. Why do the English dig for old, broken things?

– We like to find history.

– Why?

– I don't know.

He used to think it was humility, this readiness of the English to acknowledge ignorance. But he had come to understand it was the exact opposite – to be English was to move through the world with no need to impress or convince. Was this so because they had an empire, or did they have an empire because this was so? A shadow passed across the window, turning it into a mirror. Qayyum swung away and returned to the compartment, slapping the sliding door to one side. He didn't know what it was that was making him so angry. There was too much time and space in these days without routine, without the company of men waking and sleeping and eating at the same time as him, his life their lives. Even in Brighton he'd had that. But now, no escape from it – he was a Pashtun who had left his tribe behind in a gas cloud, in a trench, in the sightline of a thousand machine guns.

He didn't realise the train had stopped, or that he was sitting with his head in his hands, until he heard the flint strike. The Englishwoman was sitting across from him, a long thin tube in her mouth with a cigarette at its end. She held out a silver case to Qayyum; the cigarettes inside it thinner than any he'd seen before.

– Turkish.

He took it, grateful for anything that would allow him to stay here for a few more minutes, leaving the outside outside.

– How old are you, she asked. Nineteen? Twenty?

72

– Twenty-one.

– If I may speak to you with the wisdom of twenty-three? Things change very rapidly; this is just the beginning.

She seemed to recognise that the words were meaningless, and when she spoke again her tone was more sober.

– At any rate, you're home now.

– The emperor Babur said if a blind man walks across India he will know when he reaches Peshawar by the smell of its flowers.

They finished their cigarettes in silence. When he stood up to leave she rose, too, and held out an ungloved hand. He shook it, hoping his expression didn't reveal his discomfort at her touch, more intimate than the ministrations of the nurses. He wanted to tell her his name but she might think he expected this sympathy between them to continue once they disembarked, and so he hoisted his knapsack onto his shoulders and left without another word.

July–August 1915

Viv stepped off the train into the humid afternoon. In the time it had taken to smoke the cigarette all the other passengers had exited the platform, and now the Pathan too was striding away, so there was no one to see her turn in a circle on her heels, arms up in the air to embrace the world in the manner of Tahsin Bey when surrounded by beauty. The mountains, oh everywhere, the mountains! Dark green, almost black, mountains; blue mountains; rose-coloured mountains; and away in the distance, snow-topped mountains. Twenty-five hundred years ago Scylax came through those mountains, and saw the Peshawar Valley – this stretch of earth on which she now stood. The word 'Ours' made its way to her lips.

While revolving she had been vaguely aware of a movement on the platform, which now revealed itself to be a Pathan boy, his hair crinkled like the one-eyed man's and the Greek-influenced early Gandhara Buddhas', his almond-shaped eyes open wide in bewilderment at the spinning Englishwoman. Viv reached into her pocket and flicked a coin at the boy who caught it deftly.

– Dean's Hotel?

– Across the road. I can take you there, mem-sahib.

The view from the train had already told her that the railways tracks sliced Peshawar in two, separating the Walled City from the Cantonment. As she followed the boy out of the station it was the Cantonment they entered, with its landscape of wide roads, tree-lined avenues, church spires. Almost an English village, if not for the grand buildings set down in its

74

midst. She pointed to the red structure set just back from the road, with its four rooftop cupolas which simultaneously represented India and the Crown, and felt it some kind of triumph when the boy identified it as the Museum.

– You've been inside?

– No. It's for the English.

– Indians aren't allowed into the Museum?

– We are allowed. But –

He raised his hands in the air, palms up, expressing the pointlessness of the Museum in his life.

– What's your tribe?

– My grandfather's people were Yusufzai.

– I've been reading about you. Your ancestors fought Alexander, at Peukelaotis.

– Pew . . . ?

– You don't know who Alexander was, do you?

– An Englishman?

She shook her head. What was the cure for amnesiacs without curiosity? The young boy crossed the road, moving with the unhurried, unfaltering steps which marked those who were natives of the sun, and Viv followed. Together they walked up a long driveway with carefully tended gardens on either side which led to the pleasing simplicity of Dean's Hotel – a whitewashed barracks-like structure which promised tranquillity and tall glasses of iced drinks. It had been recommended by a Mr and Mrs Forbes of Peshawar who Mrs Spencer had found through her cousin the Bishop, recently returned to England after more than twenty years in India. They would be more than happy to welcome Miss Spencer to Peshawar and introduce her to the close-knit British society there, the Forbeses said via telegram, though during the summer most people were in Simla. It had been a relief to discover that the watchful eyes of an aged English couple who had the Bishop's stamp of approval was all that Mrs Spencer had meant when she promised to find Viv a 'conventional situation' in Peshawar. The truth was, the war had sloughed off so many rules that no one seemed to know any more what counted as unacceptable behaviour in women.

Viv turned the pocket of her linen jacket inside out, wriggled her fingers through the hole in the pocket lining and fished out a coin. The boy held up the coin she had already given him, and shook his head sternly at the offer of a second one, as though Viv was in danger of breaching a moral code.

– Do you know how far it is to Shahji-ki-Dheri?

– I can take you. Tomorrow morning, early?

The boy squinted up at the sun as he said it, but Viv suspected the answer actually meant he had no idea where Shahji-ki-Dheri was. Even so, the ground was rocking and her head pounding from the sun's glare magnified by the train window, and she certainly wasn't about to head out to a site right away. Yes, she said, and waved goodbye, certain she wouldn't see him again.

Her rooms were spacious and pleasingly modern, with electric ceiling-fans. She barely had time to notice this before there was a rapid knocking on the bedroom window, drawing her attention to a man in the flower beds holding up something which looked like a bracelet strung with red coral. She touched her wrist, thought of emerald seaweed, before opening the window. The bracelet was a length of string with jewel-like fragments threaded through it, pale burgundy speckled with dark burgundy, the pieces suggesting an entirety the size of a grape. The man – he must be the gardener, there was a basket and pair of shears near his feet – shook the string to make the fragments sway and pressed his thumb and forefinger together at the tips to indicate tiny beaks. Pointing in the direction of the second room, he made a revolving gesture with his finger and shook his head sadly.

Uncomprehending, she allowed herself to be directed into the other room. It didn't take long to understand what he was telling her – a bird had built its nest in the ceiling fan; the tiny chirping sounds which she had taken for a cricket emanated from it. If she switched on the fan it would be a massacre. The gardener, now standing outside this second room, presented her with the bracelet and placed his hands together in supplication.

She pressed her thumb against one of the speckled fragments which crumbled into fine powder. The gardener looked as if he might cry. Here was a gentler world, where the large tragedies of a military hospital didn't erode compassion for the tiniest of creatures.

Don't worry; I'd rather melt in a puddle than harm them, she said, and though they didn't speak the same language he understood the tone of her voice, and touched his hand to his forehead.

She walked back into the bedroom where the ceiling fan was rotating briskly – after sharing a hostel room with four other nurses, the space between these four walls was more than sufficient. Tying the coral bracelet around her wrist, she was grateful to be allowed this moment of largesse.

Stepping from the cool waters of the bath, she walked directly to the bed, pulling a loose Turkish robe over her head without drying off. Air from the ceiling fan rippled across cotton and wet limbs as she lay down; the curtains were carefully drawn but the window ajar so she could hear water burble from the garden hose into the flower beds just outside. Everything spoke to her of pleasure. She tried to hold herself in that shadow-place between sleep and waking where the mind drifts, excavating – Tahsin Bey was there with her, his thumbs splitting a silver fig in two, purple flesh beneath metallic skin.

The next morning Viv stepped out into a breeze which originated from two bearers snapping a tablecloth in the air, dark hands on white cloth. She had come out to see the sun rising from behind the mountains but haze smeared the sky and her presence clearly disturbed the hotel staff's early morning preparations. One of the bearers apologised – for what? Being visible? Somewhere a rooster crowed, a dog barked in response. If Mary were here they'd return to the familiar, but still amusing, topic of dogs' accents. The rolled 'r's in the bark of a poodle, the guttural growl of an Alsatian. And why was it that everything unacceptable in a man – slobbering enthusiasm, predictability, simple-mindedness – was so charming in a dog? She felt a pug's disdain, and knew it wasn't really Mary whose company she was missing.

She sat down at a table beneath a pine tree, picked up a pen and tried to think of what to write which would please Papa. When Mrs Spencer presented, as a fait accompli, Viv's trip to Peshawar all his visible anger turned towards his wife, and what Viv had received instead was his bafflement. Why? he kept saying, wanting to understand, failing to do so, being wounded by that failure. Every day Viv thought of going down to breakfast and saying, I'll return to the hospital – but then she thought of the boy with the sandy hair and the blue eyes and stopped herself. So she left with a promise: she'd be back in London by Christmas, and if the war was still on she would return to her nursing duties. Her mother sighed and shook her head when she heard that, but didn't say anything about it.

One of the bearers brushed leaves and seed-pods off the starched white tablecloth, brought her breakfast, and sent a young boy to stand behind her with a large fan in his tiny fist. In his turban and waistcoat he reminded her of the monkey similarly dressed at an *Arabian Nights* party in England two summers ago. The monkey held a Japanese fan which it swept up and down the length of its body in a manner so vulgar – head thrown back, legs spread apart – that Mary almost left the party in protest before the host had the animal taken away. Viv gave the boy a coin and told him she didn't need him. The rising heat of early morning felt like an old friend.

Setting the pen aside, she concentrated on breakfast. Tea and jam and bread in Peshawar. It was all so strange. When she had finished the bearer informed her that a boy had been waiting for her. At first she didn't know what he meant, but there he was, near the hotel entrance, the boy from the train station, with a Victoria driver who knew the way to Shahji-ki-Dheri.

Through the Cantonment the horse trotted, all creaking harness and clopping hooves, down broad streets shaded by plane trees and cypresses, their familiarity an ache. But then the Victoria drove through the arched gateway of the Walled City and Viv rose out of her seat, exclaiming loudly at the glorious colour and noise and exactly-what-you-want-it-to-be-ness of it all. Birds beating their wings against dome-shaped cages, children sucking on molasses pebbles, sugar-cane sellers slicing whistling sounds out of the air to attract buyers, water-carriers with spines curved beneath animal-skin sacks filled with liquid. Pyramids of peaches and plums in wicker baskets, carpets draped over balconies and branches, clothes lines strung between top-floor windows with men's clothes hanging from them (Native men of all ages could be seen craning their necks in the hope some female garment might have accidentally or – why not believe this? – deliberately been placed in view). There weren't in fact any men craning their necks but she would say there were when she and Tahsin Bey found themselves in each other's company again. She'd tell him tales of Caspatyrus that would make him smile that smile of exceptional warmth, and he would most certainly agree that the fabrication of stories was a form of tribute to Scylax, whose tales of India included impossible wonders.

The Victoria had stopped for no reason, and the boy – Najeeb his name was – said she should sit down. A white tent floated past, and Viv wondered if the woman within felt disdain or envy at the sight of an Englishwoman standing up in a Victoria, looking around, unimpeded. There were no other women, tented or otherwise, but looking up above the storefronts she saw some movement behind the enclosed wooden balconies; the latticework of the wood was replicated on the mesh of the tented woman's burqa. Much like the grille in the Ladies' Gallery behind which any women wanting to view parliamentary debates must sit so that men wouldn't be distracted by their presence. It must be even more hot and stuffy in those burqas than it was in the Ladies' Gallery, which she had once entered on Mary's insistence to listen to a debate on Votes for Women – that was before her father had set her right on the issue by sending her to listen to the magnificent Gertrude Bell addressing the Anti-Suffragette League. (If all women were like Ms Bell and you, men would fall over their feet in their haste to give you the vote, Papa had said when she came home to report all that had been said.) She sat down and asked the boy if he had sisters. Yes, three. Didn't they get cross-eyed behind a burqa? Their eyes learned to focus differently, he said, and she couldn't decide if this seemed plausible or not.

The Victoria progressed along the famed Street of Storytellers and Najeeb pointed out the Storytellers themselves – men sitting cross-legged on the raised floors of open-fronted stores, audiences seated across from them on rope-beds beneath trees. The stories they told were in the form of poems called badalas, Najeeb said in response to her question, and she repeated the word badala and wondered where she could find a language teacher. Hindko was the language of Peshawaris, Najeeb said, and Pashto the language of Pathans.

– So you speak Pashto, Viv said.

– At home we speak Hindko. We are more Peshawari than Pathan, but we're also Pathan. But everyone here speaks both Hindko and Pashto and many people Urdu and also English and every language of the world someone here can speak. This is Peshawar.

He said it with evident pride, making an expansive gesture which took in all the variety of the street – every manner of turban and cap and flowing garb. That man is from Tashkent, he said, and that one from Tibet; there's a Punjabi, that's an Afridi Pathan and that one is Sikh and those two Hindu. For the first time she gave him her full attention – a smiling boy with excellent but oddly pronounced English, as though most of his vocabulary came from books. He was dressed more formally than the day before in narrow black trousers, a white tunic, and a white turban with a grass stain which suggested he'd been standing on his head.

They turned into another lane and Najeeb said it was the Street of Partridge Lovers, and looked startled when she laughed.

– What else? Tell me all the street names!

– The Street of Dentists. The Street of Potters. The Street of Felt Caps. The Street of Silver. The Street of Money-Changers. The Street of Coppersmiths. The Street of Englishwomen.

– The Street of Englishwomen?

– They buy and sell Englishwomen there. We will try to avoid it.

– Take a detour through the Street of Inventive Guides if you must.

He looked delighted to be caught out, and she found she was delighted to have been teased.

He handed her a plum which he had plucked from the basket carried on a man's head in the nonchalant gesture of one to whom theft isn't understood as a crime, and she recalled attending one of Woolley's lectures in which he'd said it was important to watch one's workmen on digs in Foreign Parts because they could teach one how to understand man as he once was – how he functioned, how his brain worked in times past. If that was true why shouldn't the great men of the ancient world have some shadow in the present in addition to the slaves? She might yet find a Herodotus in this city with its Street of Storytellers and its centuries of Greek influence. Herodotus was a Carian, not a Greek! She could picture Tahsin Bey so clearly as he said it, rising to his toes, his sharply angled face a picture of outrage.

They reached another gateway, this one leading out of the Walled City – immediately the noise and rush fell away and they entered a rural world with cultivated fields on either side of a bumpy road. Somewhere in the middle of those fields was the Great Stupa of Kanishka.

Once there was the Great Stupa, seven hundred feet tall. From every point in the Peshawar Valley men and women could look up from the dust of their days to see the pillar ringed with gold which arose from its uppermost canopy of pearls. Surrounding the Stupa, a vast monastery complex. Everywhere a traveller looked there was the Buddha, carved over and over into and around the countryside, in an age when the people of this region had the vision to find the god in every stone. His serene eyes observing everything – here carved of white stone, and there of a reddish-blue which mysteriously turned golden when the sun touched it, and elsewhere the grey of Gandhara.

81

Now there was devastation cut into wheat fields. The low mound that was the remains of the Great Stupa lay abandoned, the earth around it pockmarked with trial pits and trenches, miniature stupas and rubble. The stupas were badly damaged, their carvings lacking the delicacy of the Gandhara statuary Viv had seen in the British Museum. And the long grass made it clear no one had been here in a long while. This was a place archaeologists had given up on. Too much of it destroyed, too little of value in what remained, to make recovery worthwhile. She wiped a trail of sweat off her neck; the familiarity of the morning's heat had passed and now the sun burnt so brightly it had turned the sky white.

– Miss Spencer!

An echoing quality to the boy's voice directed her to the largest of the trenches. She hurried over, scolding herself for not keeping an eye on him. When she looked into the trench she saw it had been dug deep to reveal part of a wall decorated with stucco figures of the Buddha – the boy, replicating the Buddha's cross-legged pose, was gently stroking the knee of the Enlightened One. From now on when she heard the word 'trench' she wanted only to think of this. He turned towards her, grinning a huge grin as if he had been the one to discover the stucco figures. There were steps carved into the trench and she was soon crouching beside the boy. Reaching out, she touched the Buddha's face, a shiver travelling all the way through her.

– If you like this, you should see what they have at the Museum.

– We can go there? Now?

– Don't you have somewhere to be? School?

– Summer holidays.

– And your family won't worry about you if you're gone too long?

The words tugged all expressiveness off his face. Viv wondered what 'family' might mean to him, and why he'd been alone at a train station the previous morning. Best not to make any of that her business.

She looked at her watch. The previous evening, a couple in Dean's dining room had introduced themselves as the Forbeses, apologised for not being at the train station to meet her – they'd been expecting her to send a telegram from Karachi to let them know which train she'd be on – and asked her to come to their home for lunch. Of course she'd be delighted, she'd said, and not only out of a sense of obligation; there was something about Mr Forbes – the manner of a medical professional perhaps – which she liked immensely, though the wife seemed a little on the nervy side.

– We can go there, but not now. Come to Dean's again tomorrow.

It was evening already when she shook off the heaviness of an overlong afternoon sleep, brought on by the inexplicable stew for lunch at the Forbeses', and walked out into Dean's garden. The air was scented to an almost embarrassing degree – evening jasmine overlaid on whatever else had already been there. The emperor Babur hadn't been exaggerating about blind men and Peshawar. Sitting down at a table, she looked towards the distant sentinels of the hills, clearly visible now, keeping the rest of the world at bay.

The bearer brought her a cup of tea and as she sipped it she watched the shadow of a man stride across Dean's facade. When the shadow stopped next to the silhouette of a woman holding a teacup she realised there was someone standing at her elbow.

Red-faced and sweating, with features clustered around the nose so that the cheeks and forehead appeared excessive – those were things the shadows didn't reveal. The shadow-man beamed at her, called her by name. His name was Remmick, he said; he wanted to welcome her to Peshawar. The Forbeses had told her about him. Remmick's a Political, they said, as if it were a term she should undersand; he knows everyone's business.

Once they had established that a sundowner was more suited to the time and weather than a cup of tea, Remmick the political agent asked what had brought an Englishwoman to Peshawar at the height of summer.

– I wish I had a good answer to that. I should be in London, I know. I was a VAD nurse until a few weeks ago, but I'm afraid I was rather useless, gave it up, and well, here I pathetically am.

She'd had to have this conversation with the Forbeses last night, and the speed with which Mr Forbes rushed in to tell an anecdote about a nurse he'd once worked with told her she should find a better story, if for no other reason than to spare her companions the necessity of covering up her shame. But she hadn't yet been able to think of one.

– No one in Peshawar is in a position to hold it against you that you choose to be here rather than somewhere else. How good of you to have nursed – that's more than most people have done. You should hold your head up with pride, Miss Spencer.

She inclined her head in gratitude, felt a burden lift. Two Englishmen in military uniform entered the garden. Viv looked at them, surprised by her feelings of contempt.

– Do you think they feel relieved or ashamed to be here, so far from the fight?

– Peshawar is never far from a fight.

Remmick pointed up towards the hills.

– There's a fanatic up there, name of Haji Turangzai, with a band of blood-thirsty followers. You mustn't worry about it – we're accustomed to dealing with these hotheads. But I would advise against travelling outside the city, and certainly against venturing to the Khyber Pass, without clearing it with me first.

Remmick spoke with an air of authority that was parodic in a man so young – he couldn't be much older than her – but his words had struck at something inside her. Kipling's Peshawar! The North-West Frontier! Where even the finest hotel in town was a whitewashed barracks, a reminder that the world of guns lurked beneath every veneer. It was immensely comforting to know oneself in a world in which battles followed the template laid down in books of adventure and valour. The words 'Khyber Pass' sat on her tongue, fizzing with romance.

– The war seems so far away.

– I wouldn't say that. The Haji's given us trouble before but this time round it's because the damned Turks have riled up the tribes in the name of the Caliphate. Told them to launch a Holy War against us. Forgive me, Miss Spencer. I shouldn't use such language, but they really are such damned Turks.

– That seems to be the general consensus, she said, raising her glass to her lips, and wondering how to change the subject.

She returned to her rooms just as a liveried man was on his way out. In his hands a dustpan and her waste-paper basket. She caught hold of the rim of the basket, without saying a word, and he yielded it to her. Inside, a tangle of straw and grass. Her fingers burrowed through it and encountered a beak, a tiny featherless skull. She told herself there was no such thing as omens.

If she leaned in just a few inches and placed her mouth against the Cupid's bow she might feel blood flow beneath the stone surface of the lips. But what would he want with her kiss, this man who walked away from his life the day his son was born, and became the Enlightened One?

Viv touched the face. The grey stone cool against her palm, the surface smooth except where a spade had left its mark against the forehead, just inches from the raised mole which marked the urna – she touched the scar in apology for the crimes of excavation. Her fingers traced the grooves between the tendrils of hair snaking towards the topknot. When she had first seen a Gandhara Buddha, at the British Museum, she had thought of the hair as Mediterranean but no longer – she looked over to Najeeb.

The boy was standing next to the webbed-fingered, larger-than-life Buddhas with their beautiful drapery which the museum guard claimed to have seen stir in the breeze. As she watched, Najeeb said something to the guard who crouched down and lifted the boy up onto his shoulders.

– Look, Miss Spencer!

He had spotted, and been struck by, the faint, unexpected pupil in the eye of one of the tall Buddhas – one round of the Museum and he'd already worked out that was unusual. For a

85

long time he remained motionless, studying it, until Viv clapped her hands twice, and Najeeb dropped off the guard's shoulder, agile, unconcerned by the possibility of hurt. Viv's hand on his elbow, they walked around the high-ceilinged whitewashed halls of the Peshawar Museum, and this time instead of rushing from display to display he asked her to explain those things which had particularly caught his attention. He must be near the same age she'd been the first time Tahsin Bey took her to the British Museum, and answered every question with patience.

– This is all from here, Najeeb kept repeating. This also? This also?

– Yes, all of it. We've left it here instead of taking it back to London so you can see your own history.

They walked all along the galleries, until they had circled round to the case which displayed excavations at Shahji-ki-Dheri and Takht-i-Bahi. Here, a fragmented starving Buddha; there, the goddess Hariti holding a cornucopia in one hand, the palm of the other hand resting on the upper thigh of her consort. And most prominently positioned of all, a casket – on its lid the figure of the Buddha seated on lotus leaves, flanked by the Hindu gods Indra and Brahma. Along the rim of the lid wild geese were in flight and, beneath, stood the King, Kanishka himself, in his great boots and cloak; and that old familiar form of Eros draped a garland all around the casket. She pointed the different figures out to Najeeb, explained the word 'syncretic'.

– I came to Peshawar because of this casket, Najeeb.

The boy wrinkled his nose.

– Why? It's not very nice.

It was true, the casket was far from the most beautiful object here. Too crude, too fussy. Why did Tahsin Bey choose to draw her attention to this, of all the discoveries in all the archaeological journals of the world? She couldn't shake the feeling there was something she'd missed.

– So this is a Mughal garden.

Najeeb looked at her, and shrugged.

86

– It's where I like best in Peshawar, he said, as if that were more important.

Where-he-liked-best was Shalimar Garden – though he referred to it by the less evocative local name of Shahi Bagh – a vast park with pathways, bordering long rectangular ponds, along which Najeeb and Viv walked to the central, arched pavilion. In each pond, multiple fountains kept up a steady cascade of water which cooled the eye and ear. And the summer flowers dense with colour offered up a consolation for the heat. Najeeb had promised her the Garden's wonders in exchange for those of the Museum, a boy alive to the reciprocal courtesies of his people.

– I come here after school to read, when I'm supposed to be at the mosque with the maulvi. Only my brother knows. Mr Dickens is my favourite. The maulvi doesn't care, as long as I take him his money every month. I don't like to waste my father's money but my brother says as long as I use that time to learn it isn't wrong, and I don't learn anything from the maulvi – he's so boring, he only makes me read the Qur'an out loud and doesn't explain anything.

– Sloth is always preferable to zeal when it comes to the religious-minded, in my experience. I'm sure you get a lot more out of Mr Dickens.

– Also, where he teaches me in the mosque is so hot, and here there's always shade.

– Yes, the importance of shade in Peshawar. A long-standing object of fascination for foreigners.

– It is?

Viv sat on the rim of a pond, scooped up a handful of warm water and sprinkled it onto her neck. Pulling her sketchbook out of her bag, she rested it on her knee, and was about to start drawing the two pavilions in her sight – the solid one, and its liquid reflection – when she caught Najeeb looking expectantly at her.

– Hmm? Oh, yes. There was a man called Scylax who came here long ago. Longer ago than anything in the Museum. He travelled from Peshawar all the way down the Indus, and when he went away he took stories of the tribes who lived here.

– Stories of the Yusufzai?

– Stories of shade. For instance, there was a tribe called the Otoliknoi whose ears were like winnowing fans and could protect them from the sun in the manner of umbrellas.

– What?

– Oh yes. You haven't ever seen them? No? Keep a lookout. And also for the Skyapods or Shadow-Feet. When it gets too hot the Skyapods lie down on their backs and raise one leg up. Their huge feet cast a shadow so big it gives them complete shade.

– I've never seen that.

– Next you'll be telling me you haven't seen gold-hunting ants either.

– I haven't!

He looked stricken.

– Lucky you. So much yet to discover. Where are you going?

He had darted off, in search of something or following something, she didn't know which. When she caught up with him around the other side of the pavilion he was standing above a Pathan man who was lying on his back, allowing Najeeb to manoeuvre his one raised leg this way and that.

– Look, Miss Spencer, the feet don't have to be so large. It's all about the angle of the leg and the position of the sun. See?

She had been close to Najeeb's age that bright summer's day when she saw a constable bend his head to hear something a schoolboy was saying, and the sunlight shimmered off his helmet crest, turning him mythical. She had turned to Tahsin Bey, and said, Scylax, coming to London, might have written of the Glaucocephalos – the gleaming-headed man – who had light where there should be a face and drew his power from the sun. Today, for the first time, she entirely understood Tahsin Bey's delight.

The older Pathan stood up at the sight of Viv, cuffed Najeeb on the head, and stalked away. The boy ran back to her.

– What's a winnowing fan?

* * *

88

The greater part of Asia was explored by Darius, who desiring to know of the River Indus, which is a second river producing crocodiles of all the rivers in the world – to know, I say, of this river where it runs out into the sea, sent with ships, besides others whom he trusted to speak the truth, Scylax also, a man of Caryanda. These starting from the city of Caspatyrus and the land of the Pactyike, sailed down the river towards the east and the sunrising to the sea . . .

Beneath the whirring, nestless fan, Najeeb was barely able to get through the sentence, his tongue thick as he tried to manoeuvre it around the unfamiliar names, his brain clearly defeated by the syntax. He looked up at her, despairing.

– That's Herodotus, the Father of History. Writing more than two thousand years ago. It's not a very good translation – Darius trusted Scylax especially. Kai de kai, the emphasising phrase goes. Caspatyrus is Peshawar.

– Peshawar? But there's no river here.

– The Bara River has changed course through the centuries.

– So, the Pactyike . . . ?

– Yes. You, Najeeb Gul. You are Pactyike. He's writing about the Pathans. Turn to the page with the bookmark. They – you – appear again.

Others however of the Indians are on the borders of the city of Caspatyrus and the country of Pactyike, dwelling towards the north of the other Indians . . . these are the most warlike of the Indians . . .

He stopped reading there.

– Miss Spencer, may I ask you something?

– Of course.

– Have you ever met anyone who's been to war?

– Many. Very many.

– Do they ever become the way they were before?

– I don't know. I've only known them in the middle of war, not after. Why do you ask?

89

– I just wondered. May I go now? It's getting late.

– Yes, of course.

– And may I come back tomorrow?

– Yes. Of course.

– I hear you've found yourself a civilising mission.

Remmick reached over the gate to undo the bolt, and gestured for her to go ahead of him along the garden pathway toward the 'modest' bungalow available to rent.

– You work for Empire in large ways, Mr Remmick, I work in small ways. Oh, this is perfect!

She walked past the Ionic columns supporting a red-tiled sloping roof and in through the doorway to a darkened interior. Remmick, following, closed the door behind him and touched her waist – when she quickly moved away, he apologised. Can't see a thing in here. There was a sound of something rusty being eased, and the sunlight rushed in, revealing a high-ceilinged corridor and Remmick standing beside the heavy wooden window shutters, one hand on the bolt. Beyond the corridor was a spacious room with a large writing desk at its centre, facing shutters that reached from floor to ceiling. Viv opened them and stepped out into a garden bordered with a line of trees bearing flame-coloured flowers; and at the far end, a weeping willow. Perfect, she repeated, stepping out onto the verandah.

– I still think it would be better if you were at Dean's.

– You're very kind, but I'll be perfectly all right on my own.

– Will he come here for lessons? Your civilising mission?

– His name is Najeeb, and yes.

– A Pathan is a Pathan at any age, I hope you remember that. They're not accustomed to the company of women.

– I would swear this one has Greek blood in him. I call him the Herodotus of Peshawar.

– Just make sure there's always someone else about when he's here. I'll send over staff you can trust. And also, the Pashto teacher you were enquiring about – I know you said Hindko, but most people here understand Pashto and you can use it throughout the Peshawar Valley.

– You really are very kind. When your wife is back from Simla, you both must come over for supper.

– It'll be a while before she's back.

– It'll be a while before I have this place ready for entertaining guests.

– As you say, Miss Spencer. I'm available to you at all times.

Viv pretended not to understand his meaning, and walked out into the garden, smiling when he couldn't see her; she had no intention of taking him up on his availability but it was both useful and flattering to have a man as powerful as Remmick attendant on her every need. He'd even promised to introduce her to John Marshall who planned to resume excavating Taxila when the weather changed – and once Marshall heard about Labraunda he'd ask her to join him, of course he would.

The thought of returning to London in December was fading.

Days fell into a routine: in the morning, Pashto lessons with a retired Anglo-Indian schoolteacher; in the afternoon letter-writing and dozing in darkened, thick-walled rooms; the evening, a lesson with Najeeb which might mean sitting in her garden with books or might mean an excursion to Gor Khatri, Bala Hisar, Pipal Mandi, the Museum – over and over, the Museum. At the end of the day there was almost always either a sundowner (or several) at the Peshawar Club with Remmick or an early supper at Dean's with the Forbeses. And then home before the stars were out, to read by lantern-light in her garden which must have been designed by someone of nocturnal habits, it was so rich in night-blooming flowers.

As the Allied forces faced setback after setback in Gallipoli the news reports about Armenians grew ever more dramatic. 'ARMENIANS SENT TO DIE IN THE DESERT' read a headline. 'MORE ARMENIAN HORRORS' said another. Surely the propaganda department was overplaying its hand?

She followed the shouts and splashes towards the swimming pool of the Peshawar Club. Through the trees she saw men

91

falling from the sky – muscled and young, broad of shoulder, water drops glistening on pale chests, dark necks. Officers of the Frontier Corp, on leave after weeks of protecting Peshawar from the fanatics in the mud-and-pebbled hills. One had scarcely dived from the board before the next was there to take his place. Some fell like cannonballs, some swooped like swallows. Water and air, in both they were in their element. It was the ground they wanted nothing to do with, climbing from pool to high board by way of a rope-ladder that someone had tied to the railing.

One of them – sandy-haired – sat on the high board, legs swinging, surveying the world. The Lord of Everything. Viv looped her arm around a tree, watching him, watching them all. Here was the world set right again.

They sat beneath the weeping willow, Najeeb at the school desk which he had carried in last week from God knows where, and Viv in her rattan chair. The local name for weeping willow was Majnu, Najeeb had told her the first time he came out into her garden and followed it up with a retelling of the love story of Laila and Majnu, declaimed with such pride that she hadn't the heart to tell him she knew it already. In Labraunda, Mehmet had spun the tale out over several evenings, paying particular attention to Anna, the younger of the German women, as he spoke of Majnu's undying love. Cigarettes, figs, wine, and stories beneath the Carian sky – would it ever really be possible again?

Najeeb looked up from his Greek letters, and the wind turned the pages of his exercise book, smeared the freshly inked-in date. Viv leaned forward and placed a piece of grey slate onto the book to weigh it down. Picking it up, Najeeb examined the carved hand, palm turned up. A fragment from a stupa, one of many which had Atlas holding up a platform for the seated Buddha. It was worth very little – the Sikh man who owned an antiquities store in the Walled City had presented it to her as a gift as she was walking empty-handed out of his store, to ensure she would return – but it possessed a certain charm. Najeeb placed it between the pages of his exercise book and rubbed his pencil over the page; the colour of the stone so closely resembled the grey of a lead pencil that it seemed an act of metamorphosis, turning stone into paper.

She watched him, realised how familiar his expressions, his way of holding a pencil, the angle of his back as he bent over his books had become. She had been the one to suggest he came to her during his school holidays if he wanted to hear the stories of Peshawar, but he'd been the one to insist on Greek lessons and refuse to allow the start of the school term to force any change in their routine. Why d'you let him take advantage of you, Remmick had asked, but there was nothing in all of Peshawar that delighted her more than the hunger of Najeeb's mind, the tinge of covetousness in his curiosity – apparent now as he finished the rubbing and turned the stone fragment over in his hands. Did parenthood feel anything like this, she wondered, and smiled to think of Tahsin Bey lifting Najeeb onto his shoulders to look a giant Buddha in the eye.

– Do you want to hear about a treasure hunt?

– What treasure?

– The Circlet of Scylax. Remember Scylax from our first lesson?

– Of course. The Shade Man.

– The Emperor Darius so trusted him that he gave him a circlet – that's like a crown – decorated with figs. It was a special kind of circlet, reserved for heroes and men who slay monsters. Though the fig part was unique to Scylax. Long after Scylax died, his home of Caria was ruled by a dynasty called the Hecatomnids who had the Circlet as one of their prized possessions, and stamped it onto their coins.

– And then what happened to it?

– There's the question. Alexander conquered Caria in 334 BC, the Hecatomnid period ended, and there's no further record of the Circlet. Except this.

She picked a slim, leather-bound book off the grass and, opening it to the right page, turned it towards him.

– The Fragments of Kallistos. He was a Byzantine historian,

who didn't think to leave the great work of his life in a place where the moths wouldn't nibble on it. Read what's there; I'm getting more ice.

She stood, hoisted up the steel tub placed halfway between her chair and his desk, and sloshed the cold water within it onto his bare feet, to exclamations of delight. When she returned a few minutes later, ice steaming within the tub, she would have welcomed Najeeb's assistance in carrying the weight of it across the garden but he was bent over Kallistos, in the shade of the weeping willow, his concentration too beautiful to disrupt.

– So that's why, he cried out, looking up.

– Why what?

– Why you always spend so much time in the Museum looking at that ugly thing.

– What have you found in there?

She walked round to his side of the table, picked up the book and balanced it on his head as she read words she hadn't looked at in years.

She led the holy men to the Sacred Casket mounted with the Holy One which contained the Relics but they would not be tempted. Their mission was not one of theft, and they trusted the Casket would come under divine protection. She next implored them to take the great traveller's crown of figs which was in her safekeeping, but they saw no reason to carry something which had no value to them so she went outside and buried the crown at the base of the Great Statue of the Holy One. The light of the Holy One illuminated her task, so those who watched knew this was the right course of action.

The book shifted, fell against her torso as Najeeb tipped his head back to look at her.

– I guessed right, didn't I? The Sacred Casket is the Kanishka Casket. And the crown of figs is buried beneath a statue somewhere near where the casket was found? Somewhere in Shahji-ki-Dheri?

94

– A relic casket mounted with a holy figure? You could find a thousand objects scattered around the world which match that description. And most of them would probably have a statue in the vicinity.

He looked so disappointed she tugged a lock of his hair and said, No one's found the circlet in the eighty years since Kallistos' Fragments were rediscovered in a church attic. It would almost be rude to those who've tried for decades if an eleven-year-old ferreted out its location with a single glance.

– I'm twelve now.

– Are you? When did that happen?

– Last month.

– Why didn't you say? Put your books away immediately. We're going to find you some cake. Oh, and here – happy birthday.

She placed the stupa shard in his hand. He looked up at her, not understanding, and she said, Well, why shouldn't you have it. It's your history after all, Pactyike.

Najeeb ran his thumb over Atlas' wrist, a shimmer to his eyes which it took her a moment to recognise as tears. She could see it had been pleasing before, this piece of Gandharan art, but now that it lay in his palm, transformed into both gift and heritage, it had become precious. Together with the promise of cake it had entirely wiped Kallistos from his mind.

Viv knew this about Tahsin Bey: he wasn't reckless or foolish or lazy. A relic casket with a Buddha on top wouldn't be enough to make him set aside his dreams of finding the Circlet in Labraunda in favour of a stupa that wasn't built until five hundred years after the Circlet vanished from history. So there was something else; something he'd been certain she would work out if he just pointed her in the direction of Peshawar. Caspatyrus! *Where journeys begin and end.* Not her journey – the journey of the Circlet.

She bit down on her forkful of cake, watched Najeeb press his thumb against one of the few crumbs remaining on his plate and lift it to his mouth. The other patrons of the tea-shop

– Indian and English both – kept glancing over at their table. She swapped around plates, gave him the slice she'd barely touched. It wasn't generosity; when he was eating he wasn't talking, and she needed to think.

How would a prized artefact of the Carian dynasts end up in Peshawar? And then came the answer, so obvious, so inevitable. Alexander. Of course. He would have taken the Circlet from Caria when he conquered it and carried it all the way to India – where he sent his Admiral Nearchus to sail down the Indus, following in the oarstrokes of Scylax.

– Najeeb Gul, you are a wonder!

The boy looked up, mouth full of cake; in the tea-room, whispers.

Returning home, she knew exactly the book she needed. *Buddhist Records of the Western World* – an account of several Chinese travellers' visits to India, and to Shahji-ki-Dheri. She'd read it soon after she'd arrived in Peshawar but without knowing what she was looking for despite Tahsin Bey's insertion of the words 'Sacred Casket' into his letter, which she should have recognised as an echo of Kallistos. Although really, he could have been a little more forthcoming. Regardless, now that she was sitting at Najeeb's school desk in the garden with the book open in front of her, it seemed impossible she'd missed it: In AD 518 the Chinese pilgrim Sung-Yun travelled in the company of a Buddhist novice to India on the instructions of the Empress of China, in order to bring back Buddhist holy books from a country now ravaged by 'a rude horde of Turks'. Tahsin Bey would have laughed at that, read it out loud to whoever was near by to listen – even if it was only Alice. Or perhaps he would be too absorbed, instead, in his conviction that Sung-Yun and his companion were the Holy Men whose 'mission was not that of theft'. She read all that Sung-Yun had written of Shahji-ki-Dheri, and moved on to the writings of Hiuen-Tsang, more than a century later. The rude horde of Turks and their descendants had worked their destruction – where Sung-Yun

96

found temples and stupas, Hiuen-Tsang found ruins. But the Kanishka Stupa survived and –

> To the south-west of the Great Stupa a hundred paces or so, there is a figure of Buddha in white stone about eighteen feet high. It is a standing figure, and looks to the north. It has many spiritual powers, and diffuses a brilliant light.

The Sacred Casket. The Likeness of the Holy One. The Holy Men. The Illuminating Statue. It was all there, every bit of it.

The last excavation at Shahji-ki-Dheri had taken place in 1911. Every year since then the Archaeological Survey of India, Frontier Circle reported a continuing leasing dispute with the owner of the land. The most recent report was promising – 'the compulsory acquisition of the land may be considered'. Viv looked up the Land Acquisitions Act – there was no reason it couldn't be applied to Shahji-ki-Dheri. Perhaps all that was needed was a little nudge from the right quarters.

– There's something here that's caught my attention, Mr Remmick, I wonder if you could advise me how to move forward with it.

She made a fluttering motion to indicate some flight of fancy, leaning forward slightly towards Remmick who turned an even deeper shade of red. They were the only two sitting on the verandah of the Peshawar Club, gin-and-tonics in hand, watching the sky turn a fiery orange.

– There's an archaeological site here I'm interested in. Shahji-ki-Dheri.

– The Kanishka Stupa?

– I wouldn't want to get in the way of the main stupa excavations, of course, but there's an illuminated white statue at the edge of the stupa complex which I'm interested to see if there's anything left of.

– Illuminated?

– Probably a story that arose from the sight of moonlight on

97

white marble – but it's the marble I'm interested in. Why a white marble statue in this place of grey schist? Or is it limestone? I have a theory about trade routes during the Kushan Empire.

As anticipated, his expression fixed into a pretence of interest, allowing her to skip ahead.

– Is the leasing dispute likely to be resolved soon?

– Very soon, I'd imagine. The DC is looking into taking the land away from the owner. It should all be settled by the dig season.

– Hurrah for you, Mr Remmick! That's a better answer than I'd expected. When is the dig season?

– It can start as early as November. But, Miss Spencer, I should strike a note of caution. I know there've been women archaeologists in Greece, in Turkey. Even Egypt. But this is Peshawar. Pathan men don't much like the idea of women . . .

– Don't much like the idea of women doing what?

– Don't much like the idea of women.

She thought of the soldier on the train; the ease of the silence between them right at the end. But who knew what he'd really been thinking?

– Are the English in India in the habit of having our behaviour dictated by the Natives?

– Ha! Well expressed.

He raised his glass to her.

– To the dig season!

Silence rolled thick down the mountain, smothering even the calls of the nocturnal birds. Viv collided with a garden chair, the bump of flesh on wood loud in the darkness. Piece by piece she removed every scrap of clothing until she was naked in the moonlit night, the faintest of breezes warm on her skin. Picking up one end of the garden hose she carried it back along the length of itself to the tap and, crouching down on the grass, placed the mouth of it between her shoulder blades, beneath the dip of her neck. A spine of water overlaid her own. Warm at first, but as it drew itself up from the deeper parts of the underground tank it cooled and she stood up, painting every inch of her skin with water, bending her head into it so her hair grew heavy and slicked.

She stood up, looked towards the distant mountains. Tahsin Bey stood behind her, his fingers tracing circles on her skin. The outermost circle was the girdle, the broken bowl, the circlet of mountain ranges, hills and spurs; overlapping it, the tribal areas where men killed each other before breakfast over a chicken, a bad dream, a smile; further in, the British troops protecting Peshawar from the tribesmen; then, the fields and orchards and gardens where the very summer which made the British flee to hill stations brought fruit and fiery-coloured flowers bursting into life; closer now, closer, the proud Englishness of spires and barracks; and right in the centre, the innermost circle, the eye of the storm: Vivian Rose Spencer standing in the garden of her bungalow, a shiver of pleasure running all the way through her.

July–September 1915

The familiarity of Peshawar choked off any hope that life might veer in directions Qayyum couldn't anticipate. No breeze, only heat which shrank his clothes onto his body. He thought of the snake he'd once seen shedding its skin. 'Shedding' wasn't the right word. It simply seemed to glide forward along a pebbled pathway, leaving behind a layer of scales. As though the skin it had lived in was nothing more than a sock. Qayyum had picked up the discarded skin – one piece, split along the snout. He brought the split together and held in his hands a weightless, transparent snake; even the shape of its eyes intact. When he held it up against the sunlight rainbows danced crazily along the length of it, as though something were swirling into life, and he dropped it in terror.

Steps no longer proved a challenge but he still continued to stand in the doorway to the train compartment for a long moment until some movement to his right raised the shameful possibility that someone had seen a blind man in need of help; he hopped down onto the platform – a slight plummet in his stomach before foot hit cement – and walked rapidly away, the knapsack on his back reproachfully light without its soldier's kit. The bulk of its contents were letters and mementoes from men who lived in the Peshawar Valley: a pebble from Brighton with a rose painted onto it; a photograph of a female aviator; a medal; a bullet compacted by bone; a scrap of paper with a name on it in the ragged writing of someone learning to hold a pen for the first time; a teddy bear with buttons from a soldier's uniform in place

100

of eyes. When the objects were distributed it would be the end of his service to the Army.

Leaving the station he hailed down a horse-drawn Victoria. He'd become accustomed to being greeted by salutes from children passing by and from the Victoria drivers themselves as soon as they saw the drab-and-green uniform of the 40th. Now it was the missing eye which set him apart. Even when both eyes were closed he knew it was evident something was wrong with the right one, quite apart from the swelling; a translucence to the skin.

The Victoria passed through Kabuli Gate and entered the Street of Storytellers. *If a man is to die defending a field, let the field be his field, the land his land, the people his people.* But these were not Qayyum's people – the merchants and traders, the courtesans and maulvis, the money-changers and beggars. The 40th Pathans, those were his people; not just the Yusufzai, but also the Afridis, also the Dogras. He should have fought harder to stay. So he only had one eye. What of it? Nelson had only one eye and one arm. Better to be there than here.

The Victoria approached two Afridi men holding hands – both had long hair, and the taller of the two had a flower behind his ear. In the Army, Qayyum had learned that everything about such men's appearance and deportment was unbecoming for a soldier (or for any man, one of the officers had snarled), but lying beside the stream that night at Vipers, waiting for the moon to slip out of the sky, he had seen two sepoys of the 40th – Bahadur Khan and Afroze – with fingers interlinked; and then the terrible sobbing when Bahadur Khan's fingers turned rigid. The sound had carried straight to the German gunners. And there was also this: how would his mind have survived that night without Kalam Khan lying beside him, filling his own mouth with water from the stream so he might blow cool air onto his comrade's burning face, the proximity which Qayyum had always denied the other man now his only salve.

A train of camels slowed the Victoria's progress. Qayyum's hand was a visor in front of both eyes, protecting one, hiding the other, so he didn't see the Afridi pluck the marigold from behind his ear and press it between Qayyum's splayed fingers. The petals softer than the lips of the Frenchwoman. He held it against his skin; there had been kindness in Brighton, but never intimacy.

The Victoria turned away from the broad Street of Storytellers and was soon passing by lanes too narrow for it; such little space between the structures on one side of the street and the other that it was possible for a boy to lean out of a window and ask his facing neighbour to tie his turban so that he could run down to his mother and pretend he had managed it all on his own. Almost home now. Allah forgive him, he'd rather be in the trenches.

At the top of the stairs he pushed open the wooden door and dark shapes threw themselves at him; without a sound he stepped back, still gripping the handle, pulling the door shut. Hazrat Ali, at the Battle of Khaybar, ripped a fortress door from its hinges to replace his lost shield. Qayyum's attackers called his name from the other side of the door and he commanded, Move back, move back, and this time when he re-entered they stood still, expressions uncertain, allowing him to be the one to embrace his father and mother and nod at his three sisters, all married now, looking past them for Najeeb.

The youngest of his sisters burst into tears, and stepped forward, one hand hovering over the shrapnel scars around his eyes. Qayyum caught the tips of her fingers and brought them to rest on her jutting belly. A boy, he said, and she replied, A soldier. Qayyum shook his head, looked away – how small this space was, how gloomy, with narrow bars of light falling slant-wise from the window slats onto the English-style dining table which he'd insisted on buying during his last leave, its bulk dominating the room, books at one end of it, kitchen imple-ments at the other. His mother held a Qur'an as high as her arms would allow; Qayyum ducked beneath it, his mother whispered a prayer, and he was home.

– A man wears scars as a woman wears bangles.

His mother held up her thick wrists, jangled both of them.

102

She was perhaps thirty-seven or thirty-eight, and if she were English that wouldn't make her old. But she looked the same age as her husband, twenty years her senior, who remained trim and spritely though his cheeks had the concavity which came from missing teeth. He cleared his throat; a letter-writer who spent his life transcribing other people's words, he had so few of his own.

– Najeeb went to meet you at the train station, his father said.

– I didn't see him.

The mention of sight made the old man wilt; he looked at his wife, nodding his head as if she had already said the next thing and he wanted to make it clear he agreed.

– You'll receive a pension, won't you? For the rest of your life?

– Yes, Amma.

– At least some good has come of this. When I start looking for a bride I can say, how many two-eyed men have a guaranteed income for their entire lives?

The middle sister giggled, and started to hum a wedding song. Behind her mother's back she pulled a face and crossed her eyes to let him know that the most beautiful girls in the Walled City were being saved for whole men. There wasn't enough air in this room to fill a man's lungs. He felt someone tapping his back, gently, and there was Najeeb, looking straight at Qayyum's face with an expression that didn't pretend everything was all right.

– Does it hurt?

He clasped the boy's head to his chest, and exhaled.

Qayyum sat on a bed strung with rope, bending forward towards the lantern on the ground. He lifted the glass chimney, lit a match, adjusted the flame, drawing the smell of kerosene into his nostrils. These tiny, automated rituals had become a comfort. Only when the glass was secured in place, and his body pulled into a cross-legged position allowing no proximity between his feet and the lantern, did he extract the handkerchief from his pocket. Cupping his palm he placed the weight at the centre of the handkerchief carefully within it, and unbraided the cloth with one hand. The silk draped over his palm. He pulled away the covering of cotton wool and, in the light of the full moon and the lantern, an eye stared glassily up at him.

It was the most amazing thing he had ever seen. He touched it gently with his thumb. The brown of the iris almost the same shade as the remaining eye, tiny capillaries painted onto the whites of it. Once the infection subsided, the doctor on the ship to Karachi had assured him, he would be able to wear it again. And the cluster of shrapnel scars would fade. You'll be breaking hearts again in no time. He understood now that the nurse had meant it as kindness, not an accusation.

He walked over to the matting which formed a barrier around the roof. Standing on the balls of his feet he was able to see over the matting, down to the street below and the buildings all around. Mud-and-brick houses and once brightly painted windows and doors all equally the colour of night. The construction haphazard so the upper storeys of buildings looked as if they might tumble off at any moment. Here and there, a faint lamp-glow from rooftops. Sleeping camels in the caravanserai, a boy curled against the flanks of one of the foul-smelling beasts. Did you need to learn how to slaughter in ways that were unimaginable to a Pashtun to make your country a place where every child was well fed, every home prosperous, everything a fine city or abundant farmland?

– Lala?

He tried to pretend he hadn't heard, hoping Najeeb would go away.

– Lala, they've all gone to sleep. I brought you some dinner. I'll leave it here.

The sound of a plate being set down, and the scent of something wonderful. A homecoming meal from which he'd shut himself away.

– No, stay.

Najeeb sat at the very edge of the bed-frame, watching his

brother eat. He had been the only one in the family who had met Qayyum's silence with silence instead of an increasing pitch. Even their father had tried to join in the chatter, multiplying its discordance.

– Hold out your hands. Be careful now.

Qayyum placed the handkerchief in his brother's hands. Najeeb lowered his face and brushed it against the silk.

– What is that smell?

– An Englishwoman.

Najeeb's mouth opened wide and Qayyum laughed. The first laugh in a very long time.

– She was older than our mother, and had a mouth which looked as if it had been eating lemons all her life. But she was very kind. Open it, look inside. Carefully, carefully.

Najeeb unwrapped the handkerchief as if it were a present. If he was surprised to see an eye staring at him, he didn't show it. Closing his palms protectively around it he lowered himself onto the ground, resting on his elbows, his hands as close to the lantern as was safe. For a long time he simply looked at the glass eye, rotating it slightly this way and that so he could inspect every part of its surface. In this way he could stare at a book, a butterfly wing, a rock. A stillness at the heart of his character. There were some boys in the 40th Qayyum had felt particularly protective towards; now he understood he had seen the shadow of his brother in them.

At length, Najeeb stood up, the same height as the seated figure of his brother.

– What's in there now?

– Look.

Qayyum held his thumb and forefinger like a pair of crab claws around his eye, pulling at the skin to force the eyelid open. He saw Najeeb's fingers extend towards him, found he didn't have to fight against any desire to back away. How strange – not troubling, just strange – to feel his brother's touch against the bone of the eye-socket.

But no; he had imagined it. Najeeb placed his hand over his brother's thumb and forefinger, and simply bent down and peered into the socket which was more than Qayyum could bring himself to do in front of the mirror.

– It's too dark to see anything.

– You can have a look in the morning.

– Thank you.

Najeeb sat down, leaning his weight against his brother.

– I'm sorry I wasn't at home when you arrived, Lala.

– That's all right.

– I went to the train station to meet you. You didn't see me when you stepped onto the platform, though I was right there.

– Why didn't you say something?

The sight of his scarred, one-eyed brother had frightened him. Why else? He held the boy's hand in apology, in forgiveness. Najeeb squeezed his hand in return and then picked up the plate Qayyum had eaten from, turning it over with a laugh to demonstrate that there wasn't even a sliver of onion remaining on it.

– Our mother was worried about what they were giving you to eat in the hospital.

– There were nine kitchens.

Najeeb looked impressed, and Qayyum found himself wanting to say something else, something to temper his brother's look of awe at the bounty of the English.

– Lala?

– Yes.

– Are you still a soldier?

– No.

– Do you wish you still were?

– Go to sleep, Najeeb.

The brothers faced each other on the roof; one tense and watchful, the other encouraging, slightly impatient.

– Ready?

– No, wait. One second.

Yesterday, a staccato sound on the roof had made Qayyum drop his cup of tea; when it had gone on long enough to sound more like hail than bullets he had come up to the roof to investigate, and found Najeeb holding one hand in front of his right eye while bouncing the ball with the other hand. He had bounced the ball more than fifty times in a row without fault before he realised he was being watched by Qayyum who spent his days repeating this very action, without anything of Najeeb's fluidity. Qayyum winced to think that all these days while he thought he was engaged in a private act his family below had been able to hear the aching gaps between every few bounces. Tomorrow we'll play catch, Qayyum had said and turned away.

– Now.

Najeeb threw the ball. It travelled in a slow, chest-high loop, beginning a downward path well before it reached Qayyum so that his hands were only waist-high as he caught it.

– Well done! Najeeb called out.

Qayyum looked up slowly from the cupped hands holding the child's toy.

– This is 'well done' in my life now.

He saw Najeeb turn his face away to the white sky of summer and knew his brother was wishing he were somewhere else.

– I'm sorry, Qayyum said. Najeeb shook his head but didn't look up. Qayyum wasn't sure if he was rejecting the apology or pretending there was no need for it.

– I'm more sick of me than you are.

– I'm not sick of you.

– Do you think I haven't noticed you go away after lunch and don't come back until long after the lessons with the maulvi are supposed to end?

– It's not because I'm sick of you.

– No, don't apologise. It makes me happy to think of you reading in Shalimar Bagh beside a fountain. There was an officer at Vipers – he carried a book in his pocket and in these minutes we were gathered on the slope, waiting for the order to attack, I saw him lie on his stomach, put his head in the book and go somewhere else. I envied him, and then I was happy because I knew my brother also had that in him. Whatever happens in the world, Najeeb can escape.

107

Qayyum launched the ball back towards his brother. Najeeb fumbled for it – it was obvious he only did that because he thought it a kindness.

– Lala, there's something I want to know. About when you were over there.

– Ask me anything. But don't ask me what happened on the battlefield.

He felt a slight constriction of the mouth as he spoke, as though loose stitches were looped between his lips. Najeeb stepped towards him, right hand raised, palm outwards; a formal gesture that came from outside Qayyum's world.

– Tell me about the Englishwoman who gave you the handkerchief. Was she nice? Did you practise English with her?

– Listen, Najeeb. Don't become curious about Englishwomen.

– I'm not asking it in a bad way.

– The English, they don't think there are any good ways for an Indian to want to know things about their women. Maybe they're right. Would you want Englishmen to come here and ask about our sisters?

– What would they ask?

– Are they nice? Can I practise Hindko with them?

The idea of an Englishman wanting to practise Hindko with any of their sisters was so absurd Najeeb started to laugh. His arm slung back to throw the ball to Qayyum, as though they were in a time before. Arrow-straight, it gathered speed, making for Qayyum's face, his eye. Najeeb shouted out a warning, but his brother's hands came up to catch it with the old deftness, the sound of palms closing around a speeding ball sweeter than all the sitars in the world.

Finally there came the morning when all signs of the infection had dissipated. Qayyum placed the glass eye into his socket, and stood for a long time looking in the mirror. Almost himself, but when a man's gaze on the world changes everything shifts with it. He hoisted his knapsack with the soldiers' mementoes onto his shoulders, put on his sturdiest shoes, and went downstairs.

His mother looked up from the peas she was shelling at the dining table, and her face was unknown to him. The colour came and went from it, and she lifted two fistfuls of pea pods from the pan and threw them up into the air as though they were rose petals at a wedding, her voice a cry of delight. Najeeb had been on the way out, schoolbag in hand, but he walked back into the room and embraced his mother around the shoulders.

– Amma, it's a glass eye.

Qayyum silently picked the pea pods off the floor and table and returned them to the pan, slipping his hand away from his mother's when she tried to clasp it.

Away from the noise and chaos of the city he was received in villages and small towns as the fulfilment of a dream: a Pashtun soldier returned from war. Everywhere he went he was asked to stay a night and a banquet was prepared in his honour, even when it meant slaughtering the chicken which the family relied on for eggs; the object he brought with him – pebble or bullet or photograph – was passed from hand to hand as if it were a piece of the Black Stone brought by the angel Jibreel himself. On foot he travelled through the Valley's orchards, crossed its rushing streams at their narrowest point. One day, bathing his face in the water, he felt himself rinsing Europe from his eyes. How had he thought the beauty of France superior to this – he opened his arms wide to the rivers bounding down foothills, racing each other to the Valley – this jewelled earth.

His last stop before he returned to Peshawar was Shahbaz Garhi in the Yusufzai lands, home of his forefathers. The brothers of Sepoy Khuda Buksh took the letter and the red feather from the throat of a bird which he had brought for them and told him that the man who had sent these tokens was dead; someone from the Army came to see them the previous week to deliver the news. So now you are our brother in his place, they said, as if relaying a fact rather than conveying an honour, and allowed him to enter the zenana where the older women kept their tear-streaked faces uncovered while they pressed him for news of the boy who only Qayyum had seen as a man. When it was time to leave one of the old men of the family took him by the elbow:

– There's something you should see, Yusufzai scribe.

His new brothers took him to a giant rock with shapes cut into it. Kneeling, the youngest of them used the end of his turban to wipe away dust from a small section. Faded symbols made up lines which sloped and slanted towards each other like weary battalions. Even before there was paper there were scribes amongst the Yusufzai, the old man said. But what does it say, Qayyum asked. The old man didn't know exactly but they were the words of the King, Asoka, who ruled with blood and fire until one day on a battlefield he looked at the mountain of the dead, heard the sobbing of a woman whose husband and sons had all been killed, and became a follower of the Buddha, renouncing violence and inscribing stones with his belief in peace.

His fingers lightly brushing the ancient words, Qayyum saw Asoka walking through that field at Vipers and saying to himself, No more.

There was a small hole in the canvas draped over the branches, and when the sun was directly overhead a narrow shaft of light fell into the inkhorn. Qayyum closed his fist around the buffalo horn – it was warm, heat radiating from the ink contained within.

A few days earlier his father had taken to bed with a fever and Qayyum's mother looked at her son in a way that reminded him that he had obligations beyond those of a postman. So now here he was, beneath a tree, legs squeezed under the table with the built-in inkhorn – his father's pride. As a child he'd disliked the smell of ink, associating it with the boredom of standing behind his father with a fan on hot afternoons, waving a breeze onto his neck while being careful to keep the fan from smearing the ink on the page. And the letters that were dictated were inevitably dull – someone needed money, someone was sending money, someone had arrived, someone was leaving, someone was married, someone had a child, someone was dead. Everyone was well, everyone missed someone, someone missed everyone, the chicken had stopped laying eggs, where were the bolts of silk? Occasionally news of a blood feud or murder enlivened things, but not often. He'd always known he'd choose a different life for himself – he had grown up in the shadow of a fort; how could he stay immune to the soldiers parading on maidans, boots and buttons gleaming?

But in the Army he came to understand the importance of letters, no matter how ordinary their contents. Never more so than on that day in Brighton when a sepoy from Peshawar had come hobbling into his ward, waving a piece of paper in his hand and said, Finally a letter from home. Qayyum had taken the paper and recognised the handwriting. His voice was not entirely steady as he and his father clasped hands across the world to tell the sepoy everything was well, the harvest had been good, the chicken had recovered.

As the morning became afternoon, everything slowed. The muezzin's voice wavered as he sent the call to prayer winging out from the minaret of Mahabat Khan Mosque. A blur descended onto the inkhorn. Qayyum lifted the horn from its holder, and saw a fly struggling to stay afloat in its dark waters. The ink an ocean of death. Carefully, he positioned his quill beneath the thrashing insect and lifted it out, flicking it onto the ground as soon as it was clear of the ink. The fly staggered about, blue smudges its trail, its wings rising and falling impotently. Qayyum took the pitcher near his feet, dribbled water onto his hand and from there dropped the tiniest quantity onto the fly.

– Working hard, Lala?

Qayyum snapped his wrist and the remaining water sprayed Najeeb, who responded with the giant smile.

– Instead of bathing flies, come and listen to a badala with me.

The knife-sharpener who shared the canopy with him said he'd look after Qayyum's belongings, his knife cleanly slicing the still-flailing insect in two as he spoke. Najeeb took hold of his elder brother's hand and led him towards the Street of

Storytellers, chattering away about how there were so many stories of Peshawar that none of the Storytellers in the bazaar ever told; all his life he'd heard the same old tales and maybe he should be the one to let the Storytellers know that there were other possibilities. There was a particular confidence in him that seemed to grow daily, hard to pin down; it would be necessary to make sure it didn't become arrogance. But for the moment it consisted primarily of exuberance, and Qayyum couldn't help smiling at the thought of his brother approaching an old storyteller, informing him that he had a better story than any of the old tales of the bazaar. Probably something he'd picked up at the Mission School – please let it not be a story of Christianity, or somehow that would get back to their mother who had only grudgingly given in to Qayyum's insistence that Najeeb needed to be educated in the English way if he was to progress through the world.

The brothers walked through the Street of Storytellers, Qayyum's elbows jutting out in that posture which had started as self-protection, a guarding of the space around himself, and was already becoming an attitude of ownership. He slowed as they approached the lines of Storytellers who were offering familiar fare, the stories of Peshawar unchanged through generations as Najeeb had said: 'Laila Majnu', 'Hazrat Ali', 'The Prince and the Fakir', Hadda Mulla's jihad against the English. This last story had gathered the largest crowd, and Najeeb squeezed himself in among the gathering, leaving Qayyum no choice but to follow though he'd have preferred 'Laila Majnu'.

The English approached, armed to the teeth.
　　Hadda Mulla, their foe, finally within reach.

In cover of darkness they crawled into town
　　When thunder and lightning and hail crashed down.

Everything lit up so all – all! – could see
　　The white man's forces assaulted by bees.

A handful of stings and they're overpowered,
   Is it bees or Allah's wrath that makes them such cowards?

A decade and more has passed since then
   But now hear the call for jihad once again.

Haji Sahib in the hills is gathering his forces
   Rise up! Join him! By foot or on horses.

What did it mean, this great emptiness which opened up in Qayyum's chest in response to the Storyteller's badala? A Mohmand tribesman raised his gun in the air at the end of the last couplet, the butt of a rifle catching Qayyum on the shoulder. Men around him cheered, and repeated the last line back to the Storyteller. Rise up! Join him! Qayyum turned on his heels and walked briskly away. It wasn't until he was back under the canopy, flicking away the two pieces of the fly with his toe, that Najeeb caught up with him.

– I'm sorry, Lala. I didn't know there'd be so many people.

He pushed Najeeb away, more roughly than he'd intended.

– What will our mother say if I come home without money because I've been listening to silly tales all day? Go, get out of here. Let me work.

– You're afraid of everything, Najeeb shouted, and ran away before Qayyum could respond.

Qayyum looked down at his hand, rubbing his thumb against the bump on the side of his finger formed by holding the quill in place. It had replaced the old rifle-calluses. How could Qayyum tell his brother that he hadn't walked away from the Storyteller because of the crush of people, or the threat of a rifle to his eye. He left because for a moment he pictured himself in the uniform of the British Indian Army, and what he felt was shame.

A tarpaulin flew off a donkey-cart. The load of hand mirrors caught the sun, threw circles of light up onto surrounding facades whose windows flung the glare back into the eyes of the men on the street – camel-drivers, Victoria-drivers, merchants, customers, wayfarers. Dazzling chaos. A bolting donkey, an upturned cart of turnips, a man walking into a tower of brass urns; the blur of other things falling, colliding at the periphery of Qayyum's vision. He closed his eyes for a long moment, but without any feeling of panic. Weeks of working in the bazaar, watching its everyday courtesies and camaraderie, and other people had ceased to be a threat.

In just the second or two that he wasn't looking everything moved quickly into aftermath. No signs of serious damage, but in the absence of tragedy there was nothing to leash the frayed tempers of summer. Men were stepping out of shops, dismounting bicycles, pointing at scrapes and cuts and dented brass. Ugliness in the air; any moment there would be fists or blades.

A young boy who had been trying to sell Qayyum an oxtail fly whisk from the tray he was carrying in his too small arms set it down on the pavement beside the knife-sharpener, dashed across the street to the donkey-cart, lifted out a mirror which he angled so that it struck reflected sunlight into the eyes of a man whose raised voice, directed at the cowering donkey-cart driver, was on the brink of violence. The man shielded his eyes, turned in the direction of the boy, anger swerving. Laughing, the boy lowered the mirror, his little hand covering part of its surface so that a circle of light appeared over the man's genital area, a hand silhouetted within, groping about as though trying to catch hold of something that wasn't there.

Raucous laughter broke out in the street; the boy darted back to the pavement, made a noise of indignation at the flies which had settled on his whisks, picked up the tray and was surrounded by customers, including the knife-sharpener. The man who had knocked over the brass urns helped the donkey-cart driver replace the tarpaulin, and the man who had been on the receiving end of the boy's teasing pointed towards his groin and said, First time, even my wife thought a thing that size must be my thigh, which turned him into a hero, though not because anyone believed the brag.

114

How Qayyum loved these men. Why had he ever chosen to live his life away from them?

He was still smiling when another boy approached, hair matted, clothes tattered. He held out a piece of paper and Qayyum told him to sit down; he had the look of someone who planned to race off without paying as soon as Qayyum finished reading. That almost never happened – people seemed to want to keep hold of anything addressed to them, even if they couldn't understand the symbols on the page – but there were always exceptions. But the boy just laughed and walked away, leaving Qayyum holding the piece of paper.

Your brother from the orchards has survived hell. His blade of ice will melt at your approach, and yours only.

Qayyum cupped his hands together, the paper a grainy lining between them, reciting a prayer. A missing limb, a missing eye – these were the only reasons an Indian soldier would be discharged and find himself in Peshawar again, but Allah, let it be a miracle; let it be something else. He placed his fingertip against his glass eye, astonished to find it wet with tears.

Kalam strode towards him through the orchard, arms swinging. An eye then, oh Kalam, if only I had been there to wash your wounds, to be a light in the terrifying darkness of day, to string together in whispers the names of all the gates of the Walled City as though they were prayer-beads. But just before the other man embraced him he saw that both his eyes were eyes, no artifice of glass. It could mean only one thing: it wasn't his body, but his mind which had been destroyed.

– The English have decided to stop recruiting Pashtuns.

Kalam bit into a plum, arching his neck forward so that the spray of juice wouldn't stain his clothes.

– For the Army? Qayyum asked.

The other man nodded, wiping his mouth against his sleeve so that all the juice he had carefully kept off his clothes was

115

now a dark smear near his wrist. It was the closest thing to madness he'd displayed in these several minutes during which he'd asked so considerately about Qayyum's time in Brighton, the sea voyage, the return to Peshawar.

– Too many of us mutiny, too many desert. Particularly when we're asked to fight our Muslim brothers. Don't look indignant, Lance-Naik – you should be proud to belong to a people who won't kill their brothers at the command of their oppressors.

Kalam grinned as he said it, a piece of pulp between his front teeth.

– Perhaps I belong to a people who desert because they know they can hide with the tribes where the English will never find them and have them court-martialled.

– So you've guessed it. Yes, I go tomorrow to my mother's people and do what must be done.

– What is it that must be done?

– Jihad.

This morning had brought fresh rumours of the bloody battles between the English and the tribesmen under Haji Sahib in the mountain passes and foothills; on his way to the orchard Qayyum had walked past a battalion heading towards the hills, and the sound of feet marching in unison tore at his heart as if they were the footsteps of a beloved walking deliberately away. He said this to Kalam to take that look of fierceness from his face, but his friend raised his hands sharply to ward off the words.

– You'll fight for the Europeans who want to keep their land away from invaders but when your brothers want the same thing you turn the invaders into your beloved.

– Kalam, remember that sepoy who stood up in the moonlight and started running towards the Germans, screaming a sound with no words in it?

– Of course I remember.

– Why do you remind me of him?

Kalam placed a hand on Qayyum's face, thumb stroking the scars beside his eye.

– Come with me.

The debt Qayyum owed Kalam was immense – he couldn't say no, and the other man knew it. But when he hesitated Kalam merely shook his head, and dropped his hand.

– Still a loyal soldier, Lance-Naik?

– No, Kalam. Not still any kind of soldier.

– But your loyalty is with the English.

– My loyalty is with my friend Kalam. And I know if a deserter is captured while attacking English troops he'll be executed.

– They won't capture me.

So quickly Qayyum barely had time to know what was happening, Kalam spun him round and caught him in a neck-hold, the tip of a knife pressed against Qayyum's breast.

– See, Lance-Naik? I know all their tricks, but they don't know all mine. And if their bullets find me, let them find me. I'm not afraid.

– I am. What is the world if Kalam isn't in it?

Kalam loosened his grip, pulled Qayyum closer to him. They stood that way for a while looking towards the plum trees, the mountains, the clear blue skies. There was peace here in the orchards, peace that could never be found in Peshawar with its constantly parading troops and bandoliered tribesmen. When Kalam's hand started to wander, Qayyum batted it away – it was almost ritualistic, the advance and the rejection, a shadow of the past in which there was heat in both actions. It was almost comforting. With everyone else in his life there was an abrupt severing – the Qayyum of before distinct from the Qayyum of now; but with Kalam, his life was restored to continuity.

– I tried to come to you at Kitchener.

– I know; I heard you. But I thought you were a dream made of morphine. It was only later they told me it was you, and that you believed I'd been sent away.

– Stay here. Pretend you aren't the deserter, Kalam Khan. Tend the orchards with your father. Find a beautiful wife and have lots of sons.

– It's a lovely dream.

– If we can live nightmares we can live dreams.

A pause as Kalam thought about it, and then a booming laugh.

– Lance-Naik, sir, that's the stupidest thing I've ever heard.

– I know, I know!

The pleasure of a comrade. On the days when he felt adrift in his life how would he stop himself from travelling up into the hills for a day in Kalam Khan's company? But he knew the laws which prohibited anyone in British India from communicating with members of hostile tribes. Once Kalam joined his cousins, the Mohmands, even writing to him would be a crime.

– Then will you do something else for me, brother? Kalam said.

– Anything.

– When it's planting season will you come to help my father if he sends for you? He used to hire someone, with the money I sent him from the Army, but now . . .

– Of course I will. For as long as he needs me.

Poor Kalam – twenty-one years old, a fugitive with nothing to offer the men with whom he was seeking refuge except his skill at war, no way to fulfil the obligations of a son, and no way back, no possible way back.

Qayyum rolled a leaf between his palms, releasing its scent, and saw his own life as blessed.

It was always night in the Street of Courtesans, the alley too narrow to admit sunlight. Qayyum wrapped the end of his turban around his face as he walked towards it, hunching his shoulders to make his gait unrecognisable. At this time of the afternoon only the ice-sellers did good business, so most of the doors lining the alley were open to display the women lying against pillows, propped on one elbow.

Two men waited outside a closed door, talking about the massacre of English troops by Haji Sahib's forces at Rustam. They swept down the Ambela Pass and attacked the camp, the shorter of the two said – so many dead and wounded soldiers that sixteen trucks were required to shift them to the nearest hospital. Allah keep Haji Sahib safe, said the other, and the short man threw his hands up in despair.

– How can I stay here now that you've mentioned Allah's name. You bastard, you just want to get rid of me so you're next in line. Hey, you. Scarred-man.

Qayyum had slowed to listen to their conversation – Haji Sahib's forces included Kalam – and now found the short man speaking to him, saying, Take my place. The taller man withdrew a dagger from his belt. Qayyum shook his head – a refusal to one man, a warning to the other – but his curiosity couldn't stop him from asking the next question.

– So many open doors, why are you waiting outside this one?

From across the street one of the courtesans called out:

– Some Pathans lick the shoes of the English, some want to lick other things.

Along the alley the sound of laughter from the courtesans. Any further questions Qayyum had were cut short by the door opening. A man scented in rosewater stepped out, and the woman in the room came up to the doorway, one hand on her hip, and flicked the other hand in dismissal at the courtesan across the street. Qayyum stepped back, and further back, his spine pressing against the wall. It was an Englishwoman in a long white dress, her arms encased in gloves, a bonnet on her head. Eyes grey, skin lightly freckled, age no more than twelve or thirteen.

– Good afternoon, gentlemen.

She spoke in English but her accent was of Peshawar, and brought with it the understanding that she was only part-English, her father probably a customer of one of the women in the alley.

– We haven't met.

Still speaking English, she stepped forward to Qayyum, her gloved hand extended. The man who said he couldn't stay was glowering, no longer willing to give up his place. Qayyum looked at the extended hand, and found that was a useful way to keep from looking at her face, the monstrous childishness and knowledge of it.

119

– Don't want to play, good-looking?

He squeezed his eyes closed as she brought her face closer to his, a scent on her breath which he didn't want to think about. Then something moist – her mouth, her tongue? – was on the scars near his eye.

– You taste of death.

Qayyum turned and ran down the alley, the mocking laughter of the Walled City's fantasies following after him.

The old man walked down the street in the drab and green of the 40th Pathans; the uniform hung off his frame, rolled up at ankle and wrist. He stopped to look closely at Qayyum's father who was reading a letter out loud to one of his long-standing clients, a man almost completely deaf into whose ear the elder Gul spoke, the palm of his hand resting lightly on the back of the man's head. The old man stepped around the almost-embracing duo at the desk with the buffalo horn, neck craning in an attempt to see something hidden from his view. Qayyum, sitting a few feet away on the ground where he'd been relegated since his father's return, raised a hand to draw the man's attention to himself.

– Can I help you while my father's busy?

The old soldier came up close, touched the side of Qayyum's face, just beneath his missing eye.

– A letter, will you write a letter for me?

The old man lowered himself onto his haunches, not sitting across from Qayyum but close to his elbow, so Qayyum had to twist his body round to face him.

– Address it to Sepoy Hakimullah, Mardan. We served together.

– I'll need more than that for the address.

– Just write.

– But . . .

– Write!

Qayyum picked up the pen, and waited. The man cleared his throat, held up one hand, the back of his palm facing Qayyum, and began to orate rather than speak.

– My brother, today we have the news that those brave Sikhs who were put on trial in Lahore for mutiny have received their sentences including death for some. I know if you and I had still been serving we would have been among the honourable soldiers who were ready to support their plans for revolt. But why call it revolt when really it is a fight for freedom?

Qayyum placed his pen on the ground and shook his head, no. The new laws brought into effect to help stamp out rebellion could have him jailed just for writing down this treason, and he would certainly lose his pension. But the old man continued speaking.

– You might remember that the trial itself started on 26 April of this year. On that same date our old regiment was getting torn to pieces on a battlefield in a distant place called Vipers, not knowing what they were dying for, not asking why they were dying for it. Wouldn't they have been braver, and wiser, to fight for their own land, their own freedom?

– What is this? Why are you saying all this?

– Kalam Khan sent me, glass-eye.

Qayyum picked up the paper he'd been writing on and tore it into long shreds, standing up as he did so, turning his back to the man.

– Is this how you treat a messenger from the man who risked his life for you?

– What do you want from me?

– I want to help you remove these chains from your feet. It's what Kalam wants too.

– And how will you do that?

– I'll send you to the Ottoman Empire.

– For what?

– To help turn the Indian prisoners of war who are being held there. You're a soldier – they'll listen when you tell them they're fighting for the wrong side. If they agree to join the Indian Volunteer Corps they'll win their freedom from the prisoner-of-war camps, and then they'll win all our freedom from English tyranny.

– What? The what? Indian Volunteer Corps?

– You are so blind, glass-eye. It gains numbers every day – our brothers, the Turks, promise when the time comes for Ottoman troops to sweep through Persia into India the Volunteer Corps, led by Indian generals, will be part of the army. You could be one of those men, Lance-Naik. A general in the army of Indian liberation.

– You must be mad to come and speak to me of this.

– Kalam said you're one of us, you just don't know it yet. He said if you betray us he'll slit his own throat.

– Tell Kalam to go to the Ottoman Empire then.

– He's already found his place in the world, with Haji Sahib, attacking the English here. When the Volunteer Corps comes through the Khyber Pass the two forces will combine. And what is your place in the world, Lance-Naik? Under a tree, writing letters from a man to his brother complaining about flour prices?

A hand gripped the old man's shoulder, and Qayyum wondered for how long his father had been listening.

– But there is nothing in the world more important than flour prices, his father said. Son, why don't you go home. Your mother needed help with some matter.

Out here, where he was a man whose table had a built-in inkhorn, his father possessed authority. This was his place in the world, a table beneath a tree. The old man quietened, his fierce gaze changing into the slightly resigned expression of someone who realises the moment in which he could impose his will on the situation has passed. He lifted and dropped his shoulders and turned to walk away just as Qayyum realised that the uniform wasn't hanging on the man because his youthful frame had withered away but because it was Kalam's uniform, with stains near its collar that were Qayyum's blood, spelling out a clear message: Repay the debt you owe me.

September 1915

Najeeb walked through the Hall of Statues, a prince visiting his frozen brothers, all under an enchantment which it was his destiny alone to lift. Silence, save for the rotating ceiling fan and his voice speaking to the artefacts in his simple Greek sentences which they all seemed to understand: the winged sea-monster; ichthyocentaurs and fish-tailed bulls; Tritons kneeling before the Buddha; Indra and Brahma adoring Him; a winged figure seated on a fragment of an Achaemenid column, looking out of deep-set eyes. A centaur bearing a shield. The Buddha receiving an image of the Buddha.

Of all the astonishing things in the Peshawar Museum the most astonishing of all was the Pashtun man in an English suit who walked through the Hall of Statues with an air of owner-ship and knew more about each artefact than even Miss Spencer. Mr Wasiuddin, Native Assistant at the Peshawar Museum. Yes, why not, Miss Spencer had said when Najeeb asked her if one day that might be him. Then she crossed her arms and leaned back in her chair. No, why stop there? Najeeb Gul, Superintendent of the Archaeological Survey, Frontier Circle. It's a step down from the Herodotus of Peshawar, of course, but it suits you just as well.

Pulling open the doorway to return to the ordinary world, he turned to look over his shoulder. A giant Buddha raised his hand to him in farewell. Solemnly, Najeeb returned the gesture before stepping out. The white sky of summer had finally soft-ened into blue that September morning, allowing for loitering

– the weekends, once a time of delight, were now a Miss Spencerless wasteland. He walked towards the station where Qayyum had made his heart contract when he stepped off a train with the face of a stranger, and climbed up onto the railway bridge. From here, the whole of the Cantonment was spread out – wide streets in straight lines, single-storeyed houses surrounded by gardens for people who viewed other people as nuisance rather than refuge, automobiles which looked like steel insects without wings, barracks for soldiers from whom Qayyum had started to veer away, the Governor's House across from the Museum with its gardens as large as a park which must mean the Governor really disliked other people, and everywhere, Englishmen and women whose mouths formed sounds in inexplicable ways (Miss Spencer always elongated the space between the 'n' and the 'j' in his own name). Since Miss Spencer it had started to seem less like a place in which he didn't belong, but even so it was only when he crossed the bridge and walked the short distance to the Walled City that he stopped feeling as if he were in a classroom with a teacher he didn't yet know well enough to avoid annoying.

He walked through the Street of Storytellers, stopping to listen to snatches of this badala or that, but nothing held him in place. All these old stories, not old enough. Perhaps he should go and find Qayyum. It was a heavy feeling to know that this felt like a duty rather than the most wonderful option in the world. His brother looked much as he used to before he went to war, it was true – the redness and swelling had gone from his eye, the scars around it were mere flecks which looked as if a bird had walked on charcoal and rested one claw on Qayyum's face before flying away, and most days Najeeb even forgot that half his brother's gaze was glass. But despite the healed wounds, his entire appearance was altered. It's because he wears different expressions now, their mother had tried to explain to her youngest child. Among the new expressions was that look of disquiet any time someone mentioned the English which meant that Najeeb must keep the most important part of his life from the most important person in his life.

124

An unexpected sound through the thrum of the street. A woman, calling out:

– Men of Peshawar! Oh, you men of the market! How much will you give me for my daughter?

Najeeb hopped up onto the wooden leg of a rope-bed meant for a storyteller's audience, looking over the heads of the men who were glancing this way and that at the scattering of women in burqas on the street, trying to pinpoint the origin of the shouting. The other women saw her first, all moving closer together and angling their bodies in her direction as if this were a dance they'd been practising. The men's heads turned – everyone was silent now, and the caged songs from the nearby Street of Partridge Lovers filled the air – and there she was, a very tall uncovered woman, her hair wild, holding out a child in her arms.

A moment, no more, and a man in a long-tailed turban seized her by the elbow.

– Don't do this! came a cry from a balcony looking down on the street. The carpet-seller who was a particular favourite with the English was leaning over the balustrade, one palm extended in appeal. The woman looked straight up at the carpet-seller.

– In Allah's name, save us, she said. But she left the carpet-seller no choice but to look away from her uncovered face, and as soon as he did so the man holding onto her pulled her away.

Curious, Najeeb moved among the knots of men who hadn't resumed their business and were, instead, either glancing up at the balcony or at the place where the woman had stood.

Before long he had the story. The man with the long-tailed turban was in debt, and refused to borrow money from any of the Hindu money-lenders because his piety wouldn't allow him to accept the idea of paying interest. So he'd come to an agreement with one of the prosperous merchants – in exchange for the money his infant daughter would be married to the merchant's son when she was of age. You'd think the man must be some kind of magician to have acquired both money for himself and a husband for his daughter. But the truth was that the merchant's son had some demon inside him. He'd killed his first wife; the second had killed herself. A third wife had recently been found, but she would certainly be dead or mad before that child grew old enough to leave her parents' home. And the carpet-seller? He was brother to the first wife.

Ever since Qayyum had returned from England Najeeb had started to feel that the world was filled with sadness. He saw it now everywhere. There, the boy with the crippled arm looking into a cage filled with clipped-winged birds; the man so stooped with age he had to carry a tilted mirror in his hand in order to see the reflection of the world above knee-level; the carpet-seller still on his balcony, making gestures of entreaty as though rehearsing what he could have said, what he should have said, what he would most certainly say if he had another chance to save that child from his sister's fate.

There had been a moment when the child had looked directly at Najeeb, her green eyes bewildered. She couldn't have been more than three or four years old, and already it had been determined that her life would be filled with cruelty.

I know the stories of men from twenty-five hundred years ago, but I'll never know what happens to you.

November 1915

Every day Qayyum waited for another messenger in the bloodstained uniform of the 40th to approach him. The first messenger had been preparation; the second would be the call to action. It was unthinkable for a lance-naik of the 40th to go to the Ottoman Empire to tell soldiers their loyalties didn't lie with their regiment; but it was even more unthinkable for Qayyum to deny Kalam again. Every day he twisted in his snare, waiting and waiting, but by the time the days had shortened into November he came to believe that Kalam, who loved him well enough to want the power to make him suffer but too well to prolong that suffering, had chosen in the end to allow him to live his life without wrenching him in two.

It was a strange disappointment the day he reached that conclusion. So is this it, he thought, this is my life. His father had stayed home again that day – the cold that had seeped into his bones from decades of sitting outdoors in Peshawar's winters made the onset of winter an increasing tribulation each year – and Qayyum sat at the desk with the buffalo-horn thinking, this is my inheritance, this is for ever, until the cold or the heat or the boredom kills me.

A woman sat down on the stool across from Qayyum. He wondered if she had a husband or son in the Army – in the last few months he'd lost count of the women who had come to him saying they'd heard he had been at war and would he help them in writing their letters. It wasn't just a scribe they wanted but someone who might understand their husbands' lives.

Should I tell him his father is dead? Will it make him sad if I say I want him to come home quickly? Forgive me but please be honest; is it true that white women come into the soldiers' barracks?

These women made him think, for the first time in a long while, of the girls who had been part of the neighbourhood games during his childhood, all of whom disappeared from view when they came to a certain age. In the first few days after their retreat some of them would send messages out with their younger sisters, such as, even with a burqa on I can still run faster than you; and sometimes a window shutter would open for a few seconds and some object of uncertain significance would fly out – a hairclip, an apple with a startled face carved onto it, a blank piece of paper balled up. But eventually all communication stopped. Now, if Qayyum were ever walking past the home of one of his childhood playmates and a figure in a burqa stepped out he wouldn't even wonder if it was her. Even if it was, she'd be so different she might as well be another person. Boys grew into men as a sapling grows into a tree, but girls became women as a caterpillar becomes a butterfly. His sisters most of all; they were nothing but flapping wings.

But the woman who had sat down did not flap her wings, did not ask about the Army, or even tell him who the letter was for. She only wanted him to write what she dictated with the care of someone who didn't want the letter-writer to mistranscribe a single word.

Don't apologise for the danger you put me in by sending that message. It has been the only light in my days. When my daughter is old enough for marriage I will send her to your house for protection.

He tried to keep the curiosity away from his face, as his father was skilled at doing. It was impossible to know very much about the woman from the sound of her voice except that she was young. He asked what address he should put on the envelope and she said there was no need for that. Taking

128

the letter, she walked away, and turned into the Street of Storytellers. The unexpected figure of an Englishwoman with a pith-helmet on her head and clothes which revealed almost her entire arms and part of her legs followed after her. Even here, even in Peshawar, there were different rules for the English. No, especially here.

How he missed Kalam who would mock him for sitting under a tree, sighing about his buffalo-horn inheritance, while an Englishwoman walked through the Walled City as if she had more right to it than any man of Peshawar.

The plum orchard looked incomplete without fruit hanging heavy from the trees. Time here didn't move in the sluggish way of the Walled City where days moved predictably through the minor variations which separated them. Walking the length of the orchard he realised he didn't know where he might find Kalam's father, or which of the adjoining fields belonged to him. He shouted out a greeting but there was no response, so he cupped his hands around his mouth and called out, Kalam! knowing that a father is more likely to hear his absent son's name than any other sound in the world.

He repeated the call, again and again, and finally a man appeared, Kalam's angled jawline attached to an otherwise unfamiliar face.

– Why are you calling my son?

– Khan Sahib, I'm Qayyum. Kalam's friend from the 40th. I've come to ask if you've had any news from him.

– So you're Qayyum. Khan Sahib? You didn't teach my son any of your manners.

The man's mouth twisted into a smile which was also Kalam. He walked up to Qayyum and pulled him into an embrace so fierce, so passionate it could only mean one thing; Qayyum sagged against the older man who kept him arms around him, holding him upright.

Had he been here a minute, an hour? He was on the grass, a dampness from the morning's winter rain soaking through his clothes, all the way up to his collar, or was that the tears? He held up his hand, blotting out most of the other man's face so there was only that jawline, blurred with age. Kalam's father sat down next to him and patted his back as if he were a child in need of comfort.

– Son, the old man said, my son.

– What happened? The English?

– An old family feud. Kalam's cousin stuck a knife in him and left him to bleed to death.

Blood and foam around the rabbit's mouth, its eyes wide. The sweetness of rage, here it came, flooding his veins, as Kalam's father jabbed a finger into his side to show where the knife had entered.

– You know who it was? Who did it? Qayyum asked.

– Yes. Why?

Before I didn't know why I was here, but now every German I kill will be the man who did this to you. Those were the last words Kalam had said in his ear before the ambulance took him away. Qayyum stood up, pulled on the low-hanging branch of the tree, and looked around. That endless night beside the stream, Kalam had spoken to him of the life that lay before each of them – one in the Walled City, one in the orchards. You'll visit me when the air is ripe with plums and every breath you take has a sweetness to it, he'd said. Somehow, in the middle of all that horror, he had allowed Qayyum to see a gentle future: two ageing men, sitting under a tree, occasionally bringing out a faded memory of the 40th Pathans. Kalam – his cynical smile, his hopeful eyes.

– I will avenge his death.

– You'll kill his killer?

– Yes.

– And his brothers will kill you.

– They can try.

– How many brothers do you have?

– One.

– How old is he?

– Twelve.

– When they come for you they'll kill him too.

– It's nothing to do with him.

– In their place, I'd cut his throat before he's old enough to seek revenge.

Kalam's father stood up, stretching. A man who understood the rules of the world and had long since ceased to be surprised or dismayed by them.

– Think about it for a few days.

They had buried him on the barren hillside, that boy of orchards and streams. Even in death, a deserter was a fugitive. Qayyum walked in the icy waters adjoining the plum orchard, the current pulling at his ankles.

– Ina lillahi wa inna illayhi rajiun.

We belong to Allah, and to Allah we return.

At Vipers, when the German gunners shot Afroze who chose to cry out his grief knowing the consequences rather than bear the death of a beloved in silence, a whisper burbled across the field: Ina lillahi wa inna illayhi rajiun. The men of the 40th, not all of them Muslim, whispered the words for the two dead men, and the prayer would have reached the gunners as wind on water or the sighs of ghosts. Kalam's hand on Qayyum's chest, muffling his heartbeat so the sound of it wouldn't reach the Germans.

– Ina lillahi wa inna illayhi rajiun.

Hands still cupped in prayer, he bent to the stream, filled his palms with water and poured it over his head. Again and again.

– Ina lillahi wa inna illayhi rajiun.

It was all he could do that night to walk through the Walled City instead of huddled in a quiet alley with memories for company. Near home, he heard a half-cry, more terrifying in the abruptness of its ending than in its tone, and didn't look round to see if it came from a human or animal. Even when he had two functioning eyes and a fearlessness that was almost a belief in immortality he'd known better than to make the troubles of Peshawar's nights his own. Opening the door beside the cobbler's shop, where a single candle illuminated Hari Das stitching a sole onto a shoe with a thick needle, he made his way up the steps. He heard the shouts when he was halfway up, and ran the last few steps, wrenching the door open at the top. At one end of the room his sisters huddled together to form a protective circle around Najeeb, while his mother ripped pages out of a book and threw fistfuls of paper at her youngest child. A scrap landed on a burning candle and the flame ran up the paper, briefly extending its reach to illuminate his father who was standing with his back pressed to a wall.

– Enough.

Qayyum put a hand on his mother's wrist and took the book out of her hand. It was a ruled exercise book, with symbols all over the pages which included letters of the English alphabet.

– Ask your brother, go on, ask him what he's been doing when we thought he was with the maulvi.

– Let him be. I know he goes to read in Shalimar Bagh; I told him it was all right. Leave his books alone.

– Read in Shalimar Bagh? Read in Shalimar Bagh?

She snatched the book and slapped Qayyum's shoulder with it, the sound of the cover smacking his flesh more shocking than the force of the blow.

– Every afternoon he goes into the house of a young, unmarried Englishwoman and doesn't come out for hours. Everyone in this neighbourhood knows it, they've known it for weeks. Tell him!

She gestured at her eldest daughter, who should have been at her in-laws' house preparing dinner for the family but had obviously come here just to drip venom into their mother's ear, and now had her arms around Najeeb as though she thought it was possible to be both bayonet and shield. She kissed Najeeb's hair, which conveniently kept her from responding to her mother, whose gesture became one of dismissal.

– You ask Najeeb what she wants with him, his mother said to Qayyum. Go on, ask him. I'm getting nothing but lies.

– It's not a lie! Najeeb said. Lala, please, she teaches me Classics. Explain it to our mother.

But their mother didn't even look at Qayyum, reserving the full power of her fury for her younger son.

– What is this English word, this 'Classics'? What is she teaching you, what have you been doing there?

Qayyum looked at his brother, who had broken out of his sister's embrace and was picking up the pieces of paper from the floor, his jaw tightly clenched when Qayyum expected to see him crying. Qayyum kneeled on the ground beside him, and put his hand on Najeeb's chin, tilting his face up. Soft hair was beginning to appear above his lip; why hadn't he noticed earlier that the boy wasn't entirely a boy any longer?

– I told you to stay away from Englishwomen.

He expected a look of betrayal, not this one of disdain.

– You don't know anything about her.

– I don't have to. I knew her men.

– Lala, please. You can come with me to my lessons, come and meet her and you'll see; she isn't like anyone else. Please don't make me stop our lessons. Our mother will listen to you if you tell her. It doesn't have to mean something bad when Englishwomen talk to us.

Qayyum rested his hand on his brother's shoulder. Najeeb was in that time between boy and man, lurching from one to the other in the space of a single moment. And what would happen in one such moment if the boy looked on a young unmarried Englishwoman with a man's eyes? What if an Englishman thought he caught the boy looking on one of his women in that way? Not even a Victoria Cross could give a Pashtun the right to deserve an Englishwoman's attention.

–You must do what our mother says.

He stood up, and turned away so he wouldn't have to watch Najeeb's face as his mother told him that she would walk with him to the mosque every day after lunch, and stay there until his lessons were finished, and walk him straight home. On another day, in another time, Qayyum might have had the words, the thoughts, to be his brother's champion, but Kalam was dead and his ghost pressed its mouth to Qayyum's ear. Najeeb's tears

– they had started now – were those of a child who has yet to understand the world won't shape itself to his will.

When they sat down to eat, Najeeb didn't take his accustomed position but sat on his brother's right-hand side where Qayyum couldn't see him.

The nights had turned too cold for sleeping outdoors, but Najeeb had closed the door to the room they shared and barricaded it with something – books, probably. He was at the age of grand gestures, when every emotion felt perpetual. I will always hate you, he had said, a statement not of anger but anguish.

Qayyum drew his limbs close to his torso, seeking the warmth of his own body beneath the blanket. The stars were thick in the sky, cold and alone, each one of them. Kalam, on the bare hillside, bleeding to death, would have found no comfort there. Did justice demand the same for Kalam's killer? Lure him to a lonely spot, push a blade deep into his flesh, and leave him to that terror, that overwhelming terror

– Allah

Pushing the blankets aside, he tumbled onto the ground, prostrating himself, forehead smacking brick. And if they were to come for him and find Najeeb instead and stitch his lips together and stop his breath

– Allah

And if it was him they found, only him, he should be prepared for it, he should be willing to risk anything to avenge Kalam's death but the stars, so cold, were beautiful and the night air cut him like life itself and he wanted to stay, here, in this world for ever, in the Valley which was sometimes rose and sometimes plum and always varied, infinite. He had never touched a woman in love or watched a tree grow where he had planted it or followed a stream all the way across a valley and up the mountain to the borders of snow. How could he return to a world of blood; how could he refuse Kalam's ghost

– Allah Allah Allah

Najeeb wouldn't allow Qayyum to help him with the books, not even when getting into the Victoria. He sat in the carriage, his arms wrapped around them, cheek resting on the top of the pile. As if the scent, the touch of them was something to embrace. Five books, three with hard covers, two bound in leather. One with gilt-edged pages. What world had his brother entered? Classics, Najeeb had said to him in English, as if it was a word he should know.

This morning, while Najeeb was at school, Qayyum had entered the room they shared. It hadn't been difficult to isolate Najeeb's schoolbooks from the far more expensive ones given to him by the Englishwoman. There was the one with English on one half of the page, and on the other half letters which looked like English letters but with triangles and pitchforks and other strange symbols scattered between the recognisable 'a' and 'o'. The only English letters Qayyum knew were the ones in LANCE-NAIK QAYYUM GUL. He held a corner of a creamy, gilt-edged page between thumb and forefinger. What had Najeeb been doing in the world of the English who knew so well how to make you feel that you were never so honoured as when they were the ones to honour you?

The Victoria entered the Cantonment, turned into a residential street where there was space enough for each home to sprawl across the ground instead of climbing upwards. Again he felt it, the old shame learned in France. The haphazard constructions of the Walled City a failing, a reason to sneer. He looked at his brother and wondered if any of this shame lived in him too; he could see no sign of it. Four years ago when Qayyum left to join the 40th he had thought of momentum as something he would carry with him out of Peshawar, leaving stasis behind. No one in his family would age, no one fall sick, no one acquire new habits or loves in his absence. He would be the one to come back and require rediscovering, relearning, by all around him. He hadn't entirely let go of that notion, until now.

– What's her name, this Englishwoman?

– I don't want to talk to you about her.

– There are things you don't understand.

– I understand Greek!

Qayyum pushed gently at his brother's shoulder, trying to

135

bring the laughter out of him, but Najeeb only angled his body away. Qayyum was still trying to decide if he should deliver a lecture on respecting your elders no matter what the circumstances when the Victoria stopped outside a house smaller in size than those around it, made of brick fronted by climbing plants. The brothers stepped down, and remained standing on the pavement as the horse cantered away; when it turned the corner, silence such as could only exist in an English world remained.

– Are you going to come in with me?

– I'll stay here. But don't go in. Remain where you can be seen.

– No one's looking.

– If no one was looking no one would know that you visit her every afternoon. Stand outside, give her the books, walk away.

– I don't want you looking at her when she comes out.

– Why not?

– You'll do it in a way I won't like.

– When you speak like that I know it's right to say you can't see her any more.

But he turned his back to the house all the same, and heard his brother take a deep breath and walk up the pathway. The door opened, a low murmur, a woman's voice rose and fell. And then Najeeb was striding past him at a furious pace. Qayyum had to run to catch up, and when he caught his brother's elbow and swung him round he saw a boy's sorrow, a heartbreaking thing.

– Look Najeeb, I received my pension today. Have you ever eaten ice cream? It's English kulfi. I've heard there's a shop in the Cantonment which sells it. Let's find it.

– I'm going to the Museum.

– I'll come with you.

– You won't understand anything there.

If he had yelled it out, Qayyum would have cuffed him, and taken him by the hand to find the ice cream which would return sweetness to his temperament. But he said it flatly, as if pronouncing a thought he'd long held to be true. Qayyum let go of his brother, and Najeeb walked on without looking back, pausing only to rub his elbow against a boundary wall as a Brahmin might try to rid himself of the handprint of an Untouchable.

The Museum had been built to make men feel small. Stepping into the high-ceilinged hall Qayyum was flanked by giant stone figures. At the far end, on the upper-level balcony, a Pashtun man in an English suit watched him. Qayyum looked away from him and there was another stone figure standing against the wall, holding out a stump where there should have been a hand. The smell of blood, of dead flesh. Turning, he pressed his face against the giant figure and there was another smell: stone, ancient. Qayyum stepped back to see the statue better. It was a man, the dark interior of his navel visible beneath folds of cloth at Qayyum's eye level. He couldn't keep himself from reaching out to touch it; how could you achieve that effect in stone? Stepping further back, he saw the figure had its right arm bent at the elbow, the hand raised at an angle, fingers together, palm outwards. It was a gesture he had seen Najeeb make in his direction soon after his return from Vipers.
– Is this your first time at the Museum?
The Pashtun man in the English suit, now standing beside him, asked the question. Qayyum nodded.
– What does the hand position mean?
– It's the Abhaya Mudra. A gesture of protection and fearlessness.
Qayyum replicated the gesture, felt himself step into the skin of a boy who sees his brother return from war without an eye.
– I'd be happy to answer any other questions. I'm Wasiuddin, Assistant at the Museum.
– Lance-Naik Qayyum Gul. 40th Pathans.
He didn't know why he introduced himself in that manner, but this man in the suit, these high walls, those stone figures all made it necessary.

– Najeeb's brother? Of course. You have the same look. He's in Pundit Aiyar's office, examining Kushan coins. Should I take you to him?

– Pundit Aiyar?

– The Superintendent of the Museum. Our commanding officer, Lance-Naik.

– An Indian is in charge?

– Yes.

– And my brother is in his office?

– I don't wish to interfere in family matters, and I understand the delicacy of the situation. But he has a brilliant mind, and . . .

– I'm glad you understand this is a family matter.

– Of course. Should I take you to him?

He indicated a closed door, and Qayyum said perhaps in a few minutes. First, he'd like to look around, but he didn't want to keep the Assistant from whatever he was doing. If you need anything, the man said with a dip of his head, and understood enough to leave Qayyum alone.

Several young men were walking around the hallway, pointing to this object and that, some of them writing things down as they stood in front of a cabinet or a statue. University students from Islamia College, he guessed, with very little in age separating them from him. One of them caught another in a neck-hold, laughing, and Qayyum walked swiftly past them – and past the Englishman looking at a moustached statue and patting his own moustache in comparison – to a smaller gallery beyond the main hall. Here, there was no one but him, and the stones.

Men, and winged creatures, and a bird-head with a human expression, and faces which came from the streets of Peshawar and other faces which were from somewhere else. There was beauty here, he could see, but it was a beauty that asked to be admired. Still, and distant, and nothing to do with the world outside. Live among these objects and your heart would turn to stone. He was thinking this, aware that he was building up an argument, when he stepped in front of a bearded man, sitting down, with his knee drawn up against his chest, his

138

hand clasping the back of his own head in despair. Qayyum heard his breath change, become a noise in his throat. A second figure – its face missing so it was impossible to know if it was a man or a woman – curled the fingers of one hand around the man's upper arm and rested the other hand on his chest. In the angle of the bearded man's head, turned to one side, away from the embracing figure, the sculptor told the world of the impossibility of comfort when loss pierces the heart. Qayyum covered the lower half of his face with the palm of his hand, and watched his own grief, felt the awful aloneness of it. Kalam.

A hand slipped into his, and Najeeb pulled him away from the broken statue. This, this is what you must see, he said, and took Qayyum back to the main hall, empty now.

– Here, the Buddha, this is him.

The folds of the prophet's skin suggested the former sleekness of the prince he had been; the sunken eyes bore knowledge of all the world's sorrow. All you have endured; all you must yet endure. Qayyum rested his hand against the glass-fronted cabinet and leaned in towards the Buddha's starving face, suspended over the ridged skin of his chest. Stone made flesh; no, stone made bone and skin. If a man rested his hand on that cage he might hear a heart beating within; but gently, gently, the ribs could snap from the pressure of a single finger. He shivered and stepped back; now he understood idolatry. Bismillah-ir-Rahman-ir-Rahim, he whispered, and the Buddha continued to gaze beyond him, all of Vipers there in his eyes, every dead soldier, and Kalam Khan bleeding to death, cold and alone. And beyond all the dead men, in the deepest, saddest part of the Buddha's gaze, was Kalam's killer, a man who took a life for duty, for family, for tradition.

Qayyum lowered himself to his knees, and Najeeb sat next to him, leaning on his brother's shoulder, the weight of him a tether.

He followed the sound of the axe, beyond the plum orchards to a field of furrowed soil. Kalam Khan's father squatted beside a

139

cutting stone, passing the length of a sugar cane along the stone, lopping it into pieces the length of a man's forearm. His movements so automated they might soon become careless.

– Why are you doing that?

– For planting, city man.

He dipped the axe-head into a bucket of water and ran it along the length of a whetting stone, twice, three times. Qayyum held out his hand and the man placed the axe-handle in it, standing up with a great sigh of Bismillah, his hand to the small of his back. Qayyum stepped out of his sandals, crouched low to the ground, and brought the axe-head down on the cane, two nodes from the top. The scent it released was childhood.

– Kalam asked me to help you with the planting.

– Yes.

– That was my promise to him. That's what I owe him.

– It took you three days to work this out? Are you city Pashtuns even stupider than your cousins in the tribes?

The older man wore a familiar mocking smile.

– An extra pair of hands is more useful to me than another boy dead in the hills. Did you really think I expected you to go up there to have your throat slit before you even got your knife out of your waistband? Don't look at me like an idiot. Cut! Cut! And come and find me when you've finished all of it.

Qayyum looked from the small pile of cut cane to the large quantity of sheaves still intact. He grasped hold of the longest cane he could see with a cry of Bismillah!.

Hours later, his arm ached, his back ached, the muscles of his thighs ached. He had forgotten his own body, its possibilities. Now every jolt of pain as he walked back to the plum orchards was a restoration. Kalam's father brought him hot tea and cold naan and it was a banquet. Through the late afternoon and into the evening the two men sat beneath a plum tree until the ground was made up entirely of shadows, swapping tales of Kalam the boy and Kalam the sepoy, life in the orchards and life in the Army. Eventually the old man started to talk about the old Pashtun system in which land was never owned but regularly redistributed between the tribes so none could take control over the most fertile, and every man had sufficient wealth to live with honour. It had been centuries since that system worked without corruption, but it had tottered on, with more justice within it than most systems –

– Until your English shredded it to ribbons with their laws, Qayyum Gul, in order to create a class of landowners loyal to the Crown. My grandfather lost all rights to the land he'd lived on his entire adult life, and since then my family has had to pay rent for the land we work to a man who knows as much about fruit trees as a fish knows about mountains. All Kalam's life he heard me say this – and then he joined the Army so he could bleed for the English. We deserve the yoke we wear. Of your generation, only Ghaffar Khan is a true Pashtun.

– Who?

The old man was silent for a while, then nodded firmly as if a decision had been made.

– After you've helped me plant the cane fields, you'll go and find Ghaffar Khan. He'll teach you what you need to know.

– And what do I need to know?

– How to remove your blindfold, and see your place in this world.

Once you caught the scent of Khan Abdul Ghaffar Khan you could follow it through the Peshawar Valley. Wadpagga, Sardaryab, Charsadda, Utmanzai and points in between. Twenty-five years old and already he knew how to place a light in the eyes of old men, how to make young boys whisper pieces of his story as though they were couplets of love. Within a few hours of setting out on Kalam's father's instructions Qayyum felt he was chasing the story, not the man, finding different pieces of it across the Valley: Ghaffar Khan gave up his Commission in the Guides when he saw an Englishman insult a Pashtun officer; he almost set sail for England but his mother's tears held him back; Haji Sahib of Turangzai sought him out when he was barely past twenty and together they set up a programme for education and reform; when Haji Sahib declared jihad their paths diverged,

141

and now one was a fugitive in the tribal areas and the other travelled all through the settled districts setting up schools where the Pashtuns could find education untainted by the superstition of the mullahs and the brainwashing of the English.

On the third afternoon, between Utmanzai and Mardan, winter rain was beginning to fall when Qayyum entered the mud-walled complex to which a man on the road had directed him. The sound, familiar but unplaceable, which greeted him was fat raindrops falling on a large blue tarpaulin which four tall men held at each corner, shielding the gathering in the courtyard. A square of sky between the rain and the men. Qayyum ran across the courtyard, ducked beneath the tarpaulin, which the men held up high over their heads though they were tall and the assembled men were seated and their arms must be aching. But it was for him, for Ghaffar Khan, that the extra inches were necessary. Like an angel or a djinn in height, Kalam's father had said, and Qayyum, six foot tall, found he had to turn his eyes upwards to Ghaffar Khan who stood beneath the other end of the tarpaulin. A smile of welcome for Qayyum sat between the eagle nose and close-cropped beard, even as Ghaffar Khan continued explaining how blood feuds and revenge were eating up the Pashtuns from within. As he spoke a blur in the rain resolved itself into the figure of a boy who had run from one of the doorways surrounding the court-yard to stand just a little distance from the young Khan; filled with excitement or anticipation, the boy stood on one foot, reached behind him to squeeze the other foot in the palm of his hands. A flamingo-boy; the ancient sculptors of Gandhara would have carved him into stone.

A babble of voices, a field of hands rose up when Ghaffar Khan finished speaking, but he turned his great frame towards the boy first:

– Do you bring a question?

Qayyum understood the boy was intermediary between this gathering and the women behind doors. He turned his body sideways, so no one might think he was looking in the direction of the women now that he knew where they were.

– Why didn't you join Haji Sahib in his jihad?

A number of the men looked at each other, scratched their chins, sighed a little. The question wasn't new to them.

– Taking up arms after your lands have been conquered is like building a well after your house has caught fire. The sword in tribesmen's hands will not cut this yoke from our necks. No sword will cut this yoke from our necks. If we want any chance of advancement we must . . .

And though he'd been speaking in Pashto, he switched to an Urdu idiom to end the sentence and the man holding the tarpaulin leaned towards Qayyum and said:

– What was that? What did he say?

– He said we must get rid of our wrong ideas. We must wake up from this rabbit's dream.

Qayyum stepped back into the diminishing rain, head angled back, and all the noise of the world was replaced by the plink of water droplets on a glass eye, the unexpected music of heaven.

October–November 1915

Viv raised her bow, strung with an arrow, and looked down the length of the shaft to the tip pointing directly at the minarets of Mahabat Khan Mosque. The Italian mercenary Paolo Avitabile had used the minarets as gallows to hang anyone who broke his laws, and as the moon shone on the white marble Viv thought she saw body-shaped shadows – the ghosts of those who had swung to their deaths above the eyes of all Peshawar's inhabitants. In the surrounding streets of the Old City, seventy years after Avitabile's governorship ended, children were still threatened into good behaviour with warnings that the terrible Abu Tabela would come for them in the night. It was Avitabile who had widened the streets, erected the Old City walls, brought security to Peshawar during its period of Sikh rule with the most iron of fists. They still fear him and revere him, an old major had said to Viv; he showed us the only way a man of Europe can rule the Pathans. But Remmick had disagreed – we are here to civilise, not to lose our own civility, he'd said. Then he pointed to Viv and added, some of us in large ways, and some of us in small. On certain days, Remmick was almost a friend.

Today, he wasn't among the revellers gathered at the broad walkway on top of the Mughal gateway of Gor Khatri, the highest elevation in the Walled City. The invitation cards to 'Olympian Night at Gor Khatri' had come with a handwritten note instructing each guest which Greek god they would play for the evening. Viv was Artemis, the Virgin Hunter. An

144

unsubtle joke reflecting the widespread certainty that the only reason for a young Englishwoman to come to Peshawar was the quest for a husband. Someone should explain that means finding someone who isn't already a husband, Mrs Remmick had pointedly remarked in her hearing, but since no one particularly liked Mrs Remmick or believed that Viv would choose Remmick-the-Red-faced when there were handsome bachelors around, the comment had only endeared Viv to many of the other British wives who enjoyed nothing more than an opportunity to pick sides.

She lowered the bow and arrow, placed it on the thick wall of the fortified gateway, and plucked a glass of iced sherbet from the tray of a passing bearer. The end of the summer season had transformed the sleepiness of Peshawar, bringing the British back from Simla with balls and picnics and hunts in tow. And the rapidly cooling weather brought with it the possibility of further distractions: a boat-ride down the Indus; the Taj Mahal; the Caves of Ajanta and Ellora; Taxila, where John Marshall had invited her to visit the excavations. And in the spring, the famed Peshawar Vale Hunt which, the regulars of the Peshawar Club insisted, Viv absolutely must stay for. Why suffer through Peshawar's summer and then leave just as it turned delightful? What sense did that make?

No sense at all, Viv agreed. She didn't see any need to mention that Remmick had promised he was working on sorting out the leasing problem with Shahji-ki-Dheri but it might be early in the new year before everything were settled and excavation became possible.

She looked down at the tangle of the Old City, laid out beneath. From up here it was possible to see the rooftops of all the houses, enclosed on four sides but open to the sky – or to the Olympian gods of Gor Khatri. It was like looking into a honey-combed jewellery box, many of its compartments lit up with lanterns, revealing something bright and glittering: a woman in a tunic of green and pink, sewing mirrorwork onto a shirt; a man on a rope-bed reading from a book, children at his feet; a woman combing the long hair of a shirtless man, who Viv guessed to be

Sikh, her hand on his shoulder. Which one was Najeeb's house, Viv wondered. She knew so little about his world.

Dionysus touched her elbow. The Anglo-Indian band had finally made it up the stairs with their bulky instruments and now led off with 'For Empire and for England'. Artemis joined Dionysus in a dance along the roof of Peshawar, a bright moon overhead. Sometimes she lost track of whether she was using the Peshawar Vale Hunt as an excuse to stay in Peshawar long enough to dig deep for Tahsin Bey's dream or using Tahsin Bey as an excuse to stay for the Peshawar Vale Hunt.

Najeeb brought her a roll of paper and set it down on the writing table which faced out towards the garden. May I?, he said, and carefully removed the books and typewriter and lamp so that the table was all surface. He placed a paperweight at one end, and unrolled the paper, which blanketed the table-top and trailed off onto the floor.

– The rock-edicts of Asoka, Najeeb said. From Shahbaz Garhi.

Viv bent over the rubbing of Kharoshti words, inscribed in a wave-like pattern, following the curved surface of the rock they'd been carved into.

– How did you get this?

– It's on Yusufzai land, he said proudly. This belongs to my tribe.

– Oh yes. The men who fought Alexander at Peukelaotis.

– I can't believe I thought Alexander was an Englishman!

– If he'd been alive today, he would be. I can't believe I thought you were without curiosity. My ignorance is by far the more egregious. Thank you for showing this to me.

– It's yours. I told my brother to bring it for me so I could give it to you. I said it's for my favourite teacher.

– Thank you, Najeeb. I'll treasure it.

His smile was the first gleam of a silver circlet unearthed.

Viv stepped from the treasure cave of Avtar Singh's antiquities shop, eyes blinking in the mid-morning sunlight.

146

– It will devastate my heart, Miss Spencer, to have to sell Hariti to someone else. You must spare me that.

Viv rolled her eyes at the turbaned Sikh; of late it had almost become part of her daily routine to undertake yet another round of bargaining with Avtar Singh for the Hariti statue, closely resembling the one in the Museum, which had the goddess's hand lightly resting on her consort's upper thigh, in a gesture of ownership, fingers wandering. It wasn't the position of her hand alone which made the statue erotic but also the posture of her consort, the great general Pancika, in his short military-style skirt with his legs forming a diamond – spread apart at the knees, with ankles rubbing against each other. Viv knew she didn't really have the nerve to buy such a thing, but there was a pleasure in the bargaining over cups of tea, conversation detouring via other sculptures and coins in the shop, some of which she might really purchase at some point when either she or Avtar Singh worked out how to extricate themselves from this dance around Hariti.

– Bring the price down and your heart will be spared, Mr Singh.

Placing a velvet-ribboned pith-helmet on her head she set off. With no destination in mind she meandered, turning into one alley, then another, making sure she didn't lose sight of the elevated walls of Gor Khatri which served as a landmark. Eventually she found herself in an alley that lad back to the Street of Storytellers. The shop advertising BEST ENGLISH SCHOOL UNIFORMS was familiar, and it took her a moment to work out that this was the alley down which Najeeb had pointed when he informed her, without embarrassment, that his father worked there.

Walking down the alley she saw a letter-writer sitting at a table with an inkhorn holder built into it, shaded by a tarpaulin thrown over the spreading branches of a peepul tree. How had a boy like Najeeb sprung up in a Pathan family from the Walled City where the father worked under a tree? The Indian stories of shepherd boys or slaves who become kings only made sense when you met someone like Najeeb. Did his parents have any idea of the life he

147

had stepped into, the extent to which he was leaving them behind? She'd never asked, and suspected not. She could probably walk right up to Najeeb's father and say she was Miss Spencer and receive only a blank look in return. But it quickly became obvious, even though the man had his back towards her, that this wasn't the father of a twelve-year-old boy. His hands, resting on either side of the table, were those of a young man. Perhaps Najeeb hadn't been entirely honest when he said that his father was the only letter-writer who had a desk rather than squatting on the ground. Imagine the circumstances of a life being such that owning a desk was a boast.

Her interest left the man at the table and alighted on the woman in a white burqa who had just stood up from the chair opposite him, very tall, folding up the piece of paper which he had placed on the table before moving his hands well away from it so she could pick it up without encountering his fingertips. The figure in white hurried away, before remembering that she was a woman of Peshawar and nothing in her behaviour should call attention to itself. Her pace slowed, now she was a white sheet drifting along at the tempo of the other white sheets. Viv followed her on to the Street of Storytellers. She had yet to speak to a woman from the Walled City though she had enough Pashto now to make conversation possible.

Partway down the street, approaching Kabuli Gate, the woman turned into an alley. Viv realised how ridiculous she was being and started to walk towards Kabuli Gate. But something – intuition? curiosity? an unexpected noise? – made her turn and look over her shoulder. There was the woman in the white burqa – Viv knew it was her by her height – walking back out of the alley, no envelope in hand, and crossing over to the other side of the Street of Storytellers. She stood beside a slender-trunked tree looking up at the carpet-seller's balcony, on the corner of the Street of Storytellers and the alley. It was without doubt one of the most beautiful balconies in the Walled City with roses and arabesques carved above each of the three archways of its wooden frame. At the base of the balcony, deer raced each

148

other from one archway to the next. But the woman in the burqa didn't seem interested in deer or roses; the stillness of her posture indicated a woman waiting.

Viv walked a few paces closer to the unmoving figure. Men and boys walked along past both women, sometimes hand in hand, flowers behind their ears and bandoliers across their chests. As if they had decided to be both man and woman at once, long of eyelash and broad of shoulder. Viv might as well have been shrouded in a white sheet herself for all the attention they showed her. The lack of staring is a mark of courtesy, Avtar Singh had explained to her when she expressed her irritation at being treated as though she weren't there; and then he grinned his wolfish grin and said and also, of course, the Pathans want to insist that men mustn't look at women to ensure that no man looks at their women. A throat-slitting gesture accompanied the comment.

The genial, white-bearded carpet-seller from whom Viv had recently bought a rug stepped onto the balcony. He called down to the apple-seller standing on the street below him, who threw an apple up in the air, almost directly into the carpet-seller's outstretched hand. A coin, flipped off the white-beard's thumb, followed the reverse trajectory. The carpet-seller bit into the apple, his eyes passed briefly over the woman in white across the road, and he nodded his head. It was a nod of appreciation for the apple unless you were expecting it to be something else. The woman in white remained unmoving for a few seconds after that, leaning against the tree as if she had stopped only to rest. Eventually she moved away, and turned into one of the alleyways which led to the maze-like innards of the Walled City.

A woman stands in the shade of a tree. A man surveys the street below him while eating an apple. Somewhere in there was a story which Viv didn't know how to imagine.

The letter from her mother was addressed in black ink. Someone had died, again.

Viv sat down in the garden chair, reaching overhead to pull

149

down on a branch of the willow, brushing its leaves against her face. The squawks and metallic chirps of birds, the booted feet of a regiment marching towards the barracks, her finger picking at the interwoven rattan strips of the chair as though it were a stringed instrument – all this was familiar now. The letters from England came from another world.

My dear Vivian

Mary's brother, Richard, has 'died of wounds' in Mesopotamia. She is being very Mary-like about it, speaking of her great pride in his noble sacrifice, but you know as well as I that he only signed up because she shamed him into it and I can't believe this doesn't weigh on her soul. She spoke wistfully of your absence at the funeral service – a woman needs her friends in times such as these. She is speaking of volunteering with the mobile nursing units on the Western Front. Your father is very low as well. All the boys he delivered into the world leaving it too early. It has changed him, quite suddenly.

You mustn't think it is all gloom here. Newspaper advertisements for 'Wartime Furs at Wartime Prices' lift the spirits and the competition among one's intimates for Most Patriotic Zeal continues to provide a fantastic spectacle even as those most determined to win the Cup complain bitterly of the war's effect on household staff. (The problems of the one-armed footman continue at home.)

I met Miss Murray a few days ago who said there is no place of work in England which isn't opening doors to women to make up for all the men who've rushed off to war – museums and universities included. Perhaps it's time to book your return passage? Your father was so disappointed to hear you won't be back for Christmas as you'd promised – I don't see him trying to send you away to the Front to nurse. Even if he tried, it's clear from your letters that running your own household and deciding how to spend your days has made you a woman, no longer a girl blindly following the lead of others.

Your loving mother

Oh, Mary. She rested the letter on her lap, remembered Richard, the boy with the scabbed knees who she and Mary had chased up trees in his childhood, teased when the puppy-fat fell away and he started to attract the eye of girls, relied on as an escort to parties during their university years. Richard, who disapproved of Mary's suffragette activities but still drove her to WPSU meetings and bailed her out of prison. That sweet, gentle boy. Died of wounds. She knew the sound, the smell, the agony of it. Knew the grown men whimpering for their mothers. And Richard would have called out for Mary, his older sister, the solidity to his shadow.

What am I doing here? How can I go back to that?

There were tears streaming down her face almost all the way from the Cantonment to the road to Shahji-ki-Dheri. Richard has died, she kept saying while she pedalled, as if the words might make sense of such a waste. Nearing the stupa site she passed a graveyard which a group of mourners was entering, accompanying a white shrouded body. Richard is dead. She pulled over, almost crashing into the wheat fields on the opposite side of the road, and breathed deeply, fearing she might faint.

It was only when two men walked out of the wheat field to check the memsahib was all right that she hopped back onto the saddle and continued on to the site which was suspended between cultivation and excavation as the legal and financial tussle with the landowner continued on.

She walked down into the deep ditch which she thought of as Najeeb's trench, reached into the deep pocket of her jacket and took out her notebook, its calfskin binding covered in mementoes from Turkey: the singe-mark from the leaping ember of a camp-fire in Labraunda that evening when the skies cleared and the temperature plummeted after a violent thunderstorm; the fig stain shaped like a pug's mouth; an inky thumbprint which had appeared mysteriously the first day she walked along the Carian coast, and which she thought of as the mark of a Siren; a smear of blood from the gash which opened

151

in Tahsin Bey's elbow when he scraped it against a jagged stone in the Temple of Zeus.

Kneeling in the mud, she began to sketch the figure of a stucco Buddha within an archway. She wasn't yet halfway done when she stopped, tossed her pencil aside and began to flip through the earlier pages of the notebook. Memories on every page. All at once, it was unbearable. Everything about this forgotten, crumbling site which had had its items of worth carted off to a museum so that only the half-gnawed bones remained was unbearable. She wanted Tahsin Bey here so she could pummel him with her fists. What did you mean by sending me that letter, making me come here, held hostage by your dreams. It's probably not even here! She caught hold of a fistful of mud, scooped it up and hurled it at the Buddha. There was something so satisfying about it that she did it again, and again, and again. When she finally stopped her hair was in disarray, her shirt clinging to damp skin. The stucco Buddha held her gaze, its hand raised. She touched her fingertips to his.

There had been no word from Tahsin Bey since that Christmas card. She sent letters every week, along with sketches, and photographs, and rubbings from stupas. Nothing came back but silence. Her mind ranged over all the possible explanations, and turned away from the darkest one, but not today. Today she imagined a white shrouded sheet, a body lowered into the ground, and no one thinking her important enough in his life to be told it had happened.

She rested her head against the wall of the mud trench. This too shall pass.

Time progressed, winter parties picked up, the days were sunshine and the evening breeze nipped pleasingly at her skin. One day tumbled into another. All fears slipped back into their hiding place.

Viv walked onto her verandah, humming:

152

City of Men,
City of Flowers,
Land Beyond the Mountains:
Caspatyrus, Paruparaesanna, Paropamisadae, Gandhara,
Parasapur, Purashapura, Poshapura, Po-lu-sha-pu-lo, Fo-lu-sha,
Farshabur, Peshawar.

She sat down on the wood-and-rattan chair with pivoting,
extendable arms. The first time Najeeb had seen it he'd referred
to it as Long-Armed, a direct translation of its local name; a few
days later when she'd referred to it as such, he'd turned pink
and giggled uncontrollably which told her that somehow his
boundless curiosity had discovered that the British name for it
was Bombay Fornicator, in recognition of the unseemly position adopted by those who used the extendable arms as
footrests. It had been all she could do to keep a straight face.

She looked at her watch. Najeeb should have been here by
now. When the door-knocker echoed through the house she
knew it wasn't him; his was a quick triple knock, not announc-
ing his presence so much as registering delight to have arrived
– the tempo filled with expectation. This dull thud of brass on
door suggested someone of a far less breezy temperament. But
it was him, after all. A boy wearing an expression of sorrow, his
posture straight-backed. Arms at ninety degrees, palms up, with
books piled on them, the slate fragment with Atlas's wrist on
top. She didn't know what the discordance between the intimate sadness of his face and the formality of his body meant.

– These are your books, Miss Spencer. Thank you for letting
me read them. I'm afraid I won't be able to continue our lessons,
or to see you again.

A rehearsed speech, delivered in a voice with fissures in it.

– What's happened, Najeeb? Come in, come in and tell me.

The boy glanced over his shoulder, and she followed the
angle of his eye across the garden, past the gate, and out onto
the pavement where a tall, broad-shouldered man was turned
away from the pair of them with a Pathan unwillingness to look
at an uncovered woman.

– I must go. Goodbye, Miss Spencer. I hope you won't forget your Pactyike.

– Don't I at least deserve an explanation?

He was holding the books out to her and she refused to take them. With a sigh, he placed them on the ground in front of her so he looked as though he were touching her feet in obeisance. He took the piece of slate from the top of the pile and kissed Atlas's wrist, before setting it gently back down.

– That was a gift. Am I so disdained that you must return my gifts?

He straightened, and placed the slate piece in his tunic pocket.

– It's nothing like that. Please don't think I'm ungrateful.

– But I must think that if you don't offer me any other thought with which to replace it.

– It's just that . . . it's not right, you see.

– What? That you're missing lessons with the maulvi? Is that what this is about?

He touched his upper lip, the fuzz on it which had started to appear over the last few weeks.

– I'm becoming a man. It isn't right for me to be here, alone with you.

She looked at the boy, the child, and beyond him to the broad-shouldered man. He was too far away to hear; these words were Najeeb's, uttered because he believed them.

– Then bring your sisters next time you come.

– My sisters? What will they do here?

– I'll teach them, just as I teach you.

– But they don't know any English.

– You didn't know any Greek four months ago. I didn't know any Pashto. What are you shaking your head about?

– Miss Spencer, they're girls.

– What do you think I am, for heaven's sake.

– You're English.

Then he was walking backwards along the pathway, his eyes on her face with the same concentration with which he had met the Buddha's gaze. His right hand raised to shoulder level, fingers together, palm outwards in a gesture of protection learned from a man of stone.

– Goodbye, Miss Spencer.

As the afternoon became evening she remained standing at the window, looking out onto the slate mountains through which the man with the fig circlet had entered the Peshawar Valley, the whole, unexplored world his to claim.

– Is it true you've lived among the Turks?

The judge leaned across the table of the Peshawar Club, raising his voice to be heard above the music.

– I'm sure she hasn't lived among anything of the sort – any more than I've lived among Pathans.

The judge's wife, seated beside Mr Forbes, gestured around the capacious interior of the Club where the upper echelons of British Society in Peshawar had gathered for the Winter Ball. The bearers had all disappeared into the kitchen, so the only Pathan to be seen was the one stationed beside the mounted deer's head whose task for the last fifteen minutes or so had been to retrieve the one napkin holder which a swaying man had been trying to toss onto the antlers. His aim had been growing steadily wilder, or perhaps he was deliberately aiming for the Pathan's head now.

Viv dispatched the judge's question with an inclination of her head which said his wife had correctly summed up the situation and returned what remained of her faltering concentration to the no-longer-young bachelor who was trying to impress her with some story about his valour during an encounter with fanatics along the Khyber Pass. She stood up abruptly in the middle of his story – catching Mr Forbes' look of sympathy – and, saying something which was tone rather than words, walked rapidly out to the arched portico and drew the night air deep into her lungs.

Fairy lights strung all around the garden gave the impression that the starlit sky had lowered onto the treetops.

– You're in a mood tonight.

She didn't even turn at the sound of Remmick's voice.

– And you'll be in trouble when you go home if you stand out here much longer, she said.

– A minute in your company is worth an hour of trouble at home.

– Stop it, she said sharply.

– Don't lose your friends, Miss Spencer, he replied, and walked away.

She called him back apologising, and told him what had happened that afternoon with Najeeb.

– A Pathan is a Pathan at any age, he said, but with sympathy rather than any triumph at having been proved right.

– I've been arrogant. Thinking I knew better than everyone who lives here.

– I have to say, it's a relief to hear you say that. You see now why this plan of yours – to go excavating on the outskirts of Peshawar – is such a bad idea?

– In what way?

– I've said it before. A woman leading a team of Pathan workmen . . .

– Not everyone in the Peshawar Valley is Pathan.

– Aren't your days full enough? We could find you some teaching, if you miss it; Native students, English students, whichever you prefer. Or there's plenty of cataloguing needed at the Museum. You'd be valued there.

A certainty announced itself, so clear, so well-defined, she knew it had been there for a very long time, lurking in the corner of her eye.

– You aren't actually doing anything to sort out the leasing problem of Shahji-ki-Dheri, are you?

A little shrug, a gesture of defeat.

– I did make enquiries. No one's particularly interested. General opinion has it the best finds of the site have already been discovered.

– All this while you've been lying?

– Oh come now, Miss Spencer.

156

– Oh come now, Miss Spencer?

He gestured to her to lower her voice, the air of command so unmistakable she wondered how she'd ever thought this was a man who would simply do anything she asked of him, merely because she asked it. Even so, she wasn't prepared for what came next.

– We're long past the point when the smiles you flick at me are compensation enough for everything I do for you. I found you a house, staff you could trust, I've allowed you to use all the privileges at this club that are usually reserved for a member's wife. Now you expect me to go to the Deputy Commissioner and tell him he needs to push through complicated negotiations about a crumbling piece of land simply because you're curious why a statue was white rather than grey?

– The Forbeses were helping me to find a house when you came along and told me you had the perfect one. I didn't ask you to provide me with staff – you just wanted to keep an eye on me. Oh yes, I know they report to you, Remmick, how foolish do you think I am? If you weren't going to do this for me, why didn't you just say so?

He laughed, a little bitterly.

– What man doesn't want a beautiful woman to keep believing he can do anything he sets his mind to?

– There is no shortage of men who would choose honesty over dissembling under all circumstances.

– You speak of honesty? Very well, let's be honest. There is a dance of men and women; we all recognise its rules. You, with nothing more than your smiles as reward, you were the first to break those rules.

– The dance of men and women! You make it sound so finely balanced. But you always lead, don't you?

He was standing very close to her, his hand on her waist as though it had a right to be there.

– Allow yourself to be led, Vivian. You'll enjoy it far more than you think, with the right partner.

She pushed him, hard.

– Not you, she said. Never you.

157

She stalked back inside, and told Mr Forbes she was feeling unwell, would he be good enough to escort her home?

That tree in Regent's Park which she could see from her bedroom window would have turned yellow-leafed by now. Every year she would walk out with Papa when there were more leaves on the ground than on the branches, and carefully, deliberately, they'd choose the most beautiful of the leaves and take it home to preserve it in a scrapbook she'd made with YELLOW LEAF printed on the cover in a child's hand.

If she left now there might just be a few yellow leaves still in the grass when she returned. The thought brought with it a relief, a release.

After the war, Tahsin Bey, we'll come back to Peshawar, and dig for the Circlet together.

March 1916

There was no broom for the new boy, but during the break in lessons the other students, all fourteen of them, walked out into the fields and each returned with a twig which they tied together with twine and brought to Qayyum so he could snap them into an even length. At the end of the day while some of the boys took the rugs outside the one-room structure and beat the dust from them, the others swept the ground and the new boy joined in as though it were an honour. A few weeks earlier when Qayyum had told Ghaffar Khan he wanted to teach at one of the schools his new hero had opened in the Peshawar Valley – just a short distance from Kalam's father's orchards – Ghaffar Khan had said don't forget, the most important thing you'll teach them is service. Qayyum had thought of Najeeb and the word 'service' was a weight he'd have to impose on the students' lives, but now he heard the exclamation of delight with which one of the boys found a dead ant and, with a great flourish of broom, passed it across to a boy nearer the door who swept it over to the new boy who scooped it up in his hands and proudly carried it out, the other boys applauding him on.

When Qayyum started to ride away on his bicycle he could hear the calls of the departing boys – Alif Bey Pay! The Pashto alphabet a song which they carried across the orchards to their homes where literacy had never before crossed the doorway.

Spring had come to the Peshawar Valley, and there was

159

nothing in the world that wasn't possible. Qayyum rode through a world in bloom, slowing to check the progress of the sugar cane and the plum blossoms, though he had walked among them just a few hours earlier with Kalam's father as he did every morning on his way to the schoolhouse. From orchards to gardens to city walls to the Street of Storytellers – he pedalled through the heart of the Peshawar Valley, feeling it pulse all around him, gathering its potential. Something new was coming, he was part of it. He watched a regiment marching past and there was pity in him for the Indian soldiers who didn't understand the disquiet in their own breasts.

Near the Street of Courtesans his bicycle wheel wobbled, but just in time he heard Najeeb calling out to him from across the road and, dismounting, went to meet his brother.

– Were you about to go into that alley, Lala?

– Of course not.

– Have you ever been in there?

– Keep asking questions like that and I'll send you back to the mullah.

Najeeb grinned at that, and butted Qayyum's shoulder with his head. Their mother's insistence on accompanying Najeeb to the mosque had lasted less than a week. The trick of it, Qayyum had explained to his brother, was simply to tell her everything he'd learned from the mullah that day as she walked him home. She never exactly said he should stop going, but one day she said he should go without her, and the next day she sent him to the market to buy vegetables and when he said he couldn't do that and be at his lessons at the same time she shrugged and said, potatoes come to us from heaven, and it was understood. So it was Qayyum now who took over his brother's religious instruction, teaching him as he taught the boys at school – Islam teaches us goodness, teaches us virtue, teaches us service, teaches us brotherhood, teaches us gentleness. But we are Pactyike, the most warlike of the Indians, Najeeb replied, indignant. That most unwarlike boy ever to be born into a Pashtun family. It was impossible not to laugh.

– Where are you coming from? The Museum?

–Yes. Lala, in my holidays will you take me to Shahbaz Garhi?

– Of course. I'm glad you're finally interested in seeing the Yusufzai lands.

– It's a great archaeological site. The Rock Edicts of Asoka.

Qayyum laughed, threw his hands up in a gesture of defeat. Every day more English words in Najeeb's Hindko – Classics, archaeological site, excavation, scholarship, university. Even their mother knew there was nothing to do but accept it. How do you pull the wings off a bird in flight? she'd asked Qayyum after Najeeb had sent her to the Museum on its women-only day and chattered away to her for hours after she'd returned, explaining what it was she'd seen there.

Home now, and he climbed the steps behind Najeeb towards the sounds of his mother and her eldest granddaughter, a spar-kling-eyed girl of four. They were sitting at the long table as he entered, his mother holding a doll in her hand and his niece kneeling on a chair, elbows on the table, looking at the open pages of one of Najeeb's books.

– Do you want to learn how to read?

Najeeb sat down beside her as he spoke, both of them small enough to occupy a single chair. The child nodded her head, placed her hand on the page and said, Alif, Bey, Pay. Qayyum lifted her up in his arms, away from the book, away from Najeeb's questioning gaze, and placed her on her grand-mother's lap.

– Play with your doll, little one.

Pulling the blanket close about his shoulders, Najeeb settled himself onto the rope-bed beneath a small-leafed tree on the Street of Storytellers, and respectfully greeted Ashfaq Lala. In return, the Storyteller gestured to an attending boy who approached with a blue enamel cup which the sun patterned with leaf-shapes as it passed into Najeeb's hands. Najeeb ducked his head in thanks, raising the mug to his face to take in

the scent of kahwa as the Storyteller leaned forward on his
raised platform, and began the badala:

Listen to my story, but first add sugar to your tea,
  There are salty tears aplenty here but no sweetness, you'll
    see.

It's a story of Darius, the King of over-there,
  King of Kings, King of all things, King of over here.

One morning he awakes – where there should be wife, there's
  parchment,
  Queen Atossa thus transformed! Is this hell- or heaven-sent?

The night before she lay beside him, flesh and blood and breath,
  This morning she's papyrus, the length of his bed.

What happened here, you ask? Be patient, I'm the Storyteller.
  Her ink as warm as blood, her skin oiled. What demons dwell
    here?

The King reads down the length of her, his lips near her skin.
  How long since Atossa was so smooth, so pliant, so thin.

But when he stops reading, the King of Kings he weeps,
  The Queen watches, nodding, from the alcove of the Keep.

It wasn't her at all, of course – you believe such silly things.
  She left this parchment here for him, for Darius, King of Kings.

He weeps for what Scylax has written. Scylax the Trusted One.
  His words rip the King's heart like twenty bullets from a gun.

How could the man who wore his circlet write these words of
  praise
  Not of Darius and the Persians but of that Carian slave!

162

Where do you place your loyalty, my good Peshawari men,
If you wrote of heroes today whose deeds would move your
pen?

Najeeb nodded approvingly – Ashfaq Lala was telling it better than ever before. The idea for this badala had occurred to him a few weeks ago when he was flipping through *The Encyclopaedia of Antiquity* in the Native Assistant's office at the Museum, and found an entry on Scylax with this intriguing line: *The lost biography of Heraclides of Mylasa has also been attributed to Scylax*. He had turned to the entry on Heraclides and found that he was a Carian prince who had ambushed Darius' forces and *routed them in bloody battle*. Why would anyone think Scylax the Trusted One had written a biography of such a man? He had closed the encyclopaedia, leaned back in the chair, and thought, but Qayyum would like the story – the man who served the Empire turning to the service of his people. What would Miss Spencer make of it, though? The thought brought with it a stab of sorrow. He had tried to go back to see her, wearing his sister's burqa so no one could report him to his mother, but her house was empty. Perhaps one day when he was older and the world was different she'd return and he could bring them both here together – Miss Spencer and Qayyum. They'd sit on either side of him and laugh and cry together at the story of Scylax, as interpreted by Najeeb Gul, the Herodotus of Peshawar.

Droplets of mist attached themselves like burs to Viv's sleeves as she walked away from St Dunstan's Hostel for blind service-men, and diagonally across the park towards the lamplit facade of Cambridge Terrace. All her life she had looked down from her second-storey bedroom to this piece of darkness, and yet the first time she had walked home from St Dunstan's past sunset, through the clawed shadows of trees, it had felt unknown to a greater degree than anything in Labraunda or Peshawar. Now, just a few weeks later, she barely gave it a thought.

She hadn't dreamed returning to London would feel so

163

much like freedom. How it changed the character of a city, the landscape of it, to have so many women in places they'd never been seen before – far more than when she had left. Today if a woman archaeologist were to suggest going to Cairo to work on maps no one would laugh. Gertrude Bell had joined Lawrence at the Arab Bureau, and it was whispered that Margaret Hasluck was with Intelligence too. The possibilities for Viv's life were so overwhelming she decided to resume VAD duties for a short time until she made up her mind about what else to do. It was the news of nursing shortages at St Dunstan's across the park which led to that decision. It wasn't a Class A hospital, and it was close enough to home to allow her to avoid hostel living. Convenience, rather than duty, guided her. But from her first day at St Dunstan's, service – a word which had never carried much weight in her life – revealed itself as privilege. Nothing in her life had ever made her feel more useful than placing a blind man's hand on Braille and watching his face as the shapes became letters for the first time. And if sometimes the slow pace of a Braille-learner's progress made her think wistfully of Najeeb, the thought was accompanied by only a dull pain now. He was receding. Even Tahsin Bey was receding. She hadn't written to him once since arriving in London. What was the point if the letters didn't get through to him?

A boy bicycled past, singing, Oh we don't want to lose you but we think you should go. Viv picked up her pace. Mary, soon to leave for nursing duties on the Front, was expected for supper.

When she arrived home, she could hear Mary's voice, and her father's, booming out from the parlour, partners in conviction. Viv smiled as she handed her coat to the one-armed footman. Mary and Papa were as united over pacifists as they'd once been divided over suffragettes, though when they suddenly fell silent she knew Mama had delivered a quiet, stinging blow. Nothing was as it had been before, and she thought of the colonial wives in Peshawar – their lives still mired in the nineteenth century – with pity.

164

She sent the footman into the parlour to say she'd be down in a few minutes, and went up the stairs to change out of her uniform. On her desk, beneath the framed rubbing of Asoka's Rock Edict, was today's post. She picked up the two envelopes. The first from Mrs Forbes in Peshawar had a pleasing thickness. She would read it after supper. The second, in an unfamiliar hand, was from Greece.

She stepped out onto her balcony, into the unexpectedly mild evening. Above, the thick bank of clouds reflected the flickering gaslight of streetlamps. The orange glow from streets and clouds was strong enough to read by. Opening the envelope she pulled out a sharp-edged page which gashed her thumb as she withdrew it. Holding her thumb to her mouth, she looked at the seal at the top of the page and frowned. Why would Tahsin Bey's nephew, Mehmet, be writing to her? And why from Greece?

Vivian Rose Spencer

I have this address from my uncle's book, and hope it continues to be the correct one. For a long time I've avoided writing to you, but there are things which must be said. Last April, Wilhelm sent a telegram informing my uncle of your activities in London. I was with my uncle when he received it. He was insistent that whatever the war may have forced on you, you didn't come to Labraunda as a spy and that it had been his idea, not yours, for you to join the coastal walk which made you so valuable to Intelligence. I said it was obvious that his feelings for you were strong enough to make manipulation easy. We argued about it, but in the end he made me feel guilty for my ill thoughts about you.

It didn't occur to my uncle to wonder why Wilhelm had sent a telegram – he didn't see the urgent method of communication as a warning although we knew already that Wilhelm was with Military Intelligence in Germany. ('How will archaeologists ever be trusted again' was my uncle's only note of complaint about what you had done, and he directed it mostly at Wilhelm.) At first, it didn't occur to me either. But then I asked if he might

165

have said anything to you which would create trouble if you repeated it in London to the men you were working for.

'She would never repeat it.'

Those were his words, and they made my heart stop. I thought I was the only one close enough to know his deepest secret, and even I had never heard him express it directly. I merely knew in the way we know unsaid things about people we have loved and revered all our lives. He would not hear anything I tried to say to him about you, about the danger in which he had placed himself.

It is only now, all these months later in my self-imposed exile in Greece, that I have managed to receive confirmation that the Germans intercepted a communication from London which described my uncle as an Armenian sympathiser who could be a useful informant. You were named as the source. Wilhelm found out about this after the Germans relayed the information to the Ottomans. It is possible you already know this, and regard it as just another casualty of war, one suffered by the enemy, but in case you don't: two days after receiving Wilhelm's telegram, while walking Alice through the park in accordance with his daily ritual, my uncle was shot dead. There is no doubt in my mind it was because of your betrayal. Mehmet

Viv lowered the hand holding the letter, the taste of iron on her tongue. *After the war, Vivian Rose.* His voice in her ear, its accent, its timbre. Her own voice that of a stranger when she cried out into the night.

Later, much later that evening, after her mother finally tiptoed away from her room, believing she was asleep, Viv lay openeyed in the pitch darkness. Tahsin Bey on the Split Rock of Labraunda watching the sunrise; Tahsin Bey teaching Nergiz' son bird-calls; Tahsin Bey lighting up a cigarette and telling a story of two thousand years ago as if it were still unfolding; Tahsin Bey removing clinging earth from the eyes of a stone god, his breath combining with Viv's to allow Zeus to see again;

Tahsin Bey stepping close to her, his hand on her waist, one strong forearm holding her close. Tahsin Bey's body lowered into the earth.

He was dead because of her. Wherever she went in the world, whatever she did, this would always be the truth at the core of her life.

BOOK II

TWENTIETH-CENTURY HERODOTUS

Najeeb Gul
Rose Door House
Next door to Hari Das Cobbler's
Off Lahori Gate Road
Peshawar

Qayyum Gul
Guest of Sher Mohommad Yusufzai
Shahbaz Garhi

19 November 1928

Lala

How long will your friend's wedding celebrations go on? My footsteps are an intruder in the silence of the house. You should come back soon – not only for your lonely brother but because of what it must cost your hosts to keep you well fed. How much you eat, Lala! I never noticed it before but our sisters are sending over half the quantity of food as when you're here and most of it still goes uneaten. You must have gobbled up half the chickens of Shahbaz Garhi in the week you've been away.

(I know your expression right now – one side of your mouth a smile, the other side a scowl.)

Remember when the owner of the sugar-cane fields at Shahji-ki-Dheri died and one of the men who worked his lands told you the son who had inherited showed some regret that such bad feelings had existed between his father and the English over the matter of leasing the land for excavation? Now it seems an artefact that first entered my dreams in childhood might be

173

beneath those fields. Will you find out the best way to approach the new owner for leasing the land – directly or in a roundabout fashion? With flattery, gifts or a straight gaze? Nothing has ever been more important to me than this.

I hope many people have come for the wedding celebrations, and they are going well.

Your brother

Najeeb

Najeeb Gul
Peshawar Museum
Peshawar
India

Miss V. R. Spencer
University College
London
Great Britain

19 November 1928

Dear Miss Spencer

Please forgive this intrusion. You may remember me from your time in Peshawar in 1915 when I was your student. I certainly have not forgotten you. You introduced me to the world of Scylax and Herodotus, and set me on the path I have continued to follow. (I accompanied you the first time you went to Shahji-ki-Dheri, if that aids memory.)

Following on from my degree in history from Islamia College in Peshawar I have had the good fortune of working with Dr John Marshall. I spent two years with him at Taxila before being offered the position of Indian Assistant (the role formerly known as 'Native . Assistant') at the Peshawar Museum, from where I now write to you. Mr Hargreaves is Superintendent and was the one to tell me you could be reached at University College, London.

You must be wondering why I'm writing to you after so many years. It concerns the matter of Shahji-ki-Dheri. Several years ago Mr Wasiuddin – who was Native Assistant here during your time – told me you had tried to obtain permission to excavate the stupa

175

site. I understood then that you truly did believe the Kanishka Casket and the Sacred Casket to be one and the same, and must also have deducted that the Circlet was buried there during the visit of Sung-Yun, whose 'mission was not that of theft'. It is entirely understandable you didn't wish to reveal as much to a twelve-year-old boy. Perhaps you already know that, due to the protracted dispute with the owners of the site, the excavation was levelled in 1919. There is nothing but wheat fields now where once we walked among the broken stupas and cross-legged Buddhas.

I have, only this morning, been examining the records of Dr Spooner's original excavations, and came upon a detail that may interest you. In one of the trial pits, to the south-west of the main stupa, were found fragments of white stone and a broken finger 'the size of which suggests a statue of some enormity'. Miss Spencer, I sincerely believe this to be the eighteen-foot-high white statue which you, as I, must surely have surmised to be the Great Statue of which Kallistos writes. White stone was found nowhere else on the site, and from my examination of the detailed site drawings it seems that the trial pit in question is roughly one hundred paces to the south-west of the stupa, assuming the paces are those of a small man.

I would not bring this up if I thought there was no hope of further excavations. It's true that within the Department there is no interest in returning to Shahji-ki-Dheri which yielded so little beyond the Kanishka Casket and caused such headaches, but the owner of the land with whom there were legal disputes and considerable bad blood has now passed away and his son is a man of gentler temperament. If it were possible to undertake a privately funded dig I believe he would be willing to lease out the land at a reasonable price.

I apologise again for this intrusion. It has often occurred to me to write to you but I have not wanted to presume. But now it gives me great pleasure to have occasion to thank you for all you did for me, and to hope the news I bear is welcome.
Yours sincerely
Najeeb Gul, BA (Islamia College)
Pactyike

Shahbaz Garhi
22 November 1928

Najeeb

The first rule of approaching any man: do not insult his appetite in one sentence and ask for his help in the next. (The chickens of Shahbaz Garhi are safe, and the goats are delicious.)

I have had more success here than I anticipated in promoting Ghaffar Khan's ideas of reform, due to the support of my host who is held in high regard. He has advised me against using your translations of Asoka's rock inscriptions when I talk to the men here, even though he was the one to take me to that rock for the first time when I returned from the war. Already there are rumours put about by the English and the mullahs that Ghaffar Khan's ideas of non-violence are Hindu beliefs taken from Gandhi, so it is best to talk of the Prophet only, and not confuse matters by bringing a Buddhist king into it. But before you scowl too much – I went to the rock and read the translated words while I stood in front of it, and felt a powerful peace which I know to come from Allah, no matter which of his Messengers he used to spread it through the earth.

If you go to the fields at Shahji-ki-Dheri and ask for Afzal, son of Allah Buksh, and say you are my brother, he will tell you everything you need to know about the owner of the land. I am glad for your sake that you believe you've found something valuable to you, though I wonder what this artefact is, placed into your dreams by the English who teach you their version of history.

Your brother

Qayyum

This letter is being brought to you by a man I trust. If you send a reply by his hand write freely – otherwise, speak only of wedding celebrations.

V. R. Spencer
Senior Lecturer
University College
London

Najeeb Gul
Indian Assistant
Peshawar Museum
Peshawar

18 January 1929

My dear Najeeb Gul
My memory needs no aid in recollecting you. It gives me such pleasure to know that the young Pactyike has found himself a position at the Peshawar Museum – and at such an early age. The last fourteen years of my life have involved less dramatic changes than yours (Taxila!) but I have kept myself well occupied. In addition to the lectureship post at University College I have catalogued several museum collections and taken part in a few digs: the Borg in-Nadur Temple in Malta, with my former teacher at UCL, Margaret Murray; Roman sites in Wales with my former classmate from UCL, Tessa Wheeler, and her husband Mortimer; and, most recently, the Fayum with my former student from UCL, Gertrude Caton Thompson. (Well might you think I am part of a UCL cabal!) At present, though,

179

England is by far the most interesting place to be as my old friend Mrs Mary Moore, a local councillor, plans to run for Parliament in the next elections, which will be the first to allow women voting rights on equal terms with men. I daresay this all seems very odd to you.

But to come to the point. At the time of its publication I read the Archaeological Survey Report of 1919–20, and learned that Shahji-ki-Dheri had been returned to cultivation. The news was not as distressing to me as I would have imagined and after some consideration I realised that I didn't truly believe the Circlet is there (though, yes, when in Peshawar I had great hopes). I was in some state of agitation when I came to Peshawar – wanting to believe impossible things – and I must apologise if in that state of mind I said or did anything that led you to believe, and hold on to, falsehoods. Of course you were just a child then. But how can the Assistant of Peshawar Museum (BA) really imagine that an artefact (circa 515 BC) from Caria, last heard of during the Hecatomnid era which ended in 334 BC, might come to be buried in Peshawar during the visit of Sung-Yun somewhere between AD 515 and AD 520? (There is only so much we can lay at Alexander's door.) I can only assume Mr Hargreaves shares this view else there would be no need for a privately funded dig.

Don't allow me to lead you astray any further. You are at a most privileged place and time in the history of archaeology. Concentrate your mind on what can realistically be sought after, and found.

Yrs.

Vivian Rose Spencer

Najeeb Gul
Taxila Museum
Taxila

Qayyum Gul
Rose Door House
Next door to Hari Das Cobbler's
Off Lahori Gate Road
Peshawar

15 March 1929

Lala

Thank you for sending the letter from England to me. Yes, the sender Miss V. R. Spencer is Miss Spencer from long ago. She is the one who I had hoped would lease the land at Shahji-ki-Dheri, but it seems it isn't just girls who grow into women as caterpillars grow into butterflies but in the case of the English when the butterflies age they enter a cocoon. I will try once more to convince her, but I'm not hopeful.

I know you don't understand why this means so much to me. How can I explain how it feels to hold an ancient object and feel yourself linked to everyone through whose hand it passed. All these stories which happened where we live, on our piece of earth – how can you stay immune to them? Every day here in Taxila I dig up a new story. And, yes, I'm grateful to the English for putting this spade in my hands and allowing me to know my

181

own history. But to you history is something to be made, not studied, so how can you understand?

I have received permission from Mr Hargreaves to stay with the dig in Taxila a little longer so will not return to Peshawar until the end of the month. I hope all the wedding celebrations are going well.

Your brother

Najeeb Gul
Taxila Museum
Taxila

Miss V. R. Spencer
Senior Lecturer
University College
London

15 March 1929

Dear Miss Spencer

I write to you from Taxila where a museum has recently opened to house the great findings of our excavations. I am here for a few weeks to advise on some teething problems, and am also taking the opportunity to participate in a dig. It is truly a privileged position to work both on the excavation and the curation of Gandhara artefacts. They are undoubtedly the most beautiful statuary created by human hands.

In your letter you asked how I can imagine that an artefact from Caria, lost to history in 334 BC, might come to be buried in Peshawar eight centuries later. This is how:

From Caria, Alexander took the Circlet with him to India, and gave it as a gift to Nearchus after the latter followed Scylax' route down the Indus. After Alexander's death, in the wars fought between his generals, Nearchus found himself on the opposite side to Seleucus Nicator who, following his victory over Nearchus' forces at Gaza, claimed the Circlet for himself. A few years later, when Seleucus lost control over most of Alexander's territory in India, he was forced into a treaty with the king Sandracottas who demanded the Circlet as part of the treaty terms. Sandracottas – or Chandragupta Maurya – was, as I'm sure you know, the grandfather of the great Buddhist king Asoka. When Asoka converted to Buddhism he had stupas built all across the length and breadth of his kingdom; each Buddhist stupa had a treasury, and the energy of the stupa was derived from the objects in the treasury. Is it unreasonable to think that he might have sent the Circlet from the palace treasury to a stupa treasury? And there it stayed through the centuries as Buddhism flourished in Gandhara and beyond – until the White Huns under Mihirakula overran Gandhara, burning stupas, pillaging their treasuries. Hearing of the approach of the Huns, a bhikkuni (that's a Buddhist nun) called Maya escaped from a stupa complex, carrying the treasure of the great Asoka, determined to save it from the marauders. She travelled to the Great Stupa of Kanishka, and there she met the Chinese traveller Sung-Yun. When he refused to take the Circlet to safety, she buried it beneath the Great White Statue of Shahji-ki-Dheri, trusting that the soil of that sacred place would be an even safer hiding place than its treasury if ever the Huns should attack it. And watching her was a young boy who took the story with him and kept it alive in the world until, centuries later, it reached Kallistos – but that is a story for another time.

What is history without imagination, as Herodotus teaches us? I hope this might convince you to lay out the funds for leasing Shahji-ki-Dheri.
Yours sincerely
Najeeb

18 March 1929
Peshawar.

Najeeb
Of all the fantastic tales you've ever told none is more fantastic
than that of the kindly English who dig up our treasures because
they want you to know your own history. Your museums are all
part of their Civilising Mission, their White Man's Burden, their
moral justification for what they have done here. As for the spade
they place in your hand, the honours they shower on you – the
English are too few, we too many and so they see that it is necessary for there to be a class of Indian who will revere them, feel
honoured by them, benefit from their presence and, ultimately,
serve them because if our numbers turn against them to say
'Leave' there is no way for them to stay. Our numbers are turning, brother – and even while I rejoice at this I fear for you who
will one day wake from your illusions and see you are nothing but
a subject, a yoked Pashtun who thinks the yoke is a silk cravat and
that a silk cravat is as much yours to wear as a turban.

I bear no hatred for the English. It is our weakness that is
responsible for the state we are in. How dishonoured a people
we were to allow the men of a small island who burn at the
touch of the sun to come here and be our masters. And when
the English leave, as they must, I will welcome them back into
our house as visitors and show them all the courtesy and hospi-
tality of the Pashtuns.

185

Do not attempt again to convince the Englishwoman to become part of your plans. We will play supplicant no longer, kiss their hands in gratitude for the favours they choose to bestow no longer. This is an elder brother's command.

Your Lala

V. R. Spencer
14 Doughty Street
Bloomsbury
London

Najeeb Gul
Peshawar Museum
Peshawar

21 April 1929

My dear Herodotus of Peshawar

If imagination can shape reality then it is you, not your invented
Maya, who has placed the Circlet of Scylax beneath the soil of
Shahji-ki-Dheri. I picture the boy you were circling the old
excavation site, believing a miracle exists there, beyond your
reach for reasons of mere finance. Having placed the dream in
your mind myself, and understanding something of its grip, I see
I have an obligation to at least ask: how much would it cost?

If the sum is not prohibitive I will gladly arrange for a transfer
of funds and regard it not as a favour to you but as the spur to
my long-held intentions to return to India. Perhaps in exchange
you'll accompany me to Taxila and Mohenjodaro, which I have
a great wish to see?

Will you speak to the landowner yourself? If a financial
agreement can be reached, I assume you're in a position to
obtain permission for excavating? I am unable to get away
from London until early next year so if – I hasten to stress the

'if' – all this becomes possible let's plan to excavate in the spring. What Pashto I had is largely gone but I will spend the months ahead returning to it (there is a man from Peshawar who works at the British Library – he insists his name is Durand, but of course it's Durrani).
Yours
V.R.S.

28 May 1929

To: VR SPENCER

DELIGHTED TO RECEIVE LETTER STOP COSTS FOR
LEASE AND DIG TO FOLLOW STOP WILL ARRANGE
EXCAVATION PERMISSION
NG

----

12 JULY 1929

To: N GUL

RECEIVED   FIGURES   FROM   SOLICITOR   STOP
ACCEPTABLE HAVE TOLD HIM TO PROCEED WITH
DRAWING UP LEASE
VRS

----

13 JULY 1929

To: VR SPENCER

HURRAH
NG

1 January 1930
Lahore

Najeeb
I can't describe to you what happened here yesterday at the
Congress meeting on the banks of the Ravi River. Gandhi has
called for complete independence from the English and Nehru
hoisted a flag of three colours which will be the flag of a free
India. My whole body went hot and cold when I saw it and I
thought my heart would burst open. I am so proud to be among
Ghaffar Khan's Pashtuns here to celebrate this occasion – you
should have seen us dance in celebration. Congress gatherings
have never seen anything like it.

It is not all perfect. Many of the Congress Party believe
with a certainty which might exceed that of the English that
the Pashtuns are good for nothing except war and quick
temper. They continue to express doubts that we will be
able to follow the path of non-violent resistance when we
are tested. But Ghaffar Khan tells us we must be patient and
show through example that they are wrong. We will soon
have the opportunity to do so. A resolution has been passed
for civil disobedience which will go into effect before long. I
am going from here with Ghaffar Khan to spread the word
and build support for it through the Peshawar Valley – and
in so doing, add to the numbers of the Khudai Khidmatgar.
And what is this Khudai Khidmatgar, you will ask, you my

191

brother who knows every coin unearthed in the Peshawar Valley and little else? Already I can imagine your distaste at the name. Yes, the Servants of God, Najeeb, we draw our strength from Him and will challenge any of the maulvis who claim Ghaffar Khan's actions in allying with Gandhi are not those of a true Muslim.

But to explain: It is an unarmed army – you read that correctly – which will recruit unlettered men and bring them into our struggle. Ghaffar Khan says a conversation I had with him in which I talked of the great spirit of brotherhood and discipline in the Army helped him formulate the idea for the Khudai Khidmatgar, which pleases me more than anything else in life. I have said I will be part of the Khudai Khidmatgar. I would rather stand in formation with the unlettered men than sit in committees with men of learning. Though let me confess to you that our uniform of red-brown is far less appealing to the eye than the drab and green of the 40th. But what are we to do? Ghaffar Khan's thoughts are of dye that is cheap and easily available, not of the vanity of his Yusufzai general. I am to be a general!

While I'm gone will you go to the orchards a few times to make sure Rahim is looking after everything? I trust him, but he can be lazy if he thinks no one is watching. You don't have to pretend to understand much of farm life. It will be enough for you to go there and ask him how everything is.

Now to my final and most important point. Once this civil disobedience is launched there is no telling how the English will respond. It could become unpleasant – you have not seen the ways in which they attack those they see as an enemy, but I have and there is nothing in the world more cold and pitiless. So let me order, beg, plead one more time. Tell your Miss Spencer not to come.

I am following your instructions and not trying to convince you of the intentions and motives of the English when it comes to matters of archaeology. My point now is a separate one. This is not a time for an Englishwoman with no sense of today's world to arrive in India. I know you think you understand the

world better than your zealous brother, but I am speaking from
my heart. Keep the Englishwoman away.
Your brother
Qayyum

15 JANUARY 1930

To: N GUL

PASSAGE BOOKED PLEASE HIRE TEAM TO START DIG
APRIL 5TH.
VRS

----

16 JANUARY 1930

To: VR SPENCER

CONFIRMED AWAIT YOUR ARRIVAL
NG

----

1 APRIL 1930

To: N GUL

SLIPPED AND FELL AT KARACHI DOCKS NOTHING
SERIOUS BUT DOCTOR ADVISES AGAINST TRAVEL
FOR A FEW WEEKS STOP CAN DIG BE DELAYED
VRS

----

1 APRIL 1930

To: VR SPENCER

VERY   SORRY   TO   HEAR   UNWELL   BUT   DELAY
IMPOSSIBLE
NG

----

2 APRIL 1930

To: N GUL

OH BOTHER START WITHOUT ME WILL JOIN WHEN
POSSIBLE
VRS

April 1930

The soil was dense, the work slow. From sunrise until mid-morning Najeeb and his team of men dug through history. A few feet down there was a face of bone, which made the men touch their cheekbones and noses, as if considering for the first time their own skulls. A coin from the early days of the Raj had either been placed in its eye-socket or had tumbled into it from another era. There were other small discoveries – a coin, a copper seal, a fragment of stone with a lion's flanks carved into it – mixed in with the endless quantities of white powder and white-stone fragments.

Then came the morning when he heard the ringing sound of a spade hitting something solid. The Buddha's shin, thick as a man's torso. Najeeb and the foreman used trowels and hands to work around it, revealing the Holy One's ankle, his bare feet, the slightly flexed toes. By now it was well past mid-morning and the other men departed, but Najeeb continued on, impervious to aches and thirst and the sun searing the back of his neck. He was beyond imagining results, or asking how long he would continue; there was only this motion of his shoulder and arm and the trowel which had become an extension of himself; only soil displaced all around the base of the statue. The metal of the trowel head encountered tiny pieces of rock, a sound felt in his spine. The earth cooled as he dug into it; its composition changed; a worm wound its body sluggishly through the loam. The worm stood on its tail, fleshily pink, swayed in the changed universe of light and heat in which it found itself, and he thought of the adjoining graveyard, shuddered, plucked it out and flung it as far as his arm could throw. Wiped sweating palms on his trousers, continued. The edge of his trowel-head scraped metal. On his knees now; his heart an animal throwing itself repeatedly against the cage of his ribs.

Viv Spencer stood on the roof of the pink palace and watched the rooftop cupolas slide their shadows across the garden towards the statue of Queen-Empress Victoria flanked by lions. A pith-helmeted British soldier, also carved in stone, stood guard at one corner of the property. At least some of the Indian men in the garden must look at the statues and see an enemy; impossible to know which Indians were for Gandhi and which for the King, Viv had been told by Mary's cousins with whom she was staying in Karachi. Even your Oxbridge man might go either way. There were Indian women on the lawn as well, elegant in their saris; they mainly clustered together but a few threaded their way into the knots of men where they were greeted with great flourishes of delight, which Viv didn't know whether to regard as appreciative or as a politely coded reprimand.

The palace wasn't really a palace at all, just the extravagantly named summer home of a prosperous Indian merchant who had built this mansion near the seafront. Mughal architecture, English statuary, and an underground corridor which led to a Hindu temple (and allowed the pious lady of the house to maintain purdah). Perhaps centuries from now students of history would look at this property and see syncretism, but it merely made Viv wish for the statues and stupas of Gandhara. This period of recovering from her back injury, now blessedly almost at its end, had been interminable, and strange. Such stark political opinions; so difficult to know what to make of any of it.

Viv looked over the mansion walls, across the expanse of sand dunes to the pier. A flamingo picked its way fastidiously through the waters of the Arabian Sea; another tucked a leg beneath its wings and twitched its long neck. In the stories of Karachi surely those pink birds had flown out of the stone of

197

Mohatta Palace, leaving the peacocks in the nine domes of the roof to curse their own feathers whose purpose was beauty, not flight. She brought the back of her hand to her mouth, tasted the sea on her skin. How much narrower life would be without all of India poised at the heart of the word 'Ours'. But if anyone asked her what she thought of India, of Empire, of Gandhi she remained silent. She had learned, long ago, that the easiest way to avoid causing damage was to watch and say nothing, do nothing. 'Guarded' was the word people used to describe her, though she preferred to think of it as careful. It was only amidst histories that were centuries old that she allowed her curiosity to become intervention.

– When the Muslims asked the Prophet, How should we respond to these attacks? he answered, With righteousness and patience. Righteousness and patience. These are Muslim virtues, these are Pashtun virtues.

Qayyum Gul faced the red-shirted volunteers, two dozen or more. On some faces he saw disbelief, contempt. Training, fight, army – these would have been the words that snaked through the farmland adjoining Peshawar, tugging men towards Qayyum's orchards to join the training camp for the Khudai Khidmatgar. It was unclear if the men hadn't been told the true nature of the army or if they disbelieved what they heard, but whatever the case almost half of them had arrived with guns and knives. Now they were empty-handed, and blades and barrels encircled the base of an apple tree, gleaming like the anklet of a demon goddess.

– I am not going to tell you that non-violence is compatible with Pashtunwali. I am going to tell you that in the circumstances in which we live non-violence is essential to Pashtunwali. Are you honourable enough to endure . . .

A high-pitched whistle carried through the orchards, severing Qayyum's sentence. He made a sharp gesture and the men scattered, scrambling up the nearest tree trunks and into crowns thick with leaves. Qayyum walked rapidly towards the other end of the orchard, and was inspecting a leaf, pretending to ensure that the white markings had been deposited by small birds and weren't the start of a fungal infection, when the rent-collector entered from the adjoining plum orchards, which were also Qayyum's. He thought of the apple and plum orchards as his even though every month the arrival of the rent-collector reminded him that he was merely a tenant-farmer.

Now that reminder strode towards him, beating a walking stick against his own leg, his mouth glistening with apple juice. The rent wasn't due for weeks but Qayyum didn't say anything while the rent-collector continued working on the core of the apple, nibbling at the flesh around the seeds.

– Strange rumours around, Qayyum Gul.

– There always are. Which ones have you heard?

– People say you're using these orchards to train an army for Ghaffar Khan. Of course I reply oh no, he knows the land-owner plays polo with the Deputy Commissioner and has a portrait of the King-Emperor in his Peshawar house. He wouldn't do anything that would force me to come here and tell him these orchards aren't his to work any longer.

The rent-collector waved his hand expansively around the orchard as he spoke. It was a season of abundance, branches dipping with the weight of their fruit; insects weaved drunk-enly between trees, smashing themselves against branches. Qayyum rocked back on his heels, his arms crossed, and nodded to let the rent-collector know he understood.

The rent-collector stayed a few minutes more, talking of weather forecasts and the price of sugar. When he left there was a thud-thud-thud of men-fruit dropping from the trees, and Qayyum knelt on the ground, broke off a piece of turf, and crumbled it in his palm. If this were taken away from him what would his life be – thinned, bounded in. A cloth canopy above his head instead of the branches of an apple tree. The juice of a pen, pale blue, running across his palm where there should be liquid gold, inviting to the tongue. The scratch of a nib and the clamour of salesmen; not the calls of birds, the whisper of leaves. Nothing to compare to that moment when the first fruit of the season, pulled gently, detaches itself from a branch, and rests in your palm. He stood up, faced the men.

– That man came to tell me they will take my land away if I continue to stand here and speak to you. They think they can defeat us with threats. But I will endure what losses I must endure for the sake of freedom. And you? Are you honourable enough to endure, my brothers? For the sake of freedom are you men enough to put down your guns and endure?

– Yes, came the answer, sweeter than apple, more eloquent than ink. Yes!

Najeeb rested a hand on the silver band, its embossed surface. The figures were alternate – one fruit, one leaf, one fruit, one leaf, just as on the Hecatomnid coins. Even uncleaned the delicacy was unexpected, thrilling. In places where the tarnishing wasn't so extreme he saw veins in the leaves, striations along the fruit. There would have been colour when Darius placed it on Scylax' head – fig-purple and leaf-green. He spun it. The figs danced, the leaves twirled, Scylax kneeled before Darius and felt its weight settle on him, he dipped it in the Indus with an eye out for crocodiles, placed it on the brow of Heraclides, bloodied from his ambush of the Persians. Najeeb walked his fingertips across the raised surface; a message in Braille, a greeting across the centuries:

Hello, Najeeb!
Hello, Scylax!

THE ONLY QUESTION

23 April 1930

Qayyum had never known such clarity of purpose as here, on the front line, facing the soldiers with bayonets at the ready.

He had anticipated none of this when he'd woken to a hammering on his door just after dawn, and one of his neighbours from the Congress Party told him there had been arrests during the night ahead of the proposed anti-English protest strikes scheduled for the day, and people were gathering at the Congress headquarters to decide what to do next. He dressed quickly, woke up Najeeb to say he was leaving, cautioning him to look out for trouble during the day. Najeeb, barely awake, flicked his fingers in the direction of his brother's glass eye as if it were a marble.

– Goodbye, pacifist girl.

– Goodbye, Englishman's dog.

– Better an Englishman's dog than an Englishman's Indian.

But Qayyum's thoughts were already elsewhere, and the familiar joke of his own devising echoed strangely. He wondered if there was any point warning Najeeb, once more, about the Englishwoman who was due to arrive by train that day, but the younger man had already returned to sleep, and anyway what could Qayyum say at this point.

He was en route to the Congress offices when he became caught up in the procession. Two leaders of the Congress Party, garlanded with roses, were striding towards the Street of Storytellers, with their party members and allies following behind, calling out the slogan of freedom: Inqilaab Zindabad.

What's going on, Qayyum asked a man in the khaddar uniform of the Congress Party, falling into step beside him. The man looked at Qayyum's red shirt and belt, nodded as you would to a soldier of another battalion, and said the English had come to the Congress headquarters to arrest the men a little while earlier, but someone – and here the man raised his hands in exaggerated fashion as if to say he had no idea who would do such a thing – punctured the wheels of the lorry brought to transport their leaders to prison. Shocking, Qayyum laughed, shocking vandalism! And the Congressman, trying to look grave, nodded, and said so then the leaders told the police they would present themselves for arrest at the police-thana at Kabuli Gate – and here they all were, on their way, showing the English that you can arrest two men or ten but hundreds more will follow behind and demand liberty.

But when they arrived at the police-thana the doors were closed – the policemen thought the crowd was there to storm the station. Qayyum, tall enough to see above the heads of almost everyone else present, smiled at the unfolding spectacle: Congress leaders pleading with the police, insisting they were there to be imprisoned; policemen refusing to let them in. And the crowd, larger in size now, entirely peaceful, urging the police to arrest their leaders between cries of Inqilaab Zindabad. It would be enough to make any Englishman's head spin. Finally, finally, the doors opened; the Congress leaders entered to great whoops of support from the men outside. Someone threw a handful of petals at them as if they were brides entering their marital home for the first time.

– That was fun.

Qayyum nodded in agreement with the Congresswalla standing next to him, when he saw the face of one of the Indian policemen behind the gates – terrified, blood-drained. Of course, every policeman must be thinking of Chauri Chaura, eight years earlier, when a clash between police and Congress volunteers during the first Non-Cooperation Movement led to the deaths of twenty-six civilians and twenty-one policemen, the policemen all burnt alive in their thana.

You live in your history, we live in ours. The thought made him tired, unwilling to join the group of Khudai Khidmatgar who were dancing in a circle near the jail door, and he had turned to walk away when he heard a sound which didn't make sense and looked up to see armoured cars driving through Kabuli Gate.

After that the morning spooled dramatically away from anything that was predictable – accelerating cars, men crushed beneath wheels, machine guns, fire, screams of death and slogans of freedom, bullets and stones. The Street of Storytellers turned into a battleground with the troops on one side and freedom fighters on the other. One round of bullets, one round of deaths, then a pause, negotiations – first you withdraw, no, first you withdraw – and the numbers on the Street of Storytellers grew. Not just the red-shirted Khudai Khidmatgar and their Congress and Khilafat allies but other men of Peshawar who had heard what was happening and came to witness, came to cry out Inqilaab Zindabad. Soon the street was crowded. From the balconies and roofs of buildings spectators watched, some threw stones; on the ground the King's forces – on foot, on horse, in armoured cars, all armed with rifles and bayonets and machine guns – occupied the space between Kabuli Gate and Dakhi Nalbandi. Beyond that, hundreds of Peshawaris planted their feet on the Street of Storytellers and said no, they would not retreat. If a man is to die defending a land let the land be his land, the people his people.

Hours passed; the stand-off continued. You withdraw; no, you withdraw. The men standing further back began to jostle and push. What was all this talk? Qayyum, weaponless at the front, understood that something would shift soon, something would happen. But for the moment he saw no need to stifle the unexpected love he felt for the uniformed men of the British Indian Army, seeing in each one the comrades he had lost at Vipers, and himself, too, as glimpsed through a dead eye. Earlier in the day, when the Garhwal Rifles had refused to fire on the unarmed men ranged against them he felt terror

205

on their behalf rather than any sense of victory at knowing the strategy to shame those who would cut you down without mercy if you fought back was already beginning to work. The Sikh soldiers returned to the barracks with shoulders unslumped, necks unbowed, but Qayyum knew they would already be thinking of what would follow: court martial, perhaps a firing squad. The English would not act gently with Indian soldiers who sided with revolutionaries. No one had forgotten 1857, or even 1915.

And so, rather than enmity, it was love he felt; love and pity. Pity for the lives lost when the armoured cars charged in and the troops opened fire, pity for those Indian soldiers whose minds were enslaved, pity for the families whose hearts would shatter today. Even, a kernel of pity for the English officers. That sense of honour which the English and the Pashtun had in common, as the officers of the 40th Pathans so often reminded their men, was now a weapon wielded by one against the other. Today the officers would give orders to fire on unarmed men, and almost all the soldiers would obey – but tomorrow if asked to return here and do the same, their wills would sag. Or if not tomorrow than next month, next year.

And then, he had his only moment of fear: a girl stepped out from the lines of the Peshawari men, walked through the ranks of sepoys who stepped aside as if she were a djinn whose touch might burn them, and stopped in front of an armoured car. Everyone silenced. The girl – bare-headed, plait swinging – picked up a turban lying near the wheel of the armoured car and moved back into the crowd which parted to make space for her and then closed up again in her wake. Qayyum glanced up towards the rooftops and balconies of the Street of Storytellers. Women and children were leaning down, watching. There must be something wrong in the girl's head – like the molasses-seller's son who had to continually be watched so he didn't present himself to danger as if it were a game. Whoever should have been minding the girl must have been too intent on watching the Street of Storytellers to notice her slip away. He should find her and lead her back to safety, but the press of men made it difficult to move or to know where she had disappeared.

Then the firing started, the bayonets followed. Fall back, fall back – Inqilaab Zindabad, Inqilaab Zindabad. Bullets and the screams of men, and a stench of blood. But this was nothing like Vipers, here he was fearless, here he would die if he must and he wouldn't ask why. Yet somehow the bullets didn't touch him though around him men fell; too many of them to lift up and carry away, and more soldiers had arrived, firing now even on those who were bearing the dead; impossible to hold ground any more. Fall back, fall back. Through the alleys, soldiers giving chase, two behind and one up ahead, all converging on Qayyum.

– I'll rip out my own eye before you can touch me!

He bellowed the words, reaching up and prising out the glass eye with an exaggerated gesture. The soldier up ahead pressed himself against a doorway, bayonet falling from his grasp, and Qayyum held the eye up towards him as he ran past. He could hear the other soldiers stop to ask what had happened, what had the soldier seen, and he laughed as he ran, a warrior who had found his battle.

The buoyancy left him as the sound of bullets and booted feet continued to echo through the Walled City. The troops were chasing men through Peshawar as though it were an English hunt. At any moment he might hear a bugle, or step over a corpse with its lips sewn shut. He turned into a street so narrow it allowed in no light, and a man could press himself against a doorway and become shadow.

Years earlier, Qayyum's mother had tried to find a wife for him. Everything was agreed on when the girl fell ill and suddenly died. The whispers were quick to follow – Qayyum Gul, the half-blind man, was ill-fated. Any family which gave their daughter to him would risk disaster. Enough, Qayyum told his mother. Don't search any more. There seemed an inevitability to it; his life was already moving in the direction of politics. From the moment under the blue tarpaulin when he heard Ghaffar Khan speak of the need for Pashtuns to break their addiction to violence and revenge he knew he had found a general he could follow into any battle. When the battle was over there would be time for a wife and children – men didn't age as women did. And until then, what he wanted with immediacy and couldn't always deny himself was available here, on the Street of Courtesans.

Now, for the first time he'd ever known, the street was completely silent, its doorways closed, but he saw the curtains move as he walked its length, and ahead of him a door opened and a woman's hand, flicked at the wrist, urged him to approach. The sound of booted feet, the screams of dying men drew closer as his rapid strides made up the distance between himself and sanctuary. The door closed behind him; he was in a room that he might have been in before, large enough for a bed with frilled covers, in the company of a woman with whom he might have lain upon it, though it was impossible to know; the make-up which disguised rather than enhanced the courtesan's features was absent so she was just a tired woman past youth, a bruise beneath her eye.

The curtains, identical to those which covered the back walls of all the courtesans' rooms, were open, and for the first time he saw that there was a doorway behind. Always viewing the women along the street as rivals he had never thought that their lives were interconnected and now he struggled to imagine what they might say to each other at the end of a working day. Did they compare? The thought made the blood rise hot to his cheeks even as he stepped past the curtains, down a hallway and into a large room crowded with men, some in Congress khaddar, two in red shirts, and a few who didn't wear their allegiances on their sleeves. The room itself was simple, and homely – bolsters and rugs along the floor, repeating motifs of flowers painted in a strip along the wall, faded and peeling, but only slightly. Some of the men sat with their heads in their hands, or stared vacantly ahead, but most of them spoke to each other in urgent whispers which broke off when Qayyum entered the room and started up again when they recognised him as one of their own.

208

– We're trying to understand why they sent in the armoured cars, a Congresswalla said as he made space for Qayyum to sit down. There's Civil Disobedience all across India and nothing like this has happened.

Qayyum knew the answer. It lay in all those speeches by the English officers which had made him feel such pride when he was in the Army and thought there was honour in being identified as a Martial Race: Because they couldn't believe we were unarmed; they wouldn't believe we weren't intent on violence.

– Quiet, idiots! They're here!

Even the men who hadn't heard the words of the grey-haired, hard-faced woman who rushed into the room heard the tone of it, and fell silent. Into the void where their voices had been the sound of a fist hammering on a door rushed in, and an English voice demanded entry. The grey-haired woman looked over her shoulder at the girl who had entered behind her. It was obvious by something in her that hadn't yet been erased that she was new here. The newness gave her beauty, more than her curved kohl-lined eyes or her unpainted lips the colour of crushed rose petals. The room changed, was charged with something unpleasant, slightly dangerous, which Qayyum was as much a part of as anyone else.

The hammering on the door became more insistent and the beautiful girl walked past the men and down the hallway. Despite the whispered protest of the grey-haired woman almost half the men in the room stood up and tiptoed into the hallway so they could hear what happened when the girl opened the door and spoke in English.

– What can I do for you gentlemen?

– We need to search your premises.

– Men only enter here if they pay. Although . . . so many of you? All the girls will be exhausted by the end of the day.

– We're looking for . . .

– I know what you're looking for.

It was impossible to know what she did next; perhaps the words, their tone of power, understood even by the men in the hallway who didn't know English, were enough; the

English officer said nothing more, and before the girl had returned to the hallway the soldiers could be heard marching away. One of the men caught the girl's sleeve as she passed by him.

– She's not working, the grey-haired woman said sharply.

– I'll pay double.

– Your people called for a strike. Well, we're observing the strike here.

– Triple, then.

The grey-haired woman looked around the room at all the men.

– Triple for everyone, she said.

The men – save the one who went with the girl – returned to the seating area, and were silent now, not looking at each other. Shortly afterwards a few of the women, painted for business, entered the room and one by one men stood up and followed them into the rooms which led onto the street. Like this, over the next few minutes, more than half the men vacated the room. Qayyum, looking around at those who remained, wondered how many sought their pleasure from other men, how many stayed away from courtesans for reasons of morality or fidelity, and how many were hoping that a better option might enter the room. When the next group of women walked in their number included the one he'd been waiting for, who he visited almost exclusively because years of going to her made their relationship something more than transactional, and he smiled to see her ignore the other men and jerk her head in his direction, instructing him to follow her.

They entered her room, and he sat on the bed, watching as she turned her back to him and removed her shalwar; it was both moving and arousing, as always, this facsimile of modesty. He took off his own shalwar, folded it neatly, and placed it on the foot of the bed, hearing her familiar laugh at his military fastidiousness.

– There used to be that girl here, the English one. What happened to her?

– A knife in the heart. Some say it was an Englishman, some say it was a Pashtun. Some say it was the woman whose room

210

was across the street from her, but it's men who stick knives into the hearts of women who make them weak.

– Who was her father?

She had him in her hand, though he was ready before she touched him, when she answered:

– A man like you.

He caught her forearms and would have pushed her away, but she either mistook his intention or deliberately ignored it, and then it was too late, he was a man like all the other men who came here, and the women, all of them behind the curtained doorways, knew it.

Finally, the space between one bullet and the next widened far enough for the men to leave. They were silent exiting the Street of Courtesans so there would be no need to acknowledge where they had been, what they had done, while their brothers were dying. They knew they should return to the Street of Storytellers to retrieve the dead bodies, but most of them had wives and children at home who would be worrying about them, and it was Qayyum alone who walked directly towards the site of the massacre, knowing Najeeb would have been at the Museum all day, and was unlikely to be able to return home until the soldiers returned to their barracks.

Two cats crouched beside an unexpected rivulet snaking down the street towards Qayyum, their tongues lapping at it in tandem. He thought the scent of blood was in his nostrils, until he saw the colour of the water. It wasn't necessary to understand it to know some other horror was taking place. He followed the watery blood through streets where the silence was so unnerving he was almost grateful when it was fractured by a crack of gunfire, sporadic bursts of Inqilaab Zindabad and the cries of mourners from homes where sons and husbands had returned as corpses. As he approached the Street of Storytellers, the rivulet widened, or the alleys narrowed; either way, he had no choice but to step through the warm liquid, thicker than water as in the English expression.

* * *

211

The Street of Storytellers was in flood. Water raced down its length, carrying debris along with it – shoes, planks, cloth, a half-eaten apple. A crow swooped down onto something shiny, wet its beak, and flew up with a panicked beating of wings. Firemen hosed water onto the street as the cavalry stood guard over them.

Where were the dead, the wounded? He was up to his ankles in water now; no blood, just water.

He saw a man approach the troops stationed beside the closed doors of Kabuli Gate, hands raised above his head; Return home! came the order and the man backed away. So, no one would enter or exit the Walled City tonight. Najeeb would have to spend the night in the Museum, and in the meantime his brother would try to understand what had happened here, how all the bodies had disappeared so quickly.

On the balcony of the carpet-seller's house, located at the corner of the Street of Storytellers and an alley, three men stood like gods in judgement. One of the men was pointing to something on the street; the second man, elbows resting on the balcony, covered his eyes with his hands. The third man, in a bright green kameez, stood slightly apart, his posture revealing nothing. All the other balconies on the street were empty – those three men were the only witnesses he could see.

Qayyum ducked back into the alley, cut across the smaller side streets, twice hiding in doorways to avoid soldiers, and finally emerged into the alley with the doorway to the carpet-seller's house. He was raising his hand to knock on the door when someone pushed it open and a man with a bloodied shirt walked out.

– Were you shot?

The man looked confused by Qayyum's question for a moment, then glanced down at his shirt and shook his head.

– It's not my blood, the man said. Did she give you water?

– Who?

– The girl.

– Which girl?

But before he received an answer a young man in a red-brown kameez walked out of the house, his features in disarray.

212

Qayyum knew all the Khudai Khidmatgar in Peshawar, and this man was not one of them.

– Where did you leave her? the young man asked the blood-shirted man, who responded in a tone weary with sadness.

– I'm telling you, they took the bodies away.

– I want to see where she was.

– All right. Come, I'll show you.

The two men walked onto the Street of Storytellers and Qayyum pushed open the door to the carpet-seller's house and entered. Everything here spoke of prosperity. He was on the first-floor landing when a woman's voice called out from behind a door which was slightly ajar.

– Come inside. Don't try to escape – I have a gun.

His instinct was to run, but it would be ridiculous to survive the English troops only to be shot by a woman. Qayyum pushed the door open with his foot and stood in the doorway with hands raised above his head. The shuttered room was vast, carpeted end to end, and lit with electric lamps. At the far end stood an uncovered woman in a green kameez, pointing a pistol at Qayyum.

– Come closer.

Qayyum looked down at his wet sandals, which squelched as he shifted his weight. He lifted a foot out of his sandal and – standing on one leg – dried it as effectively as possible against his shalwar, before repeating the procedure with the other foot. He wished he wasn't so aware that the woman – just a few years past girlhood but impossible to mistake for a girl – had green eyes and long, unbound hair, and was tall enough and beautiful enough to be part-djinn. He stepped from carpet to carpet as he approached her, his bare feet treading on a startled deer, a parrot's beak. Two-thirds of the way into the room, he stopped, his eyes trying to look over her shoulder or to the left of her ear but unable to keep from sliding back to her face, which had light reddish smears around the hairline. So he looked up to the ceiling instead – a mosaic of intersecting stars and circles, with pieces of mirrorwork which captured the carpet patterns and made them part of the ceiling's intricate

213

geometry. But when the woman spoke it was impossible to look anywhere but at her.

– Why are you here?

– I'm sorry. I'll leave.

Raising his hands he started to walk backwards towards the door, his eyes fixed on the ground.

– Your shirt. You're one of the Khudai Khidmatgar?

– Yes.

– Where did they take the bodies?

The desperation in her voice made him look up.

– I don't know what happened, he said. I came up because I thought someone up here might have seen. Was someone from your household . . . ?

– My husband's sister. She was down there. Diwa.

As she said the name 'Diwa' she lowered the arm holding the pistol, and stepped out onto the balcony. He strode quickly across the room to reason with her to return inside. But arriving at the balcony he saw that the fire engines had left, the street was deserted, though troops still stood guard around and on top of Kabuli Gate. The buildings had ripples of sunlight running along their facades. All the windows were shuttered, all the rooftops deserted – no one to see Qayyum standing on a balcony over an urban river with another man's wife. The woman raised the arm still holding on to the pistol, pointing it in the direction of the soldiers at Kabuli Gate. His hand on her wrist, forcing it down; the leap of her pulse against his fingers. She rotated her wrist and he saw the imprint of his fingers, red against her pale skin.

– Do you think I don't know a bullet from this gun won't carry all that way?

– It's the bullets from the soldiers' guns which I was worrying about. But I'm sorry, I beg forgiveness from my heart. I shouldn't have touched you. And your sister – Ina lillahi wa inna illayhi rajiun.

– I don't want your prayers. Where is she?

– I don't know. I'll ask. If I hear anything, I'll come back. You said she was down there – forgive me, but what do you mean?

– When men become women and approach an enemy armed with nothing but chants then it falls to a woman to take the role of Malala of Maiwand and walk onto the battlefield to show you what a warrior looks like. She was down with the men, and there was more of a man's fire in her than in all of you.

Her arms, folded together, pressed against her torso as though she were trying to staunch a wound. Ya Allah, how many women had been on the street? He had never been comfortable with Ghaffar Khan's insistence that Pashtun women must be brought into the political movement, and now he saw with complete clarity the extent to which the man he revered above all others was wrong in this matter. In the Khudai Khidmatgar training camps Qayyum knew how to teach the men to meet violence with non-violence, and insults with patience, but what words could he say to prepare Pashtun men for this: women may be shot, their wounded bodies may need to be lifted away by strange hands, you may hear them call out in pain, you may watch them die – and to all this you can respond with nothing but a cry of Inqilaab Zindabad. The havoc it would cause (that thrum of terror which ran through the Pashtuns when the girl with the plait walked out from the ranks of men). The green-eyed woman turned her back to him, and then he couldn't find a way to stay.

He returned home, the elation of earlier in the day gone. His neighbour, the cobbler Hari Das, rushed out to greet him.

– Qayyum Gul, thank God you're safe. And Najeeb? Is Najeeb with you?

– He'll have been at the Museum all day. He probably doesn't even know what's been going on.

– I saw him walk out of here this morning, wearing an English-style achkan – I didn't know where he was going. But he left only a few minutes before the first gunshots.

He had been wearing his frock-coat? For the Englishwoman, no doubt. Idiot, Najeeb, are you with her now? Toasting a tarnished piece of silver? If there was one man in all of Peshawar to avoid a protest, stride away from gunfire, it was the Assistant at the Peshawar Museum – Hari Das knew Najeeb well enough to know this. But the old man was looking at Qayyum helplessly, not really wanting an answer about Najeeb so much as seeking reassurance that everything would be all right despite this day of gunfire and blood.

Qayyum moved towards Hari Das to embrace him. But as they touched the cobbler's mouth formed an Oh of surprise; he stepped back from Qayyum, apologising, a thick needle in his hand, tipped with darkness. Qayyum glanced at his arm to see what Hari Das was staring at. There was no pain, no rip in his kameez, so whose blood was that blooming on his sleeve?

23–24 April 1930

Vivian Rose Spencer rested her hands on the keyboard of the 'Made in Berlin' piano. Her calloused palms and lined fingers had changed more than anything at Dean's since the last dance she'd danced here. She played the opening bars of 'Feeling Sentimental' in the empty ballroom and the music bounced off the polished wood floor, skimmed the long mirrors, leapt into the antique arms of the chandelier. If she looked in the mirror long enough would she find, buried deep beneath all the twirling figures and self-conscious glances that it held, the young Vivian Rose Spencer? And at her shoulder, the ghost of Tahsin Bey. He had long since ceased to be the wound in her flesh, had worked himself deeper, invisible to all onlookers, to become the brittleness of her bones, the loneliness forever in her heart.

She couldn't remember what exactly she'd dreamed earlier in the day when her train had entered the Peshawar Valley; she only knew that she'd dreamed of him, as she hadn't in a very long time, and woken up with a constricted chest and a feeling of disorientation which revealed itself to have a reason other than dreams.

The train was moving in the wrong direction. Trouble in Peshawar, the conductor had said, when she found him; the train was returning to Campbellpur. At Campbellpur station while the other English passengers stood around arguing about whether to wait there until the situation became clearer or to take the train shortly to leave for Rawalpindi Viv walked over to the Pathan couple who had disembarked from the train, and

217

was soon on her way to Peshawar, in a donkey-cart, her purse no lighter than before but her silver-handled hairbrush now in the possession of the man who used it to brush his luxurious henna-dyed beard.

How she hated him! How she hated all the men they passed on the road as they lolled and laughed and held their faces to the breeze and called out to each other in recognition and broke their journey to saunter into an orchard and pull fruit off a branch and eat it in full view of the world, juice spraying the air. All this Viv saw – as did the unspeaking woman seated beside her – through blinkered, meshed eyes. She knew she was passing through a landscape she'd encountered before (standing at the train window with her calfskin notebook, sketching stupas, comparing her observations with Arrian's) but it was almost impossible to identify any landmarks. Her brain didn't know how to translate the criss-crossed images her eyes were sending back, her head ached with the effort of trying. Beneath the burqa she clenched her fists which were themselves restricted in their movements so that if she were to try to reach out for the other woman's arm the touch between them would be doubly cloth-encased. The rage she felt on behalf of the women of the Peshawar Valley as she sweltered beneath the voluminous burqa dispelled any ambivalence she might have started to feel about Indian demands for self-rule. All these Indians talking about political change when really what this country desperately needed was social change. Why should they be allowed independence when they only wanted it for half the population? And, what's more, her back ached.

So, the relief – she had never known anything quite like it – of arriving at Dean's. The liveried man at the gate stopped the donkey-cart from entering, and Viv stood up, hitched up the burqa so that ankles and calves and shins and hemline appeared. With a sweeping gesture of his hand the liveried man waved in the donkey-cart with Viv still in that posture: half-woman, half-tent. When the donkey stopped she stepped past the long-bearded man who started once more to brush his beard as though he were still in a situation of command here in the

218

heart of British Peshawar, and jumped to the ground. With something of the same grandness with which she had cast her first vote she threw off the vile cloth, and didn't look back.

The donkey-cart departed, the gulmohar trees blazed, a bird with an iridescent throat flew past. Viv walked through a frozen world. Same, same, same – as the merchants in the Walled City might insist while trying to draw your thoughts away from the unavailable object of your desire towards an inferior replacement. Same, memsahib, same. The red-tiled roof of the whitewashed barracks-like structure might have faded slightly, but the hedge framing the driveway was the same, the tall pines in the garden were the same, the starched white uniforms of the bearers were the same, the view towards the mountains was the same, the chatter and whistles of birds were the same, even the china teacup on the garden table with its border of roses was the same.

But the most same-memsahib-same thing of all she saw, when she walked through from the ballroom into the dining room that evening, was the Forbeses, fifteen years older but unchanged save for a few extra creases in their crumpling but lively faces. Viv joined them, was touched by their delight, and said yes, she had only just arrived and yes, she would certainly have a glass of something stronger than water.

The evening wore on, perfectly pleasant, Mrs Forbes regaled her with tales of everyone from all those years ago, most of whom Viv couldn't remember, though never mind. But at a certain point – during some story about the rumours started by a missing glove at a picnic – she found herself having to concentrate very hard to shut out the increasingly raised voices from the only other table that was occupied at this early hour of the evening.

– Bolsheviks, I tell you, Bolsheviks.
– They're Muslim fanatics, not Bolsheviks.
– They'd wear green, not red, if they were Muslim fanatics. And why are there sickles on their turbans?
– It's the Islamic crescent, not a sickle.

Mr Forbes leaned across to the arguing men and said, I say,

219

there are ladies here, and the men apologised, the voices lowered.

Mrs Forbes, pretending the whole exchange hadn't occurred, moved on to the next topic that came to mind. Such an influx of Jews in Peshawar escaping the Russian Revolution. Had Viv seen the synagogue behind Dean's? Viv had not. Oh well, said Mrs Forbes, in most ways you'll find Peshawar unchanged.

Unchanging Peshawar. That had been Viv's mantra all through the previous year in London as Mary and her parents frowned at newspapers carrying stories of Gandhi and Civil Disobedience; whatever might be going on in the rest of India the Frontier was a place apart, Viv insisted. Her father had been the first one to relent and say no little Indian in a loin-cloth will stand in my daughter's way. Dear Papa – the hierarchies of his world had only been slightly shaken by the war and the women's vote; Englishmen were still at the apex, though Englishwomen now took second place ahead of Native men. Sending Viv off to Peshawar seemed to strike him as an act of defiance against Indian agitation, which would once have pleased Viv and now struck her as faintly ridiculous. Even so, she was glad he was so easily convinced. Mama and Mary, on the contrary, were unrelenting until finally her Pashto teacher Mr Durand-not-Durrani had to be invited to her parents' home for tea in order to assure the two ladies that yes, indeed, the Frontier is a place apart. Miss Spencer, he had said, you will arrive in Peshawar to find the chicken cutlets and colonial conversations and cries of the bazaar as unchanged as the enclosing hills or the shadow of Bala Hisar Fort. Certainly the cutlets and conversations were unchanged, she thought, taking a bite of her food and listening to the Forbeses talk about their summer plans for Simla.

When Mrs Forbes excused herself and walked away Mr Forbes smiled at Viv and patted her hand.

– Always dancing to your own tune, Vivian. I've admired that in you. We both have. A burqa and a donkey-cart!

How strange to be with someone who looked at her and still saw Viv Spencer, the twenty-three-year-old. She certainly didn't want that self-absorbed girl back but even so she might just go out tomorrow to find a pith-helmet and wrap a velvet ribbon around it. Give me my glad-rags! She laughed at her own silliness and Mr Forbes raised his glass to her. The gin-and-tonic must have gone directly to her head, or perhaps it was just the musk of Peshawar's night flowers.

– And don't worry too much about the nonsense you over-hear. Something unfortunate happened in the Walled City this afternoon, but it's all under control now.

– It goes on as it goes on.

– Quite.

But later when the Forbeses had returned home and Viv sat out in a surprisingly empty garden with the two men who'd been arguing about Bolsheviks the mood was darker, the tone more dangerous. She shouldn't be here, the men agreed, as they delivered warnings of the Murderous Pathans Awakened.

– But what exactly happened today?

The men shook their heads and wouldn't answer except to say she mustn't leave Dean's tomorrow on her own, and mustn't even consider entering the Walled City. It was unclear if they didn't know what had happened or were trying to protect her female sensibilities.

The younger of the men – the one who had delivered warn-ings of the Murderous Pathans in a thrilled tone which suggested desire – rubbed the ugly scar on the back of his hand.

– It's ingratitude, that's what it is. I don't mean for the roads and the railways. But we've kept India in a state of peace for so long they've forgotten to recognise it as the greatest of all gifts.

Viv bowed her head, stopped herself from trying to play the sweetest, cruellest game she knew: imagining what her life would have been if not for the war.

There were no Victorias available to take her to Shahji-ki-Dheri, the man at reception said in the morning. No, none at all. Thank you, Viv replied, and walked out to the bicycle lean-ing against one of the pine trees in the garden. Seconds later, she was whizzing down the driveway, ringing the bell and calling out to the startled gardener to say she'd return it unharmed in a couple of hours.

Oh the joy of pedalling down the tree-lined roads with their mingling scents! The ache of her back which had been a constant companion since her fall in Karachi had intensified due to the previous day's travels, but there was a pleasure in pushing past the pain, rejecting feebleness. She rang the bell at the water-buffaloes lumbering past and at the man on the side of the road using a length of sugar cane both as walking stick and breakfast. Across the railway bridge she rode, past marching troops headed towards the Walled City. As she approached it herself the troops stationed at the closed gate called out a warning and she waved to let them know yes, yes, she had been told she must stay away from there and even though she didn't truly believe there was any likelihood Pathan men would attack a woman in a crowded bazaar she would still circle the walls to get to where she was going. On she pedalled until her linen shirt was damp with sweat, through the orchards and along the canals which ringed the Walled City. Her feet slowed on the pedals near Gunj Gate. Here she was again, on the road to Shahji-ki-Dheri.

From the fields which bordered the road the sound of blades cutting through wheat were amplified scrapes of a razor against stubbled cheeks. As she approached the Great Stupa site, another sound – spades turning soil. Najeeb! she wanted to call out, but it was soon clear the spades working furiously were in the graveyard adjoining the excavation site.

Just a little way past the graveyard Viv turned onto a donkey-path, the ground pebbled and uneven. One side of the path was still luxuriously wheat-covered, the other side had been harvested. In the midst of the denuded rows, a pit. She walked slowly across the field, taking in the complete disappearance of earlier excavations. And this most recent excavation – the Spencer excavation it would have to be called – had fallen victim to the troubles of the City. No labourers, no Najeeb, no foreman, not even a watchman to be seen.

She stepped close to the edge of the pit, looked inside.

Despite the lancing emotion not far removed from desire her movements were unhurried as she descended into the maw of the site, and approached the stump of a marble stone leg. *To the south-west of the Great Stupa a hundred paces or so, there is a figure of Buddha in white stone about eighteen feet high. It is a standing figure, and looks to the north. It has many spiritual powers, and diffuses a brilliant light.*

– Oh, she said, cupping her hand around the Buddha's ankle, running a thumb along his Achilles tendon. Oh, there you are.

She was standing in a trench around the base of the statue, not very deep. Viv crouched, pressed the back of her hand against the soil as a woman might touch the pillow of a departed lover. If it were really here!

A man traced a circle in the sand with the toe of his shoe; a woman dropped fruit and leaves into that circle. Oh there it is, Vivian Rose; you've found it for me. She pulled her hand away from the soil and wiped it on her dress. Of course the Circlet wasn't really here. She wondered if Najeeb knew her curiosity about him was her primary reason for coming – her young Pactyike, the boy she'd rescued from nuns and maulvis, grown into a man whose imagination tracked the Circlet through a thousand years from Alexander to Chandragupta to Asoka to the girl who had no name until he gave her one that was Buddhist and Greek and Hindu and Muslim in origin: Maya, of the Peshawar Valley.

She climbed out of the pit and wheeled her bicycle along the donkey-path. Turning onto the paved road, she saw a small group of men dressed in the white of mourning making their way from the direction of the Walled City towards the grave-yard. They walked in two columns, flanking a donkey-cart which must have been carrying the body. Viv stopped – one foot on the ground, one on a pedal – watching the men advance towards her. There was nothing here but fields, and crows, and Pathan men, and fresh graves.

The men at the head of the procession had seen her. They raised their eyes to hers, held her gaze. Viv jumped off the

223

bicycle and ran into the wheat field, body hunched, breath coming fast. Idiot, she swore at herself, and didn't know if it was for coming out here on her own or for feeling terror because Pathan men looked at her instead of through her. She could hear the tread of the men, the wheels of the donkey-cart. By the laws of Pashtunwali you may not attack a woman, she practised saying in Pashto.

Then the steps grew fainter; the men had turned into the graveyard. Viv wiped sweat from her face, wrinkling her nose at the tang coming from her armpits. And then, a greater terror – not dozens of footsteps, not a group of Pathans among whom at least some could be relied on to insist their brothers hold fast to Pashtunwali, but only two sets of feet walking closer, stepping into the wheat field.

– We know you're here, said a man's deep voice in English. We've come to bury our dead, not to attack a woman. Please don't believe what your people say about us.

Viv didn't move, hardly dared breathe.

– Why is she hiding? said a second voice, and it was a boy speaking Pashto.

Viv gripped a stalk of wheat, used it to pull herself up. She raised her eyes to the faraway mountains, blue against an almost white sky; the first time she'd seen them she had regarded the unexpected colouring as welcome proof that she was in an inverted Europe. The unchanging familiarity of them allowed her to slow her breath as she walked out onto the path. A man was standing there; he had picked up her bicycle from the ground and was holding the very end of one of the handlebars, his face turned away from hers. The boy, ten or eleven, looked straight at her and waved his hand in greeting as she walked out of the wheat field. She caught the other end of the handlebar, and the man holding it let go as he felt her touch travel along the steel frame.

– We will accompany you back to ensure your safety, he said, still not looking at her, and she wanted to thank him, she wanted to say she was sorry about the loss which had brought him to the graveyard, but instead she jumped onto the bicycle and pedalled as rapidly as she could, away from the boy who cried out in surprise and the man who didn't.

Safety looked like the Peshawar Museum. Viv pushed open the wooden door set in the red-brick facade and there was a sweet familiarity to the weight of it beneath her palm and to the mustiness of ancient stone and fresh ink when she stepped inside. The two giant Buddhas still stood at the far end of the high-ceilinged hall, one raising its hand at her in the Abhaya Mudra. Protection and fearlessness. To enter this place was to feel all the foolish terrors of the day slip away. She raised her hand to the Buddha to return the greeting, and heard a door opening to her left, where the Native Assistant's office used to be.

– Najeeb?

Surely the man who walked through the door – young, stout, moustached – wasn't the boy she had known. No, he wasn't. He looked apologetic, and said the Assistant hadn't yet arrived, but could he be of any help? It was quickly established that he couldn't, and Viv said she would wait for Najeeb. The man's apologetic look grew even more pronounced as he explained there had been an unfortunate incident in the Walled City the previous day because of which some people were choosing to stay indoors, and perhaps the Assistant would be of that number. He was usually here by this hour, he added. Viv fished in her satchel, and pulled out a coin.

– Can you send someone to tell him I'm here? I don't intend to leave until I see him.

Although he was clearly alarmed by the pronouncement the man took the coin and dispatched the boy who had been mopping the floor to tell the Assistant that a memsahib was waiting for him in the Museum. After ascertaining there was nothing further he could do for her he gestured to the Assistant's door and said she should wait inside, and not to hesitate to call him if there was anything she needed.

The first thing Viv saw when she walked into the spacious, white-walled office was the chair placed in front of the

225

bookshelves, beside a window. A Bombay Fornicator! On the wall there were framed photographs. She walked close, curious to see whether anything in her memory matched up to the man Najeeb had grown into. In the first photograph the familiar figure of John Marshall looked sternly into the camera, his hand on the shoulder of a much younger man – almond-eyed, crinkled-haired. Najeeb Gul, she said aloud, and the slight figure smiled back at her, recognisable. The next photograph was Najeeb again, holding a stone slab with a sea-monster carved into it in the way other men might hold a large fish they'd just caught. The third frame held his university diploma.

As she turned away from the photographs something on the desk made her walk over to the imposing desk chair and sit down at it. She picked up the paperweight and ran her thumb over the wrist of Atlas. It's your history after all, Pactyike, she'd said years ago, handing a Pathan boy this crude carving to distract him from the discovery he'd made, accepting as her due the enormity of his gratitude.

Viv stepped into the gallery of Buddhas. There he was in all sizes, all stages of life from young prince to aged ascetic, his expression almost always on either side of the border which separates smug from serene. Only in the deep-set eyes of the starving Buddha did something else emerge, a humanity beyond all other humanities. How much younger she had been fifteen years earlier when the centaurs and Tritons and fish-tailed bulls had arrested her more than this face of suffering, these fragile ribs encasing the strongest of all hearts.

There was a shift in the light. The front door had opened. A Pathan woman entered, very young and very tall, a chaddar covering her head but her face unveiled. Viv, aware that she was wearing a smile of greeting excessive in its brightness, held up her hands in apology. I thought you were someone else, she said in Pashto. The woman moved towards one of the display cabinets near the entryway without responding. Probably never spoken to an Englishwoman, Viv thought, and moved into the anteroom with the statue of Hariti so her presence wouldn't

226

make the unveiled Pathan feel self-conscious. When she returned to the main gallery the woman was still there, sitting on her haunches in front of one of the cabinets, her hand reaching out to the object on the other side of the glass.

Viv circled around the room so she could see what the woman was looking at, standing back far enough that her presence didn't draw attention to itself. She knew at a glance the stucco carving at which the woman was staring, had always been repelled and fascinated by it. Men stood next to a tomb which had broken open to reveal a grotesque figure, one half of its body a skeleton, the other half a living, healthy woman. Her right breast rounded, heavy; on the left side, only ribs. The Nurseling of the Dead Woman. The Pathan woman looked up and spoke to Viv's reflection in the cabinet glass.

– What is this?

Viv didn't move closer, but allowed her reflection to be the one to speak to the woman in whose voice curiosity was the barest patina over animosity. Speaking slowly, finding work-around phrases when her Pashto failed to present the most direct options, Viv told her the story. A king's senior wives filled him with poison against a young and beautiful wife and convinced him to bury her alive in a tomb. But because she was virtuous she was able to give birth to a child after her own death and to miraculously suckle him. For three years the child remained in the tomb with his mother, until the walls crumbled and he escaped into the jungle where he lived during the day; at night he would return to the tomb. This continued for three further years until the Buddha, in his compassion, visited the boy who became a monk as a consequence. Later, the boy converted his father to Buddhism. The story says nothing more about the mother.

The Pathan made a knowing sound at that last part, and for a moment the two of them were bound in a mutual sympathy. Or at least Viv thought as much, but then the woman rose up and turned towards Viv, as Medusa might turn from a reflection to cast a man in stone, and said, Where are the bodies?

– I beg your pardon.

– The bodies. What did you do with the bodies?

– I think you're mistaking me for someone else.

– You're English.

– Yes.

– Where did the lorries take the bodies? Give her back to me. Let me wash her corpse, let me pray at her grave, let me touch her face one last time.

The woman advanced on her as she spoke, and Viv moved backwards, thinking she should run – this Medusa, this Amazon, this grief-stricken woman might do anything – but she was transfixed by the green eyes, more haunting than the work of any stonemason.

The light changed again. A man walked through the open door. Crinkle-haired and almond-eyed.

– Najeeb!

24 April 1930

When Qayyum stretched out on his mattress for the tiniest of rests he tumbled straight into dreams in which he wore the uniform of the 40th Pathans to try and reach his brother but at every gate of the Walled City a green-eyed woman held a pistol to his heart and asked why he had killed her sister. Finally at the last gate he felt the weight of a hand on his shoulder and turned round with a cry:

– Najeeb!

– Qayyum, no, it's me. Wake up now, wake up.

Qayyum raised himself onto his elbow. Through the open window, the morning light was feeble. One of the most trusted of Ghaffar Khan's men was there, his face discoloured with weariness – darkness below the eyes, pallor everywhere else.

– What is it? What happened?

– We don't have time to talk of what happened. There's work to be done.

The British still hadn't opened any of the gates, he said, but some of the party leaders from Congress and the Khilafat Committee had been in talks with them to make allowances for the burials of those who couldn't be interred within the Walled City – the Hindus who needed to take their bodies to the crematorium, and those Muslims who wished to bury their dead beside family members at the graveyard in Shahji-ki-Dheri. The funeral processions would take place in shifts, no more than one set of mourners at a graveyard at one time, and no more than ten people were allowed to accompany each body.

229

– How many have died?

– Who can say? But only a few are being taken for burial.

– What do you mean?

– Qayyum Gul, we don't have time to talk of all the injustices of the night. Get ready, we need men to go round and explain the situation to the bereaved.

– Explain what? First the British kill our men, then they decide how we can bury them?

– This is exactly what you won't say. We must be allowed to channel all the rage of the Walled City into resolve, not allow an explosion that we'll be unable to control. Can I rely on you, General?

– Yes, sir. But . . .

– Can I rely on you, General?

– Yes, sir.

The dead man was young, childhood's mark still on his features. Qayyum lowered his head in shame as he stood in front of the body explaining to the boy's father and brothers the terms of the funeral. If only Ghaffar Khan were in Peshawar, surely this wouldn't happen. But the men accepted what he said without question. They'd worried they wouldn't be allowed to the graveyard at all; any burial was better than none.

Only one of the men appeared not to listen to anything Qayyum said. He sat on the ground, holding the hand of the dead man whose face was his face. Twins, one of the men of the family whispered to Qayyum. He carried the corpse home all the way from the Street of Storytellers; he said it was like carrying his own death. Qayyum knelt in front of the unpaired twin.

– I'm sorry. To lose a brother must be the greatest of all griefs.

The man looked up at Qayyum.

– Do you have brothers?

– Yes, one.

– Was he on the Street of Storytellers yesterday?

– No. He's in the Cantonment. He must be worrying about me but I don't know when he and I can reach each other again.

– Come with us then.

– What?

– Come with us when we leave the Walled City for the graveyard.

Qayyum waited outside the house, smoking a cigarette, while the women of the family said their farewells, their voices rising through the windows as a battalion marched past. Through the smoke of his breath he watched the English soldiers' expressionless faces. It was as though they were ghosts from some other time unaware of the cries that would pierce any living heart. He ground the cigarette beneath his heel, wished he were in an orchard away from these narrow alleys. Even at this hour, so soon after sunrise, the air was heavy. The body indoors had been surrounded by cut lemons to keep a scent of freshness about it – the family had been unable to go in search of ice during the curfew.

A donkey-cart arrived, the body was brought out, stiff as wood. Qayyum walked beside the cart as it progressed through emptied streets toward Gunj Gate, watching the driver's bare foot as it rested on the donkey's rump, the toes tapping out code for 'slow down' and 'veer right'. The animal's fur was discoloured and thinned where the man's foot rested on it, but the foot itself was smooth. Only that foot, not its pair. Love wasn't composed of grand gestures; it was found in the dead cells sloughed from a man's skin for the thousandth morning in a row without expectation of even being noticed, it was a man rubbing his brother's dead hand because he didn't know how to stand aside and do nothing while his twin's skin was ice-cold, it was a boy who learned without being told to always walk on the left-hand side of a man who had lost his right eye.

The donkey-cart took a zigzagging route past the homes of those who had known the dead boy but weren't allowed to add their voices to the prayers at his grave. Windows opened all along the donkey-cart's route and the fists of mourners released rose petals onto the corpse. Qayyum had expected to find

231

himself an impostor in this funeral procession but instead, as the Walled City rained rose petals, he was reminded that grief never leaves, It merely sinks into you. A deep sorrow. It wasn't his parents he thought of as the soldiers at the gate waved him through but the man whose features he could no longer sharply recall – Kalam Khan, hardly older than the dead boy whose body rolled with the motion of the donkey-cart until his father placed a hand on its chest to hold it still, releasing the scent of crushed roses.

Qayyum would have walked all the way to the graveyard beside the donkey-cart – to treat this funeral procession as a cover for escape was an insult – but at a certain point, as they walked past the wheat fields of Shahji-ki-Dheri the dead boy's father said to him, Go to your brother, and Allah be with you. And all the men said the words which they knew were the last the boy had heard: Inqilaab Zindabad.

He didn't slow his pace until he reached the Museum grounds, where the gardener took a single look at him and held the garden pipe in his direction. Qayyum cupped his hands, splashed the cool water onto his face and neck, smoothed down his hair. No need to embarrass his brother by running in look-ing like a crazed Pashtun. He stood up, listened a moment to the birds and touched the bark of a tamarind tree. Every morn-ing he went to the orchards thinking it would be his last day there, but the rent-collector's sympathies clearly didn't lie with his King-toasting, polo-playing employer. Or perhaps the men who socialised with Deputy Commissioners and paraded their loyalty by the portraits of kings on the wall were only disguis-ing their deeper sympathies. Peshawar is filled with Scylaxes, he would say to Najeeb, who lived in as close proximity to delight as an adult as he had done as a child.

He thanked the gardener, strode towards the door, and pushed it open. Through the archway leading into the Main Hall he saw two figures; one with her back to him advancing upon the other – an Englishwoman in trousers, her hair short as a boy's. The Englishwoman turned towards him as he entered and said, Najeeb!, her voice containing too much emotion.

– I am his brother, he said, more harshly than he'd intended, and barely had time to be disturbed by her acute look of disappointment before a thought came bearing down on him, trampling all other concerns.

– You haven't seen him? Yesterday, he didn't meet you at the train station?

– The train had to turn back. I only arrived in the evening. Someone has gone to fetch him now. No, please don't go.

The last words were spoken in Pashto to the other woman who, head down, walked past Qayyum – he stepped aside to make room for her – and, ignoring the Englishwoman's comments, proceeded out of the door.

So now it was the two of them. Qayyum Gul and the famed Miss Spencer.

– I ask for your forgiveness.

She looked over her shoulder and then pointed to herself, a question in the gesture. Qayyum nodded and stepped a few steps closer to her, recalling that Najeeb had once mentioned this high-ceilinged, wooden-floored space used to be a hall where the English came to dance. He hoped her Pashto was fluent so he could say what he needed, quickly, in a language which didn't make him feel inadequate, and be done with it.

– I came to your house with my brother and stood with my back turned towards you when I should have thanked you for taking the time to teach him.

– So that was you. But it was fifteen years ago.

– That's fifteen years in which I've failed to ask for your forgiveness.

– In all the wide world there is no one like the Pathans!

He had come to hear that idea, from other Indians and from the English, as one indicating the hot-bloodedness of the Pashtuns; but here stood an Englishwoman reflecting his people back at him with warmth and admiration. He saw too

233

keenly what there was in her that Najeeb had found so appealing as a boy, and wheeled away, a lumbering creature who didn't belong in this place where both women and statues were composed of precise gestures of forgiveness and blessing. But the woman seemed to think he had started a conversation, not concluded one, and came to stand beside him in front of the starving Buddha.

– Are you a letter-writer, like your father?

He looked sideways at her, shook his head, wondering what he was supposed to do now. In Brighton he had grown accustomed to Englishwomen – had come to enjoy their company, if he was honest. But they had all been older, and the relationship of patient and nurse clearly demarcated. What was her name – he tried to remember – that nurse in whose handkerchief he still wrapped his eye at night? How shameful to have forgotten.

Everyone, even Najeeb, assumed Qayyum's stand against Empire stemmed from Vipers, the suffering he'd been led into for a fight that wasn't his to fight. But he had never felt closer to the English than on that day. Even now, he knew hatred could never truly take root in his breast so long as he remembered Captain Dalmohy shot again and again, getting back to his feet each time as though his body were an irrelevance; and Captain Christopher, dying with Urdu words of gratitude on his lips for the sepoys who had rushed to help him. It was later, at Brighton, that the questions began. It was because of the nurses. His glass eye felt gritty in its socket. Tell them a widow gave a present to a Pathan boy – let the Empire tremble at that! It was something like that she'd said, and he'd been astonished by her audacity, the dismissal of Empire. Everything had started there.

But the only young Englishwoman he'd ever spoken to was that one – how vividly the memory came back – on the train to Peshawar. He was thinking this as the Englishwoman beside him held out a cigarette case to him and offered him its contents, her hand freckled.

– Turkish. The cigarettes are Turkish.

She smiled as if this observation of his, in English, were something wonderful, showing uneven teeth, pink gums. Now he started to think he had recognised her immediately. The large blue eyes, the angular features. But no, he hadn't. When he thought of her – and sometimes he did – what he recalled was not eyes or jawline but the impatience of her gestures, the hunger of a woman trying to be a man and failing as a result to be either man or woman. But now everything about her was more measured.

– How did you first meet my brother?

– He was my welcome committee in Peshawar the first time I arrived here. Well, not really. But when I stepped off the train, there he was.

– You were right.

– I'm sorry?

– That day, when I told you I was twenty-one years old, you said this is just the beginning. You were right.

Her look of confusion disappeared the moment he pointed to his glass eye, and then her hand covered her mouth and the two of them stood and looked at each other, directly now in a way that hadn't been possible until this moment, excavating their memories for what remained there of the train journey, one speaking in Pashto, one in English.

– You sketched all the way from the Indus to Peshawar.

– I barged into your compartment!

– You offered me half your bread roll.

– You refused that, but you took the cigarette later.

And then they both said, Turkish! and laughed, as if something miraculous had happened. Qayyum thought, wait until I tell Najeeb.

– Where is he, that brother of mine? In the house with his broken statues?

– He has broken statues at home?

– At home. No. What do you mean, at home?

– Someone went to get him from his house. They say, because of all this trouble, he probably decided to stay in the Walled City. Oh, there's the fellow who went to get him.

235

Qayyum turned round, trying to fight the rising, ridiculous panic. The peon at the Museum was shaking his head at the Englishwoman, saying, The soldiers won't allow me into the Walled City.

– But he's here, Qayyum said, walking across to the peon, catching hold of his arm. He was here yesterday. He stayed in the Cantonment overnight.

The peon shook his head.

– No, he said, he didn't come in yesterday at all.

Qayyum pushed the peon aside and strode out of the door. He was here yesterday, Najeeb Gul, my brother, he was here. And the gardener: no, not yesterday. He never came. Qayyum put a hand out, felt rough bark beneath his skin. The Englishwoman had followed him out. Mr Gul? she said, and her voice was shrill, awful. He gritted his teeth against the sound, and ran out of the grounds towards the Walled City.

Kabuli Gate was closed, but as he approached it opened to allow a car driven by an Englishman to drive in. Running, he was through, and within the Walled City again.

– Stop. Stop right there.

Strange, how a command delivered in an English accent still made him want to salute. He turned towards the voice, and there was an English officer with two sepoys on either side of him, their rifles pointed at Qayyum.

– Lance-Naik Qayyum Gul, 40th Pathans. Sir!

The sepoys looked uncertainly at the officer, who signalled to Qayyum to approach him, his expression entirely disbelieving.

– On leave, are you?

– Discharged due to injuries sustained in battle, sir.

– Which battle?

– Vipers, sir. Ypres.

Of all the words known to the English, only Somme had greater power. Not King, not Country, not Christ could stand against Ypres. Even so, he didn't expect the Englishman to step forward and hold out his hand.

– My father died there. Royal Fusiliers.

236

Qayyum took the Englishman's hand, unable to discern if he was feeling anything at all beyond anxiety that a green-eyed woman might be watching him from a balcony down the street, aiming a pistol at his head.

24 April 1930

Viv picked her way among the severed hands, the headless
torsos, her shoes leaving faint prints in the dust of the
chequered tiled floor. The groupings were by body parts: arms
and feet and heads and torsos and legs of all sizes together, like
placed with like so that variety might emerge.

The stout man in the Museum had told her that it had been
Najeeb's idea to undertake the cataloguing of detritus: all the
excavated pieces too fragmented, too poorly crafted to ever
have a hope of being displayed. Such work was a labour of
labour, he said, and no one else showed much enthusiasm for it,
but Najeeb had obtained permission to turn the elongated
reception room of a departed official's house into a field of
broken stone. A notebook lay on the window ledge, and Viv
picked it up. *Item 1. Takht-e-Bahi 1911–12. Torso with drapery,
stump of left arm ending above elbow. 18.7 L. Crude. Late Kushan?*
She walked over to the cluster of torsos, located the one with
the number 1 chalked onto it, walked to the next one, read the
accompanying entry. Continued on, feeling the world steadying
around her for the first time in the day.

*Item 184. SKD 1908–9. Left hand. 5.5 L x 2.8 W. Lower-
right palm missing. Three fingers curled into fist. Index finger bent
at first and second joint. Effective foot scratcher.* Sliding her foot
out of its shoe she rested it against the extended index finger
of the upturned Gandhara hand and moved it forward and
back. There were pleasures large and small here from the
foot-scratching hand to the jigsawing together of a fish-tail

238

with a human torso to reconstitute an ichthyocentaur from Takht-i-Bahi. But her favourite thing of all was Najeeb's pairing of two abraded heads of almost identical size, one Greek in features, one Indian, separated by three centuries or more. He had laid them down in profile so they looked each other in the eye, their mouths inches apart each other. Was this an expression of his own proclivities or an acknowledgement of the passionate intimacy of Pathan men, sexual and otherwise? Who had the boy she'd adored grown into, and how long would it be before movement in and out of the Walled City would become possible again so she could find out?

But how extraordinary that his brother should turn out to be the one-eyed Herakles. She smiled at the memory of their mutual wonder, and wished he hadn't run out so abruptly. She had asked the peon what he and Mr Gul had said to each other in Hindko, and his answer was an unhelpful Nothing, memsahib, though he was more obliging when the stout man asked him to accompany Miss Spencer to the house of fragments.

A cool breeze, accompanied by the heavy clatter of water. The peon had turned the garden pipe onto the bamboo blinds of the verandah which ran along one side of the house. Viv walked over to the window and leaned out, calling out her thanks to the dark shape on the other side of the blinds. Easing herself onto the window frame, she swung her legs out and stepped down so she was in the shadowed verandah. She fanned the front of her blouse to bring some relief to her clammy skin and moved forward to look through the chink between blinds, wet bamboo against her cheek; the colours in the garden were bleached by sunlight, tree limbs sagging. Viv had a brief, glorious, image of a jugful of ice cubes which she could pour down the front of her dress, but felt too stupefied by the heat to go in search of a kitchen. Foolishly she sat down on a wicker chair, and then it was doubtful she would be able to get up again. She watched a bead-eyed lizard dart up the wall and stop, stilling entirely, as though, having sped towards

239

this spot, it couldn't remember why it wanted to be here or think of what next to do.

She must have fallen asleep in the shaded verandah because the light was muted when she opened her eyes and saw the peon bending over, his hands resting on his knees, looking at her in concern. He jumped back, apologising, and she shook her head which seemed to be the only part of her awake – everything else gripped by sleep.

– Water, she said, and he held out a glass filled with liquid. She drank more than half its contents before tossing the rest of it at her face and neck. The water was warm, but even so, it did the trick of rousing her, though she hadn't anticipated the transparent rivulets that would snake down her blouse.

– Thank you, she said.

– Memsahib, the peon responded in a tone which did no more than acknowledge she had spoken.

Memsahib. Such a peculiar word. In this country filled with titles and honorifics nothing pre-existing had suited English-women; while the ubiquitous 'sahib' came to rest comfortably on the shoulders of Englishmen, something other than 'begum-sahib' had to be devised for their female counterparts. As if to say that Englishmen and Indian men, for all their differences, could still be described in the same language but the women of the two races were so far apart that they had to be categorised separately, kept separate.

– What is your name?

– Dil-daraz.

– Dil-daraz, there was a woman in the museum with me. She would have been leaving as you arrived. Have you seen her before?

The boy slid a bare foot back and forth in the dust, and moved his head in that way which was halfway beneath a yes and a no.

– Memsahib, no, but she said to say something to you. I didn't want to bother you with it.

– What did she say?

240

– She said all she wants is to know where her sister is. If there is anything you hear, she lives in the carpet-seller's house on the Street of Storytellers. Chand Carpets, anyone can tell you which it is.

– I know Chand Carpets. Thank you, Dil-daraz.

– Memsahib, I hope this doesn't trouble you.

She shook her head, and stood up to leave accompanied by the boy, Dil-daraz – the most unlikely-looking character to have the name 'Heart's Drawer'. The space between dreams and reality was wider in India than anywhere else in the world.

The Forbeses still lived in the bungalow with a garden which was exceptional in its lushness even by the high standards of Peshawar. Viv followed the young man in white livery, who looked disorientatingly like the old man in white livery who had worked here in 1915, along the pathway shaded by trees so tall only the top of St John's spire could be seen through them. When she entered the bungalow and closed the door behind her everything was plunged in darkness, the heavy curtains muffling light more successfully than it kept out the late-afternoon heat; but gradually, outlines became objects and Viv found herself surrounded by the familiar disorder of Forbes books and Forbes shoes. And then there was Mr Forbes walking in from the door which led to the garden – the spade in his arms and the grass stains on his trousers indicating that the same person who would draw his curtains against the day would then step out and toil in it.

– Heave-ho!

Mr Forbes hoisted the spade, scooped up a few books and knocked others onto the floor to make space for Viv on the sofa. The liveried man moved forward to lift up the books, and Mr Forbes waved him away, the spade in his hand making the gesture a dangerous one, for which he laughingly apologised before sending the young man to the kitchen with instructions for tea. He excused himself as well, holding up his soiled hands in explanation. While he was away Viv made a pile of all the books on the floor, and carefully brushed away the clinging

241

mud which had transferred itself from the spade to a thick book with soft leather binding. There was a welcome peace in watching the mud fall to the speckled stone floor in a room heavy with the scent of jasmine buds, strings of which hung from the rotating ceiling fan.

– Mrs Forbes should be with us in a few minutes.

Mr Forbes, still in his grass-stained trousers but with hands that were well scrubbed, sat down on the armchair adjacent to Viv, nothing in his lined face with its ruffled eyebrows indicating that there was anything untoward about Viv dropping in during the middle of the afternoon when Mrs Forbes was undoubtedly taking an afternoon rest.

– I'm so sorry to disturb you. I just didn't know where else to go, or who else to ask.

– What is it, my dear?

– What happened yesterday on the Street of Storytellers?

– I shouldn't worry about it, Miss Spencer.

– Mr Forbes, if I can be very frank?

– Perhaps we should wait for Mrs Forbes?

– I worked as a VAD nurse in London for almost every day of the war that I wasn't in Peshawar. You can guess what I saw, what I heard. Do you think I'm not equipped to cope with news of a skirmish in the Walled City?

Mr Forbes sighed, and sat back, his fingers bridged together, trembling against the tip of his nose. He had been one of the leading surgeons in Peshawar before his retirement and though Viv had never known him during his professional life his palsy struck her as an example of life's cruelties.

– Things got out of hand.

– What does that mean?

– There was some inexperienced fool – allowed himself to get worked up by a baying mob and called in the armoured cars when it wasn't necessary. And then – well, Pathans. In so many ways the finest men you'll ever meet, but the first sign of a fight and the blood rushes to their brains.

– How many died?

The door opened and the liveried man entered with a tray on

242

which there were biscuits and the usual sort of tea for Viv, and kahwa, scented with cardamom and almonds, for Mr Forbes. Fifteen years earlier she'd asked him when he planned to move back to England and he'd repeated the word 'England' back to her as if it were a strange vegetable that he had no intention of adding to his diet. They sat silently until the Native man left the room, closing the door behind him on Mr Forbes' instructions.

– All things considered, it was something of a miracle. Several injuries. Broken bones, lacerations, that kind of thing. One fellow got his finger shot off, but if a man can't hold on to his own gun he probably deserves it. Oh, and a horse was shot dead. Mrs Forbes is particularly upset about that. But the only chap who died was a dispatch rider – Bryant. Ignored orders, and rushed in where he wasn't supposed to go. Right into the path of the armoured car. Terrible thing. And then, I regret to say . . . well, never mind.

– VAD nurse, Mr Forbes.

– The savages set him on fire.

– While he was still alive?

– Probably not, but does that matter?

– Are you saying the only Englishman who died was killed by our armoured cars?

– There's no need to sound disappointed by the ability of our troops to withstand attack.

– I'm struggling to understand, that's all. And how many Peshawaris died?

He shook his head and picked a book off the side table, turning it round in his hands, examining its bindings as though it were the Gutenberg Bible rather than a tome on military campaigns of the North-West Frontier.

– Were there any women among the dead?

– Have you been listening to some Congress propaganda? They don't waste a moment! Here comes Mrs Forbes. We mustn't talk about this in front of her.

The rules of the Peshawar Club were clear: if you were an Englishman you could apply for membership; if you were an

243

Englishwoman you could enter as the guest of a member. But there were other rules in place which governed the interaction of the Indian guards with the ruling race, and when Viv arrived after dinner at Dean's, uninvited, unaccompanied, she merely showed the guards a profile of sufficient disdain to ensure they wouldn't question her right to be there. How badly she'd behaved with Remmick, accepted his favours as if they were her due – no, as if she were doing him a favour by allowing him to claim her as his guest. No one should ever be beautiful and young at the same time; it deranged the mind. Not that it excused his behaviour, of course. She wondered where in the world he'd got to by now.

Viv stopped along the pathway leading to the familiar single-storeyed club house with its multi-arched verandah, bracing herself against a palm tree with one hand so she could remove the drawing pin which had lodged itself into the heel of her python pumps. The days of derangement had passed. Now, however fashionable her hemline and heels, she was a spinster nearing forty, one of the tragic-but-uncomplaining women in a generation which had lost its men to the Great War. This was the story assumed of her, and she supposed it was true in its own way. There had been other men since the war ended – before the war ended, in fact – but joining one's life to any of them in perpetuity always seemed to entail more loss than gain.

Indoors, the Club was as crowded as she'd ever seen it except during a ball but there was nothing of a festive atmosphere in the rooms heavy with smoke and whispers. Viv stood in the doorway, trying to decide whether or not to enter, until a slightly hysterical high-pitched laugh, which came from a man, decided it. Backing out, she walked around the club building and through the trees to the swimming pool from which no sounds of splashes and merriment issued despite the warmth of the night.

Beyond the rectangle of liquid darkness, a group of men sat on deckchairs and loungers, the ends of their lit cigarettes tracking the movements of their arms as they jabbed at the air.

244

Sounds swooped across to her, too tangled for words to emerge. All the men seemed to be speaking at the same time. She took off her shoes – the grass prickling her foot through silk – and, still unseen in the shadow of a palm tree, slipped off her rolled garters and stockings and stuffed them into her handbag. Beneath the high diving board the darkness was particularly concentrated, and it was here she sat, her legs stockinged in water beneath the knee.

Eventually she heard the muffled tread of a man's shoes on grass and though she held herself very still he walked straight towards her, stopping a few feet away to climb onto the low diving board, fully clothed. He walked to its end and, disappointingly, sat down, legs dangling just above the water's surface. He didn't look at Viv at first, but she knew he was aware of her. She had seen him – red-faced as ever – as she stood in the doorway, and it was unsurprising that he'd either seen her too or else been informed she was there by someone who knew he was a man who liked to know everything that went on in this city. There seemed barely any change in him since he'd walked into Dean's on her second day in Peshawar, which said more about how middle-aged he'd looked in his youth than how young he looked in middle age.

– I'm surprised to find you here tonight.

– I could say the same of you, Miss Spencer. How did you get here from Campbellpur?

– So you knew I was on the train.

– Of course. Why are you surprised to find me here?

– I'd thought you'd be behind locked doors, making important decisions about important things.

She couldn't make out his expression in the darkness as he removed a cigarette from its case, and patted his pockets.

– Catch.

She threw her lighter at him; it flashed silver in the darkness, and disappeared into the water. Without a word, barely a sound, he slipped off the diving board, the sleeves of his jacket briefly ballooning before the water dragged him down. Viv stood up, wondered whether to call for help from the men in deckchairs

245

who remained engrossed in their conversation, and settled instead for lying flat beside the pool, her sequinned garter looped around her wrist, and plunging her arm into the wavering darkness. Diamonds of light flared in the water; something pressed against her fingertips and she started to jerk away before she recognised the familiar shape of the lighter and closed her fist around it.

Remmick pulled himself out of the water, and lay down on his back with a squelching sound, eyes fixed on the jut of the high diving board. Viv struck the lighter, was amazed to find it working, and offered him a lit cigarette. When he didn't move she held the cigarette a few centimetres from his mouth and his head eased off the cement floor to take it between his lips, the length of a filter between her fingers and his kiss. She found herself imagining something that should be ludicrous, and by the catch of his breath knew he was imagining it too. She moved a few feet away, and everything that had started to happen stopped. When Remmick spoke his words leaned into each other, and she realised he was drunk.

– Remember when the Tochi Scouts were here on leave and one of them rode a motorcycle up the stairs of the diving board and then dropped — whoosh! — into the pool?

– Whoosh? I must have missed that.

– Really? 'Twasn't you? Could've sworn it was. Anyone else would've been thrown out of the Club, but everyone recognised those fellows spend all that time in the tribal areas, Peshawar the oasis where they can let their hair down. That's what it is, you know. An oasis. The place which isn't all those other places in the Frontier.

– Or wasn't all those other places?

He closed his eyes and there was a sound which was almost a sob.

– How bad is it? Viv asked. He held his arm up and pushed the sleeve back so she could see his wristwatch.

– What time is it?

– Nine twenty-three. No, wait, I think your watch has stopped. Must be the water. A few minutes past then.

246

– Within an hour we'll have abandoned the Walled City.

– Who?

– We. The British. We're pulling out the troops.

– Why?

– Because idiots and cowards are running things.

He crossed his arms over his chest like a pharaoh, eyes still closed.

– And you'll have to leave tomorrow. All women and children being evacuated.

– Could you please sit up and start making sense?

Several seconds passed in silence. The men in the deckchairs stood up and walked across the lawn toward the verandah, not looking in her direction, their eyes fixed in front of them in a way that made it clear they were aware of her and would take back news to the dining room of an assignation beside the pool. She tapped Remmick's forehead with the lighter. His eyes opened and he said, Go back to England.

– We did something terrible yesterday, didn't we?

He put his hands to his ears, began to hum 'Makin' Whoopie', and she shivered, wondering what could bring this man – always so assured, so solid – to this teetering place.

– The lorries, she said. The humming stopped, almost mid-note.

– Who told you?

Viv tasted blood in her mouth. It wasn't her imagination. There was blood, real blood, she was swallowing it. And an ache in her tongue where her tooth had driven into it.

– Someone in a position to know, she said, and her voice was measured, without judgement.

– What was done had to be done, he said.

She closed her hand around the solidity of the lighter. There was a lesson she'd learned many years ago, though she hadn't understood it at the time: how to coax information out of someone, how to make them believe you would never use it against them.

– If there'd been funerals this morning, all those bodies paraded around the street!

247

In her voice there was just the right mix of horror at what would have ensued and sympathy for the decision that had to be made to prevent it. There was a tiny exhalation – she understood it to be relief – from Remmick, before he responded:

– Mayhem. Absolute mayhem. The bastards, beg your pardon, would have whipped the entire Walled City into a frenzy.

– But we've lost the City all the same?

– Bolton – he's cracking up. Somehow they've got him convinced that there's a dam about to burst unless he withdraws the troops. It's madness. We've contained it. We've done what had to be done.

– How many were there in the lorries?

She placed a hand on his shoulder as she asked the question; a woman appreciative of men who did what had to be done.

– I don't know. I didn't ask.

– Where were they taken?

– Six feet under. Beyond that, I don't imagine anyone other than Caroe knows.

– Caroe?

– Man in charge of it. He'll go far.

A lone cricket chirped in the vicinity of the oleander tree.

– Shall I tell you something I never understood, she said. My mother had a friend who lost a son in the Great War; he was buried in France. This was a woman who couldn't venture more than ten feet from her house without treating it as if she was going on the Grand Tour. But on Armistice Day she heard the news on the radio, walked out of her door and didn't stop until she was at her son's grave. He'd been dead three years. Why should standing at a grave matter? But it mattered more than anything else in all the world.

Remmick sat up, then stood, entirely steady on his feet.

– You will keep your own best interests at heart, won't you, Miss Spencer?

– It's a vexed matter, to decide what those might be.

– Oh, not really. For instance: it wouldn't be in your best interests to give anyone reason to go over the unfortunate matter of your wartime record.

248

Viv stood too, and slipped her shoes onto her bare feet, which gave her the advantage of several inches over him.

– Unfortunate. So speaks the man who was sipping tea at Dean's while his countrymen were in the trenches at the Somme. And while I was nursing those men.

– You see, the question of your loyalties. I don't like bringing it up. But I kept my eye on you, after you left here. I know about the letters you sent to the War Office, accusing a man who worked there of lying to you, and of murdering – what was your phrase – a man with more nobility in his little finger than the entire War Office has in all its bloated carapace?

– I barely remember those letters. I was . . . upset.

– Yes, that was clear. And it was clear why. But if this proclivity for the King's enemies should prove to be habitual –

– Proclivity?

– You used to speak to me about him, though never before you'd had a drink or two. Men aren't such fools in matters of the heart as women like to think. So, that was the Turk. And now you're here to see the boy to whom you had that unnatural attachment. People used to talk about it – I always defended you. He was just a child. But he's a grown man now, with a Red Shirt brother.

The emptiness, the terrible emptiness of it, would it never leave her? For what had she betrayed that dear man, that mentor, that friend, that love? For men like Remmick. For the crumbs of their approval. Not just the whip-thin man from the War Office, but Papa, too, who even now was a shadow in her mind, telling her women didn't understand the weighty decisions that men must make on their behalf.

The verandah doors opened and a small group of people came out, headed by one of the men who had been sitting in the deckchairs, Remmick's wife walking beside him. Remmick turned his head at the sound of her voice, and called out, Darling, look who I found sitting out here. It's Miss Spencer.

– She's not still Miss Spencer, I'm sure, said his wife, walking rapidly across the garden. She looked at Viv's hand for a wedding ring, her glance travelling to take in her unstockinged legs and Remmick's wet clothes.

– He saved my lighter from death by drowning, Viv found herself saying, holding up the silver rectangle as though it were the guardian and proof of her chastity, and her voice was steady as the world hurtled into the cold darkness and she allowed herself to be pulled along with it towards the lights of the club building, Remmick by her side.

24 April 1930

Najeeb wasn't at home; he wasn't in either of his sisters' houses; he wasn't in Khan Sahib's clinic where planks of wood had been nailed to the wall to make extra beds for the wounded; he wasn't on the very short list of those who had been taken to the English-run hospitals in the Cantonment; he wasn't in the back room of Avtar Singh, the antique dealer's, shop, so lost in artefacts that he was unaware his brother and nephews and brothers-in-law and the cobbler Hari Das were striding around the Walled City with his photograph in hand, knocking on doors, saying, Have you seen this man? He wasn't with this friend or that friend or the boy he walked back from school with ten years earlier. He wasn't at the mosque to which he never went except for Eid prayers; he wasn't at the neighbourhood tea shop which was closed; he wasn't at any of the places to which he might go in search of Qayyum if he were the one trying to find his brother. He wasn't, no, that wasn't him in the corner of Qayyum's eye; he wasn't the man who threw that shadow against the wall; he wasn't the force which knocked over the mosque-reflecting mirror leaning against a tree so that it held the sky, placed clouds within reach. He was everywhere until Qayyum looked closer, and then he was nowhere.

Troops patrolled the perimeter wall, looking towards the hills where word of the massacre would have reached the tribes; six men from the Congress Party stood on the stairs of the

251

Municipal Library, their skin red, sun-flayed – they had been made to stand there since the morning when they tried to picket a liquor shop; round the corner came the sound of a lathi striking a man's flesh.

Qayyum kept his eyes to the ground, instructed his nephews to do the same, and moved from house to house, knocking on doors. Have you seen this man? He was wearing a frock-coat yesterday. In one of the houses a very old woman touched the photograph and said, You're lucky to have this; my son is missing and all his father can do to try and find him is take our daughter to unveil herself in front of strangers and say imagine if she were a boy. But otherwise every house was the same: No, I'm sorry, I haven't. Go to the Congress offices, go the Khilafat offices, that's where they took the bodies – but Qaayum shook his head and moved on.

It was evening already by the time Qayyum crossed the square dominated by the domed structure of Hastings Memorial. Troops stood guard around it, protecting the memory of an Englishman who had died decades earlier; a group of boys, a few feet away, spat pulpy sugar cane in the direction of the soldiers. Their aim fell short, but they didn't move closer, and the soldiers ignored them.

– Get out of here; go home.

Qayyum had hardly touched one of the boys, a gentle push to move him along, when all the boys scattered and ran, shouting Inqilaab Zindabad as if it were the chorus to a game. Qayyum walked past the monument and entered the Street of Jewellers; overhead, the flapping of a paper kite trapped in wires magnified the silence by disrupting it. Further along the street a tea-shop – Khalsa Hotel, the signboard said – was the only establishment open for business. Two long, low benches usually occupied by customers were being used as parallel tracks for a game of marbles by men whose turbans identified them as a Wazir and a Marwat – they sat facing each other, simultaneously flicking two marbles along the length of both benches, glass ricocheting off glass.

Shaking his head apologetically at the owner of the

252

tea-shop who hurried forward to ask what he wanted, Qayyum showed the marble-players the picture which was already thinning at the corner where his finger had been gripping it all day: Najeeb at Taxila, pointing at a double-headed eagle carved in stone. The Wazir shook his head and the Marwat said he looked as if he needed to sit down, drink some tea, play a game of marbles. The owner of the tea-shop wiped his hands on the end of the turban draped over one shoulder and took the picture from Qayyum.

– I saw him. Yesterday, on the Street of Storytellers. He was wounded.

– Where? Wounded how badly?

– His shirt was all blood, I don't know.

– Shirt?

– He's a Khudai Khidmatgar, yes? He was wearing a red shirt, shouting Inqilaab Zindabad. I saw him, and then he went deep into the crowd, and when I saw him again two men were carrying him and his shirt was all blood, and that's all I saw.

– No, that wasn't him.

– No? Allah alone knows – how can our minds make sense of such scenes?

A marble bounced on the ground and came to rest beside a cat curled under the stool. The animal looked up at Qayyum, a thick film over its eyes. Beneath its paw, a green-flecked cat's eye.

The Congress office was only a short distance from Hastings Memorial but darkness came quickly and the day had moved from evening to night by the time Qayyum approached the door from behind which there was the sound of raised voices, typewriters, a ringing telephone. He knocked several times before the door opened and a Congresswalla he knew – the lawyer, Abdul Hakim – stepped out, closing the door behind him, his exhausted expression giving way to a smile of surprising warmth.

– Qayyum Gul, I haven't seen you all day. I was beginning to worry you were among those we lost yesterday.

– I've been looking for my brother. I need to see the bodies. There are some which haven't been claimed?

He could barely understand his own words spoken with a tongue which felt sluggish in his mouth, but Abdul Hakim placed the palm of his hand against his own forehead in a way which suggested he understood better than Qayyum did.

– Please. Where are they? I need to know he's not among them.

– We took them to the Khilafat offices yesterday evening. So that all the dead would be in one place. To make it easier for the families.

– I'll go there, then. Thank you.

Abdul Hakim caught him by the shoulder as he started to walk away.

– We did it to make it easier for the families. We thought it would make things easier. They were in the care of the Khilafat Committee.

Qayyum didn't know what the lawyer was trying to tell him. The Khilafat Committee in Peshawar was practically indistinguishable from Congress, the membership overlapping, anti-Imperial strategies planned and executed together.

– I'll go there, then, he repeated; and Abdul Hakim said, I have a car; I'll drive you.

Military pickets remained in place but no one was attempting to stop or question passers-by any longer, and the numbers out on the street were greater than earlier in the day. Unaccustomed to car travel, Qayyum braced his hands against the dashboard. Speed blurred the night sounds together, only the muezzin's call for Isha prayers remaining distinct. The Khilafat offices were closed, no light seeping from beneath doors or through windows, but Abdul Hakim didn't even slow, as if he already knew there was no one there, and continued driving in silence through the Walled City. Perhaps he had no destination; perhaps they would drive and drive in circles, for ever on their way to the place where the bodies were laid out, and while they circled Najeeb would be neither alive nor dead.

254

The muezzin's voice rose higher. His words, stitched into the air of the Walled City, were a challenge, not a lament. Every morning Qayyum greeted the day by swearing the oath of the Khudai Khidmatgar: In the name of God who is Present and Evident, I am a Khudai Khidmatgar. I will serve the nation without any self-interest. I will serve people without regard to their religion or faith. I will not take revenge and my actions will not be a burden for anyone. My actions will be non-violent. I will make every sacrifice required of me to stay on this path.

The muezzin's voice – Ash-hadu-anna; I bear witness – turned the oath into a provocation. Why swear to God using the word 'sacrifice'? Which man had it in him to be Ibrahim? In a field a rabbit with sewn lips thrashed in the grass, its dying breaths drawn alone.

– Nearly there now, the lawyer said, turning into a street only just wide enough for his car. Almost immediately, he braked. A press of people was gathered outside the front door of a house Qayyum recognised as belonging to a municipal commissioner who was also one of the notable figures of the Khilafat Committee. One man was knocking on the door, a rhythmic repetition to the action which suggested he'd been doing so for a while; the other men – and two women – stood silently, looking up at the shuttered windows.

– So much for secrecy, the lawyer said, reversing out and driving a short distance to the parallel street.

Here he knocked on the door of the house which backed onto the Municipal Commissioner's house, and whispered a few words to the broken-nosed man who answered. The man stood to one side and gestured towards the stairs which Qayyum and Abdul Hakim climbed up to the roof. Overhead, a low-hanging moon, clustered stars. A row of bulrushes planted in troughs separated the broken-nosed man's roof from the Commissioner's, their spiked tips etched in sharp relief against the sky. Together Qayyum and the lawyer moved one of the troughs – a metallic scraping sound – and entered the property of the Municipal Commissioner.

He was standing alone at the edge of his roof, looking through the narrow slit between the khus mats which formed a wall facing the street.

– They won't go away until you tell them what they need to know, Abdul Hakim said. The Commissioner turned sharply, though it seemed impossible he hadn't heard the sound of the trough being moved, and was visibly relieved to see the Congresswalla and the Khudai Khidmatgar.

– What can I tell them? I don't know where they took them.

– Qayyum Gul's brother has been missing since yesterday.

Abdul Hakim pushed Qayyum forward slightly, and the Commissioner raised his hands, palms facing Qayyum as if to say, I'm defenceless, you can't attack me.

– He was in a frock-coat. Have you seen him?

– A frock-coat, no. No, there was no one in a frock-coat. I swear on the Qur'an. I would have remembered that.

The Commissioner's manner changed after that, becoming more confident, almost avuncular. He placed an arm around Qayyum's shoulder, and said, He's probably been arrested, so many have. We'll go tomorrow to the Kabuli Gate police-thana and find him. I'll come with you.

The relief of an explanation was dizzying. Qayyum wanted to embrace the older man, who he decided he must have loved and admired for years. This stalwart of the city. This sage who walked among the powerful and used his influence for those who had none. How fortunate it was to live in an age which demanded the best from the best, and allowed them to illuminate the world.

– Go downstairs and tell those people you'll find their brothers and sons as well, Abdul Hakim said, sitting on the lip of a trough so the bulrushes formed the high back of a throne of gold behind him.

– Do you think I had a choice? the Municipal Commissioner said.

– No? Explain it to me. Explain it to Qayyum Gul who has spent all day looking for a man who can't be found.

Qayyum wanted only to return home with his relief and tell his sisters and nieces and nephews and brothers-in-law that they would find Najeeb tomorrow, and tease him about the English frock-coat which couldn't keep him from being thrown into prison. He walked over to the khus mats, looked through a gap between them at the street below. The numbers seemed to have grown, and someone had taken the place of the man knocking on the door, without disrupting the rhythmic thud-thud thud-thud. Across the street, someone opened a window and said, Enough now, enough! and one of the women below cried out, Where is my son?

– Tell me what else I could have done, the Municipal Commissioner said. Caroe called us together – four of us – and said we had to hand over the bodies. The ones in the Khilafat offices, the ones in the Madrassa, all of them. Do you think he phrased it as a request?

– What?

– Now you hear the truth, Qayyum Gul, the lawyer said. Go on, Mr Commissioner, tell us how you tried to resist. Tell us you said take me to prison, put a bullet through my brain, but I will not be a part of this shameful, criminal act.

The Municipal Commissioner winced at the bite of the word 'Mr', but the rest of the sentence had him flicking his hand at the lawyer, dismissing him.

– What do you understand of it, Abdul Hakim? Caroe was right; he said if there's a mass funeral tomorrow no one – not the Congress, not the Khilafat Committee, not Gandhi and Ghaffar together if they were here – will be able to control the passions of the city. Haven't we had enough bloodshed already?

– Oh, oh, listen to him! He was acting in Peshawar's best interests. Oh Qayyum Gul, are you witnessing this?

– Remember Chauri Chaura, the Municipal Commissioner said, his voice stern, reminding the two other men that he was the oldest here. After your Congress volunteers burnt the police station Gandhi called off the entire Non-Cooperation Movement. Do you want something like that to happen again? Here? So that all the rest of India, all the Congress officials, can say those savage men of the Frontier! How can we trust them to be part of a movement of non-violence?

257

Abdul Hakim spread his hands in Qayyum's direction as if to say, Can you believe this?

– I don't understand. What did they do with the bodies? Qayyum asked.

The lawyer made a sound which would have been a laugh if it had contained any humour.

– Probably threw them into the nearest river or in some ditch somewhere.

– Don't start these ridiculous rumours! They were buried according to full Muslim rites. Caroe swore that.

– What, even the ones who weren't Muslim?

– Enough, Qayyum said, holding up his hand. His voice was ragged with anger when he said to the Municipal Commissioner, Those people down there, they want to bury their dead. Some way could have been found to allow them to do that.

– Really? said the Municipal Commissioner. You think after a day like yesterday Peshawari men would quietly walk behind row after row of shrouded bodies, including the body of a young girl shot dead by an English bullet. And not just any young girl. The angel on the Street of Storytellers. You should have seen the men in the office when she was brought in, the ones who recognised her particularly. I thought their hearts would burst right there.

– What girl, what angel?

The lawyer stood up.

– Didn't you see her, Qayyum? Yesterday, on the Street of Storytellers. A figure made of light stood on a balcony, dispensing water to the men on the street below; the water itself liquid light, a miracle. The English officers saw her standing there, a sign of Allah's grace, and shot her with every single gun in their artillery. She plunged from the balcony, a falling star, and only when she landed, dead, did the light extinguish, and the men saw it wasn't an angel against whose brightness they had closed their eyes even as they drank her blessing, but a Peshawari girl, blessed by the Almighty.

In the silence that followed the lawyer struck a match and in a completely different voice, flat, slightly cynical, added, That's what the man who told me about it insisted, though I know he was hiding at home all day. He extended his arm, held the match against the spiked tip of a bulrush and stepped back. A circle of brightness flared; a string of gold unspooled from the circle, wrapped itself around the dense tip of the bulrush, and the flames caught. Within seconds there was a wall of fire, the shapes of individual bulrushes visible within it.

– Have you gone mad, the Municipal Commissioner shouted, backing away from the crackling light.

– No, just letting the people down below know you're up here. You might as well go and try to explain things to them before they work out the route from your neighbour's roof. I think you'll find a way to control their passions. But I might be wrong.

With a great, spat-out curse the Municipal Commissioner descended the stairs into his house. The bulrushes were disintegrating but the night was breezeless, the flames stayed contained. A concentration of heat and brightness and beauty, unapproachable. So might an angel appear to a man, veiled in the fire of heaven.

– Which balcony was she on? Qayyum asked Abdul Hakim.

– There's no need to say anything to anyone about the girl, the lawyer said, putting a hand on Qayyum's arm. What can't be denied we'll admit, but let's not start speaking about our allies giving dead girls into the hands of Englishmen. Understand?

– Was it the carpet-seller's balcony?

– Yes.

Qayyum scooped up hot ash from the trough in cupped palms, and whispered a verse from the Qur'an, his breath scattering grey flecks.

– Their works are as ashes which the wind bloweth hard upon a stormy day. They have no control of aught that they have earned.

25 April 1930

Walking through the train station and across the railway bridge Viv was able to consider the burqa as the Invisibility Cape she had longed for as a child. Beneath the white tent she moved in an entirely private sphere. Unknown, unseen. The policeman standing near the station lavatory who had taken note of Miss Spencer as she entered paid no attention to the woman in the burqa who emerged; the Englishwomen and children who waited on the platform for the train to evacuate them from Peshawar looked straight through her; Remmick who had personally accompanied her here from Dean's was too busy sneezing loudly into his handkerchief to pay attention to a local woman whose steps didn't falter as she walked past him though she ducked her head so that the shimmer of her blue eyes wouldn't be visible beneath the face-mesh.

Beyond the bridge, at the end of a metalled road, Kabuli Gate was open, a doorway into a world entirely unlike the one she was leaving behind. Viv steadied herself against the railing of the bridge, looked over her shoulder towards the train station. She might just have enough time to return before anyone noticed she'd disappeared. Another few minutes, though, and someone would raise an alarm, the woman in the white burqa would be mentioned, Remmick would understand that she'd set out to betray him – to betray the Empire itself.

She tried to see if she could recognise Remmick among all the Englishmen gathered on the station with their wives but her latticed vision made it impossible. She pulled at the face-mesh so it was a few inches away from her eyes, squinted, cursed men, dropped her hand and continued on to Kabuli Gate.

It was true, all the troops had withdrawn from the Walled City, but the cry of 'Peshawar has fallen' which had sent everyone at the Club into such a panic the previous night seemed ridiculous as she walked through the wide-open gates and into the bustle of the Street of Storytellers. The smells of cooking meat, the calls of traders, the variety of turbans, it was all as before, but even so, something was off-kilter. It took a little while to decide that the difference was in her – in making her just another local woman, the burqa took away her very English right to be eccentric. Now she couldn't stop and stare, point to things that struck her as unusual, ask questions, enter all-male domains, expect to be treated with a certain deference (she'd never known she'd expected this) simply by virtue of her race. So it's me, she told herself. All that's different is me. But she knew this wasn't true.

She had left the Peshawar Club as soon as she was able to slip away from Remmick the previous night, returning to Dean's to sit on the ledge of her bedroom window, smoking cigarettes and drinking gin from a bottle, listening to crickets and nightbirds. If she closed her eyes she saw corpses laid on corpses, pale hands lifting the dead out of their own blood and throwing them like broken dolls into the back of a lorry. But what could she do about it? She was just a woman with no authority on either side of the city walls.

She held the gin bottle against her neck, the glass cool. There was a woman in the Walled City who would never have the chance to stand by the grave of someone she loved, or even to know where that grave was – if a tree grew above it, if children played near by, if a god no one believed in any more had left his mark just overhead. *He was buried in Bodrum, beneath a cypress tree, and in 1917 I took his walking stick and Alice's collar (she had died by then too) and interred them beneath the Split Rock of Zeus.* Wilhelm had written this to Viv after the war, an act of kindness she'd never forget. There was nothing comparative she could offer the green-eyed woman – but she could give

261

certainty where there might be doubt, knowledge where there might be confusion. Yes, there were lorries, a man named Caroe ordered it, and here is the reason why. Perhaps it would matter. After a loss every detail mattered, every acknowledgement of a wrong mattered. *The War Office has nothing to do with that man's death, Miss Spencer. I must ask you to stop sending those letters for the sake of your own reputation.*

It was well after midnight when Remmick knocked on her door. He'd come to remind her all women and children were being evacuated next morning, and she must be ready to leave first thing. As he spoke he looked around her room in the manner of a man practised at finding anything out of place and, noticing the burqa slung over the back of a chair, walked up to it and stroked the white cotton.

– Put this on, he said.

– Why?

– Put it on and take your dress off.

– Get out or I'll to scream the roof down.

He left, shrugging, but when he had gone Viv picked the burqa off the chair, and the fabric between her fingers felt like an answer.

But now she approached the carpet-seller's house and the voice in her head grew louder – Stay out of it! And then this thought, these people are not your people. She looked down the long vista, and saw only Pathans. Despite the burqa she felt exposed, and turned sharply into a street so narrow the man walking in the other direction couldn't pass her without contact. He flapped his hands at her as if she were a flock of pigeons, and she found herself reversing in rapid but tiny steps so she wouldn't trip over the hem of her burqa. It was only when a doorway opened and she saw the woman standing there, garishly made up, that she realised what he feared wasn't the contamination of her touch but a witness to what the men of the city did here. A street for everything in the Walled City. No map, only desire to steer you. The Street of Storytellers. The Street of Courtesans. The Street of Englishwomen. The Street of Inventive Guides. Her young Pactyike, her Herodotus of

Peshawar, her Civilising Mission. He was the last person in the world she wanted to see.

Beneath the burqa she was sweating, and it was impossible to wipe the perspiration from her forehead. Back on the broad avenue she saw a woman in the bright clothes of a nomad call out to a man with a wide-brimmed basket on his head who squatted down and allowed her to pluck out the most appealing melons. A man walked along the pavement with a large cone of cloth beneath his arm; from the tapered base of the cone, green and blue iridescence emerged; from the wide mouth three beaked heads peered out. A hat of melons, a bouquet of peacocks. In another time she would have viewed these sights with delight at their Oriental colour. But the melon-seller was standing beneath the burnt remnants of a Union Jack; the peacock carrier was walking towards Kabuli Gate through which the armoured cars and troops had rushed in. This was the world she was now in. Or perhaps she'd been here all along, unseeing.

She looked down to the end of the street and there was Najeeb Gul's brother, arms crossed, facing the gate leading into a police station.

Until the middle of the previous century river channels ran into the heart of Peshawar, willows and mulberry trees growing along their banks. Everywhere, headiness and shade, grown men of many nations cramming sweet purple fruit into their mouths as they walked along the Street of Storytellers. Now there was a masonry canal, carrying sewage and drain water, where the channels had once flowed. Why sigh over lost mulberries instead of giving thanks to the engineers who saved the city from floodwaters? said Qayyum and Najeeb threw his hands in the air in exasperation. Lala, why can't you see that the past is beautiful?

Qayyum took a deep breath as he saw a man in khaddar walk out of the police station and come towards the gate. The past was not the beautiful place in which he still had a brother, he could not accept that. Any moment now Najeeb would be

263

released from his cell, any moment now. But the Congresswalla merely took something out of the car parked inside the station grounds and turned and walked back in.

Qayyum had been standing outside the station ever since the Army withdrew the previous night, waiting for the policemen who had barricaded themselves inside to come out. For the first couple of hours he rattled the locked gate at regular intervals before it occurred to him that it would only terrify the policemen further. Through the night men he knew from Congress or Khilafat or the Khudai Khidmatgar urged him to join them in taking over policing duties for the city – there was a rumour the British had sent word to trans-border raiders to attack the Walled City so that the Peshawaris would beg the Army to return and save them – but he only said, I'll join you when my brother comes out, and they left him alone. An hour or more ago a delegation of Congress and Khilafat men had arrived at the police-thana. One of them scaled the walls, and opened the gate from inside, picking the lock with ease.

– No, stay here, the lawyer Abdul Hakim who was part of the delegation had said. If your brother is there we'll get him out.

The scent of melons caught Qayyum by surprise – it was a fruit-seller walking past – and he wished he were back in the orchards where he understood the world.

– Mr Gul?

He looked round, startled to hear an Englishwoman's voice, and startled further to find it coming from beneath a burqa. The voice identified itself as Miss Spencer, and he gestured sharply to her to keep her voice down. A little distance away two men were leaning against a tree, reading the newspaper *Sarhad* which had published a list of over a hundred names of the dead this morning.

– Please go back to the Cantonment.

– I'm more sorry than I can say about what happened here.

– You don't know what happened here.

The door to the thana opened again and this time the entire

264

Congress and Khilafat delegation came out, and behind them men who Qayyum hadn't seen go in – the prisoners, in khaddar and red shirts, so great a number of men it was impossible to make out each face. They opened the prison gates and stepped into the street and a great roar went up around the Walled City: Inqilaab Zindabad!

– Najeeb! Qayyum shouted over the roar. Najeeb!

A hand on his shoulder, he spun, his heart so light with relief it might fly out of his chest. But it was Abdul Hakim, shaking his head.

– I'm sorry, the lawyer said. I'm so sorry, he's not there.

The prisoners streamed past him, embracing men on the street. Inqilaab Zindabad! Qayyum held out his arm to steady himself against something and what he touched was cloth, a shoulder beneath which didn't flinch.

– Najeeb? the Englishwoman said, her voice carrying barely any sound. Please, not the lorries?

– No, Qayyum said, no. There was no one in a frock-coat. Someone would have seen him in his frock-coat.

The sentence gave him some strength and he repeated it, removing his hand from the woman's shoulder.

– Of course, she said. I'm sorry, I shouldn't have said that.

– You know about the lorries?

– Yes. But, Najeeb. Where is Najeeb?

– Do you know where the lorries went? Where they took the bodies?

– No. If I did I'd say so, of course I would. That poor woman, I can't imagine what it must be like. Where is Najeeb?

– Which poor woman?

– There was a woman at the Museum yesterday. You must have seen her when she came in. She said her sister-in-law had been taken away in a lorry.

Now he remembered the figure with her head covered, the height of her.

– Did she have green eyes? he said.

– Yes. You know her?

– Why did she come to the Museum? Her sister-in-law had

265

just died. The gates of the Walled City were closed. Why, how would she be at the Museum?

– I don't know.

He looked down the Street of Storytellers towards the balcony on which deer chased each other between borders of roses. Without a word to each other both he and the Englishwoman in a burqa started to walk towards it.

It was impossible to keep pace with the Pathan without walking like an Englishwoman. Viv allowed him to stride ahead of her, surprised when he stopped near the carpet-seller's door to wait for her.

– I can't go in and ask to see a woman, he explained, knocking on the door. A young servant boy answered and said the family wasn't back from Kohat yet, all mourners were being asked to come back the next day when they'd all be here. They aren't all in Kohat, Mr Gul said, and the boy replied that his sahib had gone to Shahji-ki-Dheri.

– Shahji-ki-Dheri?

The boy's expression grew alarmed at the sound of Viv's accent, but he answered all the same.

– Yes, he's gone there for a grave. Even if there isn't a body there should be a grave.

He held up his fist which was wrapped in a gauzy blue dupatta, a faint scent of coconut oil rising off it, his eyes filling with tears.

What have we done here?

Mr Gul was looking at her and she knew she had to be the one to ask for the green-eyed woman.

– Tell your begum-sahib I'm the Englishwoman she spoke to about the lorries.

– Come with me, the boy responded. Come upstairs.

They followed him into an enclosed courtyard of coloured glass windows and delicate lattice woodwork, and from there up one of the corner stairways, and into a cavernous room she'd been in years earlier as a customer. The boy opened the shutters, and left the room. Along the length of one wall rolled-up carpets were arranged by height like schoolchildren. She remembered the kindly, bearded carpet-seller showing her a rug which had seemed no more than ordinary. I don't think that's quite what I had in mind, she'd said. He'd smiled as if he had wanted such a response and with a single flick of his wrist, as though turning the page of an illuminated manuscript, flipped over the rug to reveal sharply delineated arabesques of reds and blues, deep as blood and twilight. Viv's delight was as much an appreciation of the salesmanship as the rug itself. Now the finely knotted arabesques were laid out in her study in Bloomsbury.

– Do you want to take the burqa off?

– Yes.

Mr Gul closed the shutters, and stood with his back to her while she removed the burqa and smoothed down her dress.

– All right, she said, and he walked away from the shutters and switched on a Tiffany lamp. A dragonfly lit up the gloom and, genie-like, a voice emerged from the lamp:

– What do you want?

Qayyum moved away from the door which had opened just feet away from him, almost tripping on a raised crease in the carpet. His imagination had claimed the woman so entirely, exaggerating the greenness of her eyes, the angle of her cheekbones, that she seemed reduced, disappointing. It was the Englishwoman she was addressing, not him.

– I'm sorry, the Englishwoman said, in English. Then, in Pashto: Forgive me, I can't find out where the lorries are. They won't tell me. But there were lorries, I know that for certain. A man named Caroe gave the orders.

– Why have you come here? Do you think I need you telling me what I already know to make it true? If you don't know where she is, get out. I don't need an Englishwoman coming in here with her 'forgive me's. What forgiveness do you deserve?

All the rage of the Walled City in her voice, and all the grief of a single heart breaking. My life would be better if I knew you – the thought was entirely out of place, and he hoped his face

267

didn't look as flushed as it felt when he cleared his throat so she would know he was there.

– We were also involved in what happened. My comrades, my brothers, the men of the Walled City.

– The Municipal Commissioners. I know. Why do you keep telling me things I know? Where is Diwa? There is no other question in the world.

He couldn't look at her. Not because she was uncovered, not because desire might strike him, not because another man might see him looking where he should not. He just couldn't look at her. And the Englishwoman across the room, he was sure she couldn't look either.

– Take this.

He felt something thrust at his chest. When he looked up and placed his arms out to take it he saw it was the blanket she'd been holding under her arm. Without explanation she walked through the door and he heard a key turn in the lock on the other side.

Miss Spencer walked across to him. What is it? Just a blanket, he answered, his voice catching. The Englishwoman placed her hands on the upper layer of the folded-over cloth, took hold of its corners, her knuckles grazing Qayyum's shirt, and stepped back, unfolding the dark fabric. Between her arms and his a frock-coat stretched out, prone, lamplight shining through the bullet-shaped hole in Najeeb's chest.

ON THE STREET OF STORYTELLERS

23 April 1930

Najeeb Gul imprints his hands with the rose carvings on the wooden door, his fingers catching in the deep whorls of a petal, and breathes in the intensity of attar. The rose-scent of springtime Peshawar – could any other city possess a season of such headiness? In England, he knows, the season of choice is autumn with its mists and mellow fruitfulness. 'Mellow'. Only an Englishman would offer up such an adjective as a delight. It speaks to their subtlety of character. He steps back, allowing himself to feel pride at the ornately carved door, paid for with his salary from the Museum, which signals prosperity. If only his parents had lived to see it.

He pats his head, feels beneath the yards of cloth for the silver band. The previous night he dreamed he was standing on a train platform, and as the train pulled in and a carriage door opened to allow out the only passenger he untied his turban only to realise he'd wound it around nothing more than the ordinary hard cap. He sets off along the alley in large strides, laughing at the cobbler Hari Das' cry of Viceroy Najeeb!, aware how impressive he looks in his long-tailed turban, gleaming white shalwar and the black frock-coat which is the pride of his wardrobe. At the train station she'll see him, she'll smile and take his arm and they'll walk together the short distance to the Museum – and there, in the Hall of Statues, between the two standing Buddhas, he'll place the end of the turban cloth in her hand and he'll spin. Round and round like a dervish, one arm bent at the elbow, palm forward, fingers spread apart. The

271

cloth unravelling from the turban. A blur, a circlet! Miss Spencer's laughter, her delight, her gratitude.

Through the alleys he goes, through one bazaar and then the other. Everything silent and bolted, so it is as though he is looking at a half-finished sketch of his city. Everything static, except for him. Oh, and a large red butterfly drifting lazily through the wafting stench of a caravan of camels.

He is grateful that the clutter of the present is largely absent so that nothing obstructs his view of the Old City walls and arched gateways, the ancient hills and mountains. What he most loves in Peshawar is the proximity of the past. All around the broken bowl of the Peshawar Valley his glance knows how to burn away time. So in a single day he might encounter the Chinese monk Fa-Hien throwing flowers into the Buddha's alms bowl at Gor Khatri while recalling the eight elephants who with their united strength could not drag the alms-bowl away from the monastery; the Kushan king Kanishka laying the foundation for the Great Stupa which the Buddha had prophesied he would build; the Mughal Emperor Babar, seated on the back of an elephant, hunting rhinos in the swampy marshland where later his descendants would create gardens; the Sikh maharaja Ranjit Singh standing on the heights of Bala Hisar Fort, surveying the city below through his one eye about which his foreign minister wrote, *The Maharaja is like the sun and the sun has only one eye. The splendour and luminosity of his single eye is so much that I have never dared to look at his other eye*; and Scylax. Sometimes, time braids and there goes Babar's spear, missing a rhino and wounding Nearchus who falls at the feet of a Gandharan sculptor carving a stupa with Atlas at its base holding up the elevated figure of the Buddha which Marco Polo sketches on a leaf stolen out of his hand by Scylax and buried deep in the ground by an unnamed heroine to protect it from the marauding White Huns.

The weight on his head grows heavier. There is a single irritation brought about by the protest strike – it denies him the chance to bring Miss Spencer from the train station straight to

272

the Street of Storytellers where 'Darius and the Betrayal of Scylax' is now a familiar and well-loved tale. But perhaps that isn't such a terrible thing after all; the last time he'd heard it told Ashfaq the Storyteller had added in extra verses to capture the new mood of the times:

On Caria's streets Scylax cursed the Persians on parade
But a crown of silver and – ! He gave them a country to invade.

In his dreams Darius throws that crown like a disc through the air,
It shears through Heraclides' neck while his lips part in prayer.

Does Scylax dream of Carian seas or of Persian fountains?
No, in every dream he dreams he's surrounded by our mountains.

Which man of Peshawar won't understand those dreams?
Our land's beauty, its perfume, makes poets write reams.

We stand here with open arms to embrace you as a guest
But instead you try to enslave us, our leaders to arrest.

Qayyum denied he'd told the Storyteller to recite those couplets but Najeeb remains unconvinced. Each day his brother moves deeper into a world in which everything touched by the British is tainted, even Peshawar's ancient history.

A commotion heads towards Najeeb in the form of several men wearing the red-brown shirts of Ghaffar Khan's unarmed army. Najeeb sometimes pretends to himself that his disdain for the Khudai Khidmatgar is primarily an urban Peshawari's response to everything that comes from the rural surroundings, including political movements, but in truth he knows he is the adoring younger brother jealous of those to whom the object of his hero-worship has turned his attention.

– Inqilaab Zindabad!

At the sound of the Khudai Khidmatgar boys' cry a window

shutter opens and an old woman darts her head out like a cuckoo in an English clock.

– What now? What's happening?

– The English have locked up our leaders at the Kabuli Gate thana. Send your sons to join the protest.

Najeeb reconsiders his route to the train station. There is a new kind of shouting. A man comes running into the alley.

– They're killing us.

One of the red-shirted boys catches the man by the shoulder. Najeeb tells himself the man is speaking in metaphor, but he knows this isn't true. Something in his expression has been stripped away or pasted on – it isn't clear which, but Najeeb knows the man, has seen him hundreds of times selling sweetmeats in the bazaar, and yet he almost didn't recognise him.

Despite his crazed air, when the man speaks he is lucid: armoured cars drove into the crowd of party workers accompanying the leaders who had presented themselves at the jail, as promised, for arrest, and there are bodies along the Street of Storytellers, how many dead, how many wounded it's hard to say. He has barely finished speaking when Najeeb takes off, running.

He runs into a tumult. Everyone in the Walled City seems to have heard what has happened, dozens making their way to the Street of Storytellers; people standing on roofs and leaning from balconies catching rumours out of air and tossing them down into the alley. A car on fire. An Englishman knocked down with a stone. A horse, something about a horse. An Englishman run over by a horse. No, an Englishman run over by a motorcycle. No, an Englishman on a motorcycle run over by a horse. No, a horse which refused to fight killed by an Englishman. An armoured car reversing into – a horse? An Englishman? A motorcycle? A gun. A stone. An unarmed crowd.

Then gunfire. Not one bullet, or two, but a machine-gun staccato. Where there were people standing on rooftops now there is sky. Through sheer will Najeeb forces past the paralysing terror and picks up speed.

274

The noise as he approaches the Street of Storytellers is too dense to separate into its components. A door opens and a woman in a bright green kameez with eyes to match steps out. He calls to her to return inside to safety, but she ignores him and continues forward. He catches the scent of walnuts and plums. The chaddar covering her head is streaked with the red-brown of the Khudai Khidmatgar. It's still wet with dye, and her face has red-brown smears where the fabric clings to her skin. A knife-blade flashes in her hand before she disappears around the corner.

Sounds from above draw his attention and he sees people moving about on a roof – the carpet-seller's roof, which commands a clear view of the Street of Storytellers. The woman with the dyed face failed to securely close the door to the house, and Najeeb hesitates only a moment before entering and making rapid progress up the stairs and through the topmost door. There are no men, only women and children up here. The women are standing on the lip of the roof and looking over the matting to the street below, the children sitting on the broad partition wall which divides this roof from the one next door. The sight of the uncovered women makes him hesitate until one, in a blue kameez with mirrorwork on its sleeves and a braid reaching down to the dip of her back, turns to look at him and then shrugs as if to say, Why not? The walnut-plum scent is strong. He passes the bucket from which it emanates. Next to it a clothes line draped with men's garments dyed red-brown. Sun strikes a dyed shirt – a heart explodes.

He walks to one corner of the roof, maintaining distance from the women; other than the one with the braid they either haven't noticed him or are ignoring him.

Below, a horse lies dead in the street, its mane drenched in blood. An armoured car is on fire, and something else, a man, is that a man beside the armoured car, his flesh charred. More armoured cars block the exit through Kabuli Gate. A crowd of hundreds of Peshawaris fills the Street of Storytellers. Soldiers with bayonets at the ready face them. In between, the dead. One of the dead starts to crawl. A group of men in

275

khaddar clothes move forward and lift him off the ground. The crowd parts to let them through and a rapid silence races through the street so that his cry can be heard all the way up to the rooftops.

– Inqilaab Zindabad!

The crowd takes up the demand for revolution. They move forward to gather up the dead. But now the English officers are shouting something and the soldiers with bayonets advance, not only forward but also in an encircling movement to place themselves at the mouths of the alleys leading into the Street of Storytellers. He'll have to find some other route in, if in is where he chooses to go.

Najeeb Gul looks over the boundary of the Walled City. A fire engine speeds towards Kabuli Gate, but everything else is at peace in the Cantonment and beyond, all the way to the distant hills. Lush fields and fruit trees and wide streets and English architecture. A man walking a dog. Someone meandering through the grounds of the Museum. At the train station, the most anxious or eager of those awaiting the train from Karachi have already arrived on the platform. He looks around the jigsaw of roofs and sees how he can leap his way onto and across the City walls. To the train station. Vivian Rose Spencer.

The escape path becomes clear in order for him to reject it. Where is Qayyum? He forces himself to look down among the dead. None of the bodies are familiar, but what does that mean? A dead Qayyum could never look familiar. If only the shadow-fearing version of his brother which had returned from France had left some residue in Qayyum's character, instead of being replaced by a man who simply chose another army, another leader to march behind, this time without a gun to protect him.

The Peshawaris in the street are passing wooden planks and boxes over their heads to the men at the front of the crowd. No, not a crowd – they are a platoon, a battalion, with a battle cry: Inqilaab Zindabad. Najeeb wants to shout at them. They are unarmed, hemmed in. He has never seen anything so ridiculous. There is a low table next to him, with a mirror and razor and mug of water on it. The razor gleams with possibility. Down

276

on the street, the men in the front rows hold up the planks and boxes like shields and start to advance. Bayonets splinter the wood, but the distraction is sufficient for the men just behind the shield-bearers to lift up the wounded and pass them back through the crowd.

There's Qayyum. Near the front of the action, of course. A soldier with a bayonet rushes him. Najeeb tastes his own heart. Qayyum holds up a plank; the bayonet catches in it. Qayyum tugs and the bayonet leaps out of the soldier's grip, its tip firmly embedded in the plank. Qayyum's strong arms can rip the bayonet from wood, turn it round to pierce the soldier's belly in a second. But he merely tosses it at the soldier's feet – wood and bayonet – and moves back into the unarmed platoon which closes around him and cuts him off from Najeeb's sight. Najeeb understands that in his brother's mind he has just made defeat impossible. He doesn't care about victory or defeat – he wants Qayyum alive.

One of the girls on the roof throws a stone. The concentration on her face is tremendous but the stone makes it no further than the shop awning beneath. One of the women pats her head with pride but points out that she's more likely to hit a Pashtun than an Englishman at this distance; taking another stone the woman slings it, low and fast, towards the troops. The street in front of the soldiers is now littered with stones, though Najeeb sees only one English soldier being helped away, blood pouring from the side of his face.

The girl with the long braid leaves the cluster of spectators and walks past the clothes line, her hand trailing along the hanging clothes as though they are in an entirely different moment, one which allows for a woman to run her fingers along a man's trouser without either disturbing her modesty or hiding her intentions. She yanks at a kameez which tumbles off the line. And then she is walking towards him, her gaze distant. As she passes by him she slings the kameez over his shoulder. She's trying to shame him into joining the men who face down bayonets, of course, but he's just grateful to be able to rid himself of the heavy black frock-coat which has trapped the

277

late morning sun. The kameez is much too large for him, which is useful for pulling it over his neck without disturbing his turban. Its cool dampness pleasing to his skin. He knows exactly the area of fabric near the shoulder which was bunched in her fist. Stepping away from the discarded frock-coat pooled at his feet, he knows it will give him a reason to return. Knows also that while everyone else was looking down at the Street of Storytellers the woman whose handprint is on his shoulder watched him unbutton and shrug off the frock-coat. What did she make of him picking up the razor to cut the undershirt away from his slim body? (He allows himself to imagine the banter of early married life: I did it because I didn't want to disturb my turban! he'll say, and she'll reply, Oh yes, oh really, then why arch your back and rotate your shoulder blades in that way which made every muscle surge, here and here and here?)

All this is a few seconds of diversion, a few seconds to imagine a future in which today is remembered for the start of love.

Gunfire again. He crashes down a flight of stairs and through a doorway, searching for a window without bars through which he can escape. There, an enclosed balcony with shutters he batters open. It takes a while before the men below hear his shouts but when they do he climbs onto the balcony railing, his back to the street. The woman with the plait enters the room, holding his frock-coat as if dancing with it in the English style, one arm at its waist, one at the wrist. They regard each other without expression and then she raises the hand which is holding his frock-coat sleeve and he sees her arm and his own wave goodbye at him.

He clamps his hands to his turban and falls. A bullet sings its ways through the place where his body had stood just a moment earlier, through the open shutters, into the room where the woman and frock-coated stranger dance. The waiting arms beneath catch him, place him on his feet. There is no way back into the room.

His red-brown shirt gives him authority in this crowd. He taps a shoulder in front of him and the man glances down, sees

278

the colour of his sleeve, and steps aside. There are thousands here, all of them men as far as he can see. What happened to the woman with the dyed face? What is her relationship to the dancing woman? Where did the bullet go? He keeps moving forward through the scent of sweat and blood.

Two men carrying bricks in their hands are arguing with two men in Congress khaddar who want them to put down their weapons.

He comes to a small group of women, all old as grandmothers. They are trying to go forward, to shame the soldiers into putting down their weapons. The men around are trying to keep them back, away from the bullets which have stopped again.

Two men, holding hands, trade couplets about cruel lovers.

He knows he is coming to the front of the crowd when these individual tableaux fall away and the red-brown and khaddar shirts increase in density. His borrowed shirt, which had dried, is wet at the armpits. It's hard to move now, these front rows packed in tightly, stepping forward together than falling back with inexplicable logic. He addresses the man next to him.

– What are we doing?

– If you don't know, go home.

It's only then he realises that every experience of his life feels pallid beside this one, including that moment yesterday in which the shape of the object in the soil of Shahji-ki-Dheri became clear.

– Inqilaab Zindabad!

He shouts the words to see what hearing them in his own voice will do to them. It feels slightly ridiculous until the men around him join in the cry. How wonderful this is.

– My brother; I must go to my brother.

He parts the shoulders of the men in front of him, and steps into the trajectory of a brick hurtling from a balcony.

23 April 1930

The bullet travels through the frock-coat, missing Diwa by millimetres, and burrows itself into a mirror. Her arm is still raised in the direction of the bewildering man who has just dived backwards off her balcony and it takes a moment to understand the smell of burnt fabric, the crackling sound towards which she turns, and the frozen sun in the mirror, glass rays shooting out from a dark circle.

This day has been the strangest of her young life.

By rights she should still have been in Kohat with her parents and brothers, celebrating her cousin's wedding. But yesterday when her eldest brother heard of the planned anti-British protest in Peshawar he said he was returning to join the nationalists and his wife, Zarina, insisted she would go along too. If it had been any other woman she would have been overruled, but Zarina had made clear the strength of her will when she entered Diwa's family home two years earlier and said she refused to marry the man her family had chosen for her, and wished to marry Diwa's brother instead. Under the laws of Pashtunwali I come here seeking the protection of your household, which can only be given to me through marriage, she had said. It was as if a woman from legend had walked through the door.

So when Zarina said she would return to Peshawar with her husband it was quickly understood that there was no point in arguing. The only one who might have tried was Diwa's mother, but she had seen many of the women of her extended family eyeing her fifteen-year-old daughter as a prospective bride for their sons and, seeing the possibility of losing her only daughter to another city as her own mother had lost her when she married her cousin the carpet-seller, she was grateful for the opportunity to send Diwa back to Peshawar under the pretext of keeping Zarina company.

Diwa hadn't minded at all, being sent back to Peshawar with her wedding clothes uncreased except where they had been folded for packing. If she could have had one wish in the world it would be this – to be at home with Zarina, and no one else. No one else demanding her time, distracting her attention. Only Zarina with her quick gestures, her stories and poems, her ability to be loved enough to be forgiven everything. Even rushing into a street filled with men, her face uncovered though Diwa's mother repeatedly warned her against doing that, even this she'd be forgiven. By now she would have found her husband and he would be plying her with endearments, his hand touching hers, both wrapped around the hilt of the dagger. My warrior, Malalai of Maiwand reborn, he'd say.

Everything is turned around today. Diwa woke up to bird-song instead of the tumult of the marketplace, smelt boiling walnuts and plum instead of tea, watched her brother leave his books in order to go out and fight. When an unknown man appeared on the roof she thought, of course, on this upside-down day, why not? But when none of the neighbourhood women or their children noticed him it started to seem possible that he was there for her, not as threat but opportunity. Opportunity for what? He looked half-crazed, sweating in his black coat. And then, more crazed, he cut his clothes off himself in order to put on the kameez she had tossed in his direction as a more ventilated option. Mad, completely mad, she decided as he ran down the stairs again, leaving the coat where it had fallen.

She knelt on the ground, fastening the gold buttons of the coat. The metal was warm, like a fired bullet. She had just watched men die, and a horse too. It was the horse she couldn't stop looking at, the horse's flanks over which she wanted to run her hand, giving it the comfort of her presence as it twitched towards death. The dying men didn't seem as real as the horse. She'd found herself looking away from them, towards the elevation of Gor Khatri, wondering how the Walled City might appear to someone on top of its Mughal gateway who could look down onto all the roofs of the Walled City, cut off from each other by enclosing walls but open to the sky. An Englishwoman had once described the view to Diwa's father as looking into a honeycomb made of jewels – but the English spoke this way about things in Peshawar that were entirely ordinary, so it didn't help. What she wanted to know was if life was proceeding as normal on the roofs a little further back from the Street of Storytellers, where no one could see the horse and the men, the English bayonets and the Peshawari bared chests. Or did everyone feel the strangeness in the air, the sense of possibility?

She stood, the coat in her arms. The crazy stranger was the height of a short man or a tall woman. Zarina's height. She took the sleeve of the coat in one hand, placed her other hand at its waist. Zarina would wear this, and they would dance as the English dance. Weeks earlier they had watched a couple on the Gor Khatri gateway twirling in the open air, and Zarina had said it was so English to dance in public, as if there was nothing intimate in their embrace, as if it was merely a social transaction and there was no danger that a limb pressed against another limb could lead to desire. No fire in their blood, she said, only half-thawed rivers of ice.

Bullets and shouts from below. Perhaps Zarina would change her mind about the English today.

Diwa continued to hold the coat close as she skipped lightly down the stairs. She'd leave this on Zarina's bed as a surprise. How soft the fabric. She rested her head against Zarina's shoulder and they spun together into the bedroom. And there was the crazy man, standing on the balcony railing, about to jump. She raised her hand in command, Don't! – but he just clutched his head as though a pair of soft palms were enough to keep a head from splitting, and fell. Then the burning smell, the crackling sound, the frozen sun.

She opens the wardrobe door. The bullet has travelled through the mirror and is lodged in the splintering wood. When she touches it, her fingers burn; she doesn't think of coat buttons in the sun, but of the metallic edge to blood, the stench of which is rising off the street.

She leans back against the wardrobe frame, hands at her temples. A man whose scent and heat is still in the coat she held close to her breast has just looked into her eyes and chosen to die. She tamps down the desire to see what the fall has done to his body, whether it has erased the madness from his features. Even as she thinks that, she understands that she is the one to have been mad these last minutes, not the man who clutched his head just as she is doing now, her brain consumed with terror. Her brother is out there, and Zarina.

Zarina, who never wanted her husband to take part in this protest, who insisted on accompanying him back to Peshawar because every second in his company was an opportunity to dissuade him from becoming a participant in this non-violent army of Pashtuns. Zarina, who took a dagger in her hand and walked out bare-faced, the dye of the Khudai Khidmatgar staining her skin not as tribute but as taunt, so that she could shame her husband, so that all the neighbourhood would say, His woman has to be the man in the family now that he's turned weak. It is unnecessary; everyone knows that Diwa's eldest brother has no real commitment to protests and political parties – handsome and good-natured enough to be spoilt by everyone around him, he sometimes flings himself upon a whim for a brief duration. If he wanted to join Congress we'd need to worry, her father said, but an army of unlettered peasants? Everyone understands this, so why can't his wife leave him alone to become dissatisfied with this new pretence at stepping out of his own life instead of creating such a scene about it. Zarina, the self-absorbed, the unseeing.

This is the first time Diwa has thought of Zarina with such anger. Her palm presses against the tip of the bullet, which is cooling now and doesn't even have the ability to break her skin, let alone cut through muscle and bone. She prises the bullet out of the wood. A spent cartridge, Zarina called her husband when she went up to the roof this morning, Diwa following behind, to see him plunging white clothes into a bucket, his hands already red-brown from the kameezes which were strung along the washing line. Now, the weight of the bullet resting in her palm, Diwa can't help thinking there's nothing so wrong with a spent cartridge.

There are sounds of adult command, and childish protest. The rooftop spectators are making their way down the stairs. One of the neighbourhood women comes into the room and closes the shutters without looking onto the street below.

– They're firing up at the roofs. Stay hidden.

For a while she does. She sits on Zarina's bed, one hand clutching a bullet, the other resting on the black coat. She is alone now. For the first time in her life she is alone in this house. What if Zarina and her brother never return? Will she just go on sitting here, holding an inert bullet in her hand while live rounds echo on the street below? How many people live in an empty house? One! She heard her father say this once. It hadn't made sense at the time. The bullets continue on and off for a while. Then they stop, or perhaps she stops hearing them. Eventually, she crosses the border from fear to boredom and is surprised to find the two emotions lie adjacent to each other. She lies down, propped on one side, the black coat resting beside her on the embroidered bedcover. While stroking the softness of the fabric, from breast to thigh, she feels something beneath the cloth, a rectangular shape. She unbuttons the coat, heat rising to her face as she works her way down the length of the garment, and feels her way along the silk lining until her fingers encounter a pocket, and pull out a metal case which she opens to find business cards.

They're written in English, and for the first time she's actively grateful she knows the language. So far its only purpose has been commercial. Her father's carpet trade has many English customers, and his blurring eyesight has left him dependent on his daughter to make sense of the pen-stroke demands which arrive from as near as the Cantonment and as far away as

Calcutta. Sometimes the letter-writers arrive themselves and when she carries in the tray of tea she is able to match up handwriting to person, smug in the knowledge she has derived of them from the written courtesies they extend or withhold, the slash or curl of their penmanship, the punctuation. All this is in the past. Over a year ago her father's blurring eyesight intercepted something in the glance of one of the Englishmen, and since then it's been her younger brother who takes in the tea tray. She wishes she had caught the glance herself; it might have made the exile seem worthwhile.

NAJEEB GUL, INDIAN ASSISTANT, PESHAWAR MUSEUM.

Najeeb Gul. That was his name. It's suddenly unbearable that someone called Najeeb Gul jumped to his death from her balcony. If only she'd known his name – she would have called out, Najeeb! and he would have stopped, climbed off the railing and come towards her. But now he lies broken on the street below. She stands up and sits down again. What is she supposed to do for him, for the dead stranger in a frock-coat who works at the Museum?

She walks over to the balcony, opens the shutters and – with a quick prayer asking for the sight of death to be bearable – looks down onto the street below. But there is no street, only a thicket of men. Of course. She is so much closer to them now than when she was on the roof. She could lower herself off the balcony and jump down onto the shoulders of the men below, who might not even notice her until they felt her tread. They are so handsome, these men of Peshawar. She notices it with pride, as though the good looks reflect back on her. How silly. And yet, this is the first time she's seen such a gathering. Men of Peshawar, in row after row. The traders of Bukhara and Tibet and Tashkent and Farghana and Delhi and Kabul and China are all absent from the Street of Storytellers. She thinks of her father, standing up here, his arms open wide to the street below, his voice filled with pride as he says, Peshawar, the Heart of the World, pointing out all the men of different nations who throng its street.

285

She thinks all this, even while trying to make sense of what's happening below. Everything seems to have stopped. Or paused. No one is leaving, but no one is fighting or calling out slogans. An elderly Peshawari man is standing on a fire truck, near Kabuli Gate, nodding at something said by the men at the front of the gathering, and then turning to address the English officers. The dead horse has turned dark in clumps, the darkness composed of something living which pulses and swarms. She turns her face away and finds herself looking straight into the raised glance of a man in the street below. Before she can retreat indoors he places his palms together and raises them in supplication.

– Water.

She nods, yes of course, they must all be thirsty, and this at least she can do.

Diwa is strong – she can carry rolled-up carpets that her younger brother is too feeble to hold on to – but even so her arms ache by the time she has carried the earthenware vessel from the kitchen and hoisted it onto the balcony railing. One hand holding it in place, she uses the other – with a certain flourish – to whip off the tin cup which she has balanced on her head. But here she is confronted by the empty space between her hand holding the cup and the man below waiting to receive it. The two of them look at each other, blinking in perplexity for a moment, and then he taps on the shoulders of the two men standing next to him and each crouches down with interlocked palms.

And there he is, raised above the crowd, close enough that her outstretched fingertips could touch his. His eyes are on the tap near the base of the earthenware vessel, but she is aware how easily he might glance up and see her watching him. As any man on the street below might glance up and see her watching him. She has become more accustomed than she'd realised, in this last year, to the invisibility conferred on her by a burqa, its gift of allowing the wearer to stare without being noticed, drinking in the unseeing sight of men. She is entirely jumbled about whether she wants him to look up at her, or not.

He closes his eyes and raises his face towards her. She angles the earthenware vessel, and opens the tap. A rope of water slips out, beginning to unbraid just before his mouth receives it, some of it splashing his cheeks and chin. She watches his throat work, gulp after gulp, until with a splutter he turns his face away and she stops the flow of water. The two men lower him to the ground, and then take turns being lifted up to drink. And so it goes on. One man after another taking position just beneath her balcony. She starts to feel desperate. There are hundreds down there, and the sun is getting hotter. Her arms ache from holding the vessel in place, her back aches. She is thirsty herself, but it seems indulgent to take a drink. She stops noticing the individual faces of the men, her concentration unwavering on the clear, beautiful water entering thirsty mouths.

Then a hand grabs at the fabric of her kameez and pulls her backwards. The earthenware vessel crashes to the balcony floor, and she hears the man who was just raised up cry out. She is being pulled back, back, away from the balcony, into the room, flailing.

– Have you gone mad?

Zarina slaps her across the face. An odd silence follows the sound of palm striking cheek, one not of shock or pain but of something dramatic shifting in a relationship and as if to confirm that things have turned on their head Zarina sits – collapses really – onto the bed and begins to weep. This woman who Diwa has always viewed as something out of a tale of valour has turned feeble at the mere scent of battle. The knife she'd carried this morning is on the bed, sheathed, merely decorative. Diwa tries to wipe the clinging red clay from her clothes, and only succeeds in smearing it.

– Now I look like a Khudai Khidmatgar too.

There is no response beyond more weeping. Not a sorrowful weeping but a jagged little-girl-who-lost-her-toys weeping. Shrugging, Diwa picks up a glass bottle filled with water and drinks, holding the mouth of the bottle a few feet away from her face. It makes her feel a sense of kinship with the men below.

287

– Where is my brother? Diwa asks.

– I don't know. I couldn't find him.

– How did you get back here?

– The soldiers let me through. They said women shouldn't be out there.

Zarina lies back, one hand covering her face which is splotchy with dye and emotion. She is clearly in need of some comfort, but Diwa is too annoyed at the manner in which her sister-in-law pulled her away from the men, as though she were a child. It's clear, she is the heroic one, the water carrier in battle, and Zarina is just a frightened girl. The three-year age gap between them seems to have reversed, and widened.

– Everyone out there could see you, Diwa. So why didn't your brother come to stand beneath the balcony and shout at you to go inside?

– Why should he? I was helping. Couldn't you see that?

– I could see you. So could all the soldiers with guns.

She reaches out for the glass bottle in Diwa's hand and presses her forehead against it.

– I thought I saw him. Your brother. I was standing under the watch-shop awning and one of the men who had been wounded, they carried him there, into the shade, trying to stop the bleeding. I couldn't see his face at first, but I saw blood everywhere, and I saw his sleeve with a long tear through it. Just like that kameez your brother won't throw away because he was wearing it the day I walked into your house for the first time.

She rocks herself back and forth silently, and once more it is Diwa who is the child, knowing that she is watching both the shining promise and the dark pain of adulthood, enmeshed. It takes a moment to realise what Zarina has just told her.

– Was he badly hurt? The man with the torn sleeve?

A tiny shrug. A shrug which says, It wasn't your brother, so what I felt was relief.

– There was a lot of blood, Zarina says.

– Did he say anything? Was he in a lot of pain?

– Why are you so interested? What's this?

Zarina lifts up the sleeve of the frock-coat, catches a whiff of something which makes her bend more closely towards the fabric. She has no sooner found the bullet hole than she sees the bullet lying on the bedcover.

– Diwa?

Diwa pulls the frock-coat into her own arms, says, Tell me about the injured man.

Zarina stands up, bullet in hand, and walks across to the shattered mirror. She places the bullet against the dark circle and it slides in.

– Where were you when this happened? Whose coat is this?

– Tell me about the injured man.

– Whose coat is this?

– Tell me about the injured man.

– What is there to tell? He was wounded, he was in pain. Probably delirious. He kept shouting, My turban, my turban.

– What about his turban?

– How should I know? He wasn't wearing one. Whose coat is this? Where were you when this bullet came in?

Diwa puts her hands to her ears and turns away. She has never before noticed how tiny this room is, how oppressive its dark walls. His turban? She has no sooner thought it than she recalls how carefully he pulled the kameez over his head, with what precision. And then the hands clasped to the turban as he fell.

She must act quickly, before Zarina can stop her, or else she could be here for hours, stuck with this cowering, shrill version of her commanding sister-in-law. Before she can give herself time to reconsider, she is on the balcony railing, calling out to the startled men below.

– Catch!

For a long terrifying moment she falls. Then she is in the arms of men, and it is all too brief before they set her on her feet and urge her to go back. She hears Zarina's voice calling to her from the balcony, but she knows this new version of her sister-in-law won't follow. She pushes through the crowd. A man puts his hand on her shoulder to stop her – it's the first of the men into whose mouth she sent a rope of water, the one with the strong hands – and she roars at him, a sound which might have had words in it but she's not sure it does. His hands spring away from her as though she's a flame. She barrels her way through the crowd, feeling herself on fire, no one must stop her, no one must even try. The men can feel it radiating off her, they step out of her way, some of them saying things she can't hear because the roaring of the fire is in her ears.

Then she's beneath the watch-shop awning, and he's there. Najeeb Gul. Standing on a crate, looking around as if searching for someone or something in the crowd. There's blood every-where – seeping through the bandage on his head, staining his clothes. When he sees her, he steps off the crate, grimacing in pain. His feet have barely touched the ground when he almost falls over and has to loop an arm around a slim tree trunk for support.

– How bad is it?

– Nothing like it looks. A brick hit my head, and I fell over onto a bayonet. The soldier looked more surprised than me. Don't worry, please, it's just a flesh wound.

– What was beneath the turban?

– It doesn't matter now.

Then he says the words which she's been hearing for so many hours she's stopped hearing them: Inqilaab Zindabad.

When she stood on the roof those words meant nothing to her. They belonged to that part of her brother's life in which he turned most tedious. But down here, amidst the musk and thrum of a suspended battle, everyone waiting for a starting gun, she finds herself moved to emotions she's never known before. She sees herself unwinding Najeeb Gul's bloodied bandage and waving it like a flag, joining in the cry of Inqilaab Zindabad. But first she wants to know what was beneath the turban.

– Where is it? The turban?

Najeeb Gul smiles. He says, Now we have to get married.

– What?

– Think of the story we'll tell our children. When they

brought me here I saw you on that balcony, dispensing water onto the parched battlefield. There was a light shining from you, I swear it.

She feels herself blush. She doesn't know if he's mad, half-delirious with pain or simply as struck as she is by the day's sense of possibility. She might agree to anything right now. She might agree to step onto a train with a man who she knows only by the scent of his clothes, the muscles of his back and the fact that he works in the same place her brothers go on school excursions. She might find herself in London with him, wearing his turban on her head. Because in London, she has heard, fashionable women wear turbans.

– When he pulled the bayonet out I fell. The turban rolled off my head.

– Where did you fall?

– Near the armoured car. It rolled beneath the wheel, just past where my arm could reach. The turban doesn't matter now. Stay here. Tell me your name.

But the fire is too much inside her. She tells him her name and lightly touches his wrist – it's some kind of promise, she feels – and rejoins the crowd. Moving forward gets harder as she nears the front. The men here are on fire themselves, and don't want to yield an inch of ground. But she keeps insisting she has a message for someone, it's important, she has to deliver it in person, and they let her go either because she's convincing or because their attention is elsewhere or because they see they'll physically have to carry her away and no man wants to be the one to lay a hand on her.

She understands so little of what's going on here. It has been an age since the bullets stopped, but everyone is still here, waiting. The man who was standing on the fire-truck has gone now, and now that she's near the front she hears an English voice say, This is your last chance. Disperse. A Peshawari voice replies, with exquisite courtesy, After you.

She can see nothing past the shoulders of the men in front of her. Then, amazingly, a space opens up and she sees it: the long-tailed turban, resting against the wheel of the foremost armoured car. She pushes her way through the tiny space, and steps out into the middle ground between her people and the English, a space wider than any valley, wider than the sky. The startled eyes of men turn to her, voices of different accents and different languages tell her to retreat, in a tone which makes it clear she is nothing but disruption. She is amazed by her own fearlessness. She darts forward, picks up the turban and places it on her head. It's a little loose, but only a little. As she pushes it down onto her skull her palms encounter some kind of band between the fabric and the hard cap. Very slowly – head up, eyes meeting the eyes of an Indian soldier with his gun trained on her – she steps back into the battalion of Peshawari men. One of the men, his beard white, pats her shoulder.

– I'm sorry for your loss. But go now. Quickly.

He thinks mourning has propelled her here, the turban a memento of a fallen brother or father. Or husband, if she appears old enough for a husband.

The men are content to step aside and let her through now that she's retreating. As she approaches the watch shop she sees that Najeeb Gul is moving towards her, his eyes on her turban, then on her face, his expression telling her she is a miracle. Diwa runs towards him. So full of elation she doesn't understand the cracking noises, the screams, the sharp pain in her spine; there is only time to wonder if Najeeb Gul's arms are reaching for her or the object on her head as he, too, stumbles and falls.

23–25 April 1930

Standing on the balcony between shards of earthenware Zarina watches Diwa charge through the crowd, straight towards the wounded man. The sun catches the mirrorwork on her sleeves, light leaps up from her arms. The man speaks to her and points, she nods in acceptance and, too far away to hear Zarina's loud cries, pushes her way to the space between the troops and protestors. If Zarina tries to follow her onto the street she'll lose sight of her just as she lost sight of her husband earlier in the day when she left the rooftop to call him back home. So there is nothing to do but watch as Diwa picks up a fallen turban – it has to be the one the wounded man had been calling out for earlier – places it on her head and disappears back into the crowd. For a few seconds Zarina loses her. Machine-gun fire rips the air; sprays of light; there she is, near the watch-shop awning, there she is.

Did she trip? Did someone pull her down below the line of fire? Did she veer away in the time it took Zarina to blink? The street is in chaos, a chessboard overturned. Some men run towards the side alleys, some fall, some move towards the bullets to help their fallen brothers. Diwa! She draws the name out from deep in her belly, but even so her voice is a thread falling limply onto the street where panic itself is a sound. She is barefoot, but there is no question of taking the time to find her shoes before running down the stairs and out into the alley, through which soldiers are chasing Peshawari men. The ground is hot, sticky; the men run past her as if she isn't there. She rounds the corner onto the Street of Storytellers where the gunfire is so loud it's as if each bullet is being fired into her ear. And the smell! Fresh blood, and hours-old blood, and something else, more rank – men, terrified, have been losing control of their bodies. The flies are thick, fearless.

So quickly, this end of the street is almost empty. The armoured cars are still in place, and troops guard Kabuli Gate but most of the noise of running feet and guns now comes from the alleyways and in the direction of Hastings Memorial. A man runs past, tries to pull her along, but she shakes him off. The ground is unpaired shoes, and men, dead and wounded, and near the watch shop a long-tailed white turban soaking in fresh blood. She runs to pick it up, touches the bloodied fabric and brings her hand to her nose. If it is Diwa's some part of her will know it; how is it possible she can't tell Diwa's blood from a stranger's? But it is only blood, it could be anyone's. There's a sound behind her and she turns to see a man in a red shirt with his back towards her, something strange about his posture which she doesn't understand until she sees the tip of the bayonet protruding from his back. He falls backwards and an English soldier pulls his bayonet clear of the body, blood thickening the blade. Someone else grabs her arm and this time she doesn't resist as a man wearing khaddar pulls her along with him, into an alley.

A doorway opens, women's hands pull her in to safety. My sister, she says, and tries to walk back out, but they stop her, hold her with force until she stops struggling. There is nothing you can do, they say.

One of them will die. This sentence is a thought she can't unthink. Her husband, her sister. One of them will die. She backs herself into a corner of the room and sits pressed against the walls, her head in her hand. Outside the bullets don't stop.

Three years ago on a day when she thought she fully understood terror, Zarina walked unrecognised down the street on which she had grown up, her body hunched over so her height wouldn't give her away. Her destination was the carpet-seller's house which overlooked the Street of Storytellers. Entering the house, throwing off her burqa, she said the words her late mother had trained her to say when the time came to be married to a murderer in repayment for her father's death: I come seeking the protection of your house which can only be given to me through marriage. The carpet-seller knew immediately who she was and she understood then that he and her mother had agreed long ago that she would come here and invoke Pashtunwali, allowing him to become responsible for her life.

It was only after the carpet-seller said she was welcome into his family that she thought to look around the room for her husband-to-be and, in the cluster of family members who were looking at her in shock, saw one adoring face – Diwa. It was Diwa who loved her first and who she loved first in the household. Zarina holds the turban close to her chest although the smell of blood is almost unbearable. Her love for her husband came later, but once she recognised it she was able to look back and understand that the seeds of it were already there when she woke up beside him on the first morning of her married life and knew that now there would always be this secret life, these altered selves, known to no one but the two of them.

Hours later the women lift her up from the corner of the room because her unmoving limbs have stiffened into their cross-legged posture. One of the young sons of the household says he'll walk home with her, but when he asks his mother to give this stranger a burqa the older woman says it's safer to be uncovered so the English don't think it's a nationalist trying to hide.

They walk all the way to the Street of Storytellers before an English soldier stops them and tells them to return home. When the boy explains the soldier says the woman can cross the road without any help; he won't be fooled by troublemakers using women as shields to allow them to move around the city freely. Zarina barely hears this exchange. In the twilight gloom she looks up and down the street, trying to make sense of it. The bodies have gone, and even as she watches there's a roaring sound and water jets out of the hose of a fire-engine at

Kabuli Gate, and then another hose, and another. Where is your house, the soldier asks. She points, and he says, Go there directly, I'm watching.

She goes as quickly as possible, bare feet splashing through the bloodied water while shoes of different sizes race past her in the opposite direction. The front door of her house is ajar, and as she enters and starts to climb the stairs she hears her husband's voice. He must be talking to Diwa – they are both here! Here, and worrying about her. But the other voice is a man's voice, coming from the balcony. She is just a few feet away when she hears him say he can't express his regret sufficiently, but he had to put her body down in order to help the wounded, and now she's gone, along with all the other corpses on the street.

Zarina runs the stiff-blooded fabric of the turban between her fingers, and swears that she will kill the man who sent Diwa into the bullets.

When her husband returns home from his fruitless attempt to get past the soldiers and look for Diwa's body she takes him into his bedroom and shows him the frock-coat with the bullet hole and the business cards lying beside it on the bed. His voice is unfamiliar with grief as he reads out what is written there: Najeeb Gul, Indian Assistant, Peshawar Museum.

– What will you do to him?

– Zarina, don't.

– Don't what?

A banging on the front door interrupts them. There aren't any servants in the house – they're all either in Kohat or still taking a few days to visit their families, unaware that some members of the household have returned – so there's no one to answer the door. It will be neighbours checking that everyone is all right and when they find out what's happened the house will fill with mourners and she and her husband will be pulled apart into the men and women's sections of the house. Pretend we're not here, her husband says. I just want to be with you tonight.

But the hammering on the door goes on and on, and finally

296

he stands up and says, I'll take care of it. He's been gone only a few seconds when the presence of Diwa in this room, in those last seconds they had together, catches her by the throat. Diwa is dead. Diwa is dead, and she is still living, and will go on living without her. This surge of pain, this rushing sense of enormity. She is dead, she will never be any less dead than she is now. How can Zarina survive even this moment – right now. She will not survive it. She opens the shutters, there's no air in her lungs. On the balcony, shards of earthenware, spilt water. She kneels, picks up a jagged piece of fired earth. From her throat, rasping sounds. And through them her husband's voice calling her name. When she turns he's standing there, gripping the upper arm of a man in a bloodied shirt, who doesn't flinch or try to move: Najeeb Gul.

– This is my fault, he says.

When he speaks she sees the point in his throat where she can jam the tip of the earthenware shard, pushing through skin and cartilage. She grips the shard, walks up close to him.

– Why have you come here?

– I saw her fall, but I didn't see what happened after. I came to see if she was –

He can't say either the word 'alive' or 'dead', and she can tell her husband wishes he had sent away this young, open-faced man instead of bringing him up here. Her husband has lived his life in a world abundant with good fortune where softness is given the name refinement. Grief is making his heart flood with tears instead of blood.

– Zarina, it's the English who killed my sister, not this man, whatever he did.

– What do you know of what he did?

She picks up the frock-coat and brings it close to her husband.

– He violated the sanctity of our home and came into our bedroom with your sister, she says. She sees her husband flinch at that and presses on. He took off his clothes. And where was she when this happened, when this man undressed himself? Ask him if he touched her, and how? What did he do to her,

297

what promises did he make, to send her flying through a crowd of strange men towards him when he was injured?

Najeeb Gul hangs his head. I'm sorry, he says, his voice an admission of everything that she had only half believed to be true. Her husband catches him by the shoulders, places a foot on his backside and kicks him to the ground. He lands hard, and his bellow of pain suggests that the wounds he received in the day have re-opened. Her husband lifts him by the collar and drags him through the corridor and down the stairs, a trail of blood smearing the floor, and steps, the man screaming in pain. Zarina follows all the way to the storage room on the ground floor, watches her husband – this man who has never raised a finger in anger – kick Najeeb Gul inside and step in after him, closing the door behind him.

And now she is terrified. It is his gentleness she loves most. Once taken out of him how can it be put back? She bangs on the door, calls his name, and it's only a few seconds later that he walks out, his face drawn, pale.

– What do you want me to do to him?

All this blood, the trail on her floor. She wants the smell of it gone.

– I don't know, she says, and his relief is unmistakable.

– We'll keep him there until my father comes back. He can decide.

Her husband bathes and binds the prisoner's wounds, takes him tea and dried fruit which is all the sustenance there is in the house, but will not say a word to or about him. Although there's a lock on the storage-room door he insists on sitting outside it, a rifle across his knee. He tells Zarina to sit with him but she can't find a way to leave Diwa's room, the girl's scent still on her pillowcase, her clothes. Somehow she sleeps, and even in her dreams Diwa is already dead.

By morning her husband's face has aged. Zarina tries to go in to see the prisoner but her husband says no, and won't give her the key. But there is something she wants from Najeeb Gul

– she wants the last hours of her sister-in-law's life. How did she grow so brave, what allowed her to run through a street of men as if nothing could touch her?

– No, her husband says, and lays his head on his knees. I'm so tired, I'm so hungry. Where did they take my sister's body?

The only thing she can attend to is hunger. She leaves the house, nothing but a chaddar to cover her head so the soldiers will think she's only a woman, incapable of making trouble. The world is empty without Diwa, no life, no sound. And nothing to buy, nothing to eat. At Kabuli Gate an English officer tells her she can't leave the Walled City, and she says it doesn't trouble her but when her employer wants to know why his children's ayah didn't come to work she'll tell him who was responsible. Who is her employer, he asks and she gives him the name of an Englishman who is a valued customer of her father-in-law, with two young children and an important position in government. The English officer speaks Urdu but doesn't know enough to tell an ayah apart from the daughter-in-law of a merchant, or perhaps all Peshawaris look the same to him today just as every Englishman is a murderer to her. Either way, he waves her through. On the railway bridge leading into the Cantonment she sees the domes of the Peshawar Museum, and then it's impossible to keep herself from going towards it.

Inside there's an Englishwoman. That's almost reason enough to leave, but the Englishwoman walks away, and Zarina can stand and look around the silent hall of idols. This is where he works, and this has something to do with the blackened metal band hidden in his turban which Diwa retrieved for him from beneath the wheels of an armoured car. She walks up to the two largest of the stone idols, wants to smash them. There'd be a satisfaction in watching them shatter on the ground, these giant unchanging figures which look onto the world with indifference, even today. But instead she turns to leave and as she's going she sees a carving on a grey panel which draws her to it – a woman neither alive nor dead, neither entombed nor in the world of the living. Gone for ever. Zarina repeats those words to herself, tries to force them into meaning.

When her mother died she learned that when the living touch a corpse they understand, through their fingertips, that the dead are truly dead; no life is left in that coldness. This the fingertips understand, but without that touch the brain flounders. How is it possible that a whole universe of habits, humour, taste, tics, loyalties, loves has gone spinning into randomness, freed from the magnetic force of Diwa's personality? Where is she lying now, has anyone said a prayer over her body, will Zarina for ever see her from beneath each burqa in the Walled City? If she must be dead let her be dead, but where is the body?

She returns home and the cook and his two sons are there, sitting outside the storage room with guns across their knees. There had been a moment in the Museum when the Englishwoman had said, Najeeb! and Zarina thought her husband had set him free. But it was the man who had come up to her balcony yesterday, and he said he was Najeeb's brother. Why had he come to her balcony? What conspiracy is there between the brothers? She shouts through the door at Najeeb Gul but he doesn't answer, and the cook says her husband has given him the key to the lock and made him swear on the Qur'an not to give it back to him or to let Zarina have it, and whatever the cook might personally believe to be the right choice in this matter the Qur'an is the Qur'an.

When her husband returns he's found out who was responsible for putting the bodies in lorries, but no one knows where they were taken. He bangs with the flat of his palm on the door of the storage room, tells the cook he'll fire him unless he gives the key back, and it is Zarina who pulls him away, tells him to be calm. The day crawls by, endless, pointless. There is a man imprisoned in the house and his presence is driving them both mad.

Another night passes. Soon, her father-in-law will return. With the withdrawal of the British the gates of the Walled City have opened and this morning the cook's older son left for Kohat to give the family the terrible news. Zarina's husband has gone to buy a grave plot in Shahji-ki-Dheri, and for now it is only

300

Zarina, the cook and his younger son in the house. She's upstairs in Diwa's room when she hears the cook calling out to her from the hallway. He never comes to this part of the house, but the world is different now.

– They'll all be here soon, he says when she comes outside to see what he wants. He's been with the family longer than her husband and any of his siblings have been alive, and Diwa has always been – always was – his favourite.

– Yes. And?

– I've sworn I won't give you the key to the room. But I haven't sworn I won't unlock it myself.

When the carpet-seller arrives he will set the captive free. Zarina knows it, her husband knows it, the cook knows it.

– I don't know, she says.

– I'll do it. I want to. How can we let him walk out of here after what he's done?

– Let me think.

– I held her in my arms when she was a baby. I don't need your permission.

He says it in kindness, lifting from her the burden of this responsibility, ensuring no one's displeasure will fall on her.

– I want to talk to him, she says.

– You talk. I'll do the rest.

They are partway down the corridor when the cook's son runs up the stairs, breathless, to say two people have arrived: a man with a glass eye and an Englishwoman in a burqa who says the begum-sahib asked her about the lorries. How can they know he's imprisoned here? It's impossible. But they must be looking for him, and someone will have said he was here during the massacre. The cook has already told her that the neighbours have been asking about the man who went up on the roof when the women and children were there. Get your gun, she commands the cook and goes to find the frock-coat with the bullet hole which will convince Najeeb Gul's brother and the Pashto-speaking Englishwoman from the Museum that the man they're looking for is already dead. Let them think the lorries took him away.

* * *

301

And then, they don't ask about Najeeb Gul. They are here to tell her about the lorries, tell her what she already knows. It's as if they want her forgiveness for the crimes of their people. How little her grief means to them if they can come here seeking a salve for their own conscience. Where is Diwa? That is the only question in the world. She pushes the frock-coat into the man's arm and steps out of the room.

The cook is in the study on the other side of the door, a gun in his arms. What do they want, he asks, and before she can answer all the weight of a tall man crashes against the door.

– Najeeb! Where is my brother? Najeeb!

His body is a battering ram against the heavy wood door. The cook holds the rifle in a firing position and tells her to unlock the door and open it.

– No, Zarina says. She hears the glass-eyed man's sorrow, the agony of it. The echo of her own heart.

– Enough, she says.

In the courtyard, the brothers embrace. They hold each other so close, so uncaring of those who are watching that the cook and his son and Zarina turn their faces away, and then have to look back because joy is something they know they won't witness again in this household for a very long time.

The Englishwoman says the younger brother's name, so softly only Zarina, standing beside her, can hear. They are facing each other – the Englishwoman and Najeeb Gul – but his eyes are closed as he grips his brother's back, his face pressed against the older man's shoulder. Soon though, he will open his eyes and see the woman studying his face, her hand pressed against her heart.

The Englishwoman pivots on her heel, walks towards the front door. No one but Zarina is watching her. In the doorway she turns, holds up her hand to shoulder height, fingers together, palm facing outwards. Zarina doesn't know what the gesture means, and yet she finds herself replicating it. The Englishwoman ducks her head in acknowledgement, covers herself in a burqa, and walks out into the street.

27 April 1930

In the whisper of pre-dawn which belonged to neither the brothel nor the mosque, Zarina walked through rows and rows of mounds with pebbled borders, wearing the white of mourning. She already knew her way to the three opulent graves with marble-bordered flower beds at the foot of head-stones inscribed with Qur'anic verses. These were the graves of the carpet-seller's parents and his sister, the girl murdered by her husband who could have been Zarina's husband too. Beside them, a mound of packed mud carpeted in rose petals. Hundreds, thousands of rose petals which Diwa's father and brothers had poured onto the mud. So many they had become something other than rose petals – a stilled red river between tombs, the ripped wing of an angel fallen to earth.

Zarina knelt, lifted up handfuls of petals, and moved them to one side. Her trowel bit down into the grave. She kept on for a few minutes, slicing the earth. When the hole was large and deep enough she placed the turban within it, its dried blood Diwa's only remains. Carefully, she covered it up again, stood, bent towards the rose petals and scooped up a handful of the warm, fleshy licks of red. By this time next year she'd have a child; she was certain it would be a girl. She'd call her Diwa and when the child was old enough she'd bring her here and tell her about the turban and the metal band of figs. And perhaps one day they'd dig them up together and the world would hear the story of Diwa – not an angel sent by Allah to give water to thirsty men but a girl, unafraid, shot

303

down by the English and disposed of by the men who shouted 'Freedom'.

The breeze stirred the petals and it was as if she were holding a tiny creature in her hands. She threw her arms up in the air, a great expansive gesture, and watched the fledgling take to the sky.

485 BC

Where are the monstrous races he promised? The
Shadow-Footed Men who lie down at midday and raise
up their broad feet to make a shadow within which
they can escape the sun? The Once-Engendering Men
with semen as black as their skin? The Mouthless
Men who live off the scent of plants? Atossa, widow
of Darius, leans over the prow of the ship, looking
into the muddy waters of the Indus' tributary. And
the fish-tailed lions, the spiny mermaids, the giant
white worms? The ants who dig up gold? Lies, always
lies with Scylax.

Along the banks of the river the Pactyike stand
with spears in hand, heads bowed as the Persian ships
sail past. The water-carrying ship draws up along-
side and one of Atossa's attendants holds out an
empty urn into which the priest pours the water of
the sacred river Choaspes. A few drops, silver with
sun and divinity, fall into the river which shimmers
to receive them. The water is calm, the priest's hand
famed for its steadiness. The unsalted water of the
Indus is sacred enough for everyone but her, and some
of the attendants whisper that it is sweeter than
Choaspes, but even so they will all, even the priest,
do what they can to have some share of that which is
permitted only to the Queen. Everywhere, everywhere
betrayal. This is the price of power.

At Caspatyrus she disembarks, and waves away all offers of food and rest.

— Bring him to me.

He is old now, his skin so leathered and creased he could be one of the monstrous races he wrote about. But he still looks at her as he always did as though she isn't really his queen no matter the words on his lips, the curve of his neck as he kneels in front of the gold and lapis-lazuli throne which four Pactyike men had carried from her ship to this grove of pomegranate trees.

— The Queen honours me. All this travel, for me?

— I've always wanted to see the Indus. Now there is peace in our kingdom, and my son is on the throne, it seemed the right time. You are incidental.

He smiles at the lie. She sent her best men to capture him, with instructions that he must be kept alive and brought to her. But when the message arrived to say he had been found in Caspatyrus and was too sick to survive the journey to Persepolis it was very clear what she had to do. Though looking at him now it's clear he isn't sick at all, just still able to convince his listeners of everything he has to say.

— Did you think you could hide from me here, Carian?

— Hide? No. I grow sentimental in my old age. I wanted to retrace the happiest footsteps I've ever taken. You were not part of my calculation.

— And who allowed you those happy footsteps? Who trusted a man of Caria? Who placed a circlet on the brow of a barbarian?

— A man wise enough to recognise that I would do exactly what he asked of me in return.

A smashed pomegranate lies near the throne. Rubies strewn at her feet in pools of blood.

— Where is the Circlet?

— Why?

— I want it back. That's why I've come.

— I don't have it.

— Why did you do it, after everything Persia had given you?

This is the real question, the only one in the world which eludes her understanding. Why did Scylax of the Fig Circlet, Scylax the Entrusted, choose to risk the wrath of Darius by writing a glorified account of the life of that Carian rebel, Heraclides, raising his ambush of the Persians to a victory greater than any of Darius or Cyrus? It had achieved nothing in the end; Caria was brought back under control, Heraclides was killed. So, why?

— Because I loved Heraclides.

— What kind of answer is that? What about Caria? What about Persia?

— Continents are cut up this way, and that way. Islands extend themselves across seas and mountains. What is any of that when compared to Heraclides?

The exhaustion of the journey has finally seeped into her marrow. She looks around at the chains of mountains, the bright green grass, the rivers and fruit-laden trees. Mountain ranges and valley together form the broken bowl of an artist, its base smeared with thick paints of green and blue and red. He didn't lie about that.

— Are there really ants which dig out gold from the sand?

— Oh yes! If you weren't going to kill me I'd show you.

She is startled by the sound of her own laughter. He stands and holds his hand out to her. The Circlet may be lost but they are not so very old yet — and the world is still full of discoveries.

Written by Najeeb Gul, Archaeologist for V.R. Spencer, Archaeologist (Qayyum wants me to add, 'and campaigner for the freedom from Empire for the peoples of India and Britain'.)

14 August 1947, Caspatyrus, Pakistan.

End Note

The explanation from Olaf Caroe, then secretary to the Chief Commissioner, of what happened to the bodies on the night of 23 April 1930, is as follows:

I received a note on 23rd April evening from Sir Norman Bolton asking me to do what I could to arrange for the burial of as many of the casualties as possible during the night, in order to avoid the danger of a fresh riot occurring over the funeral procession. I spoke to R.S. Mehr Chand Khanna and asked him to bring me some of the leading Khilafists at the Municipal Library. He brought M. Abdurrab Nishtar; M. Ataullah Jan, Municipal Commissioner; M. Aurangzeb Khan, Vakil; Qazi Mohd Aslam, Vakil.

I informed these persons what was required and asked for their co-operation as peace-loving citizens and good Muslims. They agreed to do what they could and asked me to arrange for lorries, saying they would persuade the relatives to agree. I arranged for lorries through Shahji – one of C.C.'s orderlies – who is I believe a Peshawari and a Syed. During the night in this way we sent away seven or eight bodies in lorries. Some of them had no relatives and arrangements were made to pay for a mullah and to carry through the obsequies with all regard to religious rites. The next day Qazi Mohd Aslam came to see me and said that he was making himself unpopular by assisting in the matter. He gave me to understand that he could do no more. I fancy that the association of these four men with the action

309

taken will put an end to any attempt to make capital of the incident. ('Public and Judicial Department. Civil Disobedience Campaign in NWFP. Response to Patel allegations'. British Library reference number L/PJ/6/2007)

Several eye-witnesses, interviewed in preparation for the Indian National Congress' 'Report of the Peshawar Disturbance Inquiry Committee 1930' describe seeing bodies packed into lorries while the troops fired on roofs and balconies in an attempt to keep witnesses away. The Congress' list of the dead numbered a hundred and twenty-five, including forty-three missing. The official British inquiry conducted by Justices Sulaiman and Panckridge placed the number killed at thirty.

Acknowledgements

Syeda Meher Taban from the University of Mardan was an excellent guide through old Peshawar; Nidaullah Sehrai at the Peshawar Museum was generous in answering my questions; thanks also to Salman Rahim for making the trip to Peshawar possible. Sana Haroon gave me the run of her library and filled in many blanks in my knowledge. Qayyum Gul would not have entered my imagination if not for Mukulika Banerjee's *The Pathan Unarmed*; J. Kasmin's collection of artefacts – particularly the Achaemenid lion – brought me closer to Viv. I was extremely fortunate to be able to ask both Tom Holland and Madeleine Miller for Greek translations. (Najeeb didn't have Tom's translation of Herodotus at hand, so the version he reads is G. C. Macauley's translation.) David J. Gill responded to questions from a stranger and was good enough to direct me to his *Sifting the Soil of Greece* so I might better understand the world of archaeologists before and during the war. Many other reference sources have been of great value, particularly *Indian Voices In the Great War* (selected by David Omissi), photograph and records of colonial Peshawar from the British Library, and *Peshawar: Historic City of the Frontier* by Dr Ahmed Hasan Dani. Beatrice Monti provided, yet again, a writing refuge at Santa Maddalena and also gave me the blue of the Mediterranean. Gillian Stern's editorial acumen was invaluable. Thanks also to John Freeman, Ellah Allfrey and Yuka Igarashi for editorial work on the section of this novel that appeared in *Granta 123: Best of Young British Novelists*. Thank you to all at

A. M. Heath and Bloomsbury – as well as the sub-agents, publishers, translators who help give my novels a place in the world. Finally, my deepest gratitude to my Dream Team of Frances Coady, Victoria Hobbs and Alexandra Pringle.

A Note on the Author

Kamila Shamsie is the author of five novels: *In the City by the Sea; Kartography; Salt and Saffron; Broken Verses;* and *Burnt Shadows,* which was shortlisted for the Orange Prize for Fiction and has been translated into more than twenty languages. Three of her novels have received awards from Pakistan's Academy of Letters. She is a Fellow of the Royal Society of Literature and in 2013 was named a Granta Best of Young British Novelist. Kamila Shamsie grew up in Karachi and now lives in London.

@kamilashamsie